DYATLOV PASS

DYATLOV PASS

A Novel

ALAN K. BAKER

Cover image © 2013 by Daniel Acacio

This edition published in 2013 by:

Thistle Publishing
36 Great Smith Street
London
SW1P 3BU

ISBN 13: 978-1-909869-07-3

My gaze slips sadly from hill to hill,
Slowly extinguished in the fearsome void.

– Fyodor Tyutchev, *Solitude*

PREFACE

I have tried to think of an appropriate description of the following document. It has not been easy: to call it a psychiatric report (which it was originally intended to be) is no longer accurate or appropriate, since I have included lengthy passages describing my own personal responses to the sessions I have conducted with the subject, Viktor Strugatsky, as well as the strange and unsettling discoveries I have made during the course of my evaluation of his mental state.

Of course, it goes without saying that a psychiatrist's responses are of the utmost importance in the treatment of a patient; and yet, I realise that I have gone much further than I intended in my evaluation of Strugatsky, to the extent that I have now become a part of his story. This is at least as troubling to me as the elements of the story themselves.

I should note here the preliminary facts of the case, and describe how I came to be involved. On Monday 23 February 2009, the criminal militia approached the Peveralsk Psychiatric Hospital just outside Yekaterinburg, where I work, asking for assistance in a possible homicide case which they were investigating.

Nine days previously, a man had entered the village of Yurta Anyamova, north of the town of Ivdel in the Urals. The village belongs to the Mansi people, who are indigenous to the area. The man was apparently in a state of profound shock, and was suffering from a fever from which he only recovered due to the care administered to him by the villagers.

It seems that on the previous Sunday, he had passed through Yurta Anyamova in the company of three other people. They were 68-year-old Vadim Konstantinov, a retired professor of anthropology; Veronika

Ivasheva, 28, a police sketch artist; and Alisa Chernikova, 31, a physicist working at the Ural State Technical University.

According to the headman of the village, Roman Bakhtyarov, the group had claimed to be conducting research into the so-called 'Dyatlov Pass incident', which occurred on the slopes of a nearby mountain called Kholat Syakhl fifty years ago, in February 1959. The facts of the Dyatlov Pass incident are well known to the region's historians, and I will refrain from repeating them in this preface, for reasons which will become clear.

Bakhtyarov stated that one of the village elders, a shaman of indeterminate age named Prokopy Anyamov, volunteered to accompany Strugatsky and the others on their expedition. Five days after they left Yurta Anyamova, Strugatsky returned to the village alone; he was sick and incoherent, but in his infrequent moments of lucidity, he claimed that the others had been killed in the pine forest that lies to the south of Kholat Syakhl.

The Director of Peveralsk, Dr Fyodor Pletner, agreed to admit Strugatsky for observation, and asked me if I would undertake an examination of the subject. Strugatsky was brought to the hospital, and quarters were assigned to him in the secure wing.

Following treatment for his rather poor physical condition, the result of exhaustion combined with lack of proper sustenance (it seems that the villagers had not been able to get him to take any food, either during or immediately after his fever), I scheduled a session with Strugatsky for Wednesday 25 February.

What follows is, as I mentioned at the outset, difficult to describe. I suppose it would be most accurate to call it a chronicle of my evaluation of Viktor Strugatsky, a personal memoir, one might say. But it is much more than that: it is also the story of my own growing awareness of the true nature of what he encountered in the forest, and of his mental state. I believe that the people with whom he set out for Kholat Syakhl are indeed dead; but I do not believe that Strugatsky killed them.

I am equally certain that many will find the text which follows problematic, for several reasons. Those in the psychiatric community will doubtless comment on the style of the prose; I would respond to those concerns simply by saying that the style is fitting for my purposes in writing a personal chronicle. Those in the wider scientific community will, equally doubtlessly, treat its contents with incredulity, or even contempt. For them, I have no response, other than to say that I present this material for what it is worth.

I would make one final note on the text: the particulars of the Strugatsky case have been gathered during the course of several sessions, during which our conversations were recorded. I have used these recordings to piece together his experiences, and have decided, for the sake of clarity, to present them in the third person. I have included many minor details and observations gleaned from Strugatsky's conversation, which I have edited to form what is hopefully a coherent narrative. As I mentioned at the outset, I have also included my own responses and discoveries.

What those discoveries mean, for the world and for humanity, I am unable to say; but I believe the implications of what you are about to read are of the utmost seriousness and significance.

Anatoliy Baskov
Peveralsk Psychiatric Hospital
June 2009

PART ONE

INVESTIGATIONS

BASKOV (1)

I went to the hospital's secure wing and entered Viktor Strugatsky's room. I instructed the two orderlies who had accompanied me to wait outside, and they assured me that they would come to my aid immediately, should I call for them.

The room was small and spartanly furnished, but clean and bright. Strugatsky had damaged nothing, which is not always the case with subjects whose mental state is in question, and who have been accused of serious crimes. There was a bed, an armchair, washing facilities and a small desk at which stood a wooden chair.

'Good morning, Viktor,' I said, smiling at him. 'I am Dr Baskov.'

Strugatsky was lying on the bed. He immediately sat up and put his feet on the floor. 'Good morning, Dr Baskov.'

He did not return my smile; but neither did his face display any hostility. In fact, his expression was blank, save for slightly furrowed brows, which gave him the appearance of someone pondering a minor problem of no particular significance. I noted the light tan on his face which had been remarked upon during his initial physical examination (and which suggested that he had recently spent an extended period of time in the open air), along with the numerous flecks of grey in his hair, which gave him the appearance of a man somewhat older than his twenty-eight years.

I indicated the chair by the desk. 'Do you mind if I sit down?'

'Please do.'

'How are you feeling today?'

'I'd like to get out of here.'

'I'm afraid that's not possible just yet,' I said gently.

'Not until you decide whether I'm crazy, or a murderer,' he said; and now he smiled, but it was a very small, sad smile: an expression of resignation rippling on the surface of fear and uncertainty.

'That's correct,' I replied, placing a DAT recorder on the desk.

'I've got one like that,' said Strugatsky. 'Same make.'

'Ah, yes. You're a journalist, aren't you?'

He repeated: 'Yes, I've got one like that. At least, I used to have one. It's still there.'

'Still there?'

'In the forest. Maybe it doesn't exist anymore.'

'Why wouldn't it exist?'

Strugatsky said nothing.

'Do you mind if I tape this conversation?'

'Would you refrain from taping it if I said yes?'

'It is standard procedure.'

'Then I don't mind.'

'Thank you.' I switched on the machine. 'How long have you been a journalist?'

'About four years. You think I killed them, don't you? You think I'm crazy, and I killed them.' His voice was quite without inflection as he said this. Clearly for Strugatsky, it was merely a statement of fact, like saying that the sun rose this morning.

'No, I'm not saying that. In fact, I don't know. That's why I'm here, why we're talking.'

'If I'm not crazy, then why am I locked up in a mental hospital?'

'You're here so that we can figure out what happened to you, and to your companions...'

'They were killed.'

'How?'

Strugatsky said nothing, he merely looked at me; but as he did so, I saw something in his eyes: a flash of apprehensiveness, perhaps outright fear. 'It's all right, Viktor,' I said gently. 'You can tell me.'

'That's the problem, Doctor,' he replied in a very quiet voice. 'I don't know if I can tell you.'

'Why not?'

His frown returned, deeply furrowing his brow. 'I don't know who I can tell, and who I can't. Do you really want to help me, or...?'

'Or what?' Silence. 'Yes, I want to help you, Viktor. Everyone who works here wants to help you. You're among friends. You're safe.'

'Safe?' He gave a short laugh.

I decided to try a different approach. 'Why don't you tell me a bit about yourself?'

'What do you want to know?'

'Well ... are you from Yekaterinburg originally?'

'Yes.'

'And you work for the Yekaterinburg *Gazette*.'

'Yes.'

Two monosyllabic answers on the trot. Clearly, Strugatsky considered the subjects of his personal history and occupation to be unworthy of conversation.

'And you have an interest in the Dyatlov Pass incident,' I said.

He looked up at me suddenly, as if startled. 'Not at first. But it's how it started.'

'How what started?'

He smiled again, and this time the smile was broader, almost feral. 'The train of events that have led me here, Dr Baskov.'

'Would you like to tell me how it started?'

Strugatsky stood up slowly. I was ready to call out for the orderlies, but he merely went over to the armchair and sat down. 'Don't worry, Doctor,' he said. 'I'm not a violent man.'

It took me a moment to realise that he had known I was preparing to call for help. 'That was very perceptive of you,' I said.

'Thank you.'

'Well then,' I said. 'Why don't you tell me how all this started?'

Strugatsky sighed, and said: 'All right, Doctor.'

ONE

Viktor leaned over his desk with his head in his hands, staring at the notes he had so far assembled on the Borovsky case, the noise and bustle of the office grating on his nerves. He had just got off the phone with another potential witness who didn't want to get involved, in spite of the promise of anonymity. The Yekaterinburg *Gazette* was a serious newspaper, Viktor had told him. There was nothing to worry about; his identity would not be divulged. But the man was terrified – Viktor had heard it in his voice. 'I'm sorry,' he'd said. 'I can't help you. Please don't call me again.' And he had hung up, leaving Viktor with a dead receiver in his hand, and the notes for a story that was going nowhere scattered across his desk.

He glanced up as Cherevin's raucous laugh shredded the air. The reporter was reclining in his chair on the other side of the office with his feet up on his desk, talking to someone on the phone – probably one of his girlfriends...

'Arsehole,' Viktor muttered, disgustedly pushing himself away from his desk. He walked towards the drinks machine by the door to the stairwell, his hands thrust disconsolately into his pockets.

As he passed the open door to Maksimov's office, the editor shouted out at him: 'Strugatsky! Get in here!'

Oh, shit, Viktor thought. *What have I done now? Or what* haven't *I done?*

He stopped and leaned in through the door. 'Yes, boss?'

Maksimov beckoned him inside. 'Come in and have a seat, Vitya.'

Viktor didn't like it when Maksimov called him by his nickname. Somehow, it made him sound even more like an irate schoolmaster than he normally did. Viktor stepped reluctantly into the office and sat down.

Maksimov was big, balding and frequently bad-tempered, but now he smiled. Viktor was not comforted. 'How's it going?'

'Fine.'

'What are you working on at the moment?' Maksimov asked, as if he didn't know.

'The Borovsky case...'

'Oh, yes.' Maksimov reclined in his high-backed leather chair, which creaked under his weight, and put his hands contemplatively behind his head, like some bigshot executive planning his next corporate take-over. 'The slum landlord who wants his tenants out so he can sell up to developers.'

'That's right.'

'And what progress have you made?'

Viktor shifted uncomfortably in his chair. 'Well ... it's difficult to get anyone to talk. Borovsky's goons have been going round, leaning on people pretty heavily. It's not easy to get first-hand testimony when people are that scared...'

Maksimov sighed. 'In other words, you've made no progress whatsoever.'

'Well...'

'Come on, Vitya! What do I pay you for? You've been working on this for nearly a month, and what have you got to show for it so far?' He pointed a stubby finger at Viktor. 'I gave you this assignment because I thought you could handle it! I had confidence in you, I thought you had potential...'

'I *do*, boss,' said Viktor, hating the unintentional, plaintive whine of his voice. At that moment, he'd have liked nothing more than to tell Maksimov to take this job and shove it right up his fat arse. Yes, that would have been satisfying ... had it not been for the small matter of food and rent.

Maksimov leaned forward and planted his pudgy elbows on the desk. 'How long have you been working for the *Gazette*?'

'Two years, just over,' Viktor replied quietly, half expecting to receive his notice right there and then, and regretting that he hadn't acted on his impulse and told Maksimov where to go. Better to resign with a few valedictory insults than be unceremoniously fired.

'You know, Vitya, you're not a bad journalist. I *still* think you've got promise...'

'You do?'

'Yeah. It's just that I don't think you're ready for this type of story. That was my mistake, not yours. I thought you'd be tough enough to dig where people don't want you to dig. But...' He shook his head sadly, like a father whose son had committed some unpleasant and disappointing transgression. He leaned back in his chair again, and said: 'Give your notes to Cherevin – whatever you've got so far. Let's see if he has more luck.'

'Cherevin? But he's –'

'He's what?' Maksimov said sharply.

Viktor sighed. 'Nothing. I'll give him my notes.' *Fuck it!* he thought. *He'll never let me live this down.*

He was about to stand up, grateful that at least he still had his job, when Maksimov said: 'I've got something else for you.'

'Not *another* store opening.'

The editor smiled. 'Don't push your luck, Vitya.'

'Sorry. What is it?'

'I'm thinking of running a historical piece.'

'On what?'

'The Dyatlov Pass incident.'

'I've never heard of it.'

Maksimov grunted. 'Why doesn't that surprise me? All right, a quick history lesson. It's something that happened in 1959, in the northern Urals. A party of ski-hikers set out on a cross-country trip from here in Yekaterinburg. Their objective was a mountain called Otorten ... but they never made it.'

'What happened?'

'Something killed them.'

Viktor hesitated. 'Something?'

Maksimov nodded.

'What was it?'

'The authorities called it "a compelling unknown force".'

'A ... what the hell does *that* mean?'

Maksimov chuckled. 'It means that no one had the faintest idea what happened to the hikers – but they were concerned enough to close off the area around Otorten for three years. *No one* was allowed in – at least, no civilians. Only one member of the party survived, and that was only because he fell ill during the first stage of their journey, and had to return home. His name is Yuri Yudin, and he lives in Solikamsk.' Maksimov paused before asking: 'How would you like to go and interview him?'

Viktor looked at him, and realised that this was his last chance, after which he'd be out on his arse. 'Nineteen fifty-nine?'

Maksimov nodded.

'So we're coming up on the fiftieth anniversary of this ... of the Dyatlov Pass incident.'

'Precisely. So, what do you think?'

'I think it would make a great piece,' Viktor said, trying to sound more enthusiastic than he felt. Solikamsk was nearly five hundred kilometres from Yekaterinburg.

Maksimov nodded, and slid a piece of paper across the desk. 'Yurin's address.'

Viktor took the paper and read it. 'No phone number?'

Maksimov shook his head. 'We don't have it, and it's not listed in the Solikamsk directory.'

Viktor sighed. 'So I'll have to show up on his doorstep unannounced.'

'It'll be good practice for you,' Maksimov said pointedly. He glanced at his watch. 'There's a train to Solikamsk at 10.35 this morning. You can make it if you hurry.'

Christ, thought Viktor. *You don't want me to waste any time, do you?* He nodded, stood up and went to the door.

'Vitya.'

He turned. 'Yes, boss?'

'This isn't exactly Watergate. It isn't even Anton Borovsky and his goons. I'd rather you didn't come back empty-handed again. Understood?'

'Understood.'

TWO

Viktor gathered up his notes and took them over to Cherevin's desk. 'Here,' he said. 'Maksimov wants you to handle this.'

Cherevin raised an eyebrow, accepted the bundle of papers and quickly leafed through them. 'Borovsky, eh? Too much for you to handle, Vitya?'

'Not at all, Georgiy. He's put me on something bigger. Sorry to dump this on you.'

'Oh yeah? What's he got you on?'

Viktor gave an apologetic shrug. 'Can't tell you right now – got a train to catch.'

'Where to?' Cherevin asked, but Viktor was already walking away.

Maksimov was right: he'd have to get moving if he wanted to make the 10.35 train to Solikamsk. He could have driven, but he didn't really trust his ancient Lada to get him there and back.

He left the offices of the *Gazette* and went to his apartment on Sibirskii Street to pack a bag and grab some information on the Dyatlov Pass incident from the internet. There were numerous websites which mentioned it, but most of the ones he checked covered it only briefly. There was one, however, which described it in much greater detail.

Viktor printed it and shoved the papers into his bag, along with his DAT recorder, notebook and a change of underwear in case he'd be gone more than a day.

An hour later, he was sitting in a clanking carriage, looking through the window at the grey-white, frostbitten world outside. Viktor had always been a city type, with little interest in the countryside. He'd always mistrusted its wildness, the suffocating darkness of its nights, when there is no moon and the brittle light of alien stars offers no illumination.

He thought of Nika, and how she had occasionally tried to persuade him to go hiking or skiing with her in the southern Urals. He'd always said no, and she'd feigned a look of hurt and gone with some of their friends instead. Only later had he realised that the hurt had been genuine, about a lot of things – but mostly about that final 'No', the one he'd said when she'd suggested that they move in together. Viktor had told her he wasn't ready for that yet, or some such mealy-mouthed bullshit – he couldn't even remember the exact words he'd used – but Nika had taken it as a declaration that he was no longer interested in her at all. They'd fought, and had both said some regrettable things, and she'd ended their relationship. Or maybe *he* was the one who had ended it, without even realising that he wanted to...

He opened his bag, took out the thin sheaf of papers and began to read the article on the Dyatlov Pass incident. It wasn't much in the way of research, but he would need at least *some* background information when he spoke to Yuri Yudin. He sighed and shook his head. *What am I even doing here? Going to interview some old man about a fifty-year-old mystery that no one gives a shit about anymore. For Christ's sake!*

He cursed Maksimov for giving him this job. It was a bone thrown to someone who had failed in his previous assignment, nothing more; a humiliation made all the more galling because it was justified...

He looked at the first page of the article, which was entitled: 'The Strange Mystery of Dyatlov Pass.'

The trip began just as Maksimov had said: a cross-country ski-hiking expedition, nothing unusual for the 1950s. Back then, in the years following Stalin's death, life in the Soviet Union had begun to improve a little, and the austerity of the immediate post-war years began to diminish. One of the results of this was the growth of 'sport tourism', which was a way to escape – if only briefly – the drudgery and repression of a highly restrictive society. Thousands of people took advantage of this small freedom to leave their bleak towns and cities and head off into the wilderness for a few weeks, to hike and ski, and become invisible to the eyes of the state.

The group comprised ten students and graduates of the Ural Polytechnic Institute, which was now the Ural State Technical University.

Shortly before they left the Institute, the group's leader, Igor Dyatlov, had promised to send a telegram to the sports club when they returned to Vizhai from Otorten Mountain on their homeward journey. Dyatlov expected them to reach Vizhai by 12 February; but according to Yuri Yudin, Dyatlov told him shortly before they parted company that the group might return a few days later than that. There was nothing unusual about that, either: delays were common on cross-country hiking trips.

So, when 12 February came and went with no telegram, no one was particularly concerned. It was only on 20 February, when eight days had passed with no word from Dyatlov, that the hikers' families raised the alarm and demanded that a search-and-rescue expedition be sent from the Institute. The expedition consisted of teachers and students, and later the police and army sent planes and helicopters to aid in the operation.

As Maksimov had said, Dyatlov and his friends never made it to Otorten. The searchers discovered their camp on the eastern slopes of a neighbouring mountain, called Kholat Syakhl by the Mansi people who live in the region. The article added that Kholat Syakhl meant 'Mountain of the Dead' in the Mansi language.

The camp was abandoned and in a state of total disarray. The tent had been torn down and was half-covered with snow; there was no one inside, and the searchers found that all of the group's belongings, including their shoes and most of their clothes, had been left behind.

Later investigations concluded that the tent had been cut open from the inside, as if the occupants had been so desperate to get out that they didn't want to waste even the few seconds it would have taken to untie the flaps. Outside the tent, the footprints of eight or nine people led away from the camp towards the edge of a nearby forest, but disappeared after about five hundred metres.

At the edge of the forest, beneath a tall pine tree, one of the searchers discovered the bodies of Georgy Krivonischenko and Yuri Doroshenko. Both were barefoot and dressed only in their underclothes. The charred remains of a fire lay in the snow nearby, along with several broken branches. The tree's branches had been broken off up to a height of five metres, which suggested that someone had climbed the tree to look for something. It appeared that Krivonischenko and Doroshenko had tried to locate the camp they had recently abandoned, before succumbing to the cold.

Between the pine tree and the camp, the searchers discovered three more bodies, those of Igor Dyatlov, Zinaida Kolmogorova and Rustem Slobodin. From the orientation of the bodies, it seemed likely that they had been trying to return to the camp when they died.

Following the discovery of the first five bodies, the authorities opened a criminal investigation, which concluded that they had died of hypothermia. Rustem Slobodin's skull had sustained a slight fracture, but this was not considered to be life-threatening. Of the remaining four bodies there was no sign, and it would be another two months before they were finally found buried under four metres of snow in a ravine seventy-five metres from the pine tree.

Autopsies revealed that Ludmila Dubinina, Alexander Zolotarev, Nikolai Thibeaux-Brignollel and Alexander Kolevatov had *not* died of hypothermia: Thibeaux-Brignollel's skull had been completely crushed, Dubinina and Zolotarev had numerous broken ribs, and Dubinina had no tongue.

Viktor paused when he read this. *No tongue? Jesus...*

Maybe they'd been caught in an avalanche: that could have caused Dubinina to bite off her own tongue, and might even have crushed Thibeaux-Brignollel's skull. And yet, Maksimov had said that the authorities had no idea what had killed the Dyatlov party, so presumably that hypothesis had been considered and rejected.

In spite of their terrible injuries, the bodies which were found two months after the initial discoveries exhibited no external wounds; and it appeared that those who had died first had relinquished their clothes to the others. Alexander Zolotarev was wearing Ludmila Dubinina's faux fur coat and hat, while Dubinina's feet were wrapped in a piece of Krivonischenko's wool pants.

Viktor still couldn't stop thinking that an avalanche was to blame – until he read the next paragraph. Apparently, a test of the clothing worn by two of the group revealed that it had been exposed to high levels of radiation. He wondered what could possibly account for this. There would have been no sources of radiation out there in the wilderness, where there was nothing but mountains and snow and pine forests – apart from, he supposed, the very low-level background radiation of the Earth itself. Could Dyatlov and the others have inadvertently stumbled upon a secret military test of some kind? That made sense: all manner of dirty little state secrets had come to light in the years since the end of the Soviet era. Was this one of them?

The official investigation lasted several months, but in the end no evidence of foul play could be found. It had been suggested that the party had been murdered by the Mansi as punishment for trespassing on their land; but this theory was later abandoned, since neither Otorten nor Kholat Syakhl were considered sacred or taboo by the Mansi, who in any event had a reputation for being peaceful and welcoming to outsiders.

According to the case documents, the Judicial Doctor who examined the bodies denied that any human being could have inflicted the more extreme injuries, which he believed were more consistent with a high-speed car crash. Something even stranger and more unsettling was claimed by those who saw the bodies at their funerals: their faces were inexplicably tan, as if they had been exposed to some source of heat or radiation.

Radiation again, Viktor thought.

He re-read the article, trying to retain as much information as he could. As the train approached the outskirts of Solikamsk, he put the papers back in his bag and looked out of the window at the passing buildings. One thought echoed continuously in his mind.

What the hell happened to those people?

THREE

Viktor took a taxi from the station to the address Maksimov had given him, a shabby building at the end of a run-down street. Everything seemed to be grey: from the snow on the ground to the buildings that sagged beneath a sky the colour of cigarette ash. In this place, it was easy to imagine that the last twenty years hadn't happened, that the country was still straining beneath the weight of a failing ideology. It was a depressing place, lost and forgotten by all except those who still lingered there.

Pulling his coat tight around his neck against the biting cold, Viktor climbed the steps of the apartment building and looked for Yudin's name on an intercom panel that looked as if it hadn't worked in years. He found the name, pushed the button and waited.

To his surprise, there was a metallic click, a burst of static, and a man's voice said: 'Yes. Who is it?'

'Mr Yudin?'

'Yes.'

'My name is Viktor Strugatsky...'

'What do you want?'

'I work for the Yekaterinburg *Gazette*. I was wondering if I could talk to you.'

Yudin hesitated. 'What about?'

'The Dyatlov Pass incident.'

There was no response for several moments, and it was only the faint electrical hiss of the intercom that told Viktor that Yudin was still there.

'Mr Yudin?'

'I don't want to talk to you.'

'But Mr Yudin...'

'Go away.'

The electrical hiss stopped as the connection was broken.

'Fuck!'

He stabbed the button again.

There was another click, and Yudin's voice said: 'Young man, if you don't leave me alone, I'll call the police. Do you want me to do that?'

'Please, Mr Yudin, just a few minutes of your time, that's all I'm asking...'

'Why do you want to talk about Dyatlov Pass?'

'I've been assigned to write an article on it, to commemorate the fiftieth anniversary.'

'Anniversary?' The voice snorted. 'No one cares about that.'

'Are you sure?'

There was a pause, but Yudin was still there. Another witness who didn't want to talk. Viktor felt butterflies in his stomach. If he didn't get this interview, he could kiss his job goodbye. The old man on the other end of the crackly intercom held his future in his hands, and he didn't even know it. There was something deeply unfair about a life that could turn upon such ephemeral moments.

Viktor knew that it would be virtually impossible to get to see Yudin if he didn't want to be seen, so he decided to go for broke, and throw himself on the man's mercy. 'Look, Mr Yudin, let me be honest with you. If I don't write this article, I'm going to get fired...'

'And is that my problem?'

'No. It's mine.'

'You don't need to talk to me. You can just make it up. That's what you people do anyway, isn't it?'

Christ! Viktor thought. *Give me a break, won't you?*

'I don't want to make it up. I want to tell the truth, I want to be accurate...'

'So you can keep your job.'

He sighed. 'Yes ... so I can keep my job.'

'It was a long time ago, Mr...'

'Strugatsky. Viktor Strugatsky. Yes, sir, it was a long time ago. Fifty years, this month.'

'Fifty years,' the voice echoed, then said with resignation: 'All right, young man. I'll talk to you about Dyatlov Pass, if only to get rid of you.'

Viktor sighed again. He couldn't remember the last time he'd felt such intense relief. 'Thank you.'

'Fourth floor. Number forty-eight,' Yudin said, and broke the connection.

The front door unlocked with a heavy click. Viktor pushed it open and went into the entry hall, which was only marginally less cold than the street outside. The lift was out of order, so he climbed the stairs to the fourth floor. At the end of an ill-lit and dingy corridor, he found number 48 and knocked.

Almost immediately, the door opened to reveal Yuri Yudin.

Viktor extended his hand. 'Mr Yudin. Viktor Strugatsky.'

'So you said,' the old man replied, as he reluctantly shook his hand. He looked Viktor up and down, his thin lips curled contemptuously, his nostrils flaring slightly, as if he had just caught a whiff of something unpleasant. 'Come in.'

He turned away and shuffled down a short corridor leading, Viktor saw, to the flat's sitting room.

'Would you like some tea?' he asked without looking back.

'Please, if it's no trouble.'

'Of course it's no trouble,' he muttered.

Viktor followed him into the sitting room and took the chair he indicated. The room was small and clean, the furniture old but well maintained. It looked like the home of someone who can see pretty much all of his remaining possessions in a single glance, and has taken great care of them.

Yudin disappeared into the kitchen, and came back several minutes later bearing a tray which he placed on a low table in front of Viktor.

'Thank you for seeing me, Mr Yudin,' he said, as he poured tea for them both. He merely grunted in response.

Viktor took out his recorder. 'Would you mind if I recorded our conversation?'

He shrugged without even looking at the device, so Viktor switched it on and placed it on the table next to the tray.

'What paper did you say you were from?' Yudin asked, sitting down on an ancient leather couch which had been patched up in several places.

'The Yekaterinburg *Gazette*. My editor wants to run a commemorative piece on the incident...'

Yudin laughed – a short, ugly, humourless sound. '*Incident*. What a fine euphemism!'

Viktor took a sip of the hot, strong tea. 'What would you call it?'

He glanced up, and there was a brightness in his eyes, undimmed by the long decades of his life. 'A tragedy, certainly,' he replied. 'An atrocity, perhaps. And then again ... perhaps something so strange, we don't even have a name for it.'

'What do you mean by that?'

Yudin didn't answer; he merely regarded Viktor with his young eyes, which contrasted strangely with the lines and wrinkles of his face. He'd had fifty years to think about what happened on that night, and Viktor could only guess at the thoughts that had haunted him ever since.

He picked up his cup, his hand quivering ever so slightly, and took a sip of his tea. 'What do you know about Dyatlov Pass?' he asked.

Viktor decided to play it straight. 'Not too much, I must admit. Only the basics. In fact, before this morning, when my editor gave me this assignment, I hadn't even heard of it...'

Yudin smiled and nodded. 'Understandable, I suppose. Everyone's got other problems to think about ... where the country's going, where the *world's* going ... in some ways better than it was, in some ways worse. Things have never been more uncertain, have they? During the Cold War, at least we knew who the enemy was, because we'd been told ... even if some of us wondered whether it was really true.'

Viktor didn't say anything. Sometimes, people chose roundabout ways to get to the things they wanted to tell you; and if you tried to get to the point too quickly, they felt insulted and clammed up. So he just nodded in agreement, and waited.

'Yes,' he continued, setting down his cup. 'Other problems, other questions ... and no time to think about what happened to a small group of friends out in the wilderness fifty years ago. But it wasn't always like that, you know. Back then, everyone was talking about it...'

'You mean in Yekaterinburg – or Sverdlovsk, as it was then?'

He nodded. 'The public was disturbed and curious, in spite of the authorities' efforts to play down the whole thing. They talked about it for a long time, in spite of the risks.'

'Risks?'

Yudin gave a quiet, low chuckle. 'I suppose you're too young to remember; but when they told you not to talk about something, it was a good idea not to talk about it. That's the way it was. But like I said, people were disturbed, and they talked anyway.'

'At first, they thought the Dyatlov group might have been killed by the Mansi, didn't they?'

Yudin waved his hand irritably. 'It wasn't the Mansi: they're a gentle people, they don't do things like that. And anyway, Vozrozhdenny said that no man could have inflicted those injuries...'

'Excuse me – Vozrozhdenny?'

'The Judicial Doctor who examined the bodies. My God, you really *do* have only the basic facts, don't you?'

Viktor smiled and shrugged. It was true, after all. 'Another theory suggested that they'd been caught in an avalanche...'

Again, Yudin laughed his ugly, humourless laugh. 'Young man, let me guess: you're not much for the outdoors, right?'

'That's right. How did you know?'

'Because no one who knew the first thing about this area ever accepted *that* rubbish. For one thing, the hills nearby are low and rounded, and the slope where they made their camp had a gradient of no more than fifteen degrees...'

'Which would make an avalanche unlikely.'

'Of course it would.'

'But what about the injuries?' Viktor persisted. 'It sounds like they were caused by an extreme concussive force. Dubinina had no tongue; couldn't she have bitten it off during an avalanche?'

'No.'

'Why not?'

Yudin said nothing, and his eyes lost some of their youthfulness as he lowered them to the threadbare carpet. Now he just looked like a tired old man with too many memories.

'Mr Yudin?'

'I talked to Vozrozhdenny during the investigation. I shouldn't have – I'd been told not to, but I did anyway, because I wanted to know what had happened. He told me something about Ludmila...'

He hesitated, and ran a trembling hand through his sparse hair. His voice had begun to crack, as if he were on the point of tears.

'What did he tell you?' Viktor asked, very quietly.

'Ludmila wasn't just missing her tongue. The whole of the inside of her mouth was gone.'

Viktor looked at Yudin in silence for some moments. 'What do you mean, "gone"?'

His eyes came up suddenly. 'How else do you want me to say it?' he asked sharply. 'The inside of her mouth – her entire oral cavity – had been taken out. They tried to cover that up, too...'

'The authorities?'

'The Sverdlovsk Regional Committee of the Communist Party. The official position was that, following her death, her body had succumbed to predator action. Something, they said – and animal, perhaps a fox – had bitten off her tongue. But Vozrozhdenny didn't accept that – or at least, he *would* have accepted it if it'd only been her tongue that was missing. But he had no idea what kind of animal could core out a person's entire oral cavity.' Yudin took a gulp of his tea. 'So you see, Mr Strugatsky, it definitely wasn't an avalanche that killed my friends. Apart from anything else, there wasn't any *evidence* of one. Their tent had *not* been completely buried, and there were clear footprints leading away from it, towards the edge of the forest nearby. If it had been an avalanche, the footprints would have been obliterated.'

He fell into silence as he poured more tea for himself. The lines of his old face had deepened, etching a terrible sadness and sorrow into his features. Viktor had the feeling that if he remained silent, he would be asked to leave. This was clearly difficult for the old man to talk about, and yet he obviously wanted to talk ... to someone, even the young fool who had appeared out of nowhere on his doorstep. He wanted to keep the memory of his friends alive – because they deserved to be remembered, and also, perhaps, because he felt guilty at having survived.

Maybe that was why he had admitted Viktor to his home: not to help him keep his job, but to talk to someone who was still prepared to listen.

'Mr Yudin, what do you think happened on Kholat Syakhl?'

He looked at Viktor, and there were decades of tears in his eyes. 'Do you know what that name means?' he asked.

'It's Mansi. It means Mountain of the Dead.'

'Yes ... Mountain of the Dead. The Mansi gave it that name for a reason. They don't like that mountain, and they stay away from it.'

'I didn't realise that. I thought the place held no particular significance for them.'

'Oh, it has significance! The Mansi stay away from Kholat Syakhl because they believe it's a bad place...'

'Why?'

'There's an old legend that nine Mansi men sought refuge on the mountain after a flood, perhaps the Great Flood of antiquity, and that they died on its summit. Ever since, the mountain has been ... damned, you might say. They have always avoided it when they go hunting, or follow their deer herds. I suppose that's why the investigators came up with the theory that the Mansi had killed Igor and the others; but it's not true. The Mansi avoid Kholat Syakhl, but they don't consider it a crime or a transgression to go there. And apart from anything else, the Mansi don't go around murdering hikers who wander into their territory. But you asked me what I think happened. The truth is, I don't know, and neither does anyone else – or at least, if they do, they're not talking.' As he said this, his voice descended into bitterness.

'So you think the truth *is* known, by someone.'

'Do you know the name Lev Ivanov?'

Viktor shook his head, and Yudin gave a contemptuous grunt. 'Why am I even talking to you?'

Viktor felt his heart sink. Why indeed? What was the point in any of this? Christ, what a shitty job Maksimov had given him!

'Please, Mr Yudin, I want to learn about this,' he lied. 'And I'm sure you want people to remember what happened to your friends.'

'Are you patronising me, young man?'

'No, not at all. I'm just ... I don't think this should be forgotten.'

Yudin shook his head. 'You don't believe that. You're just saying it to get what you came for and save your skin.'

Viktor couldn't think of anything to say, so he just shook his head.

Yudin waved his hand dismissively. 'Ah, what does it matter? Why shouldn't I give you your story? And who knows, maybe it *would* keep the memory alive in people's minds, even if it's through the actions of someone who doesn't really give a damn. A nice little irony, eh?' He sighed, and Viktor felt another wave of relief flood through him. 'Anyway, Lev Ivanov was the chief investigator of the deaths at Dyatlov Pass. In 1990, he gave an interview to a small Kazakh newspaper called *Leninsky Put*. He said that he'd been ordered by senior Party officials to close the Dyatlov case and classify the findings as secret. The files were only declassified in the early 1990s, and even then, there are grounds for believing that not everything was released.'

'Do you think the military was responsible?' Viktor asked. 'Some people think that Dyatlov and the others unwittingly entered a testing area, and were accidentally killed by some kind of experimental weapon.'

Yudin shrugged. 'What would be the point of testing a weapon in a place like that? The military had plenty of test areas they could have used: the Baikonur Cosmodrome in Kazakhstan, for instance, or the rocket complex at Semipalatinsk. No, the secret weapon theory doesn't hold up.'

'What about the radiation that was found on the victims?'

Yudin shook his head. 'That aspect has been embellished over the years. There was only a trace of radiation found on Ludmila and Georgy. And that was surface radiation – not penetrative, as one would expect from a weapon.'

'I see. So, what caused those small traces?'

'Camping lanterns,' said Yudin.

'I'm sorry?'

Yudin looked at Viktor as if he were some peculiarly ungifted child. 'The mantles used in lanterns contain thorium, which is mildly radioactive. They were used as wicks to keep the lanterns burning. But the point is that they were quite fragile, and would crumble to dust unless handled properly. That dust could easily have got onto their clothing.'

'I see ... Mr Yudin, you said that what happened might be something so strange, we don't even have a name for it. What did you mean by that?'

Yudin fell silent for some moments. His eyes became unfocussed beneath a pensive frown. 'I was thinking of the spheres,' he said.

'The spheres?'

'That was something else Ivanov mentioned in his interview. The declassified files contain testimony from the leader of another group of ski-hikers who were in the area on that night. They were camped about fifty kilometres south of Kholat Syakhl. He said that his group saw orange spheres floating in the sky in the direction of the mountain. Ivanov thought that the spheres were somehow connected with what happened to Igor and the others. He speculated that one of them might have left their tent during the night, seen the spheres and alerted the others. Whatever happened next caused them to flee from their camp ... into the darkness and the cold.'

Yudin saw the expression on Viktor's face, and scowled at him. 'You think I'm talking rubbish, don't you?'

Shit, now I've really blown it, he thought. 'No, Mr Yudin, absolutely not,' he said quickly. 'It's just that ... well, it sounds like those other hikers reckoned they saw UFOs.'

'And you don't believe in such things, right?'

Viktor shrugged. 'I would have to say no. I mean ... there's no evidence, is there? Nothing conclusive...'

Yudin gave a disgusted snort. 'A lot you know. The spheres have been seen on more than one occasion, throughout the region. The last sighting was just a few months ago.'

'What do you think they are?'

'Well, I certainly don't believe they're spaceships from another planet, if that's what you're thinking!'

'Not at all. No, of course not. So, what do you think? You've said you don't think a secret weapon was to blame...'

'Like I said before,' he said in a tired, exasperated voice. 'Something so strange, we don't even have a name for it.'

Something occurred to Viktor just then. 'Hold on,' he said. 'That doesn't fit. If one of Dyatlov's group had gone out, then the tent's flap would have been open, and there would have been no reason for them to cut their way out, which is what the report said.'

Yudin smiled at him. 'You're right, it doesn't fit. *Nothing* about what happened on that night fits. It's like trying to solve a jigsaw puzzle with pieces from different pictures. There's no logic to it, nothing makes sense.' His smile broadened, became almost cruel, and his voice grew vehement as he added: 'You see what you've got yourself into, young man? You'll *never* get to the bottom of it, and if you're not careful, you'll spend years thinking about it, and wondering, and speculating, and theorising, and all your speculations and theories will crowd around you during the night, and they'll never allow you any rest.' His gaze dropped again to the floor. 'But of course, that doesn't have to happen to you. Go back to Yekaterinburg, Mr Strugatsky, write your article and forget about it. That's my advice.'

'What about Lev Ivanov?' Viktor persisted. 'Is he still alive?'

Yudin shook his head. 'He died a few years ago.'

'And the members of the search party ... most of them were students at the Institute. Some of them must still be around...'

'I suppose so. Look, if you really want to pursue this, then you should talk to Vadim Konstantinov.'

'Who?'

Yudin repeated the name. 'He runs the Dyatlov Foundation in Yekaterinburg. He was only a boy at the time, about twelve, I think. But he remembers it well, and ever since, he's been trying to find out what really happened. That's why he started the Foundation: to keep the memory of Igor and the others alive. He's been petitioning the government for years to declassify the rest of the files on the incident – without much luck, I have to say. I'm sure he'll help you in whatever way he can. He lives on Yasnaya Street, number eighteen.'

'Mr Yudin,' Viktor said, 'did you ever go to Otorten or Kholat Syakhl after ... after it happened?'

'Oh yes,' the old man replied. 'I went to both mountains as soon as the travel prohibition was lifted, in the summer of 1962.'

'Did you find anything there?' Viktor asked, only realising what a stupid question it was when the words were already out.

Yudin gave a small, sad smile, lowered his eyes and shook his head. 'No. I didn't find anything. But Konstantinov did...'

'He did?'

'He led an expedition there two years ago.'

'What did he find?'

Yudin slowly brought his eyes up to meet Viktor's. He was still smiling. 'A metal graveyard,' he said.

'A ... what does that mean?'

Yudin shook his head. 'Go back to Yekaterinburg. Go and talk to Vadim. He'll tell you what he found.'

'Why won't *you* tell me?'

'Because I'm tired, boy!' he said loudly, and when Viktor looked into his eyes, he saw all the weight of the years and the unanswered questions bearing down on him as heavily as all the snows of the mountain where his friends had died. 'I'm tired, and I would like to take a nap. I always do, at this time of the day.'

Viktor didn't know what else to say, so he just nodded, and said: 'Thank you for seeing me.'

'You're welcome.'

As they walked to the door, Yudin said: 'You know what Kholat Syakhl means ... but do you know what Otorten means?'

Viktor turned back to face him. 'The mountain they were originally making for? No, I don't.'

'It's also a Mansi phrase. Its literal translation is "Do Not Go There".'

BASKOV (2)

I hardly need state that Strugatsky fascinated me, not least because, as his initial medical examination (conducted upon his arrival at Peveralsk) revealed, he appeared normal in every way – apart from the premature greyness of his hair. There was nothing out of the ordinary about his temperature, blood pressure or EKG; his coordination was well within normal parameters, as was his visual acuity and hearing, and his ability to sense different temperatures. The only departures from the norm were trivial, and no more than one would expect from his recent physical ordeal, from which he appeared to have made a virtually total recovery. His IQ, likewise, was above average, but not surprisingly so. In short, there was nothing to distinguish him from ten thousand other men of his age and background.

My task was to establish Strugatsky's mental state, while the criminal militia conducted its own investigation into the events preceding his arrival in Yurta Anyamova on 14 February. The Russian legal system allows for three classifications of a person's mental state: insanity, limited sanity, and sanity. In addition, there are four categories within the mental illness criterion: chronic psychiatric disorder, temporary psychiatric disorder, mental deficiency, and other mental disturbances.

I was therefore required to place Strugatsky within one of these categories before the decision could be taken on whether to send him for trial. It will perhaps be helpful if I briefly describe each of them. 'Chronic psychiatric disorder' includes conditions such as schizophrenia, epilepsy and other conditions that are continuous or intermittent. 'Temporary psychiatric disorder' includes substance-induced psychosis and disorders caused by infectious process, and other conditions which are reversible and have the potential for a complete recovery. 'Mental deficiency' includes both acquired and congenital intellectual deficits and other disorders, such as dementias, mental retardation and other cognitive disorders. Finally, 'other mental disturbances' include abnormalities of mental functioning and behaviour, such as character pathology, disorders of dependent behaviour, and so on.

Although I had already begun to form an opinion on Strugatsky (which at this stage tended more towards sanity or limited sanity, than insanity), I was intrigued by his fascination with the Dyatlov Pass incident. From his recollections, it seemed that he had become absorbed in it very quickly – perhaps too quickly – and I decided to watch for signs of obsessive compulsive disorder.

Following dinner the previous evening, I had done a little of my own research on the events of 1959. My wife, Nataliya, is a music teacher, and particularly promising students often come to our house for additional tuition in the evenings; so, while she was busy at the piano, I found some online material on the incident, and read it.

It was certainly an intriguing case, and one of which I had been only vaguely aware until now. The facts seemed to point to an avalanche as the cause of the nine ski-hikers' deaths – although, as Strugatsky had said, the Soviet authorities themselves seemed to have discounted this as an explanation.

I also found a number of black-and-white photographs of Igor Dyatlov and the others, which succeeded in bringing that long-ago mystery into sharper focus in my mind. Some of the photographs had been developed from a roll of film discovered at the abandoned campsite, while the rest had been taken by members of the search-and-rescue expedition. I examined each of them in turn.

The first was of four members of the party: Ludmila Dubinina, Rustem Slobodin, Alexander Zolotarev and Zinaida Kolmogorova. They were all smiling and wrapped up in their cold-weather gear, and in the background there was a line of snow-covered trees. The men were good-looking in a rugged kind of way, and the women were pretty and looked strong and healthy. In fact, I could see even in the low-quality image that Zinaida Kolmogorova was quite beautiful.

The next photograph was taken outside a log cabin. Yuri Yudin was hugging Ludmila as he prepared to leave the group and return to Sverdlovsk, while Igor Dyatlov, wearing skis and a backpack, looked on. Again, all were smiling. Even in those grainy old photos, it was clear that these people liked and cared for each other; and the fact that they couldn't have known what awaited them on the icy slopes of a distant mountain made the images all the more poignant.

The next photograph showed three members of the group setting up their camp. They were surrounded by snow, and in the background were a few trunks of pine trees. It looked extremely cold: the three people were wrapped up tightly, their faces obscured by hoods, so that it was impossible to tell who they were.

The next photo was of Igor Dyatlov himself, the leader of the group. He was smiling widely, his eyes half closed against the cold, his sparse moustache and beard only visible because of the frost clinging to them. There was something about his face that inspired confidence, and I realised that I would have had no problem following him into the wilderness, just as the others had.

Then there was a photo of Yuri Yudin. He was in profile, leaning forward, apparently writing something, with a dark cloth cap perched on the back of his head. He had a strong jaw, a wide, full-lipped mouth, and eyes that displayed humour even though he was clearly concentrating on his task. I found myself smiling at his image.

My smile faded when I saw the next three photographs. The first had been taken by a member of the search-and-rescue team on 26 February 1959, and showed an unidentified man looking at the remains of the camp. The tent was wrecked and half-covered with snow. The land sloped gently away into a grainy and ill-defined distance. The scene was one of desolation, complete and unaccountable, and it contrasted horribly with the earlier images of smiling faces and warm camaraderie. The second photograph was of a small, ragged piece of metal, which contained a pattern of squares, like a waffle iron. The caption below read: 'A metal fragment from Igor Dyatlov's Pass that some believe to be evidence in the case.' *Perhaps*, I thought. *But evidence of what?*

The third photograph was the most disturbing and upsetting of all. It showed two bodies lying side by side in the snow, face-down, clearly frozen solid. Their arms were stretched in front of them, as if they had been trying to reach out towards something when the cold finally overcame them...

———

I went to Strugatsky's room at 10.00 a.m. the following day. He was up, washed and dressed, and his demeanour suggested that he had been waiting for me with something approaching eagerness.

'Good morning, Dr Baskov,' he said, rising from the armchair, as I entered the room.

'Good morning, Viktor. How are you today?'

'Ready for our next session.' His eyes were bright and clear, and his expression was open. He seemed very enthusiastic, and I commented on this as I sat at the desk and switched on the recorder.

'I've been thinking about our conversations,' he replied as he returned to the armchair. 'It feels good to tell someone...' He hesitated. 'Well, perhaps "good" isn't quite the right word. But it helps me to get things clear in my mind.'

'I'm glad to hear that.'

'I take it you've read up on the Dyatlov Pass incident?'

'Yes I have,' I said, rather surprised.

Strugatsky noted my expression, and smiled. 'I've no great intuition, Doctor. I'd have been shocked if you hadn't. After all, that's what we're really talking about. That's the only thing that matters.'

Not for the first time, I was struck by the calmness in Strugatsky's demeanour. To be sure, he displayed brief flashes of apprehensiveness which at times bordered on paranoia, but these either dissipated or were successfully controlled quite quickly. His bearing was that of someone moving in and out of emotional equilibrium more or less at random. It was not a good sign.

'The only thing that matters?' I said. 'What about the deaths of your friends?'

'The two are inseparable.'

Interesting.

'In what way, inseparable?'

'You'll understand. I'll explain it to you.'

FOUR

Viktor thought about his interview with Yuri Yudin on the way back to Yekaterinburg. The old man was right, of course: nothing about the Dyatlov Pass incident made any sense. There were plenty of theories, but each one raised more questions than it answered. Yudin had said it was like a jigsaw puzzle made up of pieces from different pictures; but it was also like a cubist painting of an object seen from multiple viewpoints. If you focussed on any one element in isolation, it kind of made sense – but if you stepped back and took in the rest of the picture, it became bizarre and confusing, contradictory and counterintuitive.

He took out his DAT recorder and rewound to the start of the interview. There was one other person in the compartment, an elderly man who was reading a newspaper, so Viktor took out a set of earphones, plugged them in and played back their conversation.

At one point, he stopped the recording, rewound and listened again.

You'll never *get to the bottom of it, and if you're not careful, you'll spend years thinking about it, and wondering, and speculating, and theorising, and all your speculations and theories will crowd around you during the night, and they'll never allow you any rest.*

Viktor guessed that Yudin was describing his own life with those words.

By the time he got back to Yekaterinburg, it was too late to go to the Dyatlov Foundation, so he went straight home and transcribed the interview onto his computer, highlighting the parts which he thought would make good quotes for his article.

He also went online and did some background research on Vadim Konstantinov. Retired now, Konstantinov had been a Professor of

Anthropology in the Humanities Department of the Ural State Technical Institute. He had published a large number of monographs, mainly on the indigenous tribes of Siberia, and was highly regarded in his field.

At seven o'clock, Maksimov called and asked how the interview had gone. Viktor was glad to be able to tell him that it had gone well, and that he'd be seeing Vadim Konstantinov the next day. Maksimov seemed satisfied, and said he was looking forward to reading the piece. There was something in his tone of voice which implied that Viktor had better start looking for another job if he didn't like what he read.

———

The next morning, he drove to the address on Yasnaya Street which Yudin had given him. He hoped he wouldn't have to beg to be allowed in this time. He needn't have worried: when he pressed the button marked KONSTANTINOV, DYATLOV FOUNDATION on the intercom panel, a deep, strong voice burst from the speaker. 'Konstantinov.'

Viktor introduced myself, and explained why he was there.

'Come in, Mr Strugatsky!' Konstantinov said, sounding as if he'd been expecting him, and was glad he'd finally arrived. 'Ground floor, take the corridor on the left.'

When Viktor got to Konstantinov's apartment, the door was already open, and he was standing there waiting, his hand outstretched. He was tall and well-built, getting on in years now, of course, but still strong-looking and vital. He had an unruly shock of grey hair, and his features, though chiselled by time, were still animated by the restless ghost of his youth.

Viktor shook his hand and thanked him for agreeing to an interview without any notice.

'Not at all, Viktor. May I call you Viktor?'

'Of course.'

'Yuri phoned me last night, and told me you'd be coming to see me. He seemed quite impressed with you.'

'Really?' Viktor said, as Konstantinov ushered him into the apartment. 'I wouldn't have said so, myself.'

He waved the comment aside. 'Yuri's like that. He likes to give the wrong impression, sometimes. It's all that's left of the playfulness he once had. And there's always a negative within the positive, don't you think? That's the way human beings work. Come through to the study.'

He led Viktor to a large room, panelled with dark wood and comfortably furnished with a leather couch and armchairs and a low coffee table in walnut, polished to a high sheen. The walls were lined with bookshelves, and at one end of the room, in front of a pair of tall sash windows, stood an ancient-looking oak desk which was completely covered with papers and more books. Viktor could see a white-frosted communal garden through the windows.

'Welcome to the Dyatlov Foundation,' said Konstantinov as he motioned to one of the armchairs.

This wasn't quite what Viktor had expected. For some reason, he had imagined some kind of office with researchers and secretaries, and people talking on the phone to government officials and foreign news correspondents. But of course, it wasn't like that: in reality, the grandly-named Dyatlov Foundation was just a single man trying to keep alive the memory of nine people who didn't deserve to die the way they did. Konstantinov was very much on his own, and Viktor found myself warming to him even more for that reason.

As if he had read his thoughts, the elderly man smiled broadly and said: 'Doesn't look like much, does it?'

'I ... wouldn't say that,' Viktor replied lamely, with a shrug.

Konstantinov chuckled and disappeared into the kitchen. A few minutes later, he returned with a large tray.

'Coffee!' he announced, and poured two cups. It was strong, rich and utterly delicious. 'Jamaican Blue Mountain,' he said. 'I have a friend who imports it.'

'Can I have his number?'

Konstantinov gave Viktor a broad grin and said: 'No.'

Viktor indicated the recorder which he had placed on the coffee table. 'Do you mind?'

'Not at all. Now, down to business. You want to talk about the Dyatlov Pass incident.'

'That's right.'

'And you work for the *Gazette*.'

Viktor nodded.

'I know Sergei Maksimov. He's an arsehole.'

Viktor spluttered over his coffee. 'Yes, I suppose he is. But why do *you* think so?'

'I've submitted a number of articles on the incident to the paper over the years. He always knocked them back. Wasn't interested, until now. It's because of the fiftieth anniversary, isn't it?'

Viktor nodded. 'But he didn't mention your name to me. Yudin's, yes, but not yours.'

'Maybe he wanted you to work for your money, get here under your own steam. I don't know. Like I said, he's an arsehole.'

Viktor glanced around the room. 'This must be a lonely job. And frustrating.'

'Frustrating, yes,' Konstantinov replied. 'But never lonely. There's a difference between solitude and loneliness: solitude is the state of being alone; loneliness is not liking it. I don't mind it, not at all; and I have the spirits of the others to keep me company.' He gave a small embarrassed laugh. 'Not literally, of course, but their memory is still here, along with the memory of what happened to them.'

'And what *did* happen to them, in your opinion?'

He sat back in his chair. 'Ah, what indeed? If you're looking for a simple answer, I'm afraid I will have to disappoint you, for there *is* none.'

'I gathered as much from Yudin. He seems to think that it was something completely beyond the bounds of human experience.'

'And what do you think?'

Viktor shook his head. 'I can't even speculate. None of the theories stands up to close scrutiny.'

Konstantinov nodded. 'It's like a Rubik's Cube, isn't it? You think you've solved the puzzle ... and then you turn it over and see that one of the faces still has all six colours on it, and you realize that you haven't solved it at all.'

'Are you any closer to solving it?'

Konstantinov sighed and looked into his coffee cup. 'It's very difficult to solve a puzzle when some of the pieces are missing.'

'You mean the parts of the official report that are still classified.'

'Yes. Some of it was released in the early 1990s, but not all of it. But one day, I'll get them to declassify the rest.'

'You sound very confident.'

'I am.'

Viktor put down his cup and leaned forward. 'Yudin mentioned that you led an expedition to Kholat Syakhl a couple of years ago. He said that you found something ... a "metal graveyard", he called it. Could you tell me about that? Did you bring anything back?'

Konstantinov stood up and went to a large filing cabinet between two bookshelves. 'I'll tell you about it, and I'll dig out some of the fragments I brought back. But first..' He withdrew a sheaf of papers from the cabinet. 'First, you might like to have this. It's a timeline of the events before, during and after the incident, plus some other stuff you may find useful. It will help to get things clear in your mind, and it will certainly help with the article you're writing. You can keep it: I have several copies.'

He handed Viktor the papers, and walked off towards a large wooden cabinet that dominated the far end of the room. While he opened the cabinet and started rummaging around inside, Viktor laid the papers on the coffee table. He was about to begin reading the timeline, but Konstantinov began to speak, running through the events without any hesitation. Viktor supposed that he knew them so well, he could have done it in his sleep; so he left the papers where they were, poured himself another cup of coffee and listened.

'On the 25th of January 1959, Igor Dyatlov and his friends arrived at Ivdel, and stayed the night. The following day, they caught a lift with a truck heading to Vizhai. The morning after that, they set out for Otorten Mountain. The trek was classed as Category III, the most difficult and dangerous for the time of year; but they were all experienced ski-hikers, and they were confident that they could make the trip without any serious mishaps. They expected to be away for three weeks.

'On the 28th of January, Yuri Yudin became ill, and it was clear that he would have to abandon the journey and return to Sverdlovsk. This, Viktor,' Konstantinov said over his shoulder, 'is all that we know for sure, incredible as it seems. For the rest, all we have are the diaries and photographs discovered at the camp, and we must reconstruct the events as best we can, from that surviving evidence.

'For the next three days, the group skied across the land, following the herding paths of the Mansi people, until they reached the Auspia River at the edge of the highland zone. There they constructed a wooden shelter, and left some food and equipment for their homeward journey.

'On the 1st of February, they began their climb towards Otorten, but the weather turned bad, and they lost their way in the snowstorm. Late that afternoon, they found themselves on the slopes of the neighbouring mountain, Kholat Syakhl. Do you know what those names mean, Viktor?'

'Yes. Kholat Syakhl means "Mountain of the Dead" and Otorten means "Do Not Go There".'

Konstantinov nodded. He had found what he was looking for, a large wooden box about the size of an attaché case, which he brought over and placed on the coffee table. He didn't open it right away, but sat down and continued with his narrative.

'The storm was bad ... bad enough to throw them off course and onto the neighbouring mountain. They doubtless intended to set up camp for the night, and then continue on to Otorten the next morning. They pitched their tent at a point about one thousand, one hundred metres above sea level. It was cold, *damned* cold: about minus thirty degrees Celsius. Visibility must have been very poor, since they needn't have made camp in such an exposed spot.'

'Because they were close to the edge of a pine forest,' Viktor said, recalling the article he had read.

'Exactly. The forest was less than one-and-a-half kilometres downslope. But they didn't see it.'

'Or maybe they saw it but didn't want to go there.'

Konstantinov glanced at him. 'What makes you say that?'

'I'm not sure,' he replied with a shrug. 'It's something that just occurred to me. I'm sorry. I don't know why.'

'No need to apologise. I don't know why it hadn't occurred to me. Sometimes, you need a fresh perspective, I suppose.'

'It's just an idle speculation.'

'But one that's worth throwing into the pot, I think.'

Konstantinov hesitated, frowning. Viktor asked him to go on with his account.

'Having pitched their tent,' he said, 'the group settled down for the night. And then ... *something* happened. Dyatlov and the others ripped open the tent and fled into the cold and the darkness, down the slope away from the summit of Kholat Syakhl. There can be no doubt that they were all terrified, so terrified that they did not pause even to untie the tent's flaps. Whatever was happening, they knew that they had to get as far away from the tent as possible, as *quickly* as possible...'

'Which is emphasised by the fact that they were partially dressed.'

'Correct. The tracks found by the search party suggest that the group initially scattered in all directions, but came back together about three hundred metres down the slope. I believe that they converged beneath a large pine tree.'

'Where Krivonischenko and Doroshenko were discovered.'

'That's right, although we can't be absolutely certain.'

'Why not?'

'Because the footprints came to an end five hundred metres from the tent.'

'I don't understand how that could be.'

'I don't either, Viktor,' said Konstantinov with a small, sad smile. 'In any event, they lit a fire beneath the pine tree. I believe that they stayed there for some time, but someone – perhaps Dyatlov – decided that they couldn't stay there much longer: the fire wouldn't be enough to keep them alive in that freezing cold. Someone climbed the pine tree to a height of five metres, perhaps to get their bearings in relation to the camp, or perhaps in an attempt to see what was happening there.

'Three of the group – Dyatlov, Zinaida Kolmogorova and Rustem Slobodin – decided to try and get back to the camp. They never made it: they all died of hypothermia. Dyatlov was the first to succumb: his body was found three hundred metres from the pine tree. He was on his back, and was looking in the direction of the camp when he died. A hundred and eighty metres on towards the camp lay the body of Slobodin, with a slight fracture in his skull. Finally, a hundred and fifty metres on from him, Zina died. Both she and Slobodin looked like they had been crawling towards the camp when the cold overcame them.

'The others waited, and waited. And while they waited, Georgy Krivonischenko and Yuri Doroshenko also died. Or maybe it didn't happen quite like that: maybe they died first, and that's what made Dyatlov decide that they *had* to get back to the camp. I don't know; that's open to interpretation...'

'Like just about everything else in this case,' Viktor said.

Konstantinov grunted in agreement, and continued: 'It must have been after midnight by then. That's when the first transfer of clothing occurred; Ludmila Dubinina wrapped her feet in pieces of Krivonischenko's woollen trousers. The four surviving members of the party – Ludmila Dubinina, Alexander Zolotarev, Nikolai Thibeaux-Brignollel and Alexander Kolevatov – decided *not* to make for the camp. I've wondered many times why they made that decision. Were they disorientated, their minds clouded by fear and cold? Did they think they had a better chance of reaching the cover of the nearby trees than making it back up the slope? Or was something still happening in the camp that dissuaded them from returning?

'Whatever the reason, it's likely that at this point they sustained the injuries that would soon result in their deaths. Dubinina and Zolotarev suffered serious chest injuries, with many broken ribs, while Thibeaux-Brignollel's skull was shattered. They made it into the forest, doubtless carrying Thibeaux-Brignollel, who was either dead or unconscious. They managed to find cover in a ravine, where Dubinina died of a combination of her chest injuries and hypothermia. It must have been then that Zolotarev took her coat and hat in a hopeless effort to keep himself warm. Thibeaux-Brignollel would almost certainly have been dead by then, if he hadn't been killed instantly when he sustained his head injury. Finally, Kolevatov, alone and terrified – though uninjured – succumbed to hypothermia.

'At some point between their deaths and the discovery of their bodies three months later, something came upon them, and pulled out Ludmila's tongue, along with the lining of her oral cavity.'

Viktor felt his skin crawl as Konstantinov finished his narrative. 'What could have done that to her?' he asked, very quietly. 'Some kind of predator, or scavenger?'

'Ludmila's post-mortem injury is problematic,' he said. 'One can conceive of an animal removing her tongue ... but the lining of her mouth? That too is possible, I suppose, but one would think that it would have caused much more damage to her face.' He paused for some moments, and then continued: 'There's one other element in the case, which is at least as problematic as all the others.'

'What's that?'

'The search party found four wristwatches, two of which were on Nikolai Thibeaux-Brignollel's wrist. The watches all showed different times.'

'Different times?'

Konstantinov nodded. 'The ones on Nikolai's wrist showed 8:14 and 8:39. The other two showed 8:45 and 5:31.'

They sat in silence. Konstantinov's narrative had brought home the enormity of what had happened to Igor Dyatlov and his friends: the strange horror of it, the bizarre outrage. Viktor said: 'From what I've read, and from what Yudin told me, the investigating authorities kept their options wide open; they were even willing to consider some completely unknown phenomenon as being responsible for the hikers' deaths. That's what the chief investigator, Lev Ivanov, thought, isn't it?'

'You're thinking of the spheres, yes?'

Viktor nodded.

'There are some theories about them. All we know for sure is that a group of geography students were camping about fifty kilometres south of Kholat Syakhl on the night the Dyatlov group died, and saw several bright orange spheres floating in the night sky above the mountain.' He picked up the sheaf of papers, leafed through them until he found the page he was looking for, and read aloud: 'One student wrote that they also saw "a shining circular body fly from the south-west to the north-east. The shining disc was practically the size of a full moon, a blue-white light surrounded by a blue halo. The halo brightly flashed like the flashes of distant lightning. When the body disappeared behind the horizon, the sky lit up in that place for a few more minutes."' He put the papers down. 'That's a direct quote from one of the students. What it means, I don't know.'

'Yudin said that the orange spheres have been seen often. The last sighting was quite recent.'

'That's right,' Konstantinov said. 'And not just here in Russia, but right across the globe. They're one of the most commonly reported types of so-called UFOs. Ivanov believed that at some point during the night of the 1st of February, one of the Dyatlov party left the tent (perhaps to go to the toilet), saw the spheres and alerted the others. In panic, they fled their camp; but as they were running down the slope, one of the spheres exploded, causing the injuries.'

Viktor nodded. 'Yudin mentioned that, but...'

'But if it happened that way,' Konstantinov interrupted, 'why did they cut their way out of the tent? It would already have been open, right?'

'Right.'

'That's one reason why I don't agree with Ivanov's interpretation of the events. They may have seen the spheres that night – in fact, they almost certainly did – but I don't think they were killed by them.'

Viktor's eyes fell upon the box which Konstantinov had placed on the table between them. He had been so drawn in by the account that he had forgotten all about it. Konstantinov smiled at the expectancy in his face, opened the box and began to take out its contents, placing them carefully on the table's polished surface.

'In the summer of 2007,' he explained, 'I led a small party of researchers to the area, where we found what Yuri so poetically refers to as the "metal graveyard". This is just a small sample of what's there.'

Viktor looked at each of the objects in turn. Most of them were lumps of metal, battered and misshapen, as if they had once formed part of some device or vehicle that had been destroyed. One in particular drew his attention. It wasn't a piece of metal, but a torn fragment of cloth. It was heavy and dark green in colour. Viktor pointed to it. 'What's this?'

Konstantinov was regarding him intently. 'It's a piece of a soldier's uniform,' he replied.

FIVE

'So the military *was* there,' Viktor said.

'At some point, at least, yes, there's very little doubt about that,' Konstantinov replied.

'That's one of the theories, isn't it? That the Dyatlov party were killed by the military after stumbling into some kind of weapons testing area.'

'Correct, although personally I don't hold with it.'

'Because there would have been no point in testing hardware in that area.'

'Precisely,' said Konstantinov. 'If they were testing some kind of top secret super weapon, they would have done so in a properly controlled area...'

'Like Baikonur or Semipalatinsk.'

'Of course. They wouldn't have risked exposure by doing it anywhere else, no matter how remote. Don't forget that sports tourism was hugely popular back then: thousands of people across the country took part in expeditions all year round. On that very night, there was a party of skiers just fifty kilometres south of Kholat Syakhl.' Konstantinov shook his head. 'No, I don't believe there was any military testing in the area. It just doesn't make any sense.'

'Nevertheless...' Viktor said, indicating the pieces of metal on the table.

'Take a closer look,' said Konstantinov. 'Do you notice anything in particular about this material? Something about its general nature?'

Viktor shrugged. 'It looks like wreckage.'

'Exactly.'

'Could this be what's left of a missile, perhaps fired from Baikonur? Maybe a weapon that went off course?' Viktor was thinking of the orange spheres which the other skiers had seen in the sky that night. They could easily have misinterpreted missiles for something strange and unknown.

'A logical supposition,' Konstantinov said. 'But you're on the wrong track. A missile fired from Baikonur *could* have reached the Northern Urals, but there are no records of a launch at that time.'

'How do you know?'

'I've spoken with officials who know what they're talking about – from the Korolyov Rocket and Space Corporation, for instance. Nothing was launched from Baikonur on the night Dyatlov and the others died.'

'What about Plesetsk? That was the Soviet Union's main launch pad, wasn't it?'

'It was, but Plesetsk was still being built at that time. It didn't become operational until towards the end of 1959.'

Viktor regarded Konstantinov in silence for a few moments. He met his gaze with a slight smile.

'I get the feeling there's something you're not telling me,' Viktor said, returning the smile. 'Maybe you're waiting for me to think of it myself, but I guess I'm too dumb.'

Konstantinov laughed. 'Not at all! You're nearly there, but let me give you another couple of clues. First, and I don't know if Yuri told you this, but soon after the incident, the authorities asked him to identify the owner of every object found at the camp. He did so, but there were certain items which he was unable to match with any of his friends: a pair of skis, a piece of one ski, and a pair of glasses. Second, I have seen documents which lead me to believe that the criminal investigation into the deaths at Dyatlov Pass was opened on the 6th of February, *two weeks* before the search party found the camp.'

'What? You're joking!'

Konstantinov shook his head.

'So the authorities already knew that those people were dead. They already knew that the Dyatlov Pass incident – whatever it was – had occurred.'

'That's my belief. They may have hoped that the investigation would turn up some useful information; or it may have been nothing more than a useless formality they knew would yield nothing, but which they were obliged to follow. I'm not sure which, and I suspect that in the final analysis, it doesn't matter.'

The picture was quickly becoming clearer in Viktor's mind. 'I think I know what you're suggesting,' he said.

'Go on,' said Konstantinov.

'You don't think the military were to blame for what happened.' He picked up the piece of torn and frayed cloth, which appeared to have come from a soldier's uniform. 'You think the military were victims of it too, just like Dyatlov and the others.'

'Exactly!' said Konstantinov triumphantly. 'They weren't testing some bizarre, ultra-secret weapon: they were *investigating* something ... something in that particular area of the northern Urals...'

'And they ran into more trouble than they could handle.'

'That's what I believe. The authorities conducted the investigation because they knew they had to, and when Ivanov was unsuccessful – as they knew he would be – they ordered him to close the case, classified the incident as top secret – which had been their intention all along – and closed the area to civilians for the next three years. Many people think that the truth about the military's culpability in the Dyatlov Pass incident is hidden away in some government vault, but I don't believe that. I believe that the Soviet government knew that *something* was out there, and dispatched a military unit to investigate. But the unit fell victim to the object of its investigation...' Konstantinov indicated the wreckage on the table '...and was destroyed by it.'

'And the items found at the camp? The items whose owners Yudin couldn't identify?'

'I think at least two people – soldiers – came upon the camp around the time of the incident – whether it was just before, during, or just after, there's no way of knowing. Perhaps – and I'm speculating here – it was the soldiers who alerted Dyatlov and the others that something was happening, and that they should leave the area immediately. That could even account for the ripped tent: maybe Dyatlov and the others didn't cut their way out of it, maybe the soldiers cut their way *in*, in their frantic haste to warn the campers.'

'But if that's the case,' said Viktor, 'why weren't there more tracks at the camp? That's one of the key elements in the mystery, isn't it? The fact that there was no evidence that anyone else had been there. It was one of the reasons the investigators dismissed the idea that the Mansi had killed them.'

'That's true, although it is possible that in the days following the incident, another military unit arrived to remove the evidence that anyone else had been there. They obliterated the tracks left by their colleagues in the snow, but missed the skis and the pair of glasses.'

'I suppose that's possible,' Viktor said, although it didn't quite ring true to him. Once again, he felt himself coming up against the intractable strangeness of the Dyatlov Pass incident, the way that each explanation, each scenario, didn't quite account for all the elements.

Konstantinov read his expression and, a little guiltily, he voiced his concerns.

'I understand your reservations,' he said. 'But consider this: one of the members of the search party, a young medical student, said that she recalled *eleven* bodies being recovered from Kholat Syakhl, not nine. She added that the two extra bodies, which were found buried in the ravine, were removed by the army and taken to an unknown location. Unfortunately,' he added, 'I have been unable to locate this witness; nor have I been able to shed light on the identities of the two extra victims.'

'I hadn't realised that.'

'There are many different accounts of the Dyatlov Pass incident. And many of them differ in their details, to a greater or lesser extent. Some mention the extra bodies, some don't. At any rate, it would help if the government released the files that are still classified.'

'You've had no luck with your petitions?'

'None.'

'Maybe the answers *are* in those files. Maybe that's why they won't release them.'

Konstantinov sighed. 'Or perhaps all they would demonstrate is the authorities' ignorance and powerlessness in the face of whatever is in the area around Otorten and Kholat Syakhl.'

'On the other hand, even if they don't hold the answers, they might at least suggest the right *questions* to ask.'

'Yes,' said Konstantinov. 'They might.'

Viktor felt that the interview was moving naturally towards its conclusion, but there was one other thing he wanted to ask Konstantinov. 'Can you tell me something about the tan which was observed on the bodies?'

Konstantinov looked at him in silence, and for a while he thought he had inadvertently said something to offend his host. Konstantinov picked up the coffee pot, saw that it was empty and began to rise from his chair. But then he hesitated, and sat down again. 'The tan on the bodies,' he said. 'I've thought about that often.'

'At first sight, it would appear to be one of the strangest aspects of the incident. But is that really the case? Could it have been a result of their exposure to the sun? I'm not a skier myself, but I have friends who are, and they always come back from their trips with a tan ... a combination of the sun itself, and light reflected off the snow...' Viktor hesitated, and ended with a shrug.

'You're right, of course; but that wasn't the case with Igor and the others. I was only a small boy at the time, but I was very good friends with Igor. He was like an older brother, and I loved him as one. So, when it happened, when they were finally brought home, my parents allowed me to attend his funeral. I looked into his coffin, and saw the hue of his skin. It wasn't a normal tan, Viktor. I know, because in the years since, my connections have allowed me to examine bodies of people who have died of exposure, and who have lain in the winter sun for hours or days. And it was nothing like the colour of Igor's skin. Nor does that theory explain the greyness of his hair ... *the greyness of a twenty-three-year-old man's hair.*'

'What about the others?' Viktor asked. 'Had their hair turned grey as well?'

'Yes, all of them.' Konstantinov had been gazing at the empty coffee pot while he said all this. Now, he raised haunted eyes. 'There are things that happen to a child, Viktor, which set him on the course he will take through life. A book read, a picture seen, an event witnessed. A defining moment, at which all of life's potentialities collapse into a single intention – or a destiny, if you will. With me, it happened on the day I looked into my friend's coffin, and saw what had been done to him. I still remember what I was thinking at that moment: a simple question. *What happened to you? What happened?*' He smiled. 'How deceptive the simplicity of that question! It has haunted me all my life, Viktor, and I confess that sometimes I dream of Igor and the others, whose ghosts have returned to me, asking: *What happened to us?* I've spent years – decades – trying to find out. And now I wonder if I ever will.'

Viktor lowered his eyes, unable to meet that gaze that was so immensely desperate, so eerily troubled. 'I suppose...' he began, and hesitated. 'I ... suppose it depends on what's in the files that are still classified, and if you ever manage to secure their release.'

'Yes. I think it probably depends on that.'

'It's very hard to imagine what could have turned their hair grey. I mean, you hear stories about fear turning a person's hair white, but that's just a myth. It doesn't work like that: even if that could happen, the hair would have to grow out in its new colour. No one's hair instantly changes colour as a result of something they've experienced.'

'True,' replied Konstantinov. 'So the change in hair colour would have to have been the result of some external physical agency. The change in skin colour, too. Perhaps some form of radiation.'

'But Yudin said radiation wasn't a factor. He mentioned the thorium wicks of their lanterns as being responsible for the levels detected on the bodies.'

'He's right, but I wasn't talking about that. I'm talking about some other form of radiation, one that is at present unknown to us.'

'Wouldn't that be detectable by our instruments?'

Konstantinov gave a dry chuckle. 'Perhaps not, if it's still unknown to us. And there's evidence that the authorities were thinking along the same lines.'

'How so?'

'Igor and the others were buried without their internal organs: they were removed and sent for analysis. The results of that analysis, I suspect, are also in the classified files.' Konstantinov stood up, still holding the coffee pot. 'Well, Viktor, let me make some more of this delicious brew, eh? And then we'll sum up what we know and don't know.'

———

A few minutes later, Konstantinov returned and poured more coffee. 'Let's start with the official statement released by the investigating authorities,' he said.

Viktor recalled what Maksimov had said when he'd called him into his office the previous day. 'The statement said that the Dyatlov party were the victims of "a compelling unknown force".'

'Yes. It's a strange phrase, isn't it? Doesn't really mean anything, and it's never been clarified. Does it refer to a physical phenomenon, like an explosion or a shockwave of some kind? Or does it imply some mental aberration to which one or more of the group succumbed? At first sight, perhaps it can be discarded as being too vague – but we'll come back to it. The most plausible theory is, of course, an avalanche (or the *fear* of an avalanche).'

'Fear of an avalanche?'

'Some researchers have come up with an interesting scenario. Let's consider it. The party have retired for the night; the weather is bad and the wind is rising, and they begin to wonder whether they have made a serious mistake in pitching their tent in such an exposed location on the slopes of Kholat Syakhl. Then, they begin to hear a distant roaring. It sounds like thousands of tonnes of moving snow. They believe that they are in the path of an avalanche, and as the sound increases in volume, they panic. They don't think there's even time to unfasten the flaps, so they slash the sides of the tent and flee down the slope. As they reach the edge of the forest, exhausted and confused, they do not realise that there has actually been no avalanche, and that the sound they heard was that of low-flying jet aircraft – perhaps MiGs or Sukhois on a night exercise. Fifty kilometres to the south, a party of geography students sees the jets' afterburners, and later reports them as a group of circular orange lights. Believing that their camp has been destroyed, Dyatlov and the others think that their lives are in serious danger: they can't survive for long in minus thirty degrees. Slobodin climbs a tree to try and see the campsite, but he slips and sustains a slight skull fracture.

'Dyatlov decides to try and get back to the camp (or what's left of it) to retrieve their supplies, while the others gather some wood and light a small fire. He takes Kolmogorova and Slobodin with him, but they succumb to the cold before they can get there. While the others are waiting under the pine tree, Krivonischenko and Doroshenko die of hypothermia. The four survivors decide that they can't stay there. Assuming that Dyatlov, Kolmogorova and Slobodin are also dead, they press further into the forest, perhaps searching for a place to shelter. But the land betrays them: the ground falls away suddenly, and they tumble into a ravine, where they sustain their impact injuries. Thibeaux-Brignollel sustains a massive head injury and dies instantly, Dubinina bites off her own tongue during the fall, and dies soon afterwards. The last two survivors, Kolevatov and Zolotarev, lie helplessly at the bottom of the ravine until they, too, die.'

'In this scenario, the authorities' desire for secrecy makes perfect sense if they were testing brand new jet fighters in the area,' Viktor observed. 'It *does* make sense, but only up to a point. It still doesn't explain why the Dyatlov party didn't realise that there had been no avalanche, and that the loud roar was caused by overflying aircraft. I can imagine them running down the slope to the edge of the forest, turning around and wondering where the hell the snow was! And what about the geography students? Fifty kilometres isn't that far for a jet fighter; wouldn't they have realised what the orange lights were? Wouldn't the roar of the engines have told them?'

'My thoughts exactly,' said Konstantinov. 'It's an interesting theory, but it doesn't bear close scrutiny. Nor does the theory that the party were killed by the Mansi. They are not a violent people. If Mansi had come upon the camp (which is unlikely, since they very rarely enter the region during the winter, and certainly would not have been anywhere near Kholat Syakhl), they would have been more likely to ensure that the campers were safe and secure than to beat them to death! And even though they don't like Otorten and Kholat Syakhl, they don't consider it a punishable offence to go there.'

'Could they have been murdered by someone else?'

'Some researchers have suggested that. The Gulag system was still in operation at that time, of course, although its population had been reduced during Khruschev's political amnesty campaigns. The nearest labour camp was in Vizhai, from where the Dyatlov party set out for Otorten. Some have suggested that several prisoners escaped from the camp, fled into the wilderness and came upon Dyatlov and the others, and killed them. But I have to say that's very unlikely.'

'Why?'

'If you had just escaped from prison, would you make for uninhabited wilderness in polar temperatures, without basic survival equipment or food?'

'I don't know,' Viktor shrugged. 'If I were desperate enough, I might well do. Maybe I'd think that anything was better than the Gulag.'

Konstantinov smiled. 'And then, having overpowered and murdered the group – which contained seven strong, healthy men, I might add – you would presumably have availed yourself of their supplies...'

'Ah ... nothing was stolen from the camp.'

'Nothing,' said Konstantinov. 'Not their food, not their skis, not their money, not even the bottle of vodka they had with them.'

'Which leaves two remaining theories: secret weapons testing, and something genuinely unknown, something paranormal in nature.'

'All right,' Konstantinov nodded. 'Let's take them one by one. First, the weapons test scenario. Some have speculated on the type of weapon involved, suggesting that it was a prototype of some kind of air-burst concussion device, possibly with a chemical component to account for the changes in the victims' skin tone and hair colour. The initial detonation caused the party to flee the camp and seek shelter beneath the pine tree. Dyatlov, Kolmogorova and Slobodin decided to return to the camp, but died from hypothermia on the way; and Krivonischenko and Doroshenko also died from hypothermia while the others were waiting under the tree. Then, a second concussion device was detonated overhead, causing severe injuries. The survivors fled into the forest, where they stumbled into the ravine, which became their grave.'

'A concussive device,' said Viktor. 'It sounds plausible, but *is* it?'

'Absolutely. Such weapons are in existence now; the MOAB, for example.'

'MOAB?'

'It stands for Massive Ordnance Airburst Bomb. They're essentially ethylene bombs which explode in the air, and are much more powerful than traditional explosives. In fact, the effects of a MOAB explosion are similar to those of a small nuclear bomb, but without the radiation. The interesting thing about MOABs is that the explosive mixture of ethylene fuel and air, which travels faster than the speed of sound, leaves behind a vacuum which causes cerebral concussion, internal bleeding and the displacement and tearing of internal organs.'

Viktor smiled and shook his head. 'My god, there it is again: a plausible theory that doesn't fit the facts! A prototype MOAB could have caused the injuries suffered by Dubinina and the others; but if the effects of such an explosion are similar to those of a nuclear detonation, why wasn't there severe damage to the surrounding landscape? The pine forest nearby should have been flattened!'

'Quite so. And if you add to that what we've already said about the unlikelihood of testing such a device outside of a rigidly controlled and monitored area, I think we can safely abandon the prototype MOAB theory.'

'Which just leaves ... what? The paranormal? The supernatural?'

Konstantinov caught the tone in Viktor's voice, and said: 'I agree that this is the most problematic hypothesis.'

'Problematic because you can invent pretty much whatever you want to account for the known facts.'

'And people have done precisely that. Some say that Igor and his friends were attacked by alien beings, and while it's true that there have been many reports of hostile and even lethal UFO activity throughout the world – and especially in South America – I can't bring myself to entertain this explanation seriously. Of course, it's possible – even likely – that there are other civilisations in the universe, and that one or more of them possesses a technology sufficiently advanced to allow interstellar travel. But why in God's name would such beings commit the senseless murder of a small group of ski-hikers in the middle of nowhere?'

'I agree. The orange spheres notwithstanding, that explanation makes no sense. What other theories have people come up with?'

'Some commentators have noted how the Mansi fear Otorten and Kholat Syakhl, and have suggested that those fears are well-founded. Perhaps, they say, there is something there, some kind of evil spirit or agency, which Igor and the others inadvertently disturbed, or perhaps evoked by their very presence.' Konstantinov noted Viktor's expression, and smiled. 'A bit vague, that one, isn't it?'

'A bit. So, where does all this leave us? Where does it leave *you*?'

'With a lot of unanswered questions,' he replied, and for the first time since meeting him, Viktor detected bitterness in his voice. 'Why did the Soviet authorities classify the event as top secret for thirty years? Why are some of the case files *still* classified? Why did they forbid anyone from entering the area for three years following the incident? Why did the footprints vanish five hundred metres from the camp? What were the orange spheres seen in the sky above Kholat Syakhl that night? Why did the four wristwatches show different times? After *fifty years*, it's still an enigma. And until the Defence Ministry, the Russian Space Agency and the FSB decide to release whatever documents they possess, it will remain so.'

'And all we're left with is the official "explanation": that the Dyatlov party were killed by a "compelling unknown force".'

'Yes. The phrase that would seem to obliterate all rational theories. But what *does* it mean? Was it intended to hide a truth the authorities understood but wanted to keep secret? Or is it merely a euphemism, masking ignorance and fear of what was really out there? Of what may *still* be out there?'

BASKOV (3)

From what Strugatsky had said, it was quite plain to me that Professor Konstantinov subscribed – however reluctantly – to what I shall call the 'paranormal hypothesis' (for want of a better expression) as an explanation for the Dyatlov Pass incident.

I was most intrigued by the reference he had made to the curious tan observed on the bodies of the Dyatlov party, and the grey colour of their hair. Although Strugatsky's hair was not *entirely* grey, it still held rather more grey than was considered normal for a man of his years. His initial physical examination had certainly not revealed any pathology which might account for this, and yet the photograph in his personnel file at the Yekaterinburg *Gazette*, which the militia had secured for me, showed that Strugatsky had had jet-black hair.

Although I was curious as to the origin of his skin and hair colour, I decided not to ask him about it just yet, preferring to proceed gently and to allow him to come to it in his own time. (It is worth noting here that although I was well aware of the urgency with which the criminal militia viewed this case, I was reluctant to press Strugatsky for answers too quickly: previous experience had taught me that in doing so, I would run the risk of his withdrawing into silence, which would of course be entirely counterproductive.)

Following the third session conducted with Strugatsky, I decided to call Senior Investigator Stanislav Komar, who was heading the militia's investigation, and asked him if they had examined the home of Professor Konstantinov. Komar was very helpful: he clearly wanted to get to the bottom of this as quickly as possible.

'Yes, Dr Baskov,' he said over the line. 'We've made a thorough examination of the premises.'

'So Konstantinov did run something called the Dyatlov Foundation.'

'That's correct.'

'What did you find there?'

'Can you be more specific, Doctor?'

'I'm sorry. I was thinking of materials relating to the incident at Dyatlov Pass.'

'Oh, I see. Well, yes, we found plenty. Notes and documents, mostly: newspaper reports from the period, Konstantinov's own notes, which are quite voluminous. We're cataloguing them now.'

'And what about physical objects, specimens, samples, metallic fragments...?'

Komar hesitated, then: 'Yes, we found a box containing a number of items.'

'Including a piece of cloth?'

'Yes.'

'Do you have any idea what it might be?'

'We've sent it for forensic analysis, along with the metal fragments. Why are you asking, Dr Baskov? Do you think it has some bearing on your evaluation of Strugatsky?'

'I believe so. Would it be possible to let me have a copy of the forensic report, once it becomes available?'

'Of course.'

'And have you spoken to Yuri Yudin?'

'Yes. I interviewed him myself.'

'Did he corroborate Strugatsky's story about going to see him?'

'He did. He's a strange old bird, that one.'

'What do you mean?'

I could imagine Komar shrugging on the other end of the line. 'I don't know ... trapped in the past, you might say. Remembering ... constantly remembering, like all old men, I suppose. But Strugatsky definitely went to see him. He *insisted* that Yudin see him, in fact. Refused to leave his doorstep until he let him in, although once inside, he was quite polite.'

I asked Komar to forward to me any information he might have on Strugatsky's past, after which I thanked him and hung up.

I thought again about Strugatsky's account of the events leading up to his arrest. So far, they seemed to be quite accurate: a true recollection of what had happened. And then I had thought about his reluctance to tell me how his friends had died in the forest bordering Kholat Syakhl. He was clearly terrified, although of whom or what, I had no idea. I suspected that there would come a point in his narrative where fact became fantasy. I would have to be very careful to identify that point, after which my real work would begin. There was, of course, only one way to proceed: I would have to allow Strugatsky to continue with his story, to allow him to arrive at the crucial event in his own time and in his own way.

————

When I entered his room on Monday morning, Strugatsky asked me how my weekend had been. I'd been so absorbed in my thoughts that I was a little taken aback.

'Very good, thank you Viktor.'

'I'm glad to hear it. So was mine.'

'Really? That's excellent.'

'What did you do?' he asked.

'I'm sorry?'

'At the weekend.'

'My sister and her husband came to visit us...'

'Us? You're married?'

'Yes.'

'May I ask your wife's name?'

'Nataliya,' I replied. 'You said your weekend was good, too. What did you do?'

'Nothing.'

'Nothing?'

Strugatsky gave a long sigh; I had the impression it was a sigh of contentment rather than frustration. But there was another quality to it, also: something akin to sadness, regret.

'I existed,' he said. 'Sometimes we bend beneath the weight of existence – the brute fact of it. But it is good. I'm glad I exist.'

I regarded him in silence for a moment, then I asked: 'Do your friends still exist, Viktor?'

'No.'

'The militia are searching for them now. Do you think they'll find their bodies?'

'Absolutely not.'

'Why not?'

'Svarog will make sure of it.'

'Svarog? What's that?'

Strugatsky didn't reply. Instead, he lowered his gaze, which became distant, contemplative. This was what I had feared: it looked like he was beginning to withdraw into himself, apparently as a result of his mentioning the word 'Svarog.' I had to re-engage with him, so I tried another approach. 'Professor Konstantinov seemed to believe that Igor Dyatlov and his friends encountered something profoundly strange in 1959. Did you and your companions encounter anything like that?'

'Yes,' whispered Strugatsky.

'What was it?'

Silence.

'Something ... intelligent, perhaps?'

'Intelligent,' he said, 'or perhaps ... the product of intelligence.'

I leaned forward in my chair, conscious that I had made a breakthrough. 'You mean it was made by someone? An artefact of some kind?'

Strugatsky closed his eyes and frowned. He appeared to be concentrating very hard on something. 'I suppose ... you could call it an artefact ... something that has been manufactured...'

'By whom?'

'By whom?' he echoed. 'Or by *what*?'

'I don't understand.'

'It doesn't matter.'

'Yes it does, Viktor. Do you think the militia will find it?'

'If they do, they'll know I'm not crazy – that I didn't kill Vadim and Nika and the others.'

'And if they *do* find it,' I said, 'will they be killed?'

'There are things in the forest that will kill them, if they're not careful.'

'Things? Such as?'

'The mercury lakes.'

'Excuse me?'

'The mercury lakes. They'll want to stay away from those.'

'I'm sorry, Viktor,' I said. 'Are you saying that there are ... *lakes of mercury* in the forest?'

He shook his head. 'It's not really mercury ... but there are lakes, and they're filled with something that isn't water.'

'But it *looks* like mercury – is that what you're saying?'

He nodded.

'And you've seen them?'

Another nod. 'One of them. Dyatlov and the others who died on Kholat Syakhl ... they saw one as well.'

Was this the moment I had been waiting for: the point at which Strugatsky's recollections of real events shaded into fantasy? This was the first time he had alluded to something strange which he himself had encountered. And furthermore, there was no allusion in any of the material I had read to the Dyatlov party encountering anything like a lake full of mercury. I was tempted to view this as the first false note, the first hint that something really was amiss with Viktor Strugatsky.

Strugatsky was regarding me intently. 'You don't believe me, do you?' Before I could answer, he continued: 'It's all right, it doesn't matter. The militia will find it – and even if they don't, it's all in the dossier.'

'The dossier?'

'In Vadim's apartment.'

'They've found a lot of material there, including the metal fragments you described.'

He nodded in apparent satisfaction.

'What about this "dossier"? Would you like to tell me about that?'

'Yes,' said Strugatsky. 'I'll tell you about the dossier.'

SIX

Viktor thanked Professor Konstantinov for his time, and they parted with an agreement to meet again soon. He left his apartment building with an envelope containing the papers the professor had given him thrust under his arm. As he bent to unlock his car, Viktor caught sight of a figure standing in a doorway about ten metres away: a man in a heavy overcoat, who was gazing at the buildings across the street.

Viktor glanced at him again as he got into the car. There was something vaguely familiar about him. He shrugged off the feeling as he pulled out into the traffic and headed for the offices of the *Gazette*. It was time to start writing the article Maksimov had ordered.

It was only when he was halfway there that Viktor realised where he had seen the man before. It was the elderly man who had shared the train compartment with him on the way back from Solikamsk.

———

As soon as Viktor arrived, Maksimov called him into his office and asked him how it was going.

'Fine, boss. Two interviews so far with principal figures in the case.'

'Not bad,' the editor nodded. Viktor detected a hint of surprise in his voice, and couldn't resist giving him a broad smile.

'Looks like you're enjoying yourself, Vitya,' he said, and Viktor's smile faded. *Trust you to say something like that, you bastard.*

'Not really. It's an intriguing subject, but not one to make you want to click you heals and dance.'

'Indeed not,' he said. He nodded curtly towards the door, which Viktor took as an invitation to leave his office and get to work.

Viktor fired up his computer and opened a new file, but as he began to write, he found his concentration waning as he thought about the elderly man in the street. He was certain that it was the man who had been on the train. But what was he doing outside the Dyatlov Foundation? Was it just coincidence? Viktor wondered who the hell he was. A state security operative? FSB? But he was too old. An informer, then? *Shit*, he thought. *I wonder if I'm getting myself into trouble here.* But then, how could anyone have known about his assignment? Unless there was a spy in the offices of the *Gazette*...

For Christ's sake, this is ridiculous!

He stood up and went to get some coffee from the vending machine; not quite Blue Mountain, but it would have to do. It *was* a coincidence, he told himself. Nothing to worry about. He'd seen an old guy on a train, he was on his way to Yekaterinburg, and then he saw him again in the city. Big deal. So what?

He went back to his desk, sipping the vaguely unpleasant brew which seemed to taste more like soup than coffee. Cherevin was standing there, looking at the blank page on the monitor and scratching his stubbly chin in mock concentration.

'Hello, Vitya,' he said with his trademark patronising grin. 'Looking for inspiration?'

'I've got all the inspiration I need, thanks,' Viktor said as he sat down.

'What are you working on now?' he asked, his tone suggesting that he knew perfectly well.

Viktor sighed. 'I'm doing a piece on the Dyatlov Pass incident.'

'Oh right, I've heard of that. So ... you're off chasing flying saucers and monsters, eh?'

'Actually, Georgiy, I'm writing a historical piece about nine people who died horribly on the side of a mountain fifty years ago, people whose friends and families had to mourn them without ever knowing what really happened to them. No flying saucers, no monsters, just nine dead people.' *Or maybe eleven*, he added to himself.

Cherevin nodded, with that grin still on his face. 'I'm making headway on the Borovsky case. Getting results.'

'Good for you.'

'When I'm done, how would you like some help with this?'

'How would you like to kiss my arse? I'm sure Maksimov wouldn't be jealous.'

The grin didn't waver for an instant. 'Vitya,' he said as he wandered off, shaking his head. 'You're so easy!'

He was right, of course. Cherevin knew exactly how to yank Viktor's chain, and he rarely missed an opportunity to do so. Their little exchange was a reminder that he had been taken off an assignment he couldn't handle, and his professional ego was still smarting from the knock it had taken. However, as he began to write the first paragraph of his article, he convinced himself that it didn't matter. This was important, too; and while he pitied the poor bastards who were being victimised by their slum landlord, he pitied Igor Dyatlov and his friends more...

––––

By five o'clock, he had a rough first draft: just the basic events, a framework in which he could insert more detail later. The material Konstantinov had given him was invaluable, since it contained not only a timeline of the incident, but also a lot of background on the political situation in the Soviet Union at the time. There was also a list of references relating to contemporary military technology, the Gulag system, the history and culture of the Mansi people, and other subjects. By the time he was ready to leave the office, Viktor was satisfied that he had made a solid start.

He grabbed his overcoat, said goodnight to a few people, and took the lift down to the foyer. As he approached the glass door, he saw someone standing on the street outside – and stopped dead in his tracks.

It was the old man he had seen earlier. He just stood there, looking at his watch; and then he walked on, out of sight.

'Christ,' Viktor said under his breath. This *wasn't* a coincidence. The bastard was tailing him. He was under surveillance! He had an abrupt, intense feeling of primitive dread, like some ancient hunter-gatherer who had just seen a bear walking past the entrance to his cave.

Suddenly disinclined to venture out onto the street, he sat down in one of the armchairs in the foyer. The receptionist, who had been chatting to one of the security guards, glanced over at him from her desk. 'Are you all right, Mr Strugatsky?' she said.

'Yes, I'm fine, thanks, Lena,' he replied with what he hoped was a genuine-looking smile.

The guard also looked over, a supercilious expression on his square-jawed face. Viktor met his gaze for a few moments, and then looked away. *What are you looking at, you bastard? Are you in on this?*

He didn't know what to do – whether to go on out, or stay here. *Don't be such a bloody coward*, he thought. *What are you going to do, go back upstairs and spend the night at your desk? They know you're here – whoever 'they' are. You can't stay here forever.*

And then the thought occurred to him that the old man, whoever he was, was pretty lousy at tailing people. Surely you weren't supposed to *know* you were being watched. So ... what, then? Did he *want* Viktor to know? Was he trying to make contact with him for some reason?

Lena the receptionist and square-jaw had begun chatting again, but they soon stopped and glanced at him again.

Screw this, he thought, and stood up. 'Goodnight, Lena,' he said, heading for the exit.

'Goodnight, Mr Strugatsky,' she called after him.

Viktor stepped out onto the street with all the trepidation of someone walking onto the thin ice of a frozen lake, and looked to his right. The old man was walking slowly away, almost lost amid the other pedestrians in the early evening darkness. Viktor was about to hurry away in the opposite direction towards his car; but on some perverse impulse, he turned right instead, and began to follow the old man. He wasn't entirely sure why he was doing this; he certainly had no intention of confronting the old man: to do so might have tipped his hand, forcing him into some action he had until now only been contemplating. Who knew how many people were backing him up? There might be a dozen operatives scattered along the street, all younger and stronger than he was, all waiting for some pre-arranged signal to pounce on Viktor and drag him off to God knew where.

He asked himself what the hell he thought he was doing. What did he hope to accomplish by this? *I'll just follow him for a little while ... see where he goes, and if he meets anyone.* He briefly wondered if this was anything to do with his work on the Borovsky case; but he didn't think so. Borovsky's type didn't operate so subtly: they just got their goons to beat the shit out of you in the middle of the street. Viktor had seen things like that on occasion: some poor dolt, who had managed to annoy the wrong person, got his reward in full view of the passersby. It was nasty, someone's dark and perverted idea of justice, but it happened.

As he followed the old man along the street, Viktor kept glancing at the people walking towards him, ready to run like hell if any of them looked at him for longer than a second. As a precaution, he took out his cell phone and entered the police emergency number, then thrust it back in his pocket, with his thumb on the CALL button. If things got weird, he'd push the button and make a run for it, and hope that the police showed up before he was caught.

The old man turned right onto Shaumyana Street, and as Viktor followed, an idea occurred to him. If he could get ahead and find a good hiding place, maybe he could get a picture of the old man with the phone's camera. Then he would show it to Konstantinov, and see if he could shed any light on the man's identity.

Viktor crossed the street and hurried along the opposite pavement, keeping an eye on the old man as he dodged pedestrians. He was walking quite slowly, so it was easy to overtake him. Viktor kept close to the buildings, allowing the passersby to shield him, and hoping that he didn't glance in his direction. He pulled up the collar of his overcoat to further mask his face. The only problem was, he wouldn't be able to cross back again and find a good vantage point without the old man spotting him...

Eventually, circumstance smiled on him. Something in the window of a bookshop caught the old man's attention, and he paused to look at it. Viktor seized his opportunity immediately and, dodging between two passing cars, he gained the other side of the street and hurried into a narrow side alley. Crouching down behind a pair of battered rubbish bins, he took out his phone, raised it in the direction of the alley entrance, and waited.

A couple of minutes later, the old man walked past, and Viktor took a snap of his profile. He would have liked to use the phone's flash, but he couldn't risk drawing the man's attention. In another moment, he was gone. Viktor called up the phone's picture menu and looked at the photo he had just taken.

'Shit,' he whispered. The photo was all but useless: nothing more than a low-resolution smudge. He stayed there behind the rubbish bins for a few more moments, trying to decide what to do. Should he go after him again, and try for another shot? No, that was too dangerous. Should he just go up to him and ask him what the hell he was playing at? *Oh, good idea!* He'd either signal his reinforcements (if there were any), or make out that Viktor was some random maniac harassing him.

Maybe he could just describe him to Konstantinov, and see if he recognised him from the description...

Then another thought occurred to him, and he cursed himself for not having thought of it immediately. There *was* someone to whom he could describe the old man's appearance; and the results would be a lot better than a crappy cell phone picture.

On the way back to his car, Viktor called a number. After two rings, a voice said: 'Hello, Vitya.'

'Nika, how are you?'

'Not bad. Yourself?'

'Fine. Listen, I need to ask you a favour.'

'Not now, Vitya. I'm on my way home and I have a date tonight.'

'A date?'

A brief chuckle. 'Is that surprise or disappointment I hear in your voice?'

'Abject disappointment. Listen, Nika, this is important...'

'It always is with you – even when it isn't. Call me tomorrow.' She broke the connection.

There was no point in calling her again, or even texting her. Viktor sighed and put the phone back in his pocket. Veronika Ivasheva worked for the local police as a sketch artist, and she was damned good at her job. She'd graduated from the Ural State Academy of Architecture and

Arts with a degree in Art and Composition about six years ago, and this was the only way she'd been able to use her abilities (at least for a decent amount of money). It was sad, really. She was capable of so much more than sketching the ugly mugs of suspects, but that's what paid the rent.

Viktor didn't blame her for giving him the brush-off, although he was both flattered and depressed at the fact that Nika had greeted him by name when she'd picked up, which meant that he was still on her contact list.

He had hoped that she would be free that evening. He'd intended to take her to a bar, buy her a drink and ask her to sketch the old man's face from his description. He knew she would do a great job, good enough to take to Konstantinov. Fortunately, tomorrow was Saturday, so he'd be able to call her again in the morning. He just hoped she didn't end up spending the night with whoever she was seeing this evening – mainly because she'd be mad if he called too early, but also – and this wasn't easy to admit – because he just didn't like the thought of it.

Viktor drove back to his apartment on Sibirskii, constantly checking the rear-view mirror to make sure he wasn't still being followed, and hurried into the entrance hall, pausing only to check his mailbox. Through the glass, he could see a large yellow envelope. He unlocked the box and took it out, along with a couple of bills. He examined the envelope, and frowned. It was completely blank: no name, no address, nothing.

The thought occurred to him that it might be a bomb – that was how hyped and paranoid he was at that moment. He ran his hand over it, checking for any lumps or wires, but its surface was completely flat and smooth. It had obviously been hand-delivered, but it was too bulky to fit through the slot in the top of the mailbox, which meant that whoever had brought it had picked the lock.

Viktor stood in the hallway for a few more moments, looking dumbly at the envelope. Then, slowly, he climbed the stairs to his apartment.

———

He threw the bills unopened onto his desk, and carefully tore open the yellow envelope. Inside was a pale grey folder, unmarked except for an unusual symbol which had been embossed on the stiff card:

Viktor had never seen this symbol before, and had no idea what it meant. He opened the folder. It contained a sheaf of papers and several large black-and-white photographs. The papers had a variety of official stamps, and most of them looked and felt decades old. On the inside of the cover, someone had written the name and address of the Uralpromstroybank in Yekaterinburg, along with a safety deposit box account number, in small, neat characters. Beneath this was an electronic key, which had been firmly affixed to the inside of the cover with tape. It didn't take a genius to guess what the key was for, and Viktor ran a finger over it, wondering what was in that safety deposit box...

He would have begun reading the papers immediately, had he not been distracted by the first photograph, which showed a snow-covered landscape, apparently a large clearing judging by the curved line of pine trees in the near distance. At the centre of the clearing was an object which looked like an upturned bowl, and which appeared to be made of a dull metal akin to pewter. Viktor guessed that it was perhaps three metres in diameter. It protruded from the frozen ground at an angle of about 45 degrees. Assuming that the curve was constant, about two-thirds of it was buried. He turned the photograph over, and saw that a small label had been stuck onto the back. On the label, someone had written in tiny but well-formed characters: SMALL CAULDRON IN ANOMALOUS ZONE 3. PHOTOGRAPH RETRIEVED FROM IGOR DYATLOV'S CAMERA.

'Jesus Christ,' he said aloud. He put the photograph down and rapidly leafed through the printed papers, glancing at each heading as he did so. One read: POST-MORTEM REPORT ON LUDMILA DUBININA; another: PROPOSED METHODS OF METALLURGICAL ANALYSIS OF INSTALLATION IN ANOMALOUS ZONE 3; another:

RECOMMENDATIONS FOR RESPONSE TO DISCOVERY OF INSTALLATION AND CAULDRONS IN NORTHERN URALS SECTOR. There was also a detailed map of the region, with several locations marked in red.

Each sheet contained the following legend in its top left-hand corner:

PROJECT SVAROG

Viktor's mouth went dry as he realised that he was looking at the classified files on the Dyatlov Pass incident.

Whether this was all of them or just some, he had no idea; but there was clearly a lot of very sensitive information here, which appeared to have been gathered under the codename 'Project Svarog'. The meaning of that word was as mysterious to him as the strange symbol which accompanied it; but he now knew without a doubt that the old man who had been tailing him was his benefactor – if 'benefactor' was the right word. Viktor had a feeling he was looking at several decades in prison if it became known that he was now in possession of these documents.

He sat down at his desk, and remained very still for a couple of minutes, trying to gather his thoughts. He was right: the old man *had* wanted to be seen: he'd wanted Viktor to know that it was he who had left the package in his mailbox. But who was he? Viktor still suspected that he was an intelligence operative, even though he was clearly in his eighties. All right, then: an *ex*-intelligence operative? A member of the KGB before it became the FSB? If he was in his eighties now, he would have been in his thirties in 1959...

Viktor looked at the next photograph, which appeared to have been taken from the same vantage point, except that in this one, there were three people standing beside the object. He recognised Zinaida Kolmogorova, Rustem Slobodin and Alexander Kolevatov. They were all smiling, but the smiles seemed faint and uneasy – nothing like the wide grins and laughter prevalent in the other photographs of the group he had seen. He may have been over-interpreting their expressions, reading too much into them, but he had the impression that they were intrigued and puzzled by the object and were somewhat troubled by its unexplained presence and nature. The two men were standing right next to the thing, but Zinaida was standing a little way away, as if she hadn't wanted to get too close to it.

It occurred to Viktor that they had taken a big risk in photographing the metal object. Whatever it was, it had clearly been manufactured; and furthermore, it clearly shouldn't have been there. Hadn't it occurred to them that they might have stumbled into a place where *they* shouldn't have been? If Viktor had been there, he would have assumed it was something to do with the government or the military – perhaps part of the fuselage of a downed aircraft – and got the hell out of there, without taking any snaps!

As he examined the photograph more closely, a vague feeling of unease came over him, which at first he could neither define nor explain. There was something about the object, something about the metal from which it had been fashioned, that seemed *wrong*, somehow. Although it looked a little like pewter, as he looked more closely he could detect a slight mottling which reminded him of the skin of an elephant or a rhinoceros. The effect could have been the result of corrosion, but that didn't seem like the right explanation, notwithstanding the fact that the thing looked ancient.

'It's not part of an aircraft,' he said to himself. He knew it, absolutely and unequivocally, and so had the Soviet authorities.

Before concentrating on the documents, he decided to examine the rest of the photographs. Even though he had been working on this story for just a couple of days, and in spite of his apprehensiveness, he felt a powerful surge of excitement at the thought that he had been allowed access to information that had remained hidden for the last fifty years.

There were seven photographs in all, each bearing a handwritten label which identified them as having come from Igor Dyatlov's camera. Putting the first two to one side, he now examined the remainder.

The third photograph was even more perplexing, not so much for what it showed, but for what it *didn't* show. As far as Viktor could tell, it was of the night sky, and the only thing that led him to this conclusion was the line of treetops in the lower half. There were no stars visible, which didn't surprise him: the camera couldn't have been anywhere near good enough to pick them up. He turned the picture over and read the label. NIGHT SKY ABOVE FOREST TO THE SOUTH OF KHOLAT SYAKHL. POSSIBLY AN UNSUCCESSFUL ATTEMPT TO RECORD UNEXPLAINED DISPARITY.

Unexplained disparity, he thought. *What the hell does that mean?*

The fourth photograph was yet stranger and more unsettling. Again, it had been taken in the depths of the forest, and showed three people. Ludmila Dubinina and Zinaida Kolmogorova were on their knees in the snow; Ludmila was leaning forward, her hands covering her face, while Zinaida had one arm around her friend's shoulders, as if trying to comfort her. Georgy Krivonischenko was standing to one side, and was looking down at something on the ground. Viktor could make out a shapeless mass, from which a dark stain appeared to have spread out in all directions. Within the mass were thin white objects...

Bones, he thought. *God ... it's an animal, or what's left of one.* Maybe something had been attacked by a bear, and Ludmila had been shaken and upset by their discovery of the carcass. That was probably it ... although Viktor found myself wondering why this photograph had been included in the classified dossier. The label on the back of the photograph read simply: DISMEMBERED ANIMAL IN ANOMALOUS ZONE 3. CAUSATIVE AGENT UNKNOWN. *Why unknown?* Viktor wondered, until the answer occurred to him. *Bears hibernate in winter, you idiot! Whatever did this, it wasn't a bear.*

The fifth photograph showed nothing but a circular patch of whiteness against a dark background. He turned it over and read: PROBABLE FLYING SPHERE. EXACT LOCATION UNKNOWN. So the Dyatlov party *had* seen the spheres, and had even photographed one of them. He tried to make out detail within the white patch, but the thing had been either too bright, or had been entirely featureless. One thing was for sure: it wasn't the afterburner of a military jet. He put the photograph to one side, and went on to the next.

It showed what appeared to be a frozen lake at the centre of a shallow depression in another clearing. The lake was quite small, perhaps fifty metres in diameter, and of a strangely perfect circular shape. Its surface was completely smooth and flat, and of a dark gunmetal hue that, even in this old black-and-white photograph, didn't seem right. Viktor would have expected ice to be much brighter than that, almost as bright as the surrounding snow. Just as the 'cauldron' looked like it was made of something other than metal, this 'lake' looked like it was filled with something other than water. There was a man whom he recognised as Rustem Slobodin in the foreground, clearly hurrying towards the camera. This time he wasn't smiling, not even faintly: in fact, his face was contorted in an expression of absolute terror. The label on the back of the photograph said: RUSTEM SLOBODIN AND A MERCURY LAKE, ANOMALOUS ZONE 3.

Viktor wondered what that meant. How could there be a lake of mercury? Then it occurred to him that the contents of the lake might not actually *be* mercury. It seemed that whoever had written the labels on these photographs had been using words to describe objects whose actual names were unknown to him or her. The 'cauldron' wasn't actually a cauldron: it just looked rather like one. And this lake was called a 'mercury lake' because whatever it contained only *looked* like mercury. He looked again at the horrible grimace on Slobodin's face, at his wildly staring eyes and bared teeth. Clearly, the man had been in fear for his life at that moment. He had perhaps gone down to the edge of the lake to take a closer look at it ... and had turned and fled. It was obvious that something had terrified him.

And what was this 'Anomalous Zone 3'? Did it refer to the region around Kholat Syakhl, where the Dyatlov party had met their ends? And why 3? It implied that there were at least two other 'Anomalous Zones' ... somewhere.

The seventh and last photograph was by far the most striking. In fact, it was so bizarre that Viktor immediately flipped it over to see what the labeller had written. There was only one word on the back: INSTALLATION.

The object practically filled the photograph. The surrounding trees leaned away from it, as if its presence had disturbed their roots. There was a single figure standing directly in front of it. Although the figure was too far away to see who it was, Viktor was able to use it to gauge the size of the thing. It was at least twenty metres tall, and cylindrical. Its lower two thirds were composed of column-like structures perhaps ten metres wide, each of which appeared to be bevelled like the blade of a sword, and came to a sharp point six or seven metres above the ground. This arrangement was surmounted by a hemispherical dome approximately fifteen metres in diameter, on top of which sat a smaller dome about three metres in diameter. The columns were of a bright, silvery hue like burnished steel, while the two domes were altogether darker and duller.

Viktor put the photograph down very carefully, as if it were some infinitely ancient and fragile artefact, and gazed at it for several minutes. He had never seen anything remotely like this thing, which someone had decided to call an 'installation', doubtless because they had no idea what else to call it. He was struggling vainly with the outrageous notion that had immediately presented itself, and which was growing increasingly undeniable with every passing moment.

This object – building, machine, whatever it was – had not been built by human beings.

You don't know that, he told himself; but the internal voice echoing in his mind was small and weak, like that of a child refusing to accept some unwelcome fact of its existence. The object's appearance was utterly unearthly, its composition and function unknown and barely to be guessed at; and the laconic inscription on the back of the photograph only reinforced his assumption that the Soviet authorities had not been responsible for its presence. They didn't know what it was, why it was there or what it was for.

He put the photographs to one side and began to leaf through the printed papers. The post-mortem report on Ludmila Dubinina, which had been written by the Judicial Doctor, Boris Vozrozhdenny, showed that one of her shattered ribs had punctured her heart. Even without the exacerbating effects of hypothermia, she wouldn't have survived for long following the incident. As to her other injury, Vozrozhdenny stated that her oral cavity appeared to have been removed with surgical precision; and he added quite emphatically that this had not been the result of predator action. One observation in particular was striking:

I am completely at a loss to explain how this event could have occurred. There was minimal blood loss, as evidenced by the complete lack of blood within the oral cavity or in the snow immediately surrounding the body. Nor was there any observable damage to the lips or jaw. I am forced to consider the possibility, incredible as it may seem, that at one moment, Dubinina's mouth was completely intact, and at the next, the interior lining and the tongue were gone. The tongue itself has not been recovered; its whereabouts are unknown.

Viktor thought about this for a while, trying to make sense of it. He didn't like Vozrozhdenny's implication that parts of Ludmila's body had simply *vanished*; and he realised that the doctor must have been genuinely mystified and unsettled by the condition of her body even to consider making such a suggestion. In this regard, the Soviet Union wasn't so different from Russia today – or any other country, for that matter: any suggestion that paranormal phenomena might be real was frowned upon and dismissed as superstitious nonsense, at least officially. Behind the scenes, however, the government did take an interest – that much was well known from the documents that began to leak out in the aftermath of the Soviet Union's breakup.

Was Ludmila the victim of some utterly unknown and incomprehensible phenomenon? Was that one of the reasons the government closed off the region around Kholat Syakhl for three years following the Dyatlov Pass incident? But if so, why was she the only one to lose body parts? Alexander Zolotarev, Nikolai Thibeaux-Brignollel and Alexander Kolevatov had been found in the ravine right next to her, and nothing had been taken from them. Was the unknown agency that had mutilated Ludmila also responsible for Nikolai's shattered skull?

Viktor sighed, shook his head and turned next to the metallurgical analysis of the Installation. Several tests had been conducted by scientists at Beloretsk-15, a classified city in the southern Urals. He had trouble understanding some of the technical terminology in the analysis reports, but the gist was plain enough. The scientists were unable to identify the material from which the installation had been constructed, although there was an addendum which stated that several of them had suffered psychological problems subsequent to their exposure to the material, including debilitating nightmares and panic attacks (none of the scientists had any history of mental instability). Some had to be taken off the analysis project and were placed in psychiatric institutions, and two had committed suicide.

Poor bastards, Viktor thought. What was it about the material that had so profoundly and adversely affected them? The report wasn't clear on that, although it did conclude that under certain conditions, the material emitted an ultra low frequency hum, and speculated that this may have been responsible for the psychological effects observed in the investigators.

Viktor returned to the map and examined it more closely. It was a geographical survey map, highly detailed, with settlements, contours and other features marked. Someone had made small circular marks in red. One of them was on the southern slope of Kholat Syakhl (which he assumed was the location of the Dyatlov party's final camp); the others were all within the great swathe of the pine forest to the south. The annotations accompanying them matched the short descriptions on the backs of the photographs.

It seemed that the old man was not only showing Viktor what lay in the forest, but had also provided him with the means to find it. The obvious question was: Why? Someone had clearly decided that it was time for the truth about the Dyatlov Pass incident to be known. But why had it been decided that Viktor Strugatsky should be the recipient of this information? Why choose a hack reporter, when there was someone much more qualified to receive it?

Why choose him over Vadim Konstantinov?

It made no sense, unless Konstantinov was considered untrustworthy for some reason. But the old man knew that Viktor was in contact with him...

'What the hell are you playing at?' Viktor whispered.

One thing was certain: the Soviet authorities had sent people into the region where Dyatlov and the others met their ends, with the intention of conducting a comprehensive investigation of the objects and phenomena. Another certainty was that the Dyatlov party did *not* die on the evening of 1 February. They must have spent at least a couple of days in the forest ... the forest in which they had decided against setting up their camp, in spite of the shelter it would have afforded them.

Viktor sat back in his chair and looked at the dossier. *Why have you given this to me?* he thought. *And what happened to Dyatlov and the others during those days in the forest?*

BASKOV (4)

When I arrived at Peveralsk on Tuesday morning, I was surprised to find Investigator Komar sitting in the outer office, waiting for me. He was holding a large manila envelope on his lap, while my secretary, Mrs Holender, eyed him suspiciously. As soon as I entered, he stood up and offered me his hand.

'Dr Baskov, there's something I'd like to discuss with you.'

'Of course,' I replied, a little taken aback. 'Let's go into my office.' I asked Mrs Holender to have Viktor Strugatsky informed that our session would be delayed, and beckoned Komar to follow me.

I asked him to have a seat, and said: 'What's this about, Investigator?'

'I'm sorry for turning up unannounced, Doctor, but I didn't want to call.'

'Why not?'

He waved the envelope. 'This is something I'd rather not discuss over the phone.'

'What is it?'

'We found it during our examination of Professor Konstantinov's home. The contents are ... intriguing, let's say.'

He handed me the envelope, and I opened it and took out a sheaf of papers and several photographs. A single glance told me what they were.

'The dossier,' I said.

'Excuse me?'

'Good God, this looks like the dossier Strugatsky mentioned.'

'So he *does* know about this?'

'Yes, he mentioned it a couple of times. In our last session, he described to me how it came into his possession.'

'Into *his* possession? Then this didn't belong to Konstantinov?'

I shook my head. 'From what Strugatsky told me, it doesn't belong to anyone except the government.' I glanced up at him. 'I take it this is why you didn't want to discuss it over the phone.'

'Right. This is evidence in our investigation, and I don't want the bloody FSB spiriting it away – at least, not until we're finished with it.'

I leafed through the documents. 'Have your people examined these?'

He knew what I was getting at. 'Yes. They're not forgeries. As far as our experts can tell, they're genuine: paper, ink, typefaces, stamps, terminology, you name it. And there's a key and account number for a safety deposit box in the Uralpromstroybank. We've checked the box, and it's empty.'

'Yes ... Strugatsky mentioned the key and the account details.'

'Did he say anything about what had been in the box?'

'No, he hasn't said anything about it yet.'

Komar waited while I looked at each of the photographs, then he asked: 'How far have you got with your evaluation of Strugatsky?'

I summarised my findings so far, ending with his assertion that the militia might well encounter something highly unusual in the forest.

'I'm in regular contact with them,' Komar said. 'They've found nothing unusual so far...'

'Maybe they're looking in the wrong place,' I said, indicating the annotated map.

'True enough. That's why I've made a copy and had a courier take it out to them.'

'Why not just scan and email it?'

Komar offered me a grim smile. 'For the same reason I didn't want to discuss it with you over the phone.'

'Oh,' I said. 'Of course. What about Strugatsky? Would you like me to continue my evaluation?'

'Yes, please. We still need to know what happened to Konstantinov and the others, and whether Strugatsky had anything to do with it. And we'd like to know as quickly as possible, Doctor.'

'I understand your impatience, Investigator, and believe me, I sympathise. But I can't just demand that he tell us everything he knows. That's not the way a forensic psychiatric evaluation works. If I were to do that, he might well clam up and tell us nothing.'

Komar sighed. 'All right, Doctor. We'll play it your way, for now.'

I nodded, and looked again at the documents spread out across my desk. 'This is incredible,' I muttered. 'I mean ... if these really are genuine, it implies that there really is something strange out there – something *unknown*.' I glanced at Komar again. 'Can I make copies of these?'

He nodded. 'But I wouldn't tell anyone, if I were you. And when this case is concluded, I'd strongly advise you to destroy them.'

'Understood.' I closed the folder and ran my fingers over the symbol embossed on the cover. 'Have you ever heard of Project Svarog?' I asked.

Komar shook his head. 'Never. But I assure you it's something I'll be looking into.' He paused. 'Are you going to tell Strugatsky that we have this material?'

'Certainly. For one thing, he told me that it would only be a matter of time before you found it; and for another, I'll be very interested to see his reaction.'

'Why?'

'Up until now, he's been very calm and composed. There have been occasional lapses into silence, and on certain occasions, he has appeared to be deeply afraid. But for the most part, he has maintained a strong self-control. It's been very difficult to ascertain the likelihood of his culpability in the disappearance of Konstantinov and the others. One of the first things he said to me was that we think he's crazy, and that he killed them. That's the assumption he holds. It'll be interesting to see how his attitude and demeanour change when I tell him that we have the evidence that might prove both his sanity and his innocence of any wrongdoing.'

'And how, precisely, do you think his demeanour will change, Doctor?'

'That remains to be seen, Investigator,' I said.

———

Strugatsky was pacing up and down in his room when I arrived. As soon as I entered, he went to the armchair and sat down. He looked at me expectantly.

'I'm sorry I had to postpone this session, Viktor,' I said, taking my usual position at the desk.

'No problem, Doctor, no problem at all.'

'I had a very good reason for doing so.'

'I'm sure you did.'

'I had a visit from Senior Investigator Stanislav Komar of the criminal militia.'

Strugatsky sat forward in his chair. 'Yes?'

'The militia have found the dossier you described.'

He regarded me for several moments, his face entirely expressionless. 'Good,' he said presently. 'Have you read it?'

'I've looked over it.'

'Then Komar was here.'

'Yes, he was. He's just left.'

'You realise he's exposed you to a risk.'

'By showing me the dossier?'

'Yes. The government doesn't want anyone to know about what's out there.'

'Investigator Komar wants to get to the truth, Viktor. And so do I.'

'Are you sure, Doctor Baskov?' Strugatsky asked, leaning forward. 'Are you absolutely sure?'

'It's my job,' I replied. 'And it's Investigator Komar's job, too.'

Strugatsky nodded. 'Okay,' he said. 'Okay ... good.'

'Can you tell me anything about Project Svarog, Viktor?'

Strugatsky recoiled slightly, and lowered his eyes, saying nothing. I decided not to press him, at least not at this stage.

'Very well. Tell me about Veronika Ivasheva.'

Strugatsky's response took me by surprise. He lowered his head and began to weep. The tears came quite suddenly, and had clearly been triggered by the mention of her name. I sat quietly, waiting for him to recover himself. It took several minutes, during which his head remained bowed and his shoulders shook with the sobs. I took a handkerchief from my pocket and handed it to him.

'I'm sorry, Viktor,' I said, when the torrent of tears had finally ceased.

'Nika,' he said, shaking his head slowly. 'Nika...'

I leaned forward. 'Tell me about her. Tell me about how she...'

'How she became involved,' Strugatsky completed, looking at me with tear-reddened eyes. 'How I got her involved.' He sighed and composed himself. 'You and the militia are trying to decide whether I killed them. The fact is, Doctor Baskov, I *did* kill them. Not directly, not with my own hands ... but I'm the one who set all this in motion. I'm the one who asked Nika to help me. I'm the one who took the dossier to Vadim.'

'Tell me about her,' I repeated, quietly.

Strugatsky sighed. 'All right.'

SEVEN

Viktor called Veronika again the next morning at nine o'clock; to his relief, she picked up on the third ring.

'How was your date?' he asked.

'None of your damned business. So ... what's this favour you want to ask?'

'I'd rather not talk about it over the phone. Can we meet this morning, maybe have a coffee?'

She sighed. 'All right, Vitya. Meet me at Yakov's in an hour.'

'Thanks, Nika.'

She hung up.

'Short and sweet,' he muttered.

Yakov's bar and cafe was a twenty-minute walk from Viktor's apartment. That left him forty minutes. He wasn't sure what to do, since he didn't want to hang around in the streets for that long: even though the mysterious old man seemed to be benign, there was no telling who else knew of Viktor's interest in the Dyatlov Pass incident. He decided to make straight for the bar, and wait there until Veronika arrived.

Yakov's had been one of their favourite meeting places when they were seeing each other. Viktor wondered whether Nika had chosen it for that reason – a comment on their breakup, a chance to rub it in a bit more – or whether it was simply because it was a place that was well known to them both. He suspected it was the former.

After locking the dossier away in his filing cabinet, Viktor left the apartment and hurried through the streets towards Yakov's. He more than half expected to catch a glimpse of the old man, sauntering along or casually looking in a shop window, but there was no sign of him.

The bar was half full of Saturday morning shoppers when Viktor arrived, and he didn't have any trouble finding a secluded table in the rear. He ordered coffee and waited.

True to her word, Veronika arrived at ten on the dot. She quickly surveyed the place until she spotted Viktor. No smile, no wave, just a slight nod. She went over and sat down, placing her large shoulder bag on the empty chair between them.

'Thanks for coming, Nika.'

She ordered tea from a passing waiter.

'You look nice.'

Her black hair was shorter than the last time he had seen her, and she had lost a little weight. There was a flicker of amusement, cool and detached, in her almond-shaped brown eyes as she regarded him, and she offered a slight, begrudging smile.

'Thanks.'

'How have you been?'

'Fine. Why did you want to meet?'

Obviously, she wasn't interested in small talk, for which he was grateful.

'I want to ask you a favour.'

'So you said yesterday. What is it?'

'I need you to do a sketch for me, from a description I'll give you.'

The waiter brought her tea. She looked at Viktor contemplatively while she blew on it.

'A sketch...'

'Of a man I saw. I can remember his face very well. You shouldn't have any trouble.'

'Why do you want me to sketch him? What's this about?'

Viktor hesitated, unsure how much to tell her. Veronika looked at him while she sipped her tea. 'I think ... maybe the less you know, the better, Nika.'

She nearly spat out the mouthful she had just taken in her desire to laugh, and demurely put a hand against her mouth. 'Don't give me that shit, Vitya. What have you been up to?'

'I may be in danger...'

'So what? You're an investigative reporter. It goes with the job. Tell me what's going on, or I'm leaving.'

He smiled and shook his head. 'You haven't changed.'

'Why would I? We only broke up a few months ago. Does it seem like such a long time to you?'

The conversation was heading in a direction he didn't want to go, for all sorts of reasons, so he leaned forward and lowered his voice. 'Have you ever heard of the Dyatlov Pass incident?'

She arched an eyebrow, which she always used to do when he said something surprising, or stupid. 'Yes,' she said, after a moment's hesitation. 'I've heard of it.'

'Really?'

'Anyone who knows anything about the history of Sverdlovsk Province knows about Dyatlov Pass.'

'I didn't.'

She smirked. 'Yeah, well...'

He sighed. 'Anyway, I've come into possession of some documents which may shed new light on the mystery of what happened to Igor Dyatlov and the others.'

Veronika looked at him in silence for a few moments, then nodded slowly as she put down her cup. 'What documents?'

'Just ... documents.'

'Vitya...'

'All right. Medical reports, metallurgical analyses, things like that.'

'And just how did you "come into possession" of them?'

'That's why I wanted to see you – why I need this favour.'

He told her about the old man who had been following him, how Viktor had tried to take a clear picture of him and failed, how the documents had been left in his mailbox by someone who had picked the lock.

When he had finished, Veronika picked up her cup again and sipped her tea contemplatively. Finally, she said: 'You know that there was an official investigation of the incident, don't you? But not all of the information was released to the public...'

'Exactly. I believe I have that missing information. I've been in contact with a man called Vadim Konstantinov, who's been collecting material on the case for years. I need you to sketch the old man from my description, so I can take it to Konstantinov...'

'To see whether he can ID him?'

'That's right.'

'And what if he can? What if you find out who the old man is?'

'Then I'll try to make contact with him...'

'And get yourself arrested – or worse,' said Veronika. 'Listen, Vitya, if those documents are genuine, they've come to you through an illegal channel. You could be heading for a hell of a lot of trouble.'

He shrugged. 'You said it yourself: I'm an investigative reporter.'

'Why are you so interested in Dyatlov Pass? You doing a piece on it?'

He nodded. 'Things aren't going so well for me at the *Gazette*. I've got a feeling this is my last chance to turn in some good work before Maksimov shows me the door.'

'Does he know about the documents?'

'No. I haven't told anyone.'

Veronika looked at him in silence.

'So,' he said after a few moments. 'Are you going to help me?'

'What's in those documents, Vitya?' she asked. 'The answer to what really happened?'

'I'm not sure,' he replied truthfully. 'There's some pretty wild stuff in there...'

'Like what?'

'There are some photographs, which suggest that Dyatlov and the others spent some time in the forest near their final camp on Kholat Syakhl. It looks like they found some strange things there.'

'What kind of things?'

He described the photographs. It was against his better judgment to do so, of course; but Veronika was insistent, and he had no doubt that she would get up and leave if he held back. She was maddeningly inquisitive, so much so that Viktor used to joke that she was the one who should have been the reporter. Veronika listened in silence as he spoke, her eyes never moving from his.

When he had finished, she shook her head. 'Christ,' she whispered. 'You're right: that stuff is completely new, all of it. And those things they found – the Installation, the Cauldron – they've never been seen in the Urals before.'

Viktor had been looking for a waiter with the intention of ordering more coffee, but when Veronika said this, he looked back at her, frowning. There was something odd about that statement. 'Never been seen *in the Urals* before?' he said. 'What do you mean by that? Are you implying that they *have* been seen somewhere else?'

'Oh, yeah. They've been seen somewhere else – at least, according to the stories...'

'Stories? What the hell are you talking about, Nika?'

'You remember Evgeniy?'

He thought for a few seconds. 'Evgeniy ... the cop? Your friend?' Evgeniy worked the Vizovskii district; Viktor had only met him once, about six months ago.

She nodded. 'Evgeniy's a bit of an amateur historian, with a special interest in unsolved historical mysteries. It's kind of a hobby of his; he researches them in his spare time. Keeps saying that one of these days he's going to write a book about them. Anyway, he told me about the Siberian Installations a while back.'

'Where are they, exactly?'

'Mainly in an area of western Yakutia, apparently. The tribes-people in the region call it the "Valley of Death", and make a point of avoiding it. They describe strange "iron houses" in the depths of the taiga. Evgeniy told me that these things have become part of the Yakutians' legends.'

'Have any outsiders ever seen them?' Viktor asked.

'I'm not sure. There have been one or two expeditions into the region, but no conclusive proof of their existence has ever been found. It's really rough country – I mean, *really* rough, almost completely unexplored. Nothing but dense forest – snowbound in winter, full of swamps and mosquitoes in summer. I'm not sure whether any outsiders have ever managed to find them, and there's certainly no physical proof of their existence.' She smiled. 'But now ... there's evidence of them in the region of Kholat Syakhl.' Her smile grew broader. 'Wow ... wait 'til Evgeniy hears about *this*.'

'Are you crazy?' Viktor said, a little too loudly. Some of the cafe's patrons looked round at them, and he lowered his voice to a whisper. 'You can't tell him, Nika. I'm probably committing half a dozen serious crimes just by holding onto those bloody documents. And you want to tell a *cop* about all this?'

She grimaced. 'Sorry, Vitya, I wasn't thinking straight. You're right: of *course* I can't. That was dumb of me.'

'It's all right. But you know I have to be really careful with this.' He thought for a moment. 'Maybe Konstantinov knows something about these so-called Installations. I can ask him next time I see him.'

'When will that be?'

'Soon. Anyway, Nika, I've told you everything I know. Are you going to help me out, or what?'

She reached for her shoulder bag and took out a large sketch pad and a pencil. She flipped to a clean page, and as she did so Viktor saw several sketches of city scenes. They were beautiful, and he would have liked to look at them more closely. Not for the first time, he envied Nika her artistic talent.

'Fire away,' she said.

———

Ten minutes later, she turned her sketch around and showed him.

'Nika, you're a genius.'

The sketch was a near-perfect likeness of the old man.

'When are you going to see this Konstantinov character?' she asked.

'Today.'

'Mind if I tag along?'

His surprised expression made her smile. 'Tag along?'

'I'd like to meet him.'

'Why?'

'*Why?* Are you serious? After everything you've just told me?'

Viktor's first impulse was to say no. He didn't want Veronika to become involved in this. He was already playing with fire, being in receipt of leaked government documents. He had no idea how all this would pan out, and if things went badly, he didn't want her to go down with him.

The fact was, he still cared for her very much.

He tried to explain this to her, but it just made her angry.

'You're such an arsehole, Vitya! You call me out of the blue and ask for my help, and when I give it to you, it's "thanks very much and goodbye".'

'It's not like that, Nika.'

'It's *exactly* like that. Don't you realise what you've got here?'

'That's the point: I don't know what I've got here. I have no *idea* what I've got here! And it could turn out to be very dangerous.'

'But it could turn out to be absolute dynamite!'

'Yeah, and dynamite can blow up in your face.'

Veronika glared at him in silence for a few moments, then took the sketch between her thumb and forefinger, and waved it in front of him. He felt like a dog whose owner was showing him a new toy she'd just bought.

'Do you want this or not, Vitya?' she said. 'Because if you do, I come with it.'

He sighed. 'Shit, Veronika. I can't believe you're doing this.'

'Believe it.'

'Can't you see I'm trying to protect you? I've already been tailed by one man, who knows where I live. God knows who else has taken an interest in me. I don't want you involved...'

'I'm *already* involved.'

That much was true, of course. And at that moment Viktor realised that he shouldn't have agreed to meet Veronika in public; he should have asked her to go to his place, or asked to go to hers. He hoped that neither of them would have to pay for that mistake.

'Yes or no, Viktor,' she said. 'Make your decision.'

He took the sketch from her, folded it slowly and carefully, and put it in his coat pocket. 'All right,' he said. 'But first, we have to stop off at my place, to pick up the dossier and the key.'

'The key?'

'Yeah. There's a key taped to the inside cover of the folder, along with the account details for a safety deposit box at Uralpromstroybank.'

'Any idea what's in the box?'

'None whatsoever. Let's go.'

EIGHT

'I didn't expect to see you again so soon, Viktor,' said Konstantinov. 'And with such charming company, too!'

'This is my friend, Veronika Ivasheva,' Viktor said a little awkwardly, feeling like he was trying to get into a party to which he hadn't been invited. The feeling lifted, however, when it occurred to him that he was the one with the booze.

Konstantinov welcomed them into his apartment, and the appreciative glance he gave Nika as she walked past was so subtle as to be barely noticeable. He closed the door and offered her his hand. 'A pleasure, my dear.'

'The pleasure's mine,' she said with a smile.

'I didn't expect to be back so soon myself, Vadim,' Viktor said. 'But something happened yesterday, and I need your advice.'

'Oh?' he said, beckoning them through to the sitting room. 'What happened?'

'I've been contacted by someone ... someone who apparently knows an awful lot about the Dyatlov Pass incident.'

Konstantinov motioned them to sit down, but remained standing himself, his arms folded across his chest. He looked from Nika to Viktor, a deep frown wrinkling his brow. 'Who contacted you?'

'I don't know.' Viktor repeated the same story he had told to Nika in the cafe earlier, about being tailed by the old man. 'I described him to Veronika. She's a very talented artist, and she was able to draw this sketch of him...' He took out the sketch and handed it to Konstantinov, who quickly unfolded it and examined it.

His frown deepened as he whispered: 'My God. Lishin.'

Viktor leaned forward on the edge of his seat. 'Do you know this man?'

'I only met him once,' Konstantinov replied in a quiet voice. 'Eduard Lishin.' He glanced at Nika. 'Viktor is right: you do have a considerable talent.'

'Thank you,' she said, glancing back at him. She had been looking around the room with undisguised curiosity.

'It must be twenty years since we met, but ... well, you've captured him so well that there can be no mistake. This is Lishin.'

'What can you tell us about him?' Viktor asked.

Konstantinov sat down opposite them. 'He's ex-KGB. He was involved in the initial investigation of the incident in 1959. He was liaising with the Sverdlovsk Regional Committee of the Communist Party. An overseer, basically, keeping an eye on things for Moscow. He was in his mid-thirties, then. He retired from the KGB just before the Wall came down, and appears to have lived quietly and anonymously ever since. In fact, I must admit that I thought he was dead.'

'Far from it,' Viktor said. 'He's alive and well, and following me around Yekaterinburg.'

'You said you'd made contact,' said Konstantinov. 'Obviously not *direct* contact, otherwise you'd know who he is. So, what kind of contact have you made?'

'Yesterday, someone placed an envelope containing some documents in my mailbox. I think it was this Lishin.'

Konstantinov leaned forward. 'Documents?'

Viktor handed him the envelope. He took it without a word, withdrew the folder and opened it. He hesitated when he saw the key, and then examined the photographs first, looking at each of them for several long moments. When he came to the one showing the Installation, he caught his breath.

'Veronika tells me that those things have been seen in other parts of the country,' Viktor said. 'Specifically, in western Yakutia. They're well known to the indigenous tribes there...'

'She's right,' said Konstantinov, very quietly, as he went through the photographs again. He was shaking his head, as if he couldn't quite believe what he was seeing. Viktor sympathised.

'Do you have any idea what they might be, Professor Konstantinov?' asked Veronika.

'Please,' he whispered, without looking at her. 'Vadim.'

He said nothing more, so Viktor pressed him. 'Whatever they are, they're not just in Yakutia. Have you ever heard any accounts of them in this region?'

'No, I haven't. But I've made a study of this and many other legends. My profession, you understand.'

'What can you tell us about them?'

Konstantinov had put the photographs aside, and began to leaf through the printed documents. 'Would ... would you do me a favour, Viktor? Would you go and make us all some coffee? You'll find everything in the kitchen.'

Viktor smiled and said: 'Of course.' Konstantinov was itching to read those documents, and after all his long years of searching for answers to the enigma of Dyatlov Pass, it would have been cruel to delay him any further.

'I'll come with you,' said Veronika. They found their way to the kitchen, and did as Konstantinov had asked. Neither of them said any-thing while they made the coffee and filled a tray with three cups and a pot. There didn't seem to be anything to say – not then. It was as if they were waiting for some kind of pronouncement, or judgment; waiting for Konstantinov to offer his opinion on what they had brought him. It was a strange feeling, as if they had arrived at one of those defining moments he had spoken about. Only much later did Viktor come to realise how terribly accurate that feeling was.

———

When they returned with the tray, they found Konstantinov deep in thought.

'Well...' Viktor said as he sat down opposite him while Nika poured coffee for them all. 'What do you think?'

'I think this is the first real breakthrough. After all these long years ... the *first real breakthrough*. These documents are clearly genuine, and describe a phase of the Dyatlov Pass incident that no one outside the KGB even suspected. I want to thank you for showing them to me, Viktor.'

'There's no one else I *could* have shown them to ... apart from Yudin, I suppose.'

'Yuri...' said Konstantinov in barely more than a whisper. 'He and I are the only ones left who...' His voice trailed off.

Viktor repeated his earlier question. 'What can you tell us about these things, Vadim? These Installations and Cauldrons ... what do you think they are? Who made them, and why?'

Konstantinov smiled. 'I'm afraid I can't answer those questions. But I can give you some background. I can describe the myths and legends that have come out of the Yakutia region.'

'Please do. It might be helpful.'

'Yes ... it might. I have made a lifelong study of folklore in this and many other countries, and I've always been struck by the parallels with the modern world, and with the modern mysteries that are so glibly dismissed by orthodox science. Take the legends of the Yakut people. They contain many references to strange explosions and fiery spheres...'

'Spheres?'

'Indeed. And many of these legends have their origin in the strange objects that have been seen by Yakut herdsmen in the region known as *Uliuiu Cherkechekh*, or the "Valley of Death" – objects very similar to the one in this photograph. The first one appeared a long time ago – many centuries. The event is immortalised in their epic poem *Olonkho*, which tells of a great darkness that enveloped the land, accompanied by a terrible, shrieking wind, and by lightning which covered the sky.

'When the darkness lifted, the people saw a great swathe of scorched ground, at the centre of which stood a vast tower which emitted strange, high-pitched noises. Gradually, over many weeks, the tower sank into the ground, leaving behind it a huge vertical shaft. At times, an object was seen hovering over the mouth of the chasm, an object which the herdsmen called a "rotating island". Some people grew so curious that they put their fear aside, and went into the scorched region to investigate. They never returned.

'Many years later, the land was shaken by a tremendous earthquake. A great fireball appeared, and flew over the horizon to decimate the lands of a neighbouring tribe. They were enemies of the Yakuts, so it was assumed that the fireball was some kind of protecting "demon". They called it *Niurgun Bootur*, which means "the fiery champion".

'More years passed, and then another fireball emerged from the ground into which the tower had sunk, and exploded, causing earthquakes and transforming the land around the pit into a raging inferno. The rotating island returned, and hovered above the conflagration. The Yakuts and the neighbouring tribe fled in terror from the chaos, many of them succumbing to a strange illness.

'Six hundred years later, another fireball emerged from the ground and rent the sky in a devastating explosion which the *Olonkho* calls *Uot Usumu Tong Duurai*, which means "the criminal stranger who pierced the Earth and hid in the depths, destroying all around with a fiery whirlwind".

'In the eyes of the Yakut people, these phenomena became anthropomorphised, as one might expect. *Tong Duurai* became an antihero, while *Niurgun Bootur* became the protector of the people. In one section of the *Olonkho*, the "fiery champion" emerges from the ground to do battle with the "criminal stranger". But it all began with the arrival of the strange, glowing tower, which sank into the Earth.'

Konstantinov tapped the photograph showing the Installation with his index finger. 'I believe it's quite possible that these objects are the same as the one described in the epic poetry of the Yakut people. Today, the Yakuts refer to *olguis* – "cauldrons" – which still exist in the region, along with *kheldyu*, or "iron houses".'

'Have any outsiders ever seen them?' Viktor asked.

'There are several tales of modern travellers stumbling upon them,' he replied. 'Some are more plausible than others, I have to say. A man named Mikhail Koretsky from Vladivostok claimed to have been to the Valley of Death three times between 1933 and 1947. During these trips he said he saw seven Cauldrons. They were between six and nine metres in diameter, and partially buried. The vegetation around them was strange, more lush than the surrounding vegetation; the grass was twice as tall as a man, and the burdock leaves were gigantic. He claimed that he and his companions spent a night in one of the Cauldrons. Although the night passed uneventfully, within a month one of his friends had lost all his hair, and Koretsky developed two small pustules on his cheek which never healed.'

'Sounds like they were affected by the "strange illness" the Yakuts wrote about in their poem,' said Veronika.

Konstantinov offered her a slight smile. 'It does, doesn't it?'

'Does no one have a theory as to what they are?' Viktor asked. The legends and epic poetry of the Yakut people were interesting, but he couldn't believe that there was nothing beyond them and the unsubstantiated tales of a few travellers.

'The most intriguing theory is also the least plausible, unfortunately,' Konstantinov replied. 'It has been put forward by a Russian ufologist, Dr Valerey Uvarov. He believes that the Installations and the Cauldrons are connected to some kind of device, an immense power plant located deep inside the Earth...'

'A *power plant*? For what purpose?'

'To defend the planet against threats from deep space.'

'Who built it?'

Konstantinov shrugged. 'Perhaps extraterrestrials ... perhaps an ancient and unknown civilisation of advanced humans.'

Viktor shook his head. 'I'm sorry, Vadim, but I can't even begin to believe that.'

He offered them a weak smile. 'I did say it was the least plausible theory. However, consider this: according to Uvarov, this ... *defence complex*, whatever you want to call it ... destroyed the Tunguska meteorite before it hit the Earth in 1908. It also destroyed the Chulym meteorite in 1984 and the Vitim meteorite in 2002. And the Yakut legends speak of fiery emanations rising from the pit containing the glowing tower, and doing battle with powerful enemies coming from the sky.'

'So you think those legends could be describing meteorites that were destroyed before they could hit the Earth?' said Veronika.

'I'm merely saying it's a possibility. Remote, I grant you, but a possibility nonetheless.'

Viktor's gaze fell upon the documents spread across the coffee table. 'If the KGB knew about the Yakutian Installations and Cauldrons – which they clearly did, since they use the word "cauldron" to describe the object near Kholat Syakhl – then they must have sent their own expeditions to investigate them. Maybe that's why travel to the region was forbidden for three years following the Dyatlov Pass incident. Maybe that's what Project Svarog is.'

Konstantinov picked up one of the documents and examined it again.

'I've never seen that symbol before.' Viktor said. 'It might be significant. Do you know what it is?'

'Yes,' Konstantinov replied.

'Really?'

Konstantinov went over to one of the numerous bookcases and took down a large, leather-bound book, which he opened to a certain page and handed to Viktor and Veronika. The page contained a photograph of a woodcut. It looked quite primitive, but the image was clearly identical to the Project Svarog symbol:

'This,' said Konstantinov, 'is the symbol of Perun.'

Viktor frowned at him. 'Perun?'

'The god of thunder and lightning in Slavic mythology, analogous to the Norse god Thor. But unlike Thor, Perun was the supreme deity of the ancient Slavic tribes, in which respect you'd have to say he has more in common with Odin. In any event, this symbol is often carved on the roof beams of village houses to protect them from lightning bolts. In fact, it has been suggested that the circular shape symbolises ball lightning.'

Viktor glanced sharply at him. '*Ball lightning?*'

'What's that?' asked Nika.

Konstantinov looked at Viktor as realisation dawned. 'My God. Do you think there could be a connection?'

'Excuse me,' said Nika. 'Er, ball lightning...?'

'Oh, I'm sorry, my dear,' said Konstantinov, sitting down beside her. 'In essence, ball lightning is an ill-understood atmospheric phenomenon, sometimes associated with thunderstorms; but unlike conventional lightning, which occurs within a fraction of a second, ball lightning can last for many seconds. Its shape, too, is problematical; for as the name suggests, it is spherical.'

'Spherical,' Viktor echoed. 'Like the objects those geography students saw on the night Igor Dyatlov and the others died. Spherical, like this.' He held up the photograph marked PROBABLE FLYING SPHERE.

'Okay,' said Nika. 'We know what the symbol means – even if we don't know exactly why it was chosen. But what about the word "Svarog"?'

'The personification of the sky, according to ancient Slavic mythology,' said Konstantinov.

Veronika sighed. 'Whoever created Project Svarog, they were certainly into pagan mythology!'

'Yes,' murmured Konstantinov. 'Yes ... they were.'

'In any event,' Viktor said. 'It doesn't look like they found any answers – or if they did, they're not included in this dossier.'

Konstantinov regarded him in thoughtful silence for several moments, then said: 'I think there's more than enough to be going on with, Viktor.'

'But there could be more. Do you know where Eduard Lishin lives?'

Konstantinov's eyes widened, and he laughed. 'Why? Are you thinking of popping round to his place and asking him for the rest of the KGB archive?'

'Yes,' Viktor replied simply.

'I wouldn't do that, if I were you. I wouldn't even *think* about it.'

'Why not? After all, Lishin contacted *me*.'

'Yes, and I would say that you're lucky to be still alive and out of prison. Perhaps Lishin only had access to these documents, or perhaps he has access to more; but either way, he has given you what he thinks you should have. Don't push it, Viktor.'

'Maybe he's going to supply you with more at a later date,' suggested Veronika.

'Quite possibly,' Konstantinov nodded. 'But I wouldn't count on it, and I certainly wouldn't press Lishin.'

'There's something I've been trying to figure out,' Viktor said. 'Why did Lishin give this dossier to me? Why didn't he give it to you? I mean, you're the authority on the Dyatlov Pass incident, aren't you? You're the most logical candidate to receive this information.'

'I've also been thinking about that,' said Konstantinov. 'And the only thing I can suggest is that Lishin suspects that he is under surveillance by the FSB, and he couldn't risk being seen contacting me...'

'But I saw him right outside this building. If he was being watched, surely he wouldn't have risked coming anywhere near this street.'

'Unless he felt it was worth the risk,' Konstantinov replied. 'To connect himself with the Foundation in your mind.'

'But why would he even bother?' asked Veronika. 'Why didn't he just leave the dossier in Vitya's mailbox and have done with it? Why all this cloak-and-dagger nonsense?'

'There are two reasons I can think of straight away,' said Konstantinov. 'One: he knew that Viktor would either photograph him or describe him to me, and I would confirm his identity and his involvement with the Dyatlov Pass investigation. This would provide quick proof that the documents he supplied are genuine. And two: Lishin was a KGB agent almost all his working life; all this "cloak-and-dagger nonsense", as you put it, is simply the way these people think. You must understand that an intelligence agent's mind works in a certain way: Byzantine in its subtlety and complexity. In some respects, intelligence work is like a complicated game to them, and Lishin, even though an old man, is no exception.'

'There's another possibility,' Viktor said.

Veronika glanced at him. 'What's that?'

'Lishin doesn't intend simply to vanish into the shadows, never to be seen again. It could be that this dossier is his calling card, and that he *does* intend to make further disclosures at some point.'

'Vadim,' said Veronika. 'You said you met him once. How? And what happened at that meeting?'

'His was one of the names which came up in the course of my researches,' Konstantinov replied. 'I made contact with him in the early 1990s. Although he agreed to speak to me, I got virtually no information from him. I did, however, get the impression that he knew far more than he was saying, that he was struggling with his conscience ... that he *wanted* to say more, but couldn't, at least not then.'

'And now, his conscience has got the better of him,' said Veronika.

'Or perhaps there is an unknown factor which has prompted him to act,' said Konstantinov.

'An unknown factor?' Viktor said. 'What do you mean by that?'

Konstantinov picked up the photograph showing the Installation, and regarded it thoughtfully. 'Aren't you wondering why this has never been seen before?' he asked.

'I'm not sure I follow.'

'*Think* about it, Viktor. Back in the fifties, as we all know, this area was very popular with sports tourists; and it has been half a century since the incident, during which time plenty of other people have been there. Why has no one ever seen this and reported it? Or the other things the Dyatlov party apparently encountered?'

Viktor tried to think of an answer, but couldn't. He shook his head helplessly. 'I have no idea. But you're right: they *should* have been seen by someone, who would have spread the word about their presence. Otorten and Kholat Syakhl are remote, but not *that* remote.'

He thought of the Yakut legends of strange objects sinking into the ground and emerging from it. 'What if...?' he said, and hesitated.

'Go on,' said Konstantinov.

'Well ... there are three possibilities, aren't there? The first is that in the fifty years since the Dyatlov Pass incident – and for God knows how many years *before* then – no one has ever seen these objects in the region of Kholat Syakhl. I think that's unlikely, if they're really there. The second possibility is that someone *has* seen them, but they haven't said anything about it – which I think is equally unlikely.'

'And what's the third possibility?' asked Veronika.

He gave a short, embarrassed laugh. 'The third possibility, I have to say, is the least likely of all – but it's the one that makes the most sense. Somehow, whatever's out there is capable of concealing itself.' He looked at Veronika and Konstantinov in turn. 'The third possibility is that the Yakut legends are based on truth, and that these things, whatever they might be, are capable of sinking into the ground and emerging from it. If they really are machines of some kind, then they're still active. Whatever their function is, they still *work*.'

Konstantinov looked at him for a long moment, the corners of his mouth curled up in an ironic half-smile. 'You know, Viktor,' he said, 'we met for the first time only yesterday, but already I had come to the conclusion that you're a sceptic about such things.'

Viktor picked up the photograph showing the Installation. 'It's hard to argue against evidence like this.'

Veronika looked at them both. 'So ... where does all this leave us? We've got a lot of information here. What do we do with it?'

'Isn't it obvious?' Konstantinov said. He picked up the map of the region, with its red circles and annotations. 'We go there. We mount our own expedition, and we look for the answers ourselves. This didn't come from the Dyatlov camp: it must be a government document. It contains the precise coordinates of the objects lying within the forest – which further implies that whatever is there was secretly investigated. All we have to do is follow the directions...'

'X marks the spot,' said Veronika.

Konstantinov grinned at her. 'Precisely.'

'Our own expedition...' Viktor said. 'Who do you have in mind to go?'

'Well, you and me for a start – that's if you want to...'

'Yes, I want to, although I'm not sure how much use I'll be.'

'How about as chronicler? You can keep field notes, and record the observations and reactions of the other members. Important work, I assure you. Apart from which, it's through your involvement that this breakthrough has occurred, Viktor. I'd like to have you along; you deserve it.'

'All right. Who else?'

'One name springs to mind immediately: Alisa Chernikova. She's a physicist who works at the State Technical University. Quite brilliant.'

'Will she *want* to go?' asked Veronika.

'Oh yes, I think so. I've discussed the Dyatlov Pass incident with her on many occasions, and she's very intrigued by the mystery. In fact, Alisa was a member of my 2007 expedition. And she'll be even more intrigued now,' he added, patting the photographs.

'So ... three of us,' Viktor said.

'Four,' said Veronika.

Konstantinov glanced at her. 'Four?'

'You'll need a photographer as well as a chronicler. And I'm just as handy with a camera as I am with a pencil.'

Viktor didn't say anything: he had too much respect for Nika to try and dissuade her in front of Konstantinov. But he didn't like the idea of her going. They had no idea what they would find in that forest; for all they knew, they were headed for the same fate that had befallen Dyatlov and the others all those decades ago. It was a risk Viktor was willing to take; but he didn't want Nika to take it. For a brief moment, he held the forlorn hope that Konstantinov would decline her request; but instead, he smiled at her.

'That's a very good idea, Veronika; and I'm ashamed to say it hadn't occurred to me – what with the excitement of this discovery.' He indicated the scattered contents of Lishin's dossier.

Viktor exchanged a look with Nika, and when Konstantinov saw his expression, his smile faded a little.

'Then it's settled,' she said. 'When do we leave?'

'I'll need a few days to make preparations,' Konstantinov replied. 'I have to get in touch with Alisa, and explain the situation to her. And then there are supplies, equipment and transportation to be arranged. Yes, per-haps three days. And then we'll be on our way. But there's one very impor-tant thing we have to do first...' He took the key from the inside cover of the folder and held it up. 'We have to go to the Uralpromstroybank and see what's in this safety deposit box.'

NINE

Konstantinov called the Uralpromstroybank to see if it was open on Saturdays. It was, from nine until five. Viktor suggested that they drive to the bank: whatever was in that box, he didn't want to carry it around with them. The thought that Eduard Lishin might be under surveillance made him uneasy, and for that reason he asked Nika to remain in Konstantinov's apartment while they went to the bank. She didn't like it, of course, but she saw the logic of it, and reluctantly agreed.

They drove to the bank in Viktor's car. The streets were crowded with weekend shoppers, the roads thick with traffic, and it was only with some difficulty that they managed to find a parking space a couple of blocks away on Zhukova, where the bank was located.

Viktor was grateful that there were so many people around. As they walked amidst the hurrying, jostling bodies, he felt strangely protected: just another person in a crowded city on a Saturday afternoon. He tried to keep thinking that way as he and Konstantinov approached the bank; but the closer they got, the more difficult it became. He had visions of black SUVs screeching to a halt at the curbside, of hands reaching out from their dark interiors and pulling them inside while passersby looked on in sudden fear.

Viktor's heart started racing as they approached the steps leading up to the main entrance to the building, and he forced himself to maintain a leisurely pace, to do nothing that might draw attention. Now, the countless people on the street no longer seemed to offer protection: now, they were all potential agents of state security, intent on preventing the contents of that box from falling into the wrong hands. He glanced furtively at each face he passed, half expecting the person's eyes to fix upon him suddenly, while unseen hands grabbed him from behind...

And then they were up the stairs and into the foyer, across the marble floor and standing at the front desk, Viktor hoping that the young woman sitting there didn't notice the beads of perspiration dotting his brow in spite of the cold outside.

'May I help you, sir?' she said with a well-practised smile.

'Yes, thank you,' Viktor said. 'We would like to retrieve a safety deposit box held here.'

'Certainly. Please write the account number on this form,' she said, taking out a card from a drawer in the desk and sliding it towards him.

Forcing himself to breathe evenly, he filled out the card and handed it back to her. She picked up a phone and said a few words into it.

Almost immediately, a man in an immaculate suit appeared at their side. 'Would you please follow me, gentlemen?'

He led them across the foyer, through a door and along a corridor which ended in a wall of solid steel. The man took out a plastic card, swiped it through a card reader mounted on the wall and tapped out a series of numbers on a keypad next to the reader.

With a loud hiss of powerful hydraulics, the wall slowly slid aside, revealing the vault beyond. The room was large, perhaps ten metres square, and was bathed in a cold, clinical light from strips set into the ceiling. Each of the walls was lined with numbered panels of varying sizes.

The man walked up to one of these and indicated the lock, then nodded in the direction of another door. 'There are private cubicles through there. Please stay as long as you wish. When you have finished, simply replace the box and close the panel. It is self-locking. And if you require any further assistance, please press the button on the desk in the cubicle.'

'Thank you,' Viktor said.

He smiled at them and left the vault.

The panel the man had indicated was not particularly large: perhaps fifteen centimetres by ten. They walked over to it. Viktor glanced at Konstantinov, who gave him an encouraging smile, took a deep breath, inserted the key and pulled the panel open. He pulled out the steel box and carried it through to one of the cubicles. Konstantinov closed the dark blue velvet curtain behind them.

The cubicle contained a desk and chair, a telephone, fax machine and mini laptop, Viktor guessed with an internet connection. He placed the box on the desk, took another deep breath and opened it.

Inside, there was another box, apparently made of smoked glass. Alongside it lay a letter-sized envelope. Viktor was about to pick up the object, when something – perhaps some inner intuition – made him stop. Instead, he carefully opened the hinged lid of the glass box to reveal its contents.

He stopped breathing without realising it, and only started again when his lungs began to ache.

He had no idea what he was looking at.

He glanced again at Konstantinov, who raised his eyebrows and shook his head in bewilderment.

The object was about ten centimetres long and about three wide. It looked like a jewel, cut into the shape of a trapezohedron, with each of its facets interlocking with the next around its centre.

But it was not a jewel.

As Viktor stared at the thing, he had the impression that it was changing shape, assuming different multifaceted forms, even as his eyes told him that this was not so. Its colour, too, was like none he had ever seen, for although the object glowed faintly with a pale rosy hue, part of Viktor's mind told him that this was not so: that its colour was gradually shifting through the visible spectrum – *and on into the invisible*, from the infrared, through the seven visible colours, to the ultraviolet and then back again. He knew this was impossible; he knew that the human eye couldn't see in the infrared and ultraviolet, but that was the impression he had.

He experienced the sudden, undeniable conviction that this thing, whatever it was, had not been fashioned on Earth; and so shattering was the realisation that he wanted to run, to put as much distance between himself and the object as possible, to be *away from it*, and never to set eyes on it again. At that moment, Viktor was a frightened child who had taken an involuntary and unexpected step into a world whose existence he had never suspected. This impossible object was *real*; he had no idea of its origin or purpose; his only certainty was that it was doing things which no object could do in a sane and rational universe.

'What is this thing?' he whispered.

'I have no idea,' Konstantinov replied quietly. 'I can't even begin to speculate. It looks like ... almost like it's *alive.*'

Viktor looked at him, appalled; but he couldn't deny that the thought had occurred to him also.

Konstantinov took the envelope, opened it and withdrew several sheets of paper. The first sheet had the heading:

PROJECT SVAROG

1 JUNE 1959
SUMMARY REPORT NO. 131876-765
ON ARTEFACT DESIGNATED 'ANTIPRISM'

Viktor could see that Konstantinov had begun to read the contents. He put a hand on his arm. 'Not here. Let's get back to your place first.'

Konstantinov nodded reluctantly. 'Perhaps you're right.'

With shaking hands, Viktor closed the lid of the glass box and picked it up. The thought of carrying it on his person was strangely repellent, but he had no choice. He placed it carefully in an inside pocket of his overcoat, while Konstantinov put the pages back in the envelope.

Viktor returned the safety deposit box to its slot in the wall and they left the bank, Viktor counting the minutes until they could get back to the apartment.

———

'How did it go?' asked Veronika when they returned.

Konstantinov and Viktor glanced at each other. Neither of them quite knew how to describe what they had found.

She followed them into the sitting room. 'Come on, you two! Don't keep it to yourselves. What was in the box?'

'Forgive us, Veronika,' Konstantinov replied. 'We hesitate simply because we don't ... well, I think it's better if you just see for yourself.'

Viktor took out the glass box from his pocket and placed it very gently on the coffee table. When he opened it, Nika sat down slowly and looked at its contents in silence for several moments.

'What the hell *is* that?' she whispered.

'Damned if I know,' Viktor replied.

'Whatever it is,' Konstantinov said, taking out the envelope that had been placed in the box with the object, 'Lishin wanted us to have it.'

He opened the envelope and withdrew several sheets of paper, which he laid on the table so that they could all see what was written on them.

PROJECT SVAROG

1 JUNE 1959
SUMMARY REPORT NO. 131876-765
ON ARTEFACT DESIGNATED 'ANTIPRISM'

This artefact, which the Project Svarog administrators have designated the 'antiprism', was discovered in the central chamber of the Installation in Anomalous Zone 3, North Urals Sector, on 15 March 1959 and removed from the structure on 9 April 1959. Its removal was approved by Dr Leonid Kozerski, following the completion of initial analysis *in situ*. Dr Kozerski considered that the risk factor resulting from removal of the artefact was within acceptable limits, and ordered it to be transferred to Beloretsk-15, South Urals Sector. The record should state here that this was undertaken against the objections of Dr Anton Soloviev, who believes that the antiprism is a conscious being of some kind. This opinion is not shared by the Project Svarog administrators.

The antiprism was subjected to further analysis at the Exotic Materials Laboratory at Beloretsk-15. The results, however, were inconclusive, since the artefact is impervious to all forms of intrusive investigation and is undetectable by passive sensing equipment. The only positive conclusion reached was that the antiprism is rendered largely – although not completely – inert when it is placed in close proximity to crystals belonging to the trigonal crystal system, such as quartz. For this reason, it was decided that the antiprism should be stored in a quartz container when not being handled by project personnel.

The conclusion reached by the investigators was that, *in so far as it can be said to exist at all*, the antiprism is the product of a science that is far in advance of that possessed by the USSR or any other nation on Earth.

The first real breakthrough in our understanding of the antiprism's nature came about as a result of the related tragedies which befell two great heroes of the Soviet Union, Dr Yakov Chuzhoi and Dr Oleg Melnikov, who spent a greater period of time in close proximity to the artefact than any other members of the research team. Their contribution cannot be overestimated, although the price they paid for it was terrible.

A complete assessment of their cases is included in Report No. 675544-143, 'Psychological Evaluation of Yakov Chuzhoi and Oleg Melnikov', but can be summarised thus:

Dr Chuzhoi was a physicist and Dr Melnikov a materials analysis specialist; both were supremely capable in their fields and were loyal servants of the Russian people. They were charged with the investigation of the antiprism following its removal from the Installation in Anomalous Zone 3, and they performed their duties with faultless diligence and dedication. In view of the sensitive nature of their work, their movements and activities were closely monitored, both inside the Exotic Materials Laboratory at Beloretsk-15 and during their non-working periods in the city.

The changes in their behaviour were therefore noted immediately, and an emergency meeting was convened by the Project Svarog administrators at which it was suggested that these changes were the direct result of prolonged proximity to the antiprism. Several possible courses of action were discussed, and it was decided that, in view of the difficulties encountered during analysis of the artefact, Dr Chuzhoi and Dr Melnikov should be allowed to continue their work unimpeded, with the frequency of their physical and psychological evaluation sessions being increased from weekly to once every two days. The rationale for this decision was the belief that research into the nature of the artefact had been proceeding in the wrong direction, and that it would be more useful to observe the artefact's effects upon human beings in close proximity to it, than to observe the artefact itself.

This new program of observation began in earnest on 1 May 1959, and continued until the death by suicide of Dr Chuzhoi and Dr Melnikov on 23 May and 25 May respectively. The results of the observations included the following salient points:

- Following their assignment to investigate the antiprism, both men began to exhibit irrational behaviour patterns, including irritability, lapses in short term memory, insomnia, increased sensitivity to loud noises, and nervousness.
- During their psychological evaluation sessions, both men complained of bizarre nightmares during the short periods when they were able to sleep. They were initially reluctant to discuss the content of these nightmares, but once persuaded to do so, they described being trapped in a strange, convoluted landscape, and the presence of something unseen but monstrous. They invariably woke up before this 'thing' could be seen.
- Towards the end of their lives, both men claimed to hear voices during their waking hours. They described these voices as being very low-pitched – almost guttural – and speaking a language they did not understand. They also claimed to be able to see the

unidentified landscape superimposed over their waking vision, which exacerbated their psychological condition.

•   This continued to the point where Dr Chuzhoi and Dr Melnikov could no longer endure what they were apparently seeing and hearing. The decision was taken by the Project Svarog administrators to remove them from duty; but unfortunately the men took their own lives before this decision could be implemented.

Following a review of the cases of Chuzhoi and Melnikov, it was concluded that the antiprism is a communication device of some kind – although it should not be assumed that this is its only function. We have yet to ascertain what the device is in communication *with*.

The results of experiments with later test subjects have proved inconclusive (see Report No. 788432-154, 'Psychological Evaluation of Subjects in Prison Transfer Protocol 7').

 END OF SUMMARY REPORT NO. 131876-765

'Christ,' said Veronika, when they had finished reading the report. 'This thing drove two people insane.'

'At *least* two,' said Konstantinov. 'Who knows how many other unfortunates were part of "Prison Transfer Protocol 7"?'

Viktor didn't say anything. He didn't know what to consider more appalling: the fact that people had been driven out of their minds by this thing, or that the people running Project Svarog had allowed it to happen, had considered Chuzhoi and Melnikov and those nameless others to be no more than laboratory rats to be experimented upon, and the results dispassionately observed and recorded.

Suddenly, he didn't want to be anywhere near the object. He felt the same way about it as he would have felt had there been an open vial of smallpox sitting there on the table.

'What are you going to do with it, Vadim?' asked Veronika. 'It's obvious you can't keep it here – not after what it did to those others.'

'There's nothing else I *can* do with it,' he replied. 'It shouldn't be too dangerous, though: according to the report, its effects appear to be minimised by the presence of quartz – hence this container – and the adverse effects only occur after prolonged exposure to it. I don't anticipate having it in my possession for that long.'

Viktor glanced at him. 'What do you mean?'

'Lishin has provided us with the precise coordinates for the phenomena which have been observed near Kholat Syakhl; and he has also allowed us access to *this*.' He indicated the 'antiprism'. 'The man mentioned in the report, Dr Soloviev, protested against the decision to remove it from the Installation. I believe that the implication is clear: Lishin wants us to return the antiprism to the Installation.'

Veronika looked at him dubiously. 'That's quite a leap, don't you think, Vadim?'

He smiled. 'Perhaps. But that's my feeling.'

'If that's really what he wants, why doesn't he do it himself?' she said.

'If he believes he's under surveillance,' Viktor said, 'he may also believe that he'd be prevented from doing so. Vadim, you said that when you met him in the 1990s, you had the impression that he was struggling with his conscience, that he wanted to tell you something. Maybe...' Viktor shrugged. 'Maybe he's trying to make something right by doing this.'

TEN

When Viktor went to see Maksimov later that day, the editor was incredulous, and not a little pissed off. 'You want to do *what*?' he said.

'I want to join the expedition that Vadim Konstantinov is planning,' Viktor repeated.

'You want to go on a cross-country hiking trip, on the paper's time, to find out what happened to the Dyatlov party.'

'That's right. I've come into possession of some information that may help us to find the answers.'

Maksimov swept a hand across his balding head. 'Sit down, Vitya.'

As Viktor sat down, Maksimov stood up and closed the door, then returned to his desk.

'What information?' he asked.

Viktor took a deep breath. 'Classified KGB documents, provided by an ex-operative.'

Maksimov stared at him for a while, and Viktor guessed that he was debating with himself whether to ask for a name. Evidently, he decided against it, at least for now. 'How do you know the documents are genuine?'

'Konstantinov believes that they are, and so do I.'

'Oh, *Konstantinov* believes they are, and so do you. Well, I suppose that's all the proof anyone needs!'

Viktor said nothing; he merely smiled at Maksimov, which evidently took him aback. He read Viktor's expression intently, like a copyeditor scanning for typos. He opened his mouth to say something, hesitated, then sighed. 'And what's *in* these documents?'

'A lot of things that have never come to light before, including these.' Viktor had made copies of all the photographs in the dossier, which he now handed to Maksimov, who silently examined them one by one. Viktor explained what each photograph showed. The frown of irritation that had creased Maksimov's brow gradually faded. He put the photocopies down and looked at his reporter, his index finger resting on the picture of the Installation.

'What is this?'

'We don't know.'

'I think it's a hoax,' he said matter-of-factly.

'You're wrong.'

'Konstantinov's taken you in. He's cobbled all this together with Photoshop. It's his way of getting back at me for rejecting his articles.'

'That's a load of shit, and you know it.'

'*What* did you say?'

'You heard me. I'm sorry, boss, but that's not what all this is about. Konstantinov couldn't care less whether the *Gazette* published him or not. I've met him, talked to him, and I can tell you that all he cares about is finding out what really happened to Igor Dyatlov and the others.'

'Want to bet your job on that?' Maksimov said, leaning back in his chair.

'Yes, I'll take that bet.'

They regarded each other in silence for a long moment.

'Listen,' Viktor said, leaning forward. 'According to the information my contact gave me, Dyatlov and the others spent at least a day, and probably more, in the forest to the south of Kholat Syakhl. They saw and photographed these things, which obviously scared them so much that they decided not to set up their camp in the forest. And it seems more than likely that whatever's there had something to do with their deaths. And there's also evidence to suggest that the army was involved...'

'The army?'

Viktor told him about the torn piece of material that appeared to have come from a soldier's uniform, about the items found at the abandoned campsite, which Yuri Yudin had been unable to identify, and about the two extra bodies which the medical student had claimed were discovered in the ravine.

'This has become more than just a historical curiosity,' he concluded. 'Something totally extraordinary happened on Kholat Syakhl fifty years ago, and whatever caused it is still there. Konstantinov is going to go there anyway; he's gathering a small group as we speak. I think that the *Gazette* should send a representative. When we return, I'll write the story, you'll read it, and then you'll decide whether to run it or not. If you still smell a rat, then you can fire me. I don't care, because I don't believe that's going to happen.'

Maksimov thought about this. Finally, a slow smile spread across his face. 'Some ambition at last, Vitya. At last, some balls.'

'Thanks,' Viktor said, with a trace of sarcasm which Maksimov chose to ignore. Maybe ambition was a part of it: he'd have been lying to himself if he denied that. But there was more to it than merely getting a good story for the *Gazette* – much more. It was hard to believe that only a couple of days had passed since he first heard of the Dyatlov Pass incident. But in that short span of time, the mystery had infected him ... yes, *infected* was precisely the right word. And the contents of the dossier which Eduard Lishin had vouchsafed to him had only increased his determination to find out what happened on that night fifty years ago.

'You'll need a photographer to go with you,' said Maksimov, breaking into Viktor's thoughts.

'What?'

'I happen to be running a newspaper, Vitya. We'll need pictures.'

'That's already been taken care of.'

'By whom? Konstantinov?'

'You know Veronika Ivasheva?'

'The police sketch artist?'

'She's also pretty handy with a camera.'

'And an old flame of yours, right?'

Viktor said nothing.

Maksimov sighed. 'Okay, take her along if you want,' he said, as if it were his expedition, his decision to make. 'When do you plan on leaving?'

'In a few days. Konstantinov needs time to prepare, gather equipment and supplies, arrange transportation and so on.'

Maksimov nodded, and then said very quietly: 'What do you think you'll find there, Vitya?'

Viktor thought about this for a long moment, and gave the only reply he could. 'I don't know.'

Maksimov sighed. 'All this is very hard to believe, you know.'

'You think you need to tell me that? I still can't quite believe it myself. We've been given a lot of information, but it raises more questions than it answers. The whole thing is bizarre.' He picked up the photocopy of the Installation. 'I have no idea what this thing is, who built it, or what its purpose is. But it exists; it's *there*, in that forest, along with other things that are equally strange. They've been seen in Yakutia, and they've been seen near Kholat Syakhl. They *exist*.'

Maksimov regarded him in silence, then he did something Viktor wasn't expecting. He stood up and offered him his hand. 'Good luck, Vitya,' he said.

———

That night, Viktor had trouble sleeping. For a couple of hours, he tossed and turned in his bed, unable to get comfortable. He had the strange and unpleasant impression that the sheets were a funeral shroud, smothering him. He threw them off and lay there, thinking about what he was about to do, where he was about to go. And for the first time since agreeing to go with Konstantinov, Viktor thought carefully about it.

Did he really have any business going into the forest around Kholat Syakhl? Lying in bed, surrounded by impenetrable darkness, he asked himself how wise it really was to follow in the footsteps of nine people who had been killed by *something*, a 'compelling unknown force', as the official report had put it. It wasn't wise at all: it was crazy and stupid. Things always look worse in the dead of night, when one's fears and problems chase sleep away; and Viktor had no choice but to listen to the voice inside his head that repeated insistently: *Don't do it. Don't go there!*

After all, what did it have to do with him? An unsolved mystery ... nine dead people ... a compelling unknown force ... something that happened half a century ago. Half a century, for Christ's sake! *Let it lie*, the voice said. *There's no reason why you should get involved.*

'And what about Nika?' he asked the darkness.

She would go, whether he went or not. She would go, and curse him for a coward. And what would he tell Maksimov? Finally, he seemed to have earned the editor's respect. What would he think if Viktor walked into his office and told him he'd changed his mind, that he'd been mistaken, that it *was* all a put-on? Maksimov would fire him on the spot, and probably send Cherevin in his place.

'Screw that!' he muttered, and turned to the unseen wall beside his bed.

I need to find out what happened to those people, he thought. *They deserve better than fifty years of official silence; and they deserve a better epitaph than the occasional breathless discussion on an internet forum.*

Finally, he managed to drift off to sleep. But it offered no refuge. He dreamed that he was stumbling through a snow-covered landscape, naked and shivering. A fierce storm came down off an ugly, misshapen mountain on the horizon, and with unnatural speed a blizzard of ice and snow engulfed him, half blinding him with millions of needle-liken shards. He was fleeing from something he couldn't see, but which he knew was utterly loathsome, something from which he instinctively knew he had to escape at all costs. He staggered through the snow on those legs of dream which are no use at all, towards a line of trees in the white distance. He half stumbled, half crawled amongst the trees, trying to get deeper into the forest, away from whatever was pursuing him. And in the forest's rustling depths, he came upon a small mound of snow. For some unknown reason dictated by the bizarre logic of the dream, he knew he had to find out what was under that mound. And so he clawed at the snow, flinging away huge handfuls into the howling night. And when he had finished, he saw that it was the frozen body of Nika, her mouth open in a final desperate scream, her tongue missing.

PART TWO

THE FOREST

BASKOV (5)

'I'd like to talk a little about the Dyatlov party,' I said to Strugatsky at the beginning of our next session.

He had moved from his bed to the armchair, which he always did as soon as I entered his room. He shrugged. 'Why not? It's how it all began.'

'I'm curious as to how you came to be so driven to discover the true cause of their deaths.'

'I've already told you. And anyway, why does *anyone* want to find out how someone died? Why does a policeman want to solve a murder?'

'It's what he's paid to do,' I replied.

Strugatsky leaned forward and regarded me with a quizzical expression. 'Doctor, you surprise me. Is that the only reason? What about the desire for justice? To preserve order, and the safety of the public? The desire to bring the perpetrator to account, and to try to ensure that it doesn't happen again?'

'You're quite right, Viktor,' I said as I made a quick note in my pad. 'All of those things are important – more so than the policeman's monthly pay packet. Yes ... you're quite right.'

Strugatsky regarded me in silence. Then a slow smile spread across his lips. 'Oh,' he said. 'I see.'

I returned his smile. 'What do you see?'

'You're curious about whether there's something in my past ... something that made me take such an intense interest in this. Am I right?'

'That's one possibility,' I conceded.

'And then, on the other hand,' he continued, his gaze having fallen on my notepad, 'you're also wondering whether I believe that there's some danger to the public in the forest around Kholat Syakhl...'

'What makes you say that?'

'I noticed that you made a note when I mentioned the safety of the public just now. Do you think I'm a fantasist, Doctor Baskov? Do you think I see myself as a protector of humanity?'

'Do you?'

He gave a small chuckle. 'No. I couldn't even protect my friends. How could I hope to protect everyone else?'

'Would you like to talk about your childhood?'

'I've no objection, but I think you'll find it rather dull and commonplace. It was happy and uneventful. I was never cold, never hungry, never beaten, never sexually abused ... my parents loved and cared for me.'

'I'm very glad to hear it. What about the Borovsky case?'

'What about it?'

'It made you angry when Maksimov took you off it and gave it to Cherevin instead.'

'Yes, it did. I wanted to stay on it, but the fact is – like I said – I just don't have what it takes to get someone to talk when they think that something terrible's going to happen to them if they do. Cherevin isn't like that: he'll keep digging until he gets his information, and if some poor bastard ends up getting the shit kicked out of him for talking, that's just tough luck. He's got his story, and that's all that matters. Of course, people like Cherevin rationalise it by saying that everyone's better off if Borovsky and his type are brought to justice. But that's not much comfort for the people who end up in hospital, or worse. So yes, I was angry when Maksimov took me off the case.'

'Maybe Cherevin will be the one who ends up in hospital ... or worse.'

Strugatsky frowned. 'I hope not, but I wouldn't be surprised.'

'You don't think it would serve him right?'

'Listen, Doctor Baskov, I don't like Cherevin, but I wouldn't wish that on him.'

I nodded. 'I'm glad to hear that, too.' I believed I had my answer then, and it was straightforward enough. Strugatsky appeared to have transferred his concerns for the people who lived in Borovsky's buildings to Igor Dyatlov and his friends. Prevented from doing anything to rescue the tenants from their plight, he had thrown himself into a quest to find the solution to the Dyatlov Pass incident. I must admit it was not the most brilliant of observations, but it made sense to me. I believed it was a straightforward conclusion, rather than a simplistic one.

'Have you had time to read the dossier?' Strugatsky asked suddenly.

'Yes,' I replied.

'What do you think?'

'I'm not sure. The information it contains is ... unusual, to say the least.'

'Komar must have told you that the documents are genuine.'

'Yes, he did. But that doesn't mean that the information they contain is genuine, does it?'

'No ... I suppose that, from your point of view, it doesn't.'

'What about Project Svarog?' I said. 'Can you tell me any more about that?'

Strugatsky closed his eyes and rubbed his temples, as if he had just been struck by a sudden headache. 'Not yet,' he whispered.

'Why not?'

He simply shook his head.

'All right, Viktor,' I said, reluctant to press him at this point. 'Perhaps we can talk a little about Chernikova. Can you tell me how you met her?'

Strugatsky stopped rubbing his temples, sat back in his chair and looked at me. 'Alisa ... yes ... yes, I'll tell you how I met her.'

ELEVEN

Viktor and Nika met Alisa at Konstantinov's apartment shortly before they were due to leave for Kholat Syakhl. Viktor was struck by her appearance: she didn't look anything like his idea of a physicist. She was tall and elegant, with long dark hair tied back in a neat ponytail. There was something almost aristocratic in the way she carried herself, an aloofness – even arrogance. Her eyes were dark and penetrating, and she wore expensive-looking gold-rimmed spectacles.

She gave them a strained smile; her expression was intense – even troubled. Lishin's dossier lay on the coffee table, and it was quite clear from her demeanour that she had read it and seen the photographs. Viktor also assumed that Konstantinov had shown her the antiprism, and, given her profession, he was intensely curious as to what she thought of it.

Ever the considerate host, Konstantinov brought out coffee and cakes, which only added to the surreal strangeness of the situation. It was as if they were just a group of friends having a get-together, instead of a disparate collection of strangers and near-strangers contemplating the exploration of bizarre and mysterious objects in a far-off wilderness.

For want of something to say, Viktor made that observation. Alisa gave a contemplative nod, while Konstantinov chuckled and said: 'Quite so, Viktor, quite so.'

'You're a reporter, Viktor,' said Alisa.

'That's right, for the *Gazette.*'

She nodded. 'And presumably, you plan to write an article on this for your paper.'

Something in her tone of voice made him hesitate. 'I ... suppose it depends on what we find out there.'

'Ah yes,' she said. 'What we find out there ... What does your editor say about all this?'

'He suspects that it's all a hoax, that Vadim has cobbled all this together in revenge for the paper's rejection of his articles.'

Konstantinov burst out laughing. He shook his head and muttered: 'Maksimov...'

Alisa smiled thinly, and said: 'Do you think you'll be *able* to publish the results of this expedition?'

'What do you mean?'

She shrugged and indicated the dossier. 'I'm just thinking of the way you came by this information. Whatever really happened out there is still a state secret.'

Viktor didn't have an answer for that, beyond the obvious 'the people have a right to know'. Konstantinov came to his rescue. 'I think we're getting a bit ahead of ourselves, aren't we, Alisa?' he said. 'The important thing is to gather as much information as we can. Our subsequent actions should be dictated by the nature of that information.'

Alisa said nothing. Instead, she picked up a piece of spice cake and took a small bite.

'I assume Vadim has shown you what we found ... what Project Svarog calls the "antiprism"...'

'He has.'

'What do you think it is?'

'I have no idea,' she said matter-of-factly. 'I've never seen anything remotely like it. I'd like to get it into one of our labs and run a material analysis on it ... but that would be difficult.'

'It would raise too many questions in your department,' Viktor said.

'Precisely.'

'And I doubt it would do much good,' added Konstantinov. 'Project Svarog tried the same thing, and they came up empty-handed.'

Chernikova said pensively: 'It's as if it doesn't quite exist ... as if it isn't completely anchored in this universe. The colour shifts, the changes in its physical appearance, which are more the *intimations* of changes than *actual* changes.' She shook her head. 'It's incredible, and I'm quite certain that it's a technological device of some kind.'

'A communication device?' Viktor asked. 'That's what Project Svarog thought.'

'Perhaps, although it's quite clear they were guessing.' She shrugged. 'I can't say I'm in total agreement with Vadim that we should return it to the place where it was found, but if we do, I'm quite willing to entertain the possibility that it may reveal something of its true nature.'

I wonder if that would be a good or bad thing, Viktor thought.

Veronika took a sip of her coffee, and said: 'Have you decided on the route we'll take to Kholat Syakhl, Vadim?'

Konstantinov rummaged through the contents of the dossier until he found the annotated map of the region, which he spread out on the table in front of them. 'We'll proceed north to Ivdel, and then head across country to Yurta Anyamova. I've already rented a large SUV for the journey.'

'Yurta Anyamova?' said Veronika.

'It's a Mansi village, the biggest settlement in the area. Yurta Anyamova will be our last stop before the final leg of the journey to Kholat Syakhl.'

'Why do you want to stop there?' Viktor asked.

'I would like to speak with the Mansi people. They know the region, they've lived there for centuries, and they know Otorten and Kholat Syakhl. They may also know something about whatever is in that forest. Any information they can give us will be useful, I think.'

'Unless it's distorted by mythologizing,' observed Alisa.

Konstantinov smiled, and replied cryptically: 'It may be useful *because* of that.'

She didn't reply. Instead, she regarded Viktor in silence. As he met her gaze, he started to get annoyed. What was her problem? He said: 'You know why I'm going, Miss Chernikova...'

'*Doctor* Chernikova.'

'...but I'd be interested to know why *you're* going.'

'Isn't it obvious?' she said.

'Not to me.'

'Curiosity, of course. I'd like to know what the antiprism is, what those things in the forest are, why they're there, and why the Soviet government chose to keep their existence a secret. I'd also like to know exactly what Project Svarog was ... or is. Mind you,' she added, 'I suspect that my motives for wanting to find out are rather different from yours.'

Konstantinov saw Viktor's expression, and said: 'You mustn't mind Alisa, Viktor. She doesn't trust journalists.'

'I'm sorry to hear that, *Doctor* Chernikova,' he said. 'Would you mind telling me why?'

She sighed and sat back in her chair, crossing her legs. 'I've given many interviews to journalists, both from the print media and television. In my experience, they always simplify things to the point of idiocy, couching difficult concepts in the language of infants.'

'I've read plenty of books and articles on popular science,' Viktor replied. 'And I've never found their language idiotic. Perhaps you should consider that not everyone has advanced degrees in physics, that they *need* certain concepts to be simplified to some extent, so that they can at least begin to understand them. Aren't they to be respected for that?'

'Perhaps some of them are – the ones who take a genuine interest. A *very* small minority, I might add. For the rest – journalists *and* their readers – science in general, and physics in particular, is nothing more than a source of titbits of information to make their lives less boring. They're always on the lookout for the latest fad, something to generate a bit of interest before moving on to the next thing. Take the LHC, for instance – that's the Large Hadron Collider at CERN.'

'I know what the LHC is.'

'It's the most complex and magnificent experiment in the history of humanity. And how did the media handle it? By moaning about the cost and spreading scare stories about the possibility of accidentally creating a black hole that would swallow the Earth!'

Viktor was about to say something, but Chernikova cut him off.

'And *then*, when there was a coolant leak which caused the experiment to be temporarily shut down for repairs, all they could do was make snide comments about damp squibs and such like. Since then, we haven't heard a thing. And why not? Because the media have already moved on in search of the next big thing to babble about.'

'And that's why you think I'm here,' Viktor said. 'Because I'm looking for the "next big thing to babble about".'

'Are you going to tell me I'm wrong?' she asked with a thin smile.

He smiled back. 'Would you believe me if I did?'

'Well,' said Konstantinov. 'I'm glad to see you two are hitting it off. More cake, anyone?'

Veronika gave a slightly embarrassed laugh.

'Seriously though, Alisa,' he continued. 'Viktor is the reason we are all here. The dossier was given to him. He could easily have kept it for himself, but instead he turned it over to me. I believe his integrity speaks for itself.'

Chernikova gave a desultory wave of her hand – whether to concede the point or dismiss it, Viktor couldn't tell. Nor could he tell whether the physicist had taken a genuine dislike to him, or whether she was just yanking his chain for some reason. Maybe she was just trying to gauge him and his motives, since her general dislike of journalists seemed heartfelt enough.

The truth was, he did feel rather out of place there; and he was sure that his sense of not belonging would only grow worse when they got under way. There were two academics: an anthropologist and a physicist; and Nika was an accomplished photographer. All of them possessed talents and experience that would doubtless prove extremely useful on the expedition. But what did Viktor have? True, he was the one who had brought the dossier to Konstantinov; he was the catalyst which had got this whole thing started. And yet, even that was overstating the case: the mysterious Eduard Lishin was the *real* catalyst, and Viktor had simply been the conduit through which Konstantinov had received the information so vital to his research into the Dyatlov Pass incident.

Konstantinov had said that his function as chronicler of the expedition would be an extremely important one. He supposed that was true, in principle; although it was surely something that any of the others could have done. He began to wonder whether Konstantinov had given him the job for no reason other than because he felt he owed him the chance to participate in the expedition.

He felt a curious mixture of resentment and appreciation at the idea that he was being *allowed* to participate. It was an uncomfortable combination, and one which he saw no way of resolving. Maybe that would change once they were in the forest...

And that thought brought to mind another uncomfortable fact: that he was no outdoorsman. Konstantinov and Chernikova had already been to Kholat Syakhl, and Veronika was a pretty good skier, and had been on many hiking trips in the southern Urals. How would Viktor cope on an extended trip into the frozen wilderness?

His thoughts were interrupted by Chernikova, who had taken out a pack of cigarettes. 'I'm going outside for a quick one. Care to join me, Viktor?'

'I don't smoke.'

She shrugged. 'Join me anyway.'

'You can smoke in here, if you like, Alisa,' said Konstantinov.

'It's all right, Vadim. Come on, Viktor.'

She stood up and went out through the door leading to the communal garden at the rear of the apartment. Viktor shrugged at the others, and paused momentarily when he saw the frown that had clouded Veronika's features. He followed Alisa outside.

The small lawn and surrounding shrubbery beds lay beneath a brittle filigree of white, in that perfect stillness of winter. The sky was equally serene – silent, pale and featureless, like a canvas on which a picture was yet to be painted. Chernikova lit a cigarette and exhaled a combination of smoke and condensation into the cold air. 'I gave you a bit of a rough time in there, Viktor. Sorry.'

'That's all right,' he said, a little taken aback. 'If you've got a problem with journalists, I understand.'

She took another drag, and said: 'What do you think about all this?'

'To be honest with you, I don't know. Three days ago, I'd never heard of the Dyatlov Pass incident. I was working on another story...'

'What about?'

'A slum landlord who's been victimising his tenants. I was taken off the story and told to go and interview Yuri Yudin for a historical piece to commemorate the fiftieth anniversary of the incident.'

'Why were you taken off the story?'

He hesitated and then offered her a weak smile. 'I didn't have the stomach for it. I couldn't bring myself to get people to talk when they were terrified of doing so. Not much of an investigative journalist, I suppose.'

She regarded him in silence for a few moments.

'Anyway,' he continued, 'what do *you* think about all this?'

'I find it difficult to believe. I've looked at the documents, and they appear to be genuine, as do the photographs – although of course there's no way to be sure without examining the negatives.'

'You think this might be a hoax?'

'If it is, it's certainly not perpetrated by Vadim. But Lishin ... he's another story. Who knows how these people think, what their motivations really are? Even the antiprism ... I'd state my reputation on it being the product of an unknown technology. But experts have been taken in by hoaxes before, and in spite of my beliefs – which I have to say are based only on a cursory examination of the object – I can't help wondering whether it's part of some incredibly elaborate disinformation exercise.'

'A disinformation exercise? For what purpose?'

'I don't know, but it's not without precedent. There have been experiments, here and in Europe and the United States, to map and analyse the vectors through which unusual belief systems propagate, and how they are assimilated by the population. It's all to do with finding new ways of controlling people's opinions, about managing their reactions to certain information.'

'Well ... you can't get much more unusual than *this*,' he said. 'But what about the Yakuts? They claim to have seen similar things in their region.'

'That's what troubles me,' said Chernikova. 'I can't bring myself to believe that it's a deception: it's far too elaborate. Nor, however, can I quite bring myself to believe that they are what they appear to be.'

'And what do they appear to be?'

She took a long pull on her cigarette, and then looked at him. 'Artefacts,' she said. 'Artefacts of a completely unknown civilisation.'

'Extraterrestrial?'

'Who knows? But something makes me doubt it.'

'How so?'

'I've seen the photograph of the "Installation", as it's called, and the "Cauldron". They don't look ... *advanced* enough. I don't know, but they just don't look like the work of a culture that is or was sophisticated enough to have developed interstellar travel. The antiprism, yes. But not them.'

'But can we make such assumptions about the technology and aesthetics of truly alien minds?' he asked, thinking of Yuri Yudin's words. *Something so strange, we don't even have a name for it.*

'No, we can't; you're right about that.'

She had nearly finished her cigarette. She smoked in silence for some moments, the tobacco crackling softly in the cold air.

'Look,' Viktor said. 'I understand your reservations about journalists, but I'm not here looking for a big scoop that'll get my name up in lights.'

She glanced at him with a slight smile. 'You're not?'

'I want to know what happened to Dyatlov and his friends. *That's* what I'm curious about. Maybe we'll find the answer, maybe we won't. Maybe I'll be able to write a story about this, and be able to publish it without getting us all locked up. Or maybe not. But that's not my main concern. I just want to *find out.*'

Chernikova regarded him with that half-smile still on her lips. 'Then your attitude is more in line with Vadim than with me.'

He recalled what Konstantinov had told him, and pictured a twelve-year-old boy looking into the coffin of his friend, a corpse with strangely discoloured skin and impossibly grey hair.

'Yes,' he said. 'I suppose I am.'

'That's good. It provides a little more balance to our group. Maybe we'll find the answers, and maybe we won't,' she added, echoing his own words. Her smile broadened, but now it held no humour. 'Or maybe we'll end up like Dyatlov and the others.'

———

A couple of days later, they left Yekaterinburg and drove north towards Ivdel. Viktor didn't see Lishin again in those two days; maybe he had disappeared back into the woodwork, or maybe he was still observing him, but doing it properly, so he wouldn't know. Viktor suspected it was the latter. At any rate, as they left the city, he found himself wondering whether any of them would see it again.

The SUV Konstantinov had rented was a Toyota, big and powerful. It was loaded with camping equipment and enough supplies for a week out in the wilderness. Konstantinov had said that they wouldn't need to be out there for longer than that. He referred to their trip as a 'preliminary reconnaissance'; the first, he hoped, of many journeys into the heart of Kholat Syakhl's mystery.

At first, they didn't know where to store the antiprism. Alisa suggested that they might as well just put it in the glove compartment, which was as good a place as any. Viktor briefly wondered whether the object would interfere with the car's electrical systems, but that turned out not to be the case: the antiprism – whatever it was, wherever it came from – appeared to be completely inert in that respect. And so they put it in the glove compartment, along with a photocopy of Lishin's map: accessories to a journey that, just a few days ago, Viktor could never even have imagined making.

Alisa suggested they should call it the Konstantinov Expedition, and they all smiled at that, including Vadim, who nevertheless shook his head and waved it aside.

Konstantinov was driving, with Alisa up front beside him. Viktor was in the back seat with Veronika. Alisa was leafing through the rest of the photocopies of Lishin's dossier (Konstantinov had considered the originals to be too valuable to take with them), and periodically reading extracts aloud. They had read them already, of course, but Alisa couldn't resist doing so again. She was like a kid with a new comic, leafing through the pages, stopping here and there to re-examine something particularly intriguing.

She was especially fascinated by the last document, the one entitled RECOMMENDATIONS FOR RESPONSE TO DISCOVERY OF INSTALLATION AND CAULDRONS IN NORTHERN URALS SECTOR, and she read parts of it aloud in an almost reverential tone.

"'In view of the similarities between the Installation and Cauldrons which have been discovered in the northern Urals region, and those which are known to exist in Anomalous Zone 2 in western Yakutia, we recommend that the area around Mountain 1079 (also known as Kholat Syakhl) be quarantined for a period of not less than three years, in order to allow proper analysis of the structures and their effects on the surrounding environment.

"'Following the implementation of quarantine protocols and the designation of this area as Anomalous Zone 3, a research facility should be established, which will be manned by Project Svarog personnel. This facility will be responsible for the retrieval and analysis of the materials from which the Installation and Cauldrons are fashioned, and of any artefacts found inside the Installation.

"'The deaths of Igor Dyatlov and his eight companions have established unequivocally the danger to human life which exists in Anomalous Zone 3. This fact, combined with the Zone's relative proximity to large population centres (unlike Anomalous Zone 2) means that it is imperative that its nature be quickly and properly ascertained.

"'Zone 3 Station should be constructed of prefabricated modules which can be deployed in the target area, and fully equipped with all necessary equipment and supplies, in a matter of days. Project Svarog personnel and the detachment of troops which will guard and protect them will be supplied with hazardous materials suits, which they will wear whenever a Cauldron is approached or the Installation entered."

'To my mind,' Alisa said over her shoulder, 'this is the most intriguing aspect of the whole thing: the implication that the Installation has an interior – that it can be *entered*.'

'I take it we won't be doing that on this trip,' said Veronika.

Alisa glanced at her, but said nothing.

Viktor decided that her point needed reinforcing. 'The report recommended that protective gear be worn whenever an Installation was entered. So we're not going to *do* that, are we Vadim?'

'I agree that it wouldn't be the wisest course of action,' he replied over his shoulder. 'No, as I said, this is a preliminary excursion only. All right, Alisa?'

She offered him a smile. 'Yes, of course. But it's also worth bearing in mind that the quarantine was lifted after three years. Did Project Svarog maintain a presence in the area afterwards? Was it disbanded? Why was the so-called Anomalous Zone 3 opened once again to the civilian population?' She continued to leaf through the dossier for a few moments, then continued: 'There *must* be other documents. This is just a taster, I'm sure of it.'

Konstantinov murmured his agreement.

'Do you think Lishin has them, Vadim?' Nika asked.

'Yes, I think he does, and probably much more besides. People like him think ahead. Remember that when the Wall came down, all bets were off. The whole country was up for grabs, including the archives of the intelligence community. No one knew what was going to happen, so everyone who was in a position to do so made their own insurance arrangements. A lot of files went missing around that time, and I do mean a *lot*. Lishin was no different from many other operatives, who saw their chance to grab their share of a potentially valuable commodity, for conversion to hard currency at a later date.'

'Except that Lishin hasn't asked for any money,' said Alisa.

'No ... he hasn't,' said Konstantinov.

'Why do you think that is?' asked Veronika. 'Do you really think it's because of his conscience?'

Konstantinov swung the car out to overtake a large truck which was carrying a load of lumber. 'I think it's the most logical explanation. And it's quite evident that money is not an issue for him.'

'Perhaps,' said Alisa. 'Or perhaps he knows that what he has is beyond price, and that there's no way you could afford to pay him what it's really worth. No offence, Vadim.'

'None taken. Either way, Lishin has obviously decided that the time has come to release at least some of his material on Dyatlov Pass.'

'Which raises the question: why?' said Alisa, glancing over her shoulder at us. 'Why *now*?'

Viktor looked across at Nika, and saw that she had turned away and was looking out through her window at the traffic on the highway.

BASKOV (6)

As I have already mentioned, Senior Investigator Komar allowed me to make copies of the documents in Lishin's dossier, which I placed in the secure filing cabinet in my office at Peveralsk. I was well aware that I was taking a considerable risk in doing so – the same risk which Viktor Strugatsky had taken in holding onto them, and which Komar had taken in passing them on to me. The penalties for distributing state secrets may not have been quite as severe as during the Soviet era, but they were severe enough. Lishin's secret dossier was like a stick of dynamite that had been left in the open for too long, exposed to the elements: if it were not handled carefully, it would explode, taking us all with it.

On Thursday morning, I sat at my desk and examined the documents again. I tried to concentrate, but it was very difficult: my mind was clouded with thoughts of my wife, Nataliya, and our life together. Of course, I never discussed the details of patients' cases with her, nor did she ever wish me to; but such was her wisdom, her kindness, that Nataliya always knew when something was troubling me, and always found a way to touch upon the subject without actually broaching it directly. I suppose that at such times, we were like poets speaking to each other in metaphors ... or spies using subtle codes; and while I always found such conversations to be helpful, on this occasion I knew that I could not even hint at what was troubling me. Naturally, I could not hide my unease from my wife, but when she tried to find a way to talk about it, I refused to respond, and told her merely that everything was fine, and that she shouldn't worry. With a smile and a kiss, I shut her out. Knowing that it was necessary didn't make it any easier to watch the hurt flickering in her eyes.

Secrets breed other secrets; such is their nature. And for the first time, I realised that they also breed hostility; and hostility was exactly what I felt: towards myself, towards Strugatsky, and Komar, and the bundle of documents and photographs that had beckoned five people into the wilderness of the northern Urals.

The copies of those documents lay before me on my desk, each asking the same question in a different way. *What was in the forest around Kholat Syakhl?*

I had done some additional research on the origin of the word 'Svarog'. It is from Slavonic mythology: Svarog was the personification of the sky in the religion of the pagan Slavs, and its root, *svar*, meaning bright and clear, is related to Sanskrit. It was believed that Svarog gave birth to two children, Dazhbog (the Sun) and Svarogich (Fire), and that it was he who kindled the flames of lightning during thunderstorms, and who brought the gift of terrestrial fire to humans. It was Svarog who caused the Sun to appear each morning, re-lighting the celestial torch which had been extinguished in the evening by the demons of shadow.

I wondered why this word had been chosen to designate what was clearly an effort to investigate the objects that had been discovered in the northern Urals. Svarog was the god of the sky; Svarog *was* the sky, in the cosmology of the ancient Slavs. Did this mean that Project Svarog was established to investigate something that had come from the sky? I recalled Strugatsky's words concerning the Yakut legends of strange objects that had fallen to Earth from the heavens, and which are still worshipped as heroes and feared as dangerous adversaries.

I looked again at the symbol in the top left-hand corner of each page in the dossier: the symbol of Perun, the god of thunder and lightning, the supreme deity in the ancient Slavic pantheon; the symbol which people had once carved into the wooden beams of their houses as protection against lightning strikes...

Svarog, personification of the sky.

Perun, god of thunder.

The symbol of Perun, protection against lightning.

Its shape – circular – possibly a representation of ball lightning.

The glowing spheres seen in the sky on the night of the Dyatlov Pass incident.

What did all this mean?

I called Senior Investigator Komar on his mobile phone, and asked if there had been any further developments with the militia team that was searching the forest where Strugatsky's companions had disappeared. He replied that the search was still ongoing, that nothing unusual had been discovered.

'That's strange,' I said. 'I wonder if you're looking in the right place.'

Komar understood the significance of that apparently innocuous phrase. I was really asking if he had guided his team to the locations that had been circled on Lishin's map.

'We are, Doctor ... at least, I *think* so, but it's a very large area, and these things take time. Are you making any progress with Strugatsky?'

'Some ... but as you say, these things take time.'

'Understood, but it's worth remembering that time isn't something we have in huge supply.'

'I know, Investigator. We'll talk again soon.'

After I had hung up, I thought about that brief conversation. I had detected frustration and confusion in Komar's voice. He had told his people that Strugatsky had volunteered information on the route he and his companions had taken through the forest, and had ordered them to concentrate their search in that area. The truth was that he had consulted the map, not Strugatsky. And yet still they had found nothing; no Cauldron, no Installation, no lake filled with something that looked like mercury ... and no bodies.

This lack of results didn't square with the existence of the dossier itself, and what it contained. As I went back over the notes which I had transcribed myself from my taped conversations with Strugatsky, I began to wonder whether Alisa Chernikova had been on the right track when she had spoken of the Soviet government conducting an elaborate psychological experiment. But if that was the case, then what was the anti-prism, and what had happened to Chernikova and the rest of Strugatsky's companions? Had he really suffered a psychotic episode and murdered them? No hypothesis rang completely true. As I flipped further back, I came upon Yuri Yudin's words.

You'll never get to the bottom of it, and if you're not careful, you'll spend years thinking about it, and wondering, and speculating, and theorising, and all your speculations and theories will crowd around you during the night, and they'll never allow you any rest.

I wondered whether that would prove to be just as true of the 'Konstantinov Expedition' as it was of the original Dyatlov Pass incident.

I glanced at my desk clock and saw that it was time for my next session with Strugatsky.

When I entered his room, the first thing he said was: 'Have they found anything?'

I shook my head. 'I'm afraid not, Viktor.'

His shoulders sagged a little, and I wondered whether it was from disappointment or relief. I asked him that question.

'A little of both, I suppose,' he replied with a faint sigh.

'Investigator Komar has ordered his men to concentrate their search in the areas indicated on Lishin's map. Can you explain why they haven't found anything?'

Strugatsky hesitated before replying: 'Yes, I think I know.'

I waited for him to continue, but he fell silent, and simply sat in the armchair, looking at the floor. 'Can you tell me?' I prompted.

'It's difficult, Doctor. Please understand, if I told you now – if I just came out with it – you really would think I'm crazy.'

'Does it have anything to do with your theory that the Installations are capable of movement? That they're machines of some kind that are still active?'

Strugatsky smiled and shook his head. 'We often say stupid things when we don't have all the facts, don't we?'

'Of course – it stands to reason. And you had very few facts to go on when you made that suggestion.'

'I felt so pleased with myself. Like Sherlock Holmes and Woodward and Bernstein all rolled into one. I thought that that *had* to be the solution. The Installations and Cauldrons looked like they'd been manufactured, like someone had *built* them; Dyatlov and the others had seen them, stood right next to them, and yet the things hadn't been seen again for fifty years, even though the region was open to the public, and people went back there on many occasions ... sports tourists, skiers, hikers, you name it. Yeah ... I thought that had to be the answer: the Installations and the Cauldrons were capable of burying themselves and re-emerging from the ground. But that wasn't the answer ... that's not what they're doing.'

'What *are* they doing, Viktor?'

He shook his head again. 'Not yet, Doctor.'

'I won't think you're crazy.'

He regarded me in silence for a few more moments, then said: 'I have to do this in my own way, to tell you what happened in ... in sequence, to describe the events in the order in which they happened. It'll make more sense to you that way, believe me.'

'All right,' I said. I switched on the recorder, which I had placed on the desk as usual. The thought occurred to me that Strugatsky was insisting on describing the events 'in sequence', as he put it, so that he would be able to maintain consistency in the story he had concocted. Or perhaps he was telling the truth, and to jump forward to what happened later to him and his companions would force me to mistakenly consider him a liar or a dangerous lunatic.

'When we left off yesterday, you and the others had just left Yekaterinburg, and were *en route* to Ivdel. Would you like to continue from there?'

'The journey was long and uneventful, Doctor. Nothing happened until we reached the village.'

'The village?'

'Yurta Anyamova, the Mansi settlement. I guess you could say that that's where the story *really* begins.'

TWELVE

They left Ivdel behind and continued north, and as they drove along the Federal Highway, the pine forest gradually grew deeper and thicker all around them. The trees were like snow-covered towers reaching up into the pale sky, and the ground below wore its mantle of snow like a white pelt.

Not long after they had left Ivdel, Konstantinov took the SUV off the highway and headed into the forest. For the next six hours, they drove slowly and carefully amongst the trees. At this time of year, there was no mud, and the swamps had frozen solid, but all the same it was tedious and laborious going. Occasionally, they came to a rickety bridge spanning a frozen or sluggishly-moving river, which Konstantinov negotiated with even greater care. And all around, the trees rose up into the featureless white sky in perfectly straight, silent regiments.

No one said very much during this part of their journey. While Konstantinov concentrated on his driving, the rest looked out through the windows at the forest which had swallowed them. The moan of the car's engine, rising and falling like a labouring animal, couldn't dispel the sense of the profound silence that surrounded them. There was something palpable in its primordial depth, as if it were a part of the air, something one could reach out to and feel, like the air's bitter coldness.

Viktor felt uneasy and restless. He knew he didn't belong there – if any human did. He felt like a prisoner who was being carted off into the woods to suffer an unknown fate; but there was no escape, no way of changing course now. Lishin had seen to that when he left the dossier in Viktor's mailbox; he had stuffed their destinies into a manila envelope and vanished into the depths of the city they had left behind, leaving them alone.

Viktor thought about Alisa's question. Why *now*? Lishin must have had a good reason: people like that have a good reason for everything they do. The world was like a game of chess to them, and they prided themselves on the subtlety of their strategies. That said, he couldn't shake the feeling that they had been invited to participate in some kind of endgame.

Veronika broke into his thoughts. 'How big is Yurta Anyamova, Vadim?' she asked.

'Not big,' he replied, as he turned the steering wheel to avoid a snow-covered outcrop of rocks. 'About thirty people live there.'

'And it's the biggest settlement in the region?' she said with a note of incredulity.

'That's right. The Urals Mansi are a dying people. According to the last census, there are only about a hundred and ninety of them left, scattered across the land in small villages.'

'What does the word "Mansi" actually mean?' Viktor asked.

'It means "human being", although they're better known by their original name of Voguls. They go back centuries; they're first mentioned in written records as a distinct group in 1396, but they're also mentioned, along with the Khants, by the chronicler Rogovich of Novgorod three hundred years earlier. Rogovich, however, didn't differentiate between the Khants and the Mansis, who were collectively known as the Jugra people.'

'Why are they dying out?'

'Things didn't go well for them during the Soviet era, and in the last couple of decades, the situation hasn't improved. The winters are hard, and it's very difficult to maintain contact between the settlements. The Mansi are forced to rely on their traditional hunting skills to survive. It's almost impossible for them to find potential spouses unless they leave their villages and marry Russians. Many are trying to do just that, and the result is a demographic crisis, demonstrated not least by the decline in native speakers of their language.'

'So they speak Russian?' Viktor said.

'Oh yes, the Mansi are completely bilingual; but more and more Russian words are creeping in, and many anthropologists believe that the day will soon come when Russian supplants Mansi completely.'

'That's sad,' said Alisa. 'Languages and traditional ways of life shouldn't be allowed to die.'

While he agreed with the sentiment, Viktor was a little surprised that Alisa had voiced it: it seemed somehow incongruous, given her vocation. But then, he asked himself, why should a physicist be any less sympathetic to the preservation of language and tradition than anyone else?

'Yes, Alisa,' said Konstantinov. 'It is very sad.'

'Isn't the government doing anything to help?' she asked.

'The regional government is trying. There are plans to help the Urals Mansi to forge lasting contacts with the people of the neighbouring region of Khanty-Mansiisk, which is home to a related group of people.'

'I hope they succeed.'

'So do I,' Konstantinov replied. He pointed through the windscreen. 'Look.'

Viktor couldn't make out what he was pointing to at first, but as they slowly drove past, he saw that the stump of a pine tree had been crudely carved into the head and shoulders of a man, the facial features no more than lines etched into the wood. In spite of its lack of sophistication (or perhaps *because* of it), he was struck by the power of the image: there was a feral rawness in the crudeness of the face; the beady eyes stared into the depths of the forest, and the rough gash of the mouth was curved upward slightly in a smile every bit as enigmatic as the Mona Lisa's.

'One of their idols,' said Konstantinov. 'We're close, now.'

As they drove on, the trees began to thin out a little, until they finally gave way to a wide clearing whose snow-covered ground undulated gently towards the line of forest on the far side. The clearing was filled with squat, sturdy-looking log-built houses. They looked ancient, and although they were obviously well-built, their gabled roofs appeared to sag under the weight of the snow which had settled upon them, as if one more harsh winter would finally bring defeat, and they would sink once more into the ground that had given birth to them.

Konstantinov brought the car to a halt and switched off the engine. 'We'll wait here,' he said.

'Why?' asked Alisa. 'Do you think they won't be friendly?'

'Oh, they'll be quite friendly,' he smiled. 'However, it isn't very good manners to park right in the middle of their village without so much as an introduction, eh?'

'No, I suppose it isn't. So, how long are we supposed to sit here?'

By way of an answer, Konstantinov opened his door and got out of the car. Alisa threw Viktor and Nika a bemused glance over her shoulder, and did the same. They followed her out into the freezing cold, and they all stood in front of the car, waiting.

After only a few moments, people began to appear in the doorways of the houses, regarding the visitors with obvious curiosity. Konstantinov raised a hand and waved to them. To Viktor's surprise, they waved back. He had expected the villagers to remain perfectly still, to see their arrival as an unwelcome intrusion at best, and a threat at worst. But they were smiling broadly, as if the newcomers were old friends whom they had been expecting.

'Follow me,' said Konstantinov, and began walking across the clearing towards the villagers.

As they drew nearer, one of the villagers stepped forward and approached. He was tall and slender, with finely chiselled features which gave him an ascetic look. In fact, he looked more like an Orthodox priest than a member of a remote and isolated society. His eyes were bright and intense, and the smile he offered was razor-thin. Like the rest of the villagers, he wore a heavy fur-lined overcoat.

'The headman,' whispered Konstantinov.

'I am Roman Bakhtyarov,' the man said in Russian as they halted before him.

Konstantinov offered him his hand, which he shook after a moment's hesitation. 'I am Vadim Konstantinov. Is this Yurta Anyamova?'

'It is. And you are welcome here.'

'Thank you.'

Konstantinov introduced the rest of them, and Bakhtyarov nodded to each in turn. If that had been Viktor, he would have asked them what they were doing there, why they had come; but Bakhtyarov must have assumed that they would tell him soon enough – or maybe he was just too good-mannered to ask straight away.

'Have you had a long journey?' he asked.

'Very long,' Konstantinov replied. 'We have come from Yekaterinburg.'

Bakhtyarov looked at him in silence for a moment, then said: 'In that case, you must be hungry.'

Konstantinov smiled at the Mansi headman. 'We are very grateful for your hospitality.'

Bakhtyarov nodded. 'You will be guests in my house. Follow me.'

The other villagers nodded to them as they passed. Viktor's gaze fell upon an old man, who was watching them even more intently than his fellows. His face was deeply lined, like an old rock that had seen many hot summers and harsh winters, and he was smiling. It was a strange smile, a secret smile, as if he knew exactly why they were there; and suddenly Viktor had a curious feeling, like he was some visiting dignitary, or perhaps a visitor from another world. He could see the curiosity written upon the villagers' faces. They didn't possess that strange certainty he saw in the old man's eyes. Perhaps they were wondering if they were from the government, bringing some new plan to help their society avoid its lingering death.

But they weren't there to help those people: they were there to gather information from them, anything they could tell them about this land where they had lived for more than a thousand years. And Viktor felt a profound sense of guilt wash over him, and he avoided their eyes as he followed Bakhtyarov and Konstantinov.

The headman took them to his house, which stood near the line of trees surrounding the clearing. He opened the door and led them inside, and Viktor was surprised at how comfortable the interior appeared to be. The bare log walls were covered with animal pelts, as was the floor, and in one corner there was a wide hearth in which a fire burned brightly and welcomingly. Above the fire hung a pot in which something bubbled quietly. A rich, gamey smell pervaded the room.

'Sit,' said Bakhtyarov as he crossed the room and began to stir the contents of the pot. It was only then that Viktor noticed the number of chairs the room contained: there were five, enough for the four visitors and their host. *As if he's been expecting us*, Viktor thought as they all sat down.

Bakhtyarov began spooning the contents of the pot into wooden bowls.

'What is it?' asked Alisa.

Konstantinov glanced at her in apparent irritation.

'Boar,' replied Bakhtyarov, and Alisa gave a quiet murmur of satisfaction. The headman turned at the sound, and smiled at her. 'I hope you enjoy it.'

'I'm sure we shall,' said Alisa, accepting a bowl and spoon. 'Thank you.'

The stew was delicious, the beefy taste and texture of the boar complemented by an unfamiliar mixture of winter herbs and berries. Bakhtyarov observed their appreciative expressions and smiled again. 'I assumed this would be more to your taste than the Patanka I would have prepared if I'd been eating alone.'

Konstantinov hesitated, his spoon halfway to his mouth. 'You knew we were coming?' he said.

The headman nodded as he spooned stew into his own bowl. 'Have you ever tried Patanka? It's frozen raw fish – my favourite is muksun – thinly cut and served with spices and berries. But it's a little strange if you're not used to it.'

'Forgive me,' Konstantinov continued, 'but ... *how* did you know?'

'Prokopy told me.'

'And who is Prokopy?' asked Alisa.

Bakhtyarov didn't answer immediately. Instead, he offered the same thin, virtually humourless smile with which he'd greeted them on their arrival. 'Eat,' he said presently. 'Unlike Patanka, this isn't very good when cold.'

They ate in silence, while the fire crackled in the hearth, and Roman Bakhtyarov looked at each of them in turn. Viktor tried to gauge his expression, but his features were completely blank, as if in passive acceptance of a situation that was beyond his control.

Konstantinov finished his meal, and held the empty bowl in his lap.

'More?' asked Bakhtyarov.

'No, thank you. Is Prokopy the shaman of this village?'

Bakhtyarov nodded.

'How did he know we were coming?' asked Viktor.

The headman merely looked at him with that razor smile.

'That's not important, Vitya,' said Konstantinov. 'What is important is *why* we have come. Did Prokopy tell you that?'

'He said that you're looking for an answer.'

'An answer to what?' asked Veronika.

'To a question that was asked fifty years ago. You want to know how they died.'

Viktor felt himself go cold. There was such a calm matter-of-factness in the headman's voice, such complete awareness. He had expected Konstantinov to have to explain everything: what had happened to Dyatlov and the others on Kholat Syakhl, why they were so interested, everything. But Bakhtyarov appeared to know this already.

Konstantinov leaned forward. 'Do *you* know how they died?'

Bakhtyarov said nothing.

Konstantinov tried again. 'Do you know what's in the forest around Kholat Syakhl?'

'That's a difficult question to answer,' Bakhtyarov said quietly. 'I can describe it to you ... but I don't know what it *is*. Kholat Syakhl and Otorten ... do you know what those names mean?'

Konstantinov nodded.

'They are well-named.'

'We understand. Your people named them.'

'Yes ... a long time ago. For many generations, we have avoided them. They are bad places, bad for anyone who goes there. The ones who came in 1959 ... they realised that. It was the last thing they realised.'

'You seem to know all about the incident,' said Alisa.

Bakhtyarov fixed her with an unblinking stare. 'We know. We still speak of it. The Mansi who were living here at the time helped to search for Igor Dyatlov and his friends, although they, too, are all dead now. It has become a part of the history of our people. It is important to us...'

'Because the Mansi were originally blamed.'

'Because Igor Dyatlov and his friends died strangely, and we mourned them,' replied Bakhtyarov. 'If our people had seen them, spoken to them, we could have warned them to stay away. But unfortunately, that didn't happen. They went to the mountain alone, and that's where they died.'

'How *did* they die?' said Konstantinov. 'What killed them?'

'Why do you want to know?' asked Bakhtyarov suddenly. 'Why is it important to you?'

'Igor Dyatlov was my friend,' Konstantinov replied. 'All my life, I have been haunted by this question. And now...' He hesitated.

'Now?' prompted Bakhtyarov.

'We have been given certain documents by an ex-government agent. They prove that there is something tangible out there in the forest, something *real* ... something that is still dangerous.'

'If it's dangerous, why do you want to find it?'

Alisa stepped in. 'We have two reasons: to explore a phenomenon which is unknown to science, and to ascertain how dangerous it really is.'

Bakhtyarov was silent for some moments, then he shrugged. 'It's dangerous enough to make us stay away. Perhaps you should, too.'

Alisa shook her head. 'We can't do that.' She glanced at Konstantinov, and Viktor knew that she was wondering why they had bothered to come here.

Konstantinov knew it too, and he said: 'I understand that you have our best interests at heart, but we have to do this. *I* have to do this. Is there anything you can tell us about the forest around Kholat Syakhl that might help us?'

Bakhtyarov again offered them his thin, enigmatic smile. 'It's getting late, and Prokopy wants to meet you,' he said.

BASKOV (7)

Following my session with Strugatsky, I did some background reading on the Mansi people of the Urals region. I must admit that I was surprised that the 'Konstantinov Expedition' was welcomed by the people of Yurta Anyamova. In fact, I was surprised at their reputation for gentleness and friendliness in general. Given their treatment by the state during the twentieth century, I found myself wondering whether I could have maintained such a gracious attitude to outsiders.

As is so often the case throughout the world, the Mansi have the unfortunate distinction of living on land containing important natural resources. Their troubles began in the 1930s and 1940s, with the Soviet authorities' dislike of their folk customs and shamanistic religion; but in the 1960s, when oil and gas deposits were discovered in the Khanty-Mansi National District, they had to contend with the development of industry and new towns, along with a massive inflow of geologists, oil workers and road builders. This was followed by the catastrophic pollution of their environment: in 1960 alone, six million hectares of grazing land were destroyed by oil spills, and 200,000 hectares of water were polluted, reducing their fish stocks by ninety percent.

Not surprisingly, the Mansi received none of the financial benefits of this industrial boom. By 1990, the state had exported more than twenty billion US dollars' worth of oil and gas from the region, none of which found its way into the pockets of the people who had lived there for centuries. In fact, many Mansi had been forced to move out of the Khanty-Mansi National District, while those who remained experienced terrible difficulties in adapting to their changed environment. The Russification which began in the early 1970s, especially in schools, cast further doubt over the future of the Mansi people, and in 1980 less than half still followed their traditional way of life; the rest did odd jobs or were unemployed. Many turned to alcohol or committed suicide.

As Konstantinov had mentioned, large numbers of Mansi women had left the area, looking for employment in Moscow and other big cities, undermining the balance of the sexes in their communities. Over the decades, the plight of the Mansi has been made worse by the derisive attitude of Russians towards them, and some have decided to concentrate on protecting their language and traditions, while others have abandoned them and now try to live as Russians.

And yet, these people had welcomed Strugatsky and the others into their village without hesitation; their headman had shared his food with them as if they were old friends who had known each other for years. It was quite remarkable, really, and I mentioned this to Strugatsky at the start of our next session.

'Well,' he said, 'they're a remarkable people. I'd barely been aware of their existence before I started all this. And they had our best interests at heart, even though they didn't know us. There's no reason why they should have cared about anything we did, anything that happened to us, but they *did* care – especially Bakhtyarov.'

'Yesterday, you mentioned that they had absorbed the Dyatlov Pass incident into their history. Do they know what really happened in 1959?'

'They know that it was nothing sane.'

'What do you mean by that?'

'I mean that people who live in the remote places of the world understand the world's true nature much better than we do.' He gave a short, humourless laugh. 'We think we're so smart, that we have all the answers – or if we don't have them, at least we have the brains to figure them out eventually...'

'But you don't think that's true.'

'About many things, it is ... of course it is. But there are things that we'll never understand, things we weren't *meant* to understand.'

'Like the Dyatlov Pass incident?'

'Yes.'

'And like what happened to you in the forest?'

'That too,' said Strugatsky in a quiet, resigned voice.

I decided it was time for a more direct approach. 'Listen, Viktor,' I said. 'You know why you're here, why we're talking. Soon, I will have to present a report on your mental state to the criminal militia, so that they can decide whether to place you on trial for murder. You understand that, don't you?'

'Of course I do,' he replied without looking at me.

'And you've been very helpful, so far. I've been impressed with your recollection of events, and your cooperative attitude ... but I must be honest with you: right now, I'm no closer to reaching a conclusion than I was the day we first met.'

He glanced at me. 'But you've read Lishin's dossier. You know that everything I've said is true.'

'Agreed. But the existence of that dossier, and everything it contains, doesn't tell me anything about what happened when you went to Kholat Syakhl.'

Strugatsky thought about this for several moments. Then he sighed and said: 'Well, Doctor Baskov, in that case nothing I'm going to tell you from now on will make any difference. In fact, it will most likely confirm the theory that I killed them. I'm going to tell you exactly what happened, and by the time I'm finished, you'll have no choice but to consider me insane.'

I was rather taken aback by this forthright statement. 'I'm not sure I understand, Viktor. Yesterday, you said that if you described everything to me in sequence, it would make more sense to me. And now you're saying that it will lead me to conclude that you're mentally unfit to stand trial.'

In fact, I found myself wondering whether this was actually Strugatsky's strategy, to force me into just such a conclusion. Perhaps he considered me his means of escaping a life in prison... But that still didn't ring true to me. For one thing, there was no conceivable motive. The Konstantinov Expedition consisted of Strugatsky, Vadim Konstantinov, Veronika Ivasheva and Alisa Chernikova, with the Mansi shaman Prokopy Anyamov apparently joining at the last minute. Konstantinov was a retired professor of anthropology whom Strugatsky clearly held in the highest regard; Ivasheva had been his lover, and he obviously still had great affection for her; he hardly knew Chernikova, and he didn't know Anyamov at all. What possible reason could he have had for murdering them?

'Maybe I deserve to stand trial,' he said. 'Maybe I shouldn't tell you any more, just let things take their course. Maybe prison's the best place for me.'

'You don't believe that.'

He glanced at me sharply. 'Don't I? You don't know what I believe!'

'I think you blame yourself for the deaths of Konstantinov and the others – *if* they're dead. But I also think that, deep down, you know that there's nothing you could have done to save them.'

Strugatsky simply laughed and shook his head.

I leaned forward. 'Tell me I'm wrong. *Tell me*, Viktor.'

'I'll tell you one thing right now, Doctor. If Komar's men find what they're looking for, I'll be out of here within the hour.'

'And if they do find something, and we do release you, what then?'

'I'll probably suffer a tragic accident,' he said simply.

'You mean *you'll* be killed?'

He shrugged.

'By whom?'

'By the people who know what's really out there – who've *always* known.'

'The Kremlin? The FSB? Project Svarog?'

'I'm sorry you've become involved in all this, Doctor – really I am.'

'It's my job to be involved, Viktor.'

'I shouldn't have said anything. I should have kept my mouth shut, right from the first day. I wasn't thinking straight. I'm sorry,' he repeated.

'Do you really think I'll be in danger?' Although I was sceptical of his fears, my thoughts flew to Nataliya, and I felt a sudden knot of apprehension in my stomach.

'I hope not, but...' He lapsed into silence, and stared at the floor. There was a haunted, defeated look on his face, despairing and helpless.

'Let's continue,' I said. 'You were telling me yesterday how you arrived at the village and met Roman Bakhtyarov. What happened then?'

Strugatsky raised his desperate eyes to me, and gave a deep sigh.

THIRTEEN

When the visitors had finished their meal in Bakhtyarov's house, he invited them to attend a calling-song, to be sung in their honour by the shaman, Prokopy Anyamov. Viktor could see that Konstantinov was surprised and delighted at this, and as they left the headman's house, he asked Vadim what it meant. He told Viktor that such songs were intended to call the Mansi spirits and deities to Earth, and to ask for their protection.

Bakhtyarov led them to another house, a little larger than his. As he entered, Viktor saw that the place was already full of people – he guessed the entire village – who were sitting patiently on the floor, clearly awaiting their arrival. Everyone smiled at them – especially the children, whose eyes were large and full of curiosity, and they smiled back, and seated themselves in the vacant spaces that had been saved for them.

One of the villagers stood up and moved to the centre of the room, and Viktor saw that it was the old man with the face like ancient stone whom he had seen when they first arrived. The old man began to sing a song in a powerful voice whose reedy strains rose above the wind which had begun to sigh loudly through the trees surrounding the village. He sang in Russian, and Konstantinov told the others that this was an additional honour.

The shaman sang, and Viktor felt his mind falling into the words, seduced by them, willingly ensnared in the strange pictures they created:

Grown in the morning
on the headland grown by golden lawn
grown in the evening

on the headland grown by golden lawn;
on hills covered with the feathers of spring grouse rooster,
on hills covered with the feathers of autumn grouse rooster;
in the height of a running cloud,
in the height of a striding cloud,
my sacred house in moon colours,
my sacred house in sun colours
on a golden chain's dear end
hangs there,
on a golden silver's dear end
it hangs there.
When from the southern throat a throatly wind
starts to blow,
with the clinking sound of a little silver,
towards the dear waters of the northern Ob
it moves there.
When from the northern throat a throatly wind
starts to blow,
with the banging sound of a big silver,
towards the dear waters of the southern Ob
it moves there.
In the inside
of the sacred house of moon colours,
of the sacred house in sun colours,
close by
the hoofly table with golden hooves,
upon
the hoofly table with golden hooves
into the sacred book of spring squirrel hide,
into the sacred book of autumn squirrel hide
seven golden letters
the master is writing,
six golden letters
he is writing there.

When Prokopy Anyamov had finished the song, Viktor told Konstantinov that it was one of the most beautiful things he had ever heard. 'I'm not certain what it means, though,' he added.

'It was a song addressed to Tari-pes'-nimala-s'av, a deity whose name translates as World Surveyor Man,' Konstantinov replied in a hushed tone. 'It describes his abode near the River Ob. The shaman wishes to ask that World Surveyor Man protect us.'

Bakhtyarov said something in Mansi to a man who was sitting next to him, and the man produced a large pottery jug and began pouring a white liquid into beakers, which he passed around.

'What's that?' Veronika whispered to Konstantinov.

'Fermented mare's milk. I should warn you, it's an acquired taste.'

'It sounds like it,' Alisa murmured as she accepted a beaker with a weak smile.

It wasn't quite as bad as Viktor had feared, although he decided he wouldn't be asking for the recipe, and Alisa's weak smile vanished altogether when she took a sip. It was pretty strong stuff, too, and a few minutes after draining his cup, Viktor realised that it would be a good idea to step outside and get some fresh air.

When he made his excuses, the villagers smiled, and some of them laughed out loud.

'Maybe you should have sipped it,' said Bakhtyarov, which elicited more laughter.

'I think you're right,' Viktor said, rising a little unsteadily to his feet. 'If you'll excuse me...'

Christ, that's wicked stuff! he thought as he left the building and took several deep breaths of the icy evening air. He spent a few minutes walking back and forth, trying to clear his head, looking at the houses huddled together in the clearing, like ancient forest animals trying to keep warm. The wind had dropped away to nothing – there wasn't the slightest breath; the surrounding trees stood perfectly still, wearing their fur-like cloaks of frost and snow.

The muffled voices behind him momentarily grew clearer as the door opened and closed, and Alisa walked towards him, taking out a cigarette and lighting it.

'Better get back in, or you'll miss the next round,' she said.

'Not a chance!' Viktor laughed.

She took a deep pull on her cigarette and looked at him through the smoke. She smiled at him, but it seemed to be a smile more of contempt than affection – almost a sneer, in fact. On such an attractive face, the expression was quite startling, and Viktor looked away in embarrassment, feeling his heart quicken in his chest.

'So, Viktor ... how did you become a newspaper reporter?'

'Why do you ask?'

She shrugged. 'If we're going to be spending the next week together, it might be nice to know something about you.'

'Well ... I'm curious, and I like to write. I suppose that in a perfect world I'd have been a novelist...'

'Have you tried?'

'Oh yeah! I tried for a long time. And then one day I realised that it just wasn't going to happen. But I didn't want to stop writing, so journalism seemed like the next best thing.'

She took another drag on her cigarette, nodding absently.

'How did you become a physicist?'

'Why do you ask?' The grin she flashed at him was a little friendlier this time, he thought.

'Same reason.'

'I'm curious too: about the universe, about how it began, *why* it began. My father's a biologist, so I was brought up to respect scientific principles, rational thought...' She cast a glance back at the house.

'Which is why you think we're wasting our time here,' he said.

She didn't answer.

'So why didn't you become a biologist?'

'I suppose I wanted to go deeper into reality's mysteries, to try to answer the most fundamental questions.' She smiled again. 'I guess you could say I was always more curious about atoms than animals.'

She finished her cigarette, but instead of dropping the butt on the ground, she carefully placed it back in the packet. 'What's the story with you and Veronika?'

'What do you mean?' Viktor asked, a little taken aback.

'Are you still seeing each other?'

'What makes you think we were *ever* seeing each other?'

'It's my job to observe things, Viktor, and I'm very good at it.'

He rubbed his temples, trying to get rid of the slight ache that had begun to throb behind his eyes. 'We ... er ... it didn't work out. We're just friends.'

'I think she still wants more than that.'

Suddenly, Viktor had had enough of this conversation. He didn't know if Alisa was coming on to him, or just messing around, and right then he didn't care to find out. Her amused expression certainly didn't offer any clues. 'Let's go back inside,' he said.

'I think I'll stay out here for a while,' she replied, taking out another cigarette.

'Then I'll see you later.' He was about to turn away when Alisa suddenly frowned and took hold of his arm.

'Look, Alisa,' he said. 'I don't want to...'

'Sh! Listen!'

He wondered what she was playing at, and was about to ask her, when he became aware of something in the air, a faint sound that was slowly increasing in volume. He looked at Alisa. 'What's that?'

She shook her head and whispered: 'I don't know.'

The sound seemed to come from all around, a low-frequency hum that he sensed as much in his bones as in his ears, and which rose and fell in a slow, incessant rhythm, like a heartbeat or the breathing of something vast and alive.

Viktor looked up into the overcast sky. The setting sun had turned its colour from pale ash to dark slate. He had the impression that the sound was coming simultaneously from nearby and a great distance away. 'It's like a transformer or a generator of some kind,' he said. 'What the hell *is* that?'

'It does sound artificial,' Alisa agreed. Then she looked down. 'It's in the ground as well.'

It was true: he could feel the pulse pressing up through the soles of his heavy boots. With each faint throb, he had the feeling that ants were crawling beneath his skin, climbing the bones in his legs.

'We should tell Vadim,' he said.

'I already know,' said a voice behind them.

Viktor turned to see Konstantinov and Bakhtyarov standing in the doorway of the house.

'We could hear it from in there.'

'Do you know what it is?' Viktor asked, his question directed as much to Bakhtyarov as Konstantinov.

The headman stepped into the open. 'Sometimes,' he said, 'I tell myself that it is the sound of the World Surveyor Man, who is the son of Numi-Torum, the god of the sky. And sometimes I believe that it is Numi-Torum himself, watching over us. But in my heart, I know that isn't true.'

'So you've heard it before,' said Alisa.

'Yes ... we've heard it on many occasions.'

'It sounds artificial, like it's being made by some kind of machine. Do you know where it's coming from?'

Bakhtyarov pointed to the north. 'Otorten and Kholat Syakhl. We cannot see the mountains from here ... but we can *hear* them on some evenings. This is why we have always feared them, back into the days of our remotest ancestors. This is why Otorten means Do Not Go There, and Kholat Syakhl means Mountain of the Dead. This is why we keep away.'

As if in response to Bakhtyarov's words, the horizon to the north lit up with what looked like a flash of lightning. They all waited for the sound of thunder that should have followed.

But none did.

The air remained still and silent, but for that strange pulsing hum.

Konstantinov and Veronika joined Alisa and Viktor, and together they watched and listed, and as they did so, Viktor became aware of Bakhtyarov watching them.

The sky lit up again, momentarily banishing the encroaching night and transforming the clouds into glowing sheets of mottled grey.

'What do you think, Alisa?' said Konstantinov.

'I think it's an energy discharge of some kind,' she replied, her voice calm and uninflected. Clearly, her initial shock had given way to the composed rationality of the scientist.

'Agreed, but it must be enormous ... and I don't understand why there's no accompanying sound.'

Viktor looked at Bakhtyarov, and saw that the shaman Anyamov had come out of the house and was now standing beside him. The two of them were looking at each other, and Viktor tried in vain to interpret the expressions on their faces.

The shaman approached them. 'Do you still want to go there?' he asked. His voice was gentle, and seemed to be pitched a little too high for a man of his age.

Konstantinov glanced at him. 'Yes, we still want to go.'

Viktor looked at the others. No one contradicted him, although Veronika looked like she would gladly have supported anyone who did. She saw that he was looking at her, and gave him a weak smile. He could see the apprehension in her eyes. She was clearly wondering what the hell they were getting themselves into.

Viktor could have taken her aside, then. He could have asked her if she wanted to continue, or if she'd rather stay there in Yurta Anyamova until the expedition returned. Was she waiting for him to do that? Was she hoping that he'd offer her that option?

But Viktor said nothing. He just stood there and returned her smile, and his was just as weak, just as anxious and hesitant as hers.

Prokopy Anyamov stepped forward. 'Then I will go with you,' he said.

Everyone looked at him, including Bakhtyarov, who shook his head and said: 'No, Prokopy.'

The shaman smiled and nodded. 'They will need someone to look after them, Roman. Someone to guide them, to tell them where they should and shouldn't go ... where the dangers lie. I know this land, better than anyone in Yurta Anyamova, better even than you. It's right that I should go with them, to offer them all the protection I can.'

'*Can* you protect them, Prokopy?' asked Bakhtyarov.

Anyamov placed a hand on the headman's shoulder. 'I must try.'

Bakhtyarov looked at the visitors, and Viktor could see anger in his eyes. 'You shouldn't have come here,' he said. 'You should go back to your city now. You should go, and never come back. You should have left us alone!'

No one made any response.

No one but the sky, which flashed silently again as the strange, unexplained hum gradually faded away, and the silence of the forest returned.

———

In spite of his anger with them, Roman Bakhtyarov insisted that they spend the night in his house. They were guests in Yurta Anyamova, albeit uninvited and unwanted ones, and it was still his duty to offer them shelter.

Viktor didn't sleep very well that night. He couldn't stop thinking about the sound they had heard, and the flashes of light, and what they were and what they meant. Veronika lay next to him, and he could tell by the sound of her breathing that she wasn't sleeping too well either.

You can still back out, he thought. *You and Nika don't have to go.* But still he lay there, not moving, not saying anything, listening in the silence, straining to hear the sound that had come to them from the distant mountains.

But the sound didn't return. At least, not that night.

Sometime after midnight, he drifted into a shallow, uneasy sleep, and was groggy but thankful when the dawn seeped in through the windows and Bakhtyarov stirred.

He said very little as they rose and got ready to leave; but Viktor saw the expression on his face as he watched them make their preparations, a mixture of anger and pity, it seemed, which was not alleviated by the sight of Prokopy Anyamov waiting outside his house when he opened the door.

The old man simply stood there, his face impassive except for the faintest of smiles playing upon his thin, pale lips. He was dressed in heavy furs against the biting cold, and he carried an animal skin bag and a circular object: his shaman's drum.

Bakhtyarov stepped outside, closing the door behind him, and the visitors heard the two of them speaking in the Mansi language, one voice plaintive, the other calm and resolute. Viktor looked at Konstantinov, who was watching the door and listening. Although he already guessed the answer, he asked him what they were saying.

'Bakhtyarov is trying to dissuade Anyamov from coming with us ... to no avail, it seems.'

'Do we really need him, Vadim?' asked Alisa. 'This isn't exactly a spiritual quest...'

Konstantinov turned to her. 'Isn't it?'

The physicist made a sound, half chuckle, half dismissive grunt. 'Of course not! This is a scientific expedition. I'm surprised at you. If we hadn't made this bizarre detour and stopped here for the night, we would have nearly been there by now.'

'A scientific expedition?' said Konstantinov. 'Yes, I'll grant that ... but I wouldn't be so sure that that's all it is.'

Alisa sighed. 'What on earth do you mean by that?'

'Simply that whatever is out there may not be a scientific phenomenon.'

'Ridiculous! *Every* phenomenon is scientific.'

'You're very sure of yourself, aren't you?' said Veronika. It was the first time she had spoken that morning. 'What about that sound we heard last night? And the light in the sky?'

'As I said: an energy discharge of some kind,' Alisa replied without looking at her. 'Similar to lightning. And the sound could have been seismic activity.'

'That wasn't seismic activity,' Viktor said.

Alisa turned to him. 'Really? And how would *you* know? Are you a seismologist?'

He felt a sudden flare of irritation. 'No, are *you*? And anyway, you said yourself that it sounded like some kind of machine was making it...'

'Merely a first impression, Viktor. But even if that's true, it reinforces my point, don't you think?'

'Be that as it may,' said Konstantinov, 'I still think we should accept Anyamov's offer to accompany us. As I said back in Yekaterinburg, the Mansi know this region, and they know those mountains and the forest surrounding them. I repeat to you that any information they can give us will be useful.'

'And *I* repeat to *you* that that's all well and good, unless that information is distorted by mythologizing.'

'I'm not going to debate this with you any more, Alisa.'

She was about to respond, but there was something in Konstantinov's tone which evidently made her think better of it.

At that moment, the door swung open. 'Are you ready?' asked Bakhtyarov.

'We're ready,' Konstantinov replied.

Bakhtyarov made no move to enter the house; it was as if he wanted them out before he could bring himself to return to his home. Viktor didn't know if this impression was accurate, but just the thought of it made him angry. It was as if they were carriers of some disease, and he had a vision of the headman opening all of his windows and giving the place a good airing to get rid of their taint.

And suddenly Viktor wanted to be gone from there, since it was so obvious that they were no longer welcome – quite the opposite, in fact. He felt a curious sense of kinship with Alisa at that moment: he didn't like the fear that appeared to have descended upon the village, nor was he appreciative of Roman Bakhtyarov's attitude. It was insulting and condescending, and carried the implication that they were just ignorant city-dwellers who were too dumb to realise what trouble they were getting into. It was fair enough that he was concerned for Prokopy Anyamov's safety, but it was clear that he considered them a danger to his friend, and that made Viktor even angrier.

He's blaming us for the old man wanting to come along, he thought. *But I don't care. I don't give a shit one way or another. It's his decision, not ours!*

Bakhtyarov watched them with a grim expression as they filed out of his house, as though they were a gang of burglars he'd caught red-handed. Konstantinov said a few words of thanks to him. He merely nodded, without saying anything.

As they walked through the centre of the village towards the SUV, Viktor noted the complete absence of people. Something told him that they weren't still in bed, that they were up and about, but didn't want to see them. Maybe Bakhtyarov had forbidden them from coming outside...

Bakhtyarov accompanied them to the car, and waited while they all climbed in. Konstantinov took the wheel, and when he had shut his door, Bakhtyarov motioned for him to wind down the window.

'How long will you be gone?' he asked.

'About a week,' Konstantinov replied.

'And you will bring Prokopy back.' It was more a statement than a question.

'Yes. You have my word: we will *all* return, with a good story to tell.'

Alisa, who was sitting up front again, leaned across and said: 'Perhaps you can write a song about it.'

Konstantinov threw her a withering look and started the engine.

'I don't think we'll be invited for dinner again when we *do* come back,' she said as the car pulled out of the village.

'I wouldn't blame him if he forbade you from ever setting foot in Yurta Anyamova again,' Konstantinov said in a disgusted tone.

Alisa shook her head, but said nothing more. She had made her point, and although Viktor was inclined to agree with her that they should never have bothered to come here, he couldn't help feeling sorry for Konstantinov. He understood most the profound strangeness that was waiting for them in that forest; and he was gathering all the tools he possibly could in order to prepare for it – including the ancient knowledge of a shaman...

As they left Yurta Anyamova behind and headed into the depths of the forest, Viktor glanced at Prokopy Anyamov, who was sandwiched between him and Veronika; but he just kept looking straight ahead through the windscreen at the slowly passing trees, that faint smile still playing upon his lips.

Nika, to her credit, was the first to speak to him. She introduced the rest of them, and told him she was very glad he was coming with them. He smiled at her more broadly, and his eyes glittered like an amused child's, but he didn't say anything.

In fact, Prokopy Anyamov didn't say a word until they drew near to Kholat Syakhl.

BASKOV (8)

Over the weekend of 6-8 March, I reviewed the transcripts of my conversations with Viktor Strugatsky. The thing that struck me most was the strange inexorability of his journey towards the forest where his companions had disappeared. It was as though he had been powerless to prevent it, his curiosity about – his *obsession* with – the Dyatlov Pass incident taking over and drawing him ever closer, like the scent of some South American pitcher plant.

Aside from the vague hints and allusions to something indescribably strange and inimical, Strugatsky's narrative possessed a powerful logic and internal consistency, albeit one that was overshadowed by the bizarre behaviour of Eduard Lishin, who for some unknown reason had seen fit to provide him with information which was still considered a state secret. And yet, even that apparently false note seemed to be supported by investigator Komar's discovery of the dossier among Professor Konstantinov's effects.

My initial question as to whether Strugatsky possessed a fantasy-prone personality was rendered moot by this discovery. The dossier existed – *still* exists; I have read its contents, examined the strange photographs which it contains. Komar has confirmed that they are not forgeries. I know that there was and is much more to the Dyatlov Pass incident than the public was ever led to believe by the Soviet authorities.

As a psychiatrist, I have never believed in the paranormal, and have always been satisfied with the principle of Occam's razor: the human mind and the mechanisms by which it possesses consciousness and self-awareness are wonderful and mysterious enough without recourse to supernatural agencies to explain the strange events and perceptions which so frequently intrude into people's lives. I found myself in agreement with Alisa Chernikova, who had said that every phenomenon is scientific: in other words, that everything that happens in the world, without exception, is amenable to rational description and explanation, given sufficient data.

This, of course, was my initial attitude to the Strugatsky case, and I had started out with every confidence that I would be able to ascertain his mental state and offer sound and accurate advice to the criminal militia. It simply hadn't occurred to me that he would lead me into a world whose existence I had not even suspected, and whose strangeness and abnormality offered an affront to every rational principle to which I had subscribed throughout my professional life.

I spent most of that weekend in my study at home. After eight years of marriage, Nataliya was quite used to such reclusive behaviour on my part when I was faced with a particularly intriguing or complex case. Nor did she show any sign of annoyance when I was uncharacteristically quiet during meals. Her understanding attitude was not lost on me, however, and I promised myself that I would make it up to her, and made a mental note to suggest a holiday in one of the Black Sea resorts – perhaps Sochi, with its beautiful parks, waterfalls and spas – when all this was over.

I tried to forget what Strugatsky had said about suffering some 'accident' at the hands of the authorities. I tried to tell myself that his fears were unfounded, notwithstanding the fact that he had been in possession of state secrets. I didn't believe that it would come to that: I was certain that the case would be resolved another way, although at that stage I had no idea how. In spite of these bland assurances to myself, however, I still felt vulnerable in a way I had never felt before. It was a little like the feeling I experienced during sessions with violent inmates at Peveralsk – but only a little. In those situations, I was always face to face with the person who presented the potential threat, and I was always backed up by muscular orderlies who would come to my aid at a moment's notice.

Now the threat was invisible, and may not even have existed at all. But its very nebulousness made me feel exposed and fearful – more for Nataliya than for myself – and I wondered if it was such a good idea to go to the Black Sea, or anywhere else, for that matter...

I tried to shake myself free of these morbid worries, and decided to do some background reading on the so-called Installations and Cauldrons which were believed to exist in the Yakutia region. I found several online articles; the longest was by Dr Valery Uvarov, who was head of the Department of UFO Research at the National Security Academy in St Petersburg. I remembered that his name had come up when Strugatsky had taken Veronika Ivasheva to meet Konstantinov for the first time, and that he was the author of some wild theory about an ancient device buried deep inside the Earth.

The article began with a description of the Upper Viliuy River in northwestern Yakutia, which Uvarov claimed was the site of a 'tremendous cataclysm' which occurred 800 years ago, and which now contains strange metal objects of unknown origin partially buried in the permafrost. The Yakut people have avoided this area of swamps and impenetrable taiga, which covers 100,000 square kilometres, for centuries, since they are well aware that there is something powerful and dangerous there.

In 1936, an old merchant named Savvinov showed his granddaughter, Zina, one of these objects in an area called Kheldyu (or 'iron house'). Within an archway apparently constructed of reddish metal there was a spiral staircase leading underground into a large chamber containing the entrances to a number of rooms with metallic walls. Savvinov told Zina that even in the harshest winters, it was always warm inside the 'iron house'.

In previous years, some of the local hunters would take advantage of this, and would sleep in the metal rooms; but they soon became ill and died, confirming the Yakut belief that the region was a 'bad place' which even wild animals avoided. The knowledge of their exact locations, once possessed by old men who had been hunters in their youth, was now lost, and only certain place-names hinted at their existence.

In 1971, for instance, two researchers named Gutenev and Mikhailovsky who lived in the town of Mirny in Yakutia described a meeting with an old hunter, who told them that between two rivers, called Niugun Bootur ('fiery champion') and Atadarak ('place with a three-sided harpoon'), there is a half-buried object which apparently gave the latter river its name: a large, three-pronged device or artefact, the origin and nature of which are unknown.

Uvarov goes on to claim that in the 1950s, the Soviet military conducted a series of atomic bomb tests in the remote, sparsely populated region. In 1954, a 10-kilogram nuclear device was detonated. The yield was 2,000 – 3,000 times greater than expected, as if a 20 – 30-megaton bomb had exploded. The scientists were at a loss to explain this massive discrepancy. 'After the tests,' writes Uvarov, 'restricted zones were established in the area and secret work was carried out for some years.'

Could this be the origin of Project Svarog? I wondered.

I searched the article for references to the flying spheres to which Konstantinov had alluded, and which were allegedly witnessed by the group of geography students on the night of the Dyatlov Pass incident.

I found them in a lengthy discussion of the famous Tunguska event, which Konstantinov had also mentioned, and which occurred on the morning of 30 June 1908. On that morning a column of blue light, as bright as the sun, split the sky over central Siberia approximately 1,000 km north of the town of Irkutsk and Lake Baikal. Tungus natives and Russian settlers in the region reported seeing the titanic flash and hearing a rumbling sound like artillery, followed by a blast wave that knocked them off their feet and shattered windows hundreds of miles away.

The first report of the explosion appeared in the Irkutsk newspaper on 2 July 1908, two days later. In part, it reads:

> ... the peasants saw a body shining very brightly (too bright for the naked eye) with a bluish-white light ... The body was in the form of 'a pipe', i.e. cylindrical. The sky was cloudless, except that low down on the horizon, in the direction in which this glowing body was observed, a small dark cloud was noticed. It was hot and dry and when the shining body approached the ground (which was covered with forest at this point) it seemed to be pulverized, and in its place a loud crash, not like thunder, but as if from the fall of large stones or from gunfire was heard. All the buildings shook and at the same time a forked tongue of flames broke through the cloud.

All the inhabitants of the village ran out into the street in panic. The old women wept, everyone thought that the end of the world was approaching.

An eyewitness in the village of Vanovara, S B Semenov, also provided a vivid and detailed description of what he experienced:

I was sitting in the porch of the house at the trading station of Vanovara at breakfast time ... when suddenly in the north ... the sky was split in two and high above the forest the whole northern part of the sky appeared to be covered with fire. At that moment I felt great heat as if my shirt had caught fire; this heat came from the north side. I wanted to pull off my shirt and throw it away, but at that moment there was a bang in the sky, and a mighty crash was heard. I was thrown to the ground about three *sajenes* [about seven metres] away from the porch and for a moment I lost consciousness ... The crash was followed by noises like stones falling from the sky, or guns firing. The earth trembled, and when I lay on the ground I covered my head because I was afraid that stones might hit it.

A farmer in the Kezhma region, about 200 km south of the impact site, related his own experience of the blast:

At that time I was ploughing my land at Narodima [six kilometres west of Kazhma]. When I sat down to have my breakfast beside my plough, I heard sudden bangs, as if from gun-fire. My horse fell on its knees. From the north side above the forest a flame shot up. I thought the enemy was firing, since at that time there was talk of war. Then I saw that the fir forest had been bent over by the wind and I thought of a hurricane. I seized hold of my plough with both hands, so that it would not be carried off. The wind was so strong that it carried off some of the soil from the surface of the ground, and then the hurricane drove a wall of water up the Angara. I saw it all quite clearly, because my land was on a hillside.

The colossal explosion registered on seismographs at stations across the Eurasian continent, measuring 5 on the Richter scale. Through comparison of these data with seismograms of the Novaya Zemlya and Lop-Nor nuclear weapons tests, the physicist Ari Ben-Menahem determined that the Tunguska impactor had 'the effects of an Extraterrestrial Nuclear Missile of yield 12.5±2.5 megatons', about 30 times more powerful than the atomic bomb that destroyed Hiroshima, and about one fifth as powerful as the largest ever hydrogen bomb explosion.

Over the years, many researchers have claimed that the Tunguska impactor was not a meteorite or comet, but an extraterrestrial spacecraft that had encountered difficulties during its approach to Earth and had crashed, the detonation of its engines causing the colossal explosion. Those researchers cite the apparent changes in trajectory of the object reported by many of the witnesses to the event – changes which do not occur during a meteorite or comet strike.

Dr Uvarov does not subscribe to this theory: he maintains that there were *several* objects moving through the sky on the morning of 30 June 1908, all of them approaching the impact site from different directions. According to Uvarov: 'It was the discrepancies in the accounts of eyewitnesses – who at one and the same time observed objects above areas of Siberia far remote from one another, moving on different courses but towards a single point – that confused researchers, prompting the hypothesis that it was probably a spaceship that had been manoeuvring above the Siberian taiga.'

At the Stepanovsky mine, near the town of Yuzhno-Eniseisk, one witness was standing next to a small lake when he claimed to experience a sudden, overwhelming fear. The ground began to shake, and the water in the lake drained away to reveal a hole which was opening in the lakebed. The witness fled, and when he looked back he saw a column of bright light rising from the lake, at the top of which was a spherical object. There was a terrible roaring and humming, and the witness received radiation burns to his face.

Radiation burns, I thought. *Like Dyatlov and the others...?*

In his article, Uvarov makes the connection with the *Olonkho* epic. I returned to my notes and read again Konstantinov's description of this ancient poem:

When the darkness lifted, the people saw a great swathe of scorched ground, at the centre of which stood a vast tower which emitted strange, high-pitched noises. Gradually, over many weeks, the tower sank into the ground, leaving behind it a huge vertical shaft. At times, an object was seen hovering over the mouth of the chasm, an object which the herdsmen called a 'rotating island'. Some people grew so curious that they put their fear aside, and went into the scorched region to investigate. They never returned.

Many years later, the land was shaken by a tremendous earthquake. A great fireball appeared, and flew over the horizon to decimate the lands of a neighbouring tribe. They were enemies of the Yakuts, so it was assumed that the fireball was some kind of protecting 'demon'. They called it Niurgun Bootur, which means 'the fiery champion'.

According to Uvarov, the archives of the Irkutsk Magnetic and Meteorological Observatory contain notes written by one A K Kokorin, who was an observer at a weather station on the River Kezhma, about 600 km from the Tunguska impact site. Kokorin's notes for 30 June support the idea that there was more than one object in the skies above Siberia on that day:

> At 7 AM, two fiery circles of gigantic size appeared to the north; four minutes after appearing, the circles disappeared; soon after the disappearance of the fiery circles a loud noise was heard, similar to the sound of the wind, that went from north to south; the noise lasted about five minutes; then followed sounds and thundering, like shots from enormous guns, that made the windows rattle. Those shots continued for two minutes, and after them came a crack like a rifle-shot. These last sounds lasted two minutes. Everything took place in broad daylight.

Uvarov goes on to cite several other eyewitness accounts of the Tunguska event, all of which mention bright flying spheres, which he calls 'terminator spheres'. He suggests that it was these objects, which carried a powerful electromagnetic charge, that the eyewitnesses saw hurtling through the sky along different trajectories, and all converging on a single point: the Tunguska impact site. They had been generated within the body of the planet, and had been delivered to the surface through pillars of energy emanating from vertical shafts of incredible depth, which the Yakut people call 'the laughing chasms'.

Whether the impactor itself was a meteorite or comet was irrelevant. What was important was that the terminator spheres had intercepted and destroyed it before it could strike an area of high population.

In support of his theory, Uvarov cites the presence of 'microspherules' containing a large quantity of nickel, which were later found distributed over a vast area of the taiga. These tiny objects, ranging in size from 5 to 400 microns, are all that is left of the Tunguska impactor. 'Reasoning about the mechanism by which the terminators operate,' he writes, 'we can assume that with their powerful electromagnetic charge they were supposed to attach themselves to a flying meteorite *and alter its trajectory* so that it passed out of the Earth's atmosphere. If the meteorite's trajectory was such as to make deflection impossible, the terminators simply destroyed the rocky splinters – literally melting the meteoritic substance, which subsequently hardened into tiny spherules.'

I recalled that Konstantinov had mentioned the destruction of two other meteorites in more recent years, at Chulym in 1984 and Vitim in 2002, and I found references to these events in Uvarov's article.

The Chulym event occurred on 26 February 1984. A meteorite crossed the skies over Siberia at an altitude of about 100 kilometres, following the same trajectory as the Tunguska impactor 76 years earlier. As the meteorite approached, the passengers on a bus travelling along the Mirny Highway watched a pillar of fire emerging from the ground, while fisherman on the River Chona saw two shining spheres emerge from behind the hills bordering the Valley of Death to the north. The spheres rose vertically and disappeared into the clouds. A few minutes later, the meteorite apparently exploded over the River Chulym, a tributary of the Ob. A subsequent expedition found no trace of the meteorite, other than large numbers of silicate microspherules, similar to those discovered in the Tunguska region.

In September 2002, a United States Department of Defence satellite detected a large meteorite approaching the area of Bodaibo in the Irkutsk region of Russia. The satellite also detected a bright object at an altitude of 62 kilometres, moving at an angle of 32 degrees to the horizon, which was apparently on a collision course with the incoming meteorite. The unknown object appeared to collide with the meteorite at an altitude of 30 kilometres, and there was a powerful explosion.

There were many eyewitnesses to this event. An electrical worker named Yevgeny Yarygin, for instance, who was on duty at the distribution centre in the town of Muskovit, was manning the switchboard room when he and his colleagues heard a distant noise 'like the roar from an aircraft', followed by a strange glow which they saw through the south-facing window. Something as bright as a welding torch was ascending from behind the hills to the southeast, leaving a wake which Yarygin described as maroon in colour. After about ten seconds the glow, which had completely illuminated the overcast sky, diminished and then went out.

Yarygin and his friends went outside, where they heard an explosion so loud that it shook the plaster from the building. The initial sound had come from the region where the glow was first seen, but the explosion came from the opposite direction – that is, the direction in which the glow had been moving.

Several other eyewitnesses also reported a strange, rumbling roar apparently coming from somewhere underground, followed by the ascent of a brightly glowing light which moved off into the sky, and finally a terrifically loud explosion. Their locations and the timing of their sightings suggested that more than one object was seen, all of which appeared to be heading in the same direction, towards the point at which the meteorite exploded.

When I had finished the article, I sat in silence for several minutes, hardly knowing what to think. Uvarov's theories about 'terminator spheres' and ancient planetary defence systems were utterly outlandish; surely no more than science fiction. And yet, the testimony of dozens of eyewitnesses – to the Tunguska, Chulym and Vitim events – could not be ignored, and strongly implied that something much more complex and mysterious than meteorite strikes had occurred at those locations.

I glanced at my desk clock; it was 11.40 PM. I shut down the computer and rubbed my eyes, feeling rather lost and confused, and unsure of how much of all this I could or should believe. I had the strange sense of a profound dichotomy: that it was either complete nonsense, or the most important information I had ever read – that there was no middle ground.

I took out a blank sheet of paper and made some notes:

Unidentified spherical objects clearly form a continuous motif, threading its way from the Tunguska event, through the Dyatlov Pass incident and on into the present.

They're a constant feature – What are they?

Appearances:

- *Tunguska, 1908 – They intercept and destroy the impactor before it can strike a densely-populated area.*
- *Northern Urals, 1959 – They are seen in the sky above Kholat Syakhl on the night the Dyatlov party die.*
- *Chulym, 1984; Vitim, 2002 – Again, they intercept and destroy meteorites before they can complete their impact trajectories and strike the Earth.*

Date unknown – The Soviet government creates a top secret project, codenamed 'Svarog'. Its purpose is unknown, but it is uniquely suited to investigate the Dyatlov Pass incident.

The name 'Svarog' refers to an ancient Slavic sky deity.

All documents relating to the project appear to bear this symbol:

The symbol of Perun, god of thunder and lightning in the pagan Slavic religion.

It is conjectured that the shape is intended to represent the phenomenon of ball lightning, and is used to ward off lightning strikes: a symbol of protection.

The Soviet government obviously knew this when they chose the symbol for Project Svarog.

Questions:

- *Is Project Svarog intended to protect, or to investigate something which protects?*

- *Assuming they exist, what is the origin and nature of Uvarov's 'terminator spheres'?*
- *If the defence system which they allegedly constitute is as old as Uvarov implies, who built it?*
- *What was Eduard Lishin's motive for releasing information on Project Svarog to Strugatsky and Konstantinov?*
- *Did the spheres kill certain members of the Dyatlov party? If so, WHY?*

As I was looking over these notes, there was a loud knock at the front door. I glanced up sharply, wondering who on earth could be calling at this late hour. Nataliya was in bed, and I hurried from my study before whoever was there could knock again and wake her up.

Senior Investigator Komar was standing on the doorstep, hands thrust deeply into the pockets of his overcoat, the collar turned up against the biting chill of midnight.

'I'm sorry to call on you at home, Dr Baskov,' he said, his breath misting in front of his frowning face. 'But there's something I need to discuss with you as a matter of urgency.'

'Of course, Investigator,' I said, stepping aside to let him in. 'Can I get you anything?' I asked quietly as I led him across the hall towards my study.

He glanced towards the stairs, and replied equally quietly: 'Nothing, thank you.'

I offered him a chair.

'What can I do for you?'

Komar took a deep breath. 'Something has happened to three of my men.'

I sat on the edge of my desk, facing him. 'Your men? The ones at the mountain?'

He nodded. 'They were brought back to Yekaterinburg today. They're very ... sick.'

I looked at him in silence for a moment. 'In what way sick?'

'It looks like radiation poisoning, but...'

'But what?'

He didn't reply; instead, he sat back in the chair, sighing heavily and running a hand through his hair. 'I don't know,' he muttered presently.

'Have you seen them yourself?'

'Yes. I was at Novaya Bolnitsa hospital when they were brought in. At first sight, it looked like they had been exposed to radiation, but now I'm not so sure.'

'What do you mean? Forgive me, Investigator, but have you ever seen a victim of radiation exposure?'

He gave me a grim smile. 'My brother-in-law was a member of one of the fire crews who went into Chernobyl after the accident. Yes, Dr Baskov, I *have* seen a victim of radiation exposure ... but this was different.'

I waited for him to continue, and when he looked at me, his eyes were filled with horrified questions.

'Their skin isn't burned – not as such. It's ... *tanned*. A deep, unnatural orange.'

My mouth went dry as I asked: 'And their hair?'

'Grey. And that's not all. They're able to talk ... and when asked what happened to them, they all described seeing something in the sky.'

'What thing?' I asked.

'Glowing spheres,' said Komar. 'Hanging in the air directly above them.'

I went to the drinks cabinet in a corner of the room and poured us both a stiff shot of vodka. Komar accepted the glass without a word and knocked it back in one swallow.

'What are you going to do?' I asked.

'When is your next session with Strugatsky?'

'Tomorrow.'

'What time?'

'Ten o'clock.'

'I want to be there. In fact, I want to be there at every session from now on. I want to hear what happened from Strugatsky direct.'

'Agreed,' I said, although the presence of a criminal militia officer during psychological evaluation sessions was most irregular. In fact, I didn't have a choice, and Komar knew it. If I had refused, he simply would have arranged for the sessions to be terminated and Strugatsky to be transferred to prison. That, of course, would have been a less than satisfactory arrangement, and Komar knew that, too. If we wanted Strugatsky to share his experiences with us, then Peveralsk was by far the better environment.

Komar did me the courtesy of thanking me, and so it was with a certain amount of reluctance that I added: 'On one condition.'

'Which is?'

'That you allow me to conduct the sessions precisely as I would have done had you not been there; that you allow Strugatsky to describe the events he witnessed, or in which he participated, in his own way and at his own pace.'

Komar gave me a dubious look.

'Trust me, Investigator,' I said with what I hoped was a reassuring smile. 'We'll get more out of him that way.'

Komar nodded. 'All right, Doctor. We'll do it your way, but I want to know exactly what happened to my men. And if the doctors who are treating them now can't provide me with any answers, I assure you that Strugatsky will.'

———

Komar arrived at Peveralsk at 9.50 the following morning, and together we went to Strugatsky's room. His reaction when he saw Komar was interesting: he gave a shallow sigh, closed his eyes and nodded, as if he knew – or intuited – that something important had happened.

'I believe you know Senior Investigator Komar, Viktor,' I said as we sat down. 'He is going to be present during the rest of our conversations.'

'What's happened?' Strugatsky asked.

'What makes you think that something has happened?' asked Komar.

'Why else would you be here now? Something has happened out there at the mountain. What is it?'

Before Komar could reply, I said: 'Three militia officers have fallen ill while searching the forest at one of the locations on Lishin's map. They describe glowing spheres in the sky.'

'Where were they when it happened?'

'They were in the vicinity of what the dossier calls the mercury lake,' said Komar.

'Did they find the lake?'

'No.'

Strugatsky simply nodded.

Komar leaned forward and said in a loud voice: 'What happened to my men?'

'This must mean that the region is still active for some reason...'

'Active?'

I put my hand on Komar's shoulder and shook my head. He gave me a severe look, sat back in his chair and folded his arms.

'Viktor,' I said, 'it appears that Investigator Komar's men have encountered the same phenomenon as the Dyatlov party. Is there anything – anything at all – that you can tell us about what it is, and if there's any treatment that can be administered?'

'It's a form of electromagnetic radiation, highly localised,' he replied. 'I think it comes from the spheres.' He hesitated, then looked at Komar. 'How close were your men to them?'

'I'm not sure, but it seems that they were pretty close. They had separated from the rest of the squad, and were searching an area of forest by themselves. Yesterday, the squad called in, saying that three men had become ill and requesting an immediate medical evacuation by helicopter.'

'You must have encountered something like this when you were there, Viktor,' I said, indicating his hair. 'Although on you the effect seems much less pronounced. Why is that?'

Strugatsky didn't answer. Instead, he turned to Komar. 'Don't your men have any radiation detection equipment, Investigator?'

Komar shook his head. 'No, nothing like that,' he muttered.

Strugatsky gave a mirthless chuckle. 'No, of course not. That's not the kind of investigation you had planned, is it?'

'We were searching the area for the bodies of possible homicide victims,' he said through gritted teeth. 'We weren't looking for aliens or monsters or unidentified forms of radiation. It was a murder investigation!'

'But not anymore,' Strugastky replied, meeting Komar's gaze calmly. 'Now it's something else, isn't it, Investigator?'

'What kind of equipment did Chernikova take to Kholat Syakhl?'

'Standard detection devices. I'm sure you know what they are.'

'Remind me.'

'She had a Geiger counter with a Geiger-Mueller probe, a MicroR meter with sodium iodide detector, a portable multi-channel analyzer, an ionization chamber, a neutron REM meter with proportional counter, and a radon detector.'

'How did she get hold of all that stuff?'

Strugatsky shrugged. 'She was a physicist. She had access to a lot of equipment at the university. She borrowed it, although whether she had her department's permission I don't know. I kind of doubt it, since we didn't exactly advertise our intention to go to Kholat Syakhl.'

Komar stood up and left the room, taking out his cell phone as he did so.

When he returned a minute or so later, Strugatsky smiled at him and said: 'Making sure your team are properly equipped? Better late than never, eh? Although it won't do any good. The only radiation there is the unknown form which comes from the spheres. And there's no defence against that.'

I decided that Komar had contributed more than enough to the conversation. 'Viktor, I'd like to put this to one side for a while, and continue from where we left off on Friday – you remember? You were saying that the shaman, Prokopy Anyamov, was silent throughout the rest of your journey to the mountain. When our session ended, you were approaching Kholat Syakhl. Would you please continue from there?'

Strugatsky glanced from me to Komar. 'All right, Doctor.'

FOURTEEN

Their route took them through a cold and silent landscape of dense forest and tall outcrops of snow-capped rock. Viktor had never been here before, of course, and the place looked like another planet to him – especially the rocks. Konstantinov said that they were more than 300 million years old. They were twisted by time and geological forces into strange shapes; and yet there was a weird regularity to them: in places they formed walls, immense and sagging, as if they were the ruins of ancient castles built by a race that had long since vanished from the Earth. There were turrets and ramparts leaning crazily into each other, great slabs of striated stone and vast, grey towers. The bedding patterns of the rock faces gave the impression that they had been built of irregular bricks hewn by an unknown and surreal intelligence.

All around, the trees of the primeval forest stood snow-covered and silent. Viktor felt like the forest was watching them ... or perhaps something *in* the forest. It was a horrible feeling: a feeling of being a tiny, vulnerable creature entering a place that was vast, both in extent and age ... a place where no human had any business going.

And above the needle-like pinnacles of the trees, away in the distance, Kholat Syakhl, its rounded summit nudging the grey sky ... the Mountain of the Dead.

Konstantinov brought the car to a halt, and they all looked at it through the windscreen; and Viktor wondered what else that ancient white sentinel had witnessed, besides the deaths of nine defenceless people a geological heartbeat ago.

As if wanting to break the strange spell that had descended on them, Konstantinov said: 'We should keep going. We need to set up camp before nightfall, and there's something I want to show you before we do.'

'What do you want to show us?' asked Veronika.

'The reason we've come here,' he replied, before putting the car into gear and gunning the engine.

A little while later, they stopped again at another rock outcrop. But this one was different: a large metal plaque had been affixed to it, containing a bas-relief of a man's head in profile, fashioned in the monumental, angular style of Soviet-era art.

Konstantinov stopped the car and switched off the engine. They all got out – even Prokopy – and walked up to the plaque. They read the inscription.

IN MEMORY OF THE NINE WHO LOST THEIR LIVES AT PASS 1079, NOW RENAMED DYATLOV PASS IN THEIR HONOUR

IGOR DYATLOV
GEORGY KRIVONISCHENKO
YURI DOROSHENKO
ZINAIDA KOLMOGOROVA
LUDMILA DUBININA
RUSTEM SLOBODIN
ALEXANDER ZOLOTAREV
NIKOLAI THIBEAUX-BRIGNOLLEL
ALEXANDER KOLEVATOV

In his mind's eye, Viktor put a face, alive and smiling, to each of those names ... and then he thought of the other photographs, the ones showing the camp, abandoned and destroyed, and the poor, pathetic frozen bodies half buried in the snow. At that moment, he didn't know which was more appalling: the idea that they had died senselessly, the victims of a mindless natural phenomenon; or that they had been deliberately killed by something unknown and unfathomable, something with consciousness and intelligence.

There was silence all around, the deep, crystalline silence of a winter wilderness. Viktor couldn't decide whether to think of it as sacred or sinister; and at that moment, in that place, it seemed that there was a very fine line between the two.

Then Prokopy Anyamov did a strange thing. He walked right up to the plaque, placed one hand upon it and began speaking very quietly in his language. He lowered his head and closed his eyes, as if in prayer. None of the others said anything, to him or to each other; they simply stood and watched until he had finished. Presently, he turned away from the plaque and, without looking at them, walked back to the car and got in.

Viktor looked at Konstantinov. His eyes were fixed on the plaque, his face expressionless; but at that moment Viktor thought that he looked older than before, as if the years had finally caught up with him and overcome the passion for the truth that had animated him until then. He had the air of a man who was approaching the end of a long and exhausting journey, and who was still uncertain as to what he would find at his destination.

'Vadim,' he said quietly. 'We should go ... make camp.'

Konstantinov glanced at him as if surprised, as if he had been woken from a troubled sleep. 'Yes,' he said, looking up briefly into the sky. 'It'll be getting dark soon.'

———

'Where do you suggest we set up camp?' asked Alisa when they had returned to the car. There was a slight hesitancy in her voice, which suggested that she was as affected by their surroundings as Viktor was. He could detect nothing of the subtle condescension that had shaded her demeanour up until now. Was it a sign of sympathy or respect for Konstantinov, or perhaps apprehension? Now that they had arrived at Kholat Syakhl, bearing knowledge that there really was something profoundly wrong with this place, did she really want to be here?

Konstantinov took out Lishin's map. 'Here,' he said, indicating a certain location. 'Just inside the tree line. A convenient place from which to make excursions to the points that are marked.'

Viktor leaned forward and looked where he was pointing. 'That's the place where Georgy Krivonischenko and Yuri Doroshenko were found.'

'That's right. As you can see, the locations which are marked on the map are all about an hour away by car, given the nature of the terrain: the Installation, the Cauldron, the mercury lake, Zone 3 Station.'

'Where do you think we should go first?' asked Veronika.

'The Station,' Konstantinov replied without hesitation.

'Why there?'

'Two reasons, Nika. One: there may be something there that will tell us what Project Svarog was doing here, something they might have left behind when the Station was abandoned. That may be unlikely, but we need to check – and we'll need photographs of it. And two: given the nature of the other things, I want to start by investigating something that's actually still here. Something that doesn't appear and disappear at will.'

'Something made by humans,' said Alisa. 'You want to walk before you start running.'

Konstantinov gave her a thin smile. 'Yes ... you might say that.'

He handed the map to Alisa, started the engine and pulled away from the rock face and the memorial plaque.

———

The sky had begun to darken by the time they reached the edge of the pine forest where the bodies of Krivonischenko and Doroshenko, bare-foot and dressed only in their underclothes, had been found during the first search-and-rescue expedition in February 1959. Viktor got out of the car and looked at the trees on the edge of the forest. He recalled that someone had climbed one of them, perhaps Krivonischenko, or perhaps Doroshenko, in an apparent attempt to locate their abandoned camp ... or maybe to get a look at something that was happening there.

He turned and looked up the slope towards the nearby summit of Kholat Syakhl, his gaze coming to rest on the spot where the Dyatlov group had pitched their tent on that night. An image came suddenly into his mind of nine people running towards him, their faces twisted in panic...

He shuddered and turned quickly away from the scene, and saw Prokopy Anyamov standing beside the car, watching him, his face devoid of expression.

The others had opened the SUV's rear doors and were pulling out the tent. Viktor went to give them a hand, and together they unpacked and pitched the tent just inside the tree line. Within an hour, they were finished. During that time, no one noticed that Anyamov had slipped silently away from the group. Now they saw him emerging from the trees, carrying an armful of twigs and broken branches, which he placed a few metres from the tent.

'For the fire,' he said.

'Thank you, Prokopy,' said Konstantinov.

The shaman arranged the branches on the snow-covered ground, and with a smile accepted the lighter which Alisa wordlessly offered him. Within a few moments, the fire was burning brightly, and as Viktor felt its warmth on his face, he began to feel his spirits rise a little. As he watched the sparks dancing away from the flames, up into the cold evening air above their little camp, he found himself thinking how strange it was that fire could do that. As a species, humanity didn't like the dark, even those who professed to have no fear of it. There was something deep inside which recoiled from it, understanding with primitive animal awareness the threat which it embodied. But a roaring, crackling fire gave reassurance that the natural world could be an ally as well as an adversary, reminding us that there was always a way to keep the things in the dark at bay.

Almost always.

Veronika set up the gas stove and lit it, and they cooked their first meal in the wilderness: tinned sausage, beans and rye bread. It wasn't up to Roman Bakhtyarov's wild boar stew, but it was hot and satisfying, and Konstantinov rounded it off with a pleasant surprise. With a subdued flourish, he produced a packet of his Blue Mountain coffee and brewed a large pot, which everyone, including Prokopy, sipped gratefully from aluminium mugs which only detracted a little from the flavour.

When they had finished, Alisa lit a cigarette and leaned back in her camping chair, blowing the smoke up into the air. 'So,' she said, 'what's the plan for tomorrow? The Zone 3 Station?'

'I think that's the best place to start,' Konstantinov replied.

Prokopy Anyamov nodded. Alisa caught the movement, and smiled at him. 'Glad you agree.'

The shaman returned her smile.

'Prokopy,' said Konstantinov. 'Back in Yurta Anyamova, you said that you would be able to guide us here, to help us to avoid the most dangerous areas. What did you mean by that?'

'What I said.'

'But how do you *know* which places are safe, and which not?'

'We have lived here for many years,' Anyamov replied. 'This is our land, our home ... it's the place where we belong, and although many of us leave to go to the cities, there will always be Mansi here.' He nodded towards the rising flank of Kholat Syakhl, white against the sullen grey of the cloud-strewn sky. 'This place wants to be left alone, and so we leave it alone. But still it is part of our world, and I can see our world in ways you would not understand. I can see things you can't see, hear things you can't hear. I don't want to be here, but I come because you will do better with me to guide you. This is all you need to know. For the rest, I will keep my own council.'

Konstantinov nodded. 'I understand.'

Alisa looked from him to Anyamov, smiled and shook her head. 'I'm sure we all appreciate your help, Prokopy,' she said.

The shaman returned her smile. 'It's not necessary that you should appreciate my help. What is necessary, at this moment, is that you look at the sky.'

'The sky? What do you mean?'

Anyamov's smile grew broader. 'It is necessary that you look at the sky,' he repeated.

They all looked up.

'The clouds are clearing,' said Alisa, and threw a sardonic grin at the shaman. 'Did you do that?'

'No.'

'I guess this means it's going to get even colder,' said Veronika as she pulled the collar of her padded coat tighter around her neck.

Anyamov looked at her. 'Yes ... but it means something else as well.'

Konstantinov leaned forward in his chair. '*What* does it mean, Prokopy?'

The shaman didn't answer: he merely looked up, that enigmatic smile still playing upon his lips.

The clouds were parting to reveal the blackness of the night sky. In fact, Viktor thought that they were moving a little too quickly, considering that there was no wind, not even a light breeze.

In fact, they shouldn't have been moving at all.

'Look at the stars,' said Anyamov.

They were bright and sharply defined, glittering needle points ranged in their thousands across the black vault of space. One never saw stars like that in a city, where the light pollution from buildings and streetlamps obscured most of them, washing the sky with a ubiquitous sodium glow.

'My God,' said Konstantinov.

'It's beautiful,' said Veronika.

'That's not what he means,' Alisa whispered, and Veronika and Viktor looked at her. She was still gazing up at the sky, as were Konstantinov and Anyamov.

But only Anyamov was smiling.

'What is it?' Viktor asked.

Konstantinov said nothing, merely shook his head in obvious confusion.

'Tell us!'

'It's the stars,' said Alisa, her voice tremulous, disbelieving. 'They're wrong ... they're all wrong!'

'What the hell do you mean by that?' Veronika demanded.

'I don't recognise any of the constellations. This ... this isn't the sky as seen from Earth.'

Konstantinov shook his head. 'This is impossible.'

'Yes,' said Alisa in a small voice, almost a child's voice, filled with wonderment and fear. 'It's impossible, but it's true nevertheless. The stars are wrong ... the stars are all wrong.'

PART THREE

THE ANOMALOUS ZONE

BASKOV (9)

'He's lying,' said Komar after the session had ended and we had returned to my office.

'You think so?'

Komar gave me an incredulous look. 'Of course! What other explanation could there be? I mean, *different constellations in the sky?* That's completely ridiculous.'

'I wonder whether they could have suffered a shared hallucination,' I said, half to myself. 'Or perhaps Konstantinov and Chernikova were simply mistaken...'

Komar shook his head. 'I doubt Konstantinov would have made such a mistake, and Chernikova? She was a physicist. There's no way *she* could have looked at the sky and not recognised any of the constellations. It's strange, though: up until now, Strugatsky's story has been supported by the facts.'

'You mean your discovery of the Project Svarog papers?'

He nodded. 'Even that antiprism thing has supporting documentation. We've established that they're genuine, by which I simply mean that they're not forgeries; as to the veracity of what they *contain* ... well, that's another matter.'

'According to Strugatsky, Alisa Chernikova suggested that they might be part of some elaborate psychological experiment...'

Komar grunted. 'It wouldn't be the first time.'

'However,' I continued, 'I think we must also consider the possibility that it's all true.'

'What? You're joking!'

'Far from it.' I opened my secure filing cabinet, took out the copies I had made of the papers in Lishin's dossier and handed one of the photographs to Komar. It was the one labelled: NIGHT SKY ABOVE FOREST TO THE SOUTH OF KHOLAT SYAKHL. POSSIBLY AN UNSUCCESSFUL ATTEMPT TO RECORD UNEXPLAINED DISPARITY. 'There's this, for one thing,' I said.

Komar took the photograph. 'Yes, but this shows nothing but blackness. We can hardly take it as evidence that something strange really did happen to the sky.'

'Agreed, but I'm thinking more about the wording of the label than the photograph. Doesn't it strike you as odd? "Possibly an unsuccessful attempt to record unexplained disparity." Whoever wrote that label either knew or suspected something about why this particular photograph was taken.'

I opened a drawer in my desk and took out the article by Valery Uvarov which I had read the previous evening, and which I had printed after Komar left my house. 'Take a look at this,' I said, handing it to him.

He flipped through the pages. 'What is it?'

'More evidence that there may really be something genuinely strange in the Northern Urals.'

He looked at the papers dubiously.

'Just read it, Investigator ... and don't forget that three of your men are suffering the effects of apparent radiation exposure.'

He glanced sharply at me. 'I can assure you I haven't forgotten that, Doctor Baskov.'

'Of course not. I'm sorry. How are they?'

'I checked with the hospital this morning, before coming here. Their condition is still serious ... the doctors are doing what they can, but they've never seen anything quite like it.'

'What about the rest of your team?'

'I've ordered radiation detection equipment to be sent up there, along with protective suits. The operation is on hold until they arrive.'

'A wise precaution.'

Komar looked at me in silence for a few moments. 'All right, Doctor, let's assume for now that Strugatsky is telling the truth about what happened on their first night at Kholat Syakhl, and that the sky really did become unrecognisable. How the hell could that *happen*?'

I gave an uneasy laugh. 'You're asking the wrong person.'

Komar spread his arms wide and looked around the office. 'You're the only one here. You're the only one I *can* ask.'

'Chernikova worked at the Technical University. I take it you've already interviewed her colleagues...'

Komar nodded.

'Well, you might like to ask them about this...'

'Right,' he snorted. 'And get laughed out of their labs.'

'I doubt it. You don't have to tell them everything, and if you make it clear that you're speaking merely theoretically, you may find them more than willing to speculate. Professional scientists are just like everyone else in that respect – they love to talk about the things that interest them. I've no doubt that Chernikova's colleagues will be quite accommodating if you phrase your questions in the right way.'

He sighed. 'I suppose that's not a bad idea. And I'll also have a look at this.' He waved the article I had given him before folding it and putting it in the inside pocket of his overcoat. 'When is your next session?'

'Same time tomorrow.'

'Right. I'll see you then, Doctor.'

———

After Komar had left, I listened again to the session on my tape recorder. I sympathised with the Senior Investigator: what had initially been a straightforward case of missing persons and possible homicide had been transformed into something else entirely, something as bizarre as it was complex. I hoped he sympathised as much with me.

This much was true: taken at face value, the alteration of the sky as described by Strugatsky was totally inexplicable. It made no sense whatsoever outside the pages of science fiction. And yet ... I recalled an interview I had read with an American writer some months previously, in which he had said that the world is becoming a science fiction novel. I smiled at the recollection: evidently, his words were truer than he supposed.

I thought again about the strange, grinding hum which Strugatsky and his companions had heard while in Yurta Anyamova. I supposed that the flashes in the sky could have been distant lightning – distant enough for the accompanying thunder to have been drowned out by the mysterious sound which apparently was coming from somewhere much closer.

It reminded me of something I had read about several years previously. I couldn't quite put my finger on it, couldn't quite recall the details, although I did recall that it had happened somewhere in the United States. I went onto the internet and Googled the keywords MYSTERIOUS HUM.

I scanned the first page of results, my eye falling almost immediately on the phrase 'Taos Hum'.

That was it.

Taos, New Mexico was (or is) the most well-known location of the so-called 'Hum Phenomenon', a low frequency sound with a rhythmic pulse, which has been heard at numerous locations across the globe, but most often in America, Britain and continental Europe. In 1993, the citizens of Taos became so disturbed and exasperated by the hum that they petitioned Congress to launch an investigation into the phenomenon, which was variously described as being like the sound made by an idling diesel engine, a refrigerator, and distant thunder.

Congress eventually acquiesced to the wishes of the Taos residents, and asked several scientists from a number of scientific institutions, including the Phillips Air Force Laboratory and the Los Alamos National Laboratory, to investigate. According to Thomas Begich, a respected writer, educator and political activist who runs the New Age website Earthpulse.com, the *Taos Hum Investigation: Informal Report* was written by Joe Mullins of the University of New Mexico and Horace Poteet of Sandia National Laboratories.

The report stated the intentions of the investigators: first, to interview people who claimed to have heard the hum, and to note its description, frequency and effects on the hearer; second, to establish how widespread the hum was by determining the distribution of people in Taos and the surrounding communities who claimed to have heard it and those who did not; and finally, to attempt to isolate and determine the cause of the hum.

The investigators established several key facts about the hum; for instance, that it always began abruptly, as if generated by some mechanical device which had been switched on; it was heard by a small number of people (about two percent of the population); it was extremely low on the frequency scale (between 30 and 80Hz).

The people interviewed by the investigative team consistently complained of nausea and dizziness whenever they heard the hum, and also headaches, disorientation, insomnia and nosebleeds. They were also psychologically disturbed by its very existence: they were deeply concerned that it didn't appear to be natural in origin, and many suspected that it had something to do with the military installations in and around New Mexico. Others theorised that it had something to do with the US Department of Defence or that the US Navy's ELF (Extremely Low Frequency) stations in northern Michigan were to blame.

At this point, the team was joined by James Kelly of the University of New Mexico's Health Sciences Centre, a hearing research scientist who concluded that there were 'no known acoustic signals that might account for the hum, nor are there any seismic events that might explain it'.

The team then focussed on an examination of the hearers' inner ears, with the intention of establishing whether they were suffering from some form of low-frequency tinnitus. The results, however, indicated that this was extremely unlikely.

While a definitive explanation for the Taos Hum was unforthcoming, Joe Mullins concluded that 'we're slowly building up the background of electronic noise ... we're going to more and more cordless things, all electromagnetic transmitters. Whether that's the cause of the hum, we don't know, but we can't write it off.'

I noted with mild surprise that several websites had downloadable sound files of the Taos Hum. For some reason, it hadn't occurred to me that the sound might actually have been recorded by someone, that I might actually be able to hear the phenomenon myself.

I opened one of the files and turned the volume up on my computer. It was an incredibly eerie sound, and I felt an odd sense of apprehension, even there in my office, as I listened to it. That it was artificial in nature there could be no doubt, and I shuddered as I imagined hearing it while walking down a street, or in my house. The rhythmic pulse which punctuated the underlying metallic groan was both irritating and vaguely threatening, and I admit that I was quite relieved when the sound file ended after half a minute or so.

I inserted a flash drive and saved the file to it, with the intention of playing it to Strugatsky in our next session. I wanted to see if it was at all similar to the sound he and the others had heard in Yurta Anyamova.

As usually happens when one uses the internet, I began clicking on hyperlinked references to related subjects – in this case, unidentified sounds. There was a wealth of material on them. The two which caught my eye had not occurred on land, but in the deep ocean. They were known as the 'Slow Down' and the 'Bloop'.

The Slow Down was recorded on 19 May 1997 on a hydrophone array in the Pacific Ocean. During the Cold War, the United States Navy established a vast network of underwater listening devices in order to detect and track Soviet nuclear submarines. This array, known as the Sound Surveillance System (SOSUS), was composed of hydrophones placed at 3,000km intervals in a deep layer of ocean called the 'deep sound channel', where the combination of low temperature and high pressure allows sound waves to propagate across great distances. When the Cold War ended, the US Navy allowed the SOSUS to be used for scientific research.

The Slow Down was detected by three hydrophones at a distance of some 2,000km, and slowly descended in frequency over a period of about seven minutes (hence its name). The sensors were able to triangulate its location at approximately 15° S, 115° W. This type of signal had never been detected before, and has not been detected since. Its origin is completely unknown.

A few months later, SOSUS detected another mysterious ultra-low frequency sound on several occasions at about 50° S, 100° W. The sound rose rapidly in frequency over a period of about one minute, and was apparently generated 3,000km from the nearest sensor. Completely at a loss as to its origin, the researchers called it the 'Bloop'.

Many scientists maintain that the characteristics of the Bloop match those of a living creature, although the fact that the sound was detected from such a great distance means that such an animal would have to be truly colossal – much larger than the blue whale, the largest known animal on Earth.

I was about to disconnect from the internet, when something else caught my eye: a link to something called 'the Vela Incident'. Intrigued by the name, I clicked on the link and continued to read, quickly realising that this might have some bearing on the strange flashes of light which Strugatsky claimed to have seen while in Yurta Anyamova.

The Vela Incident occurred in the early morning of 22 September 1979, when a US Atomic Energy Detection System satellite called Vela 6911, equipped with two silicon photodiode sensors known as 'bhangmeters', detected a pattern of intense flashes in a remote part of the Indian Ocean. These flashes were rapidly followed by a fast-moving ionospheric shock wave which was detected by the Arecibo Observatory in Puerto Rico, and a muffled sound which was detected by the US Navy's SOSUS array, which at that time was still engaged in the detection and tracking of Soviet submarines.

The pattern of the flashes seemed to indicate that a nuclear device had been detonated above the Indian Ocean, since no other known phenomenon produced such a pattern. An atmospheric nuclear detonation produces a characteristic double pulse of light; the first lasts no more than a millisecond, and is followed by a second, more prolonged flash.

The data gathered by Vela 6911 suggested that the explosion occurred in the vicinity of Bouvet Island, which lies between South Africa and Antarctica. According to the webpage I had found, the tiny, uninhabited ice-covered island was home to a Norwegian automated weather station, and in 1964, an abandoned lifeboat of unknown origin was discovered there, filled with supplies.

The blast was calculated at 2 – 4 kilotons, and while no nuclear-capable nation admitted responsibility, intelligence reports suggested that Israel was the likeliest candidate. However, subsequent flights over the area by US Air Force research aircraft failed to detect any fission products, which are always associated with nuclear explosions.

A committee of scientists convened by President Jimmy Carter to investigate the Vela Incident concluded that it was by no means proven that a nuclear device had been detonated. They considered two factors as problematic: the lack of fission products in the aftermath of the event, and the fact that the two bhangmeters carried by Vela 6911 had recorded the flashes at distinctly different intensities (no explanation for this discrepancy was ever discovered).

Instead, the committee suggested that the satellite might have been struck by a micrometeorite, which dislodged a number of particles which then reflected sunlight back into the sensors. They also suggested that a lightning 'superbolt' might have struck the ocean, mimicking the appearance of a nuclear explosion (although they accepted that this was extremely unlikely given that the Vela flashes contained 400 times more energy than the most powerful lightning strike).

I sat back in my chair and thought about these mysteries. Until then, I had considered the Dyatlov Pass incident and the case of Viktor Strugatsky in a purely detached, professional way, with little or no direct bearing on my life outside the Peveralsk Psychiatric Hospital. But after only a few minutes of the most basic and cursory research on the internet, I had found references to phenomena which eerily matched those described by Strugatsky ... and that was not even to consider the possible significance of Project Svarog. I suddenly felt myself to be in the same predicament as that for which I had pitied Komar: what had begun as a straightforward evaluation of a murder suspect's mental state had become a puzzle that was frighteningly bizarre and clearly global in extent...

———

The next day, I waited in my office for Komar to arrive before beginning the tenth session with Strugatsky. He didn't come, however, and I called him on his cell phone, intending to ask him if there was some problem. In view of his adamant desire to be present at the rest of the sessions, I assumed that something serious must have happened, perhaps to do with the three men who had become ill while searching the forest around Kholat Syakhl.

There was no answer, and so I left a message saying that I hoped everything was all right, and asking him to come straight to Strugatsky's room if he managed to get here in the next hour. I also instructed the orderlies to allow the Investigator to join me if and when he arrived.

Strugatsky gave me a quizzical look as soon as I entered his room. 'No militia today, Doctor?'

'It appears that Investigator Komar has been delayed for some reason.'

'Really? You don't know why?'

'I'm afraid not.'

'I think we can guess, though.'

'You're referring to his men?'

Strugatsky nodded. 'I can't believe they went there without taking any precautions.'

'They weren't expecting ... this,' I replied. 'It's understandable enough.'

'They knew about the Dyatlov Pass incident – what happened to them. They knew why *we* went there ... what the hell were they thinking?'

'They didn't realise that there's something genuinely dangerous and unexplained there...'

'But *you* realise it, don't you? You realise it *now*.' Strugatsky noticed the laptop I was holding. 'Why have you brought that?'

I put the computer on the desk and switched it on. While it was booting up, I said: 'Yesterday, I went online and did a bit of background reading about unidentified sounds. I was intrigued by your description of the hum you and the others heard in Yurta Anyamova. Have you ever heard of the Taos Hum?'

He shook his head.

I gave him a brief explanation while I selected the relevant sound file and opened it. 'I'd like you to listen to this, and tell me if it's in any way similar to the sound you heard.'

We both listened to the eerie, metallic sound drifting out of the computer's speakers. Strugatsky's features remained expressionless, but I could see the blood slowly draining from his face.

'Well?' I said, when the file had played.

'It's...' He hesitated. 'It's not quite the same ... but not that different, either. The pulse is very similar.' He frowned at me. 'And this has been heard in New Mexico and ... and other places too?'

I nodded. 'No one has been able to identify its origin, but it's apparently very widespread.'

Strugatsky sat back in his chair and rubbed his face with one hand. 'I didn't realise that,' he whispered.

'What is it? What does it mean? Did you and the others find out, Viktor?'

He said nothing, merely stared, first at me and then at the computer.

'Would you like me to play it again?'

'No!' he said loudly. Then, more quietly: 'No, thank you Doctor. Once was enough.'

I glanced at my watch. 'It looks like Investigator Komar won't be joining us today. Why don't you tell me some more about that first night at Kholat Syakhl? About the stars ... how they appeared different.'

'There's not much more to tell – at least, not about that.'

'But it's likely that Igor Dyatlov and the others saw the same thing, and tried to photograph it.'

'Yes, I think they did.'

'Do you have any idea how such a strange thing could have happened? Did anything happen subsequently to provide some clue?'

Strugatsky laughed at this. 'Oh, there were clues, Doctor Baskov. There were plenty of *clues*.'

'Then let's continue.'

FIFTEEN

None of them slept very well that night. The tent was large enough to sleep five very comfortably, but that was the last thing on anyone's mind. They were all thinking of the sky, the impossible patterns of the stars, and how something like that could possibly happen. Of course, it made no sense, and both Veronika and Viktor tried several times to persuade Vadim and Alisa that they were mistaken.

But it was no use: after all, Alisa was a physicist who was intimately acquainted with the night sky, with the patterns of its constellations, and she was absolutely adamant that it was all wrong, that nothing was recognisable ... and so Nika and Viktor stopped trying to persuade her otherwise. In fact, like most people, Viktor have a passing acquaintance with the better-known constellations – Orion, Ursa Major and so on – and he couldn't find them. *They simply weren't there.* Alisa had pointed to the regions of the sky where they should have been, but the stars were scattered in unfamiliar shapes there. It was as if they had been taken off the Earth and placed on a world in a completely different part of the galaxy. At least, that was what Alisa said.

Right then, they knew that this was what Dyatlov had tried to capture with his camera, this 'unexplained disparity', as the label on the photograph described it. And yet, they were still on Earth, still sitting outside a tent on the slopes of a mountain in the Urals. They hadn't moved – *the sky had moved.*

If this can happen, thought Viktor, *what might happen next?*

Veronika set up her camera on a tripod and angled it up as far as it would go, then set it for a long exposure: that way, it would be able to capture the starlight. Vadim congratulated her on her presence of mind, and said that the resulting picture would constitute powerful evidence that Anomalous

Zone 3 had been well-named, that there really was something here that defied the laws of physics as currently understood by humanity. He added that, by using sufficiently powerful software, it might even be possible to ascertain the position in the galaxy from which such star patterns could be seen.

For his part, Prokopy Anyamov said and did nothing: he merely sat there, looking up at the sky with that enigmatic smile. If he knew something that the rest didn't, he was keeping it to himself. Viktor glanced at him and thought of asking him what all this meant; but something told him that it wouldn't be any use. Somehow, he knew that Prokopy would simply turn that smile on him, and remain silent.

Prokopy was the only one who didn't toss and turn periodically throughout the night. Veronika was lying next to Viktor, and at one point she reached out and took his hand, and didn't let go until morning.

Sometime towards dawn, Viktor managed to drift off into a light and uneasy slumber, and half-formed dreams began to skitter through his mind, the vague, still-born images flashing in and out of existence, vanishing at the instant he became aware of them.

There was the mountain, standing alone at the centre of a vast, featureless landscape ... and awful, shapeless things seeping down from an unfamiliar sky ... there were Dyatlov and the others, waking suddenly in their tent, cutting through its sides in sudden, uncontrollable panic, clawing their way out into the snow and looking up, their faces grimacing in terror, the expressions so intense they made them look almost alien, not human anymore but transformed by a perfect, ultimate fear into something else, something insensate and primal.

Viktor woke up and lay there in the dark, listening to the sound of his own breathing and that of the others, feeling smothered by his sleeping bag but too cold to unzip it. He strained to listen for other sounds in the freezing night outside, sounds of something approaching, sounds that would switch on the panic reflex in his own mind...

But there was nothing.

Only the darkness, and the breathing, and an occasional restless sigh, and Nika's hand in his.

———

As dawn arrived, he began to relax, feeling less under siege from unknowable enemies. He might have been able to get some proper sleep then; but it was too late for that. Konstantinov was stirring, unzipping his sleeping bag, sitting up.

'Good morning,' he muttered without enthusiasm.

Alisa yawned, stretched and rubbed her face. 'Sleep well, everyone?'

'Far from it,' Viktor replied.

'That's to be expected in such unfamiliar surroundings,' said Konstantinov. 'Don't worry – tonight will be different. We've got a long day ahead of us – a long *week* in fact. We'll sleep better tonight.'

'Where's our friend?' asked Alisa.

Viktor looked at her. 'What?'

'Where's Prokopy?'

The spare sleeping bag in which the shaman had been sleeping was empty.

Alisa looked at them. 'I didn't hear him go out.'

Konstantinov unzipped the entrance to the tent (Viktor wondered how the hell Prokopy had managed to do that without any of them noticing) and went outside.

'Can you see him?' Alisa called as she wriggled out of her sleeping bag. 'Is he there?'

'No,' said Vadim.

They joined him outside and looked around at the trees. 'We need to find him,' said Viktor.

'Why?' asked Alisa.

'What do you mean "why"?' he snapped. 'He might be in trouble.' He turned to Vadim. 'And how did he manage to leave the tent without making any sound?'

'Maybe he spirited himself away on a vision quest,' Alisa muttered.

'Please, Alisa,' said Vadim. 'You're not helping.'

She sighed loudly and theatrically. 'Or maybe he's gone to collect more firewood for this evening. Maybe he knows it'll be dark by the time we get back, and he wants to be prepared. Did you think of that?'

Vadim smiled. 'Actually, no, I didn't.'

'Then let's get some breakfast organised while we wait for him.'

'Good idea,' said Veronika, and fired up the gas stove.

Viktor still wasn't so sure about Alisa's explanation. In any other wilderness in the world, it would have made sense, and he wouldn't have given it another thought. But not here. He was still thinking about what they had seen the previous evening, and he told himself that from now on, no rational explanation for anything that happened could be relied upon even to approach the truth.

He looked up at the sky, but the clouds had returned, drawing a veil of uniform grey across whatever lay beyond. He called out Prokopy's name, once, twice, three times, ignoring the amused look Alisa was giving him. His voice sounded flat and dead, absorbed by the snow which surrounded them, falling into the cold silence. He peered into the depths of the forest, searching for movement.

And then he caught sight of the shaman, about fifty metres away. He had emerged from behind a tree and was just standing there, looking at them.

'There he is!' he said.

Konstantinov turned and looked, and beckoned to him.

But Prokopy didn't move: instead, he beckoned to them.

'I think he wants to show us something,' said Vadim. 'Viktor, come with me.'

Viktor followed him through the trees towards the shaman, who was still standing there, perfectly still, watching their approach. His old, lined face was impassive as they drew up next to him, and when Vadim asked him if he had been collecting firewood, he shook his head.

'You asked me what I meant when I said that I would be able to guide you here, to help you to avoid the most dangerous places.'

'That's right,' said Vadim. 'I did ask you that.'

'This is what I meant,' Prokopy said, and pointed straight upwards.

They looked up at the tree beside which they were standing.

The object must have been hidden by the surrounding branches – that's why they hadn't seen it as they approached. At first, Viktor didn't know what they were looking at ... and when he finally realised, when at last his mind managed to interpret it, he gasped and took an involuntary step back.

'Dear God,' Konstantinov whispered. 'Oh dear God...'

Hanging amongst the branches in the upper reaches of the tree was something that had once been a bear. But it was not a bear now ... in fact, it could not even be properly called a carcass. The only part of it that was remotely recognisable was the head, and yet even that was warped, twisted and inexplicably ruptured. Its frozen body was a distorted mass of blood-stained bones and matted fur, and its limbs were impossible to discern in the absolute ruin of its form.

But the thing that horrified Viktor the most, the thing that made him want to turn and flee the forest at that moment, was the thing's hindquarters. What had once been the bear's lower abdomen and hind legs were now unaccountably stretched into a long, thin strand, which hung down like some nightmarish vine from the branches.

'What happened to it?' He glanced from Prokopy to Konstantinov, who was gazing up, his mouth open in disbelief. 'What the hell *happened* to it?'

'It went to a dangerous place,' said the shaman.

'No shit,' whispered Viktor.

'What's going on?' said Alisa. She and Veronika were approaching through the trees.

'Brace yourselves for an unpleasant sight,' said Konstantinov, and pointed up.

The two women looked up into the tree. Veronika turned away, bent over and vomited. Viktor went to her and put an arm around her shoulder, which she shook off wordlessly.

Alisa turned to Prokopy. 'Do you know how this happened?'

'As I said to Viktor, it went to a dangerous place.'

'What kind of place? Where is it? What's there?'

'Things there are not as they are here.'

'What the hell is that supposed to mean? Stop talking in riddles.'

'Still think he's no use to us, Alisa?' said Viktor.

He could tell she was about to let fly at him, but then she stopped herself, and instead looked up again at the thing in the tree. 'I don't know what to think. We need to get it down, so I can examine it more closely.'

'*What?*' said Veronika as she wiped spittle from her chin with a shaking hand. 'It looks like it's been through a fucking meat grinder – what more do you need to know?'

Alisa gave her a mirthless grin. 'It might help to know what *kind* of meat grinder, don't you think?'

'As far as I can tell,' said Konstantinov, 'it was fully grown. What we're seeing is clearly not the result of predation. So ... what could destroy such a beast so completely?'

'And having done so,' Viktor added, 'what could then throw what's left twenty metres up a tree?'

'Perhaps it wasn't thrown there,' said Vadim. 'Perhaps it *fell* there.'

'Oh, that's a big relief,' said Veronika as she turned and walked away.

'Nika, where are you going?' asked Viktor. 'I don't think any of us should go wandering –'

'Relax, Vitya!' she said over her shoulder. 'I'm going to get my camera. I take it you'll be wanting snaps.'

Alisa pointed to the long thin strand which was all that was left of the animal's hind quarters. 'This is *very* strange. It looks like a piece of chewing gum that's been pulled apart.' Her voice grew quiet, and it was clear that she was now talking more to herself than to them. 'Nothing like this has ever been seen, anywhere in the world ... no animal can do that ... no *known* animal, that is ... but nothing native to the Earth could be even remotely capable of doing this to a fully-grown bear. So ... if not an animal, then a *force* of some kind...'

'"A compelling unknown force,"' said Vadim. 'Somehow, that phrase doesn't sound quite as nebulous as it once did.'

Alisa didn't respond; she simply continued to stare up into the tree.

Veronika came back with the camera. When she saw her, Alisa held out her hand. Nika ignored her and began taking pictures.

'Be sure to get it from every angle,' said Alisa.

'That's what I'm doing,' Nika muttered.

Viktor watched her work, suddenly proud of her for so quickly overcoming her initial fear and revulsion.

Alisa walked to the tree trunk and put both hands on it, as if she were preparing to climb it. 'How are we going to get it down?'

'I don't think that would be a good idea,' said Prokopy.

Alisa glanced at him. 'Why not?'

'It was put there for a reason. You shouldn't disturb it. There may be consequences if you do.'

Viktor could tell she was about to ask him what consequences, but evidently she decided she wouldn't get any response worth hearing.

'I agree with Prokopy,' said Konstantinov. 'It's clearly frozen solid anyway, and there's no way to thaw it, not out here. We should be content with photographs, for now at least.' He looked up again at the bear's remains. 'Poor creature. What could have happened to it?'

'I'll tell you what I think,' said Veronika, still taking pictures.

Viktor glanced at her. 'What?'

'I know it sounds crazy to say it, but I think Dyatlov and the others got off lightly.'

———

No one felt like eating breakfast, so they climbed into the SUV and headed for the coordinates of Zone 3 Station. Alisa was sitting up front with Konstantinov again. She never asked anyone else if they'd like to take the front seat; Viktor supposed she took it as her due, since she was a veteran of a previous expedition to Dyatlov Pass.

It was slow going at times: in many places the trees stood too close together to allow the car an easy passage, and Konstantinov had to make constant minor detours through areas where they were distributed a little more sparsely. Occasionally, Prokopy would lean forward and say: 'Not that way,' and Vadim would glance at him in the rear-view mirror and swing the steering wheel round without hesitation to take them in a different direction.

When Vadim did this for the third time, Veronika asked the shaman how he knew which places to avoid.

'I have been here before,' he replied.

'I thought this place was forbidden to your people,' she said.

'It was not in physical form that I came. I directed my spirit here, as part of my initiation.'

'The test you underwent to become a shaman?' said Vadim.

'Yes.'

'What happened?' asked Nika. 'What did you see?'

'It is not good to tell others of such things. Forgive me, but that is all I can say.'

'Of course,' said Nika. 'I understand.'

'I've been thinking about the bear,' said Alisa, as if she hadn't even been listening to Prokopy.

'And...?' said Konstantinov.

'The way it was ... *stretched* ... there's only one known force that could conceivably damage something in that way.'

'What's that?' asked Viktor.

'Gravity.'

'*Gravity?*'

'A vast differential in gravitational tidal forces existing within a very small volume. It's the only thing I can think of that might account for the condition of the carcass's hind quarters.'

'I don't understand,' said Veronika. 'How could gravity do that?'

Alisa hesitated before answering, and when she did, Viktor noticed that her self-confident demeanour had slipped a little, as if she couldn't quite bring herself to believe what she was saying. 'It can do that if it's strong enough ... but there's only one place in the universe where it *is* strong enough ... inside the event horizon of a black hole.'

No one said anything for several moments.

Then Nika said: 'A black hole?'

'I know it sounds insane...'

'That's putting it mildly.'

'But there's nothing else I can think of to account for that ... that catastrophic stretching and compression. Shit, I wish I could get that carcass to a lab right now ... examine it properly.'

'Excuse me, Alisa,' said Konstantinov, 'but are you saying that there might be a black hole here on Earth ... *in this forest?*'

She sighed and ran a hand through her hair. 'No, I'm not saying that. That's impossible: if there were such an object here, we'd know about it, believe me. In fact, it would already have plunged to the centre of the

Earth due to its colossal mass. There's no way it could remain on the surface. And yet...'

'And yet?'

'What appears to have happened to the bear is exactly what would happen to an object passing through a black hole's event horizon.'

'What exactly *is* an event horizon?' asked Nika.

'It's the spherical boundary around a black hole's central singularity, which is the point at which spacetime becomes infinitely curved. The event horizon is the boundary inside which nothing – not even light – can escape the singularity's gravitational pull. You can't see anything inside an event horizon, hence the name. But if an object were to traverse the horizon, the differential between the gravitational forces acting on each end of the object would stretch it into a long filament – physicists sometimes call the process "spaghettification" – which would ultimately break down into its component atoms as it fell into the singularity.'

They all remained quiet as they took this in and considered it.

Presently, Konstantinov said: 'All right, Alisa, let's say you're right, and something like that really did happen to that poor creature. What could account for it? You've already said that it can't be an actual black hole, although the effect appears to be comparable. So ... what was it?'

'An anomaly of some kind: a highly localised region of intense gravity – that's my best guess, without properly examining the carcass.'

Viktor thought of what had happened to Ludmila Dubinina, Alexander Zolotarev and Nikolai Thibeaux-Brignollel. 'Could something like that have killed the members of the Dyatlov group who didn't die from hypothermia?'

'I don't think so,' Alisa replied. 'Their injuries were nowhere near severe enough. Something else killed them. But it's clear that Dyatlov and the others found something similar to what we've just seen.'

'You're thinking of the photograph – the one showing them with the animal's carcass.'

She nodded. 'It's obvious that the phenomenon was present in the forest in 1959.'

'And how could such a phenomenon occur?'

'Not naturally, Vadim,' she replied.

'A product of intelligence?'

'Most likely.'

'Hostile?'

'I doubt it.'

'Why?'

She looked across at him, and offered her mirthless smile. 'Because the human race is still here.'

BASKOV (10)

I had to marvel at the resolve of Strugatsky and the others to remain in the forest after what they had seen. Some might consider their actions reckless and foolhardy, and I must admit that the thought crossed my mind, too. I honestly don't believe that I would have stayed there a moment longer after finding the remains of the bear. But the 'Konstantinov Expedition' pressed on in spite of the obvious dangers lurking in the forest. Reckless they may have been; but they were undoubtedly brave as well.

It may be apparent to the reader that by now I had begun to pass beyond my initial scepticism regarding Strugatsky's claims. I may also be considered foolish and credulous for doing so, for beginning to accept at face value the testimony of a man whose mental state I was, after all, attempting to evaluate. Nevertheless, I believe I was justified in doing so.

The photographs taken by the Dyatlov party in 1959 alone implied that something extremely unusual existed in the forest around Kholat Syakhl; and when one added to this the other documents in the Lishin dossier, the similarities between the sounds heard in Yurta Anyamova and other mysterious humming noises heard elsewhere in the world, and the exposure of three of Komar's men to an unknown form of radiation, the case for Strugatsky's truthfulness was only strengthened.

That this reinforcement of his testimony obliged me to consider accepting that the stars had somehow changed their orientation on that first night in the forest, and that a bear had somehow been exposed to a localised field of colossal gravitational force, was of course extremely problematical to me. There were no mechanisms by which these events could have occurred – at least, none that are currently known to science.

When I considered this, I confess that I felt a sudden, profound unease sweeping down upon me. We often think of the universe as existing *out there*, apart from the world and the concerns of humanity, and that the mysteries it contains are separated from us by unimaginable distances. But now I wondered if that were really true. Our Earth is *in the very midst of the universe*, and who is to say that those mysteries do not apply to *this* world as well as those drifting through the ultimate depths of space?

It was then that I began to worry about the kind of report I would be obliged write for the criminal militia. They were waiting for my advice on whether to bring a prosecution against Strugatsky, and I wondered what they would think if I concluded that not only was he mentally fit to stand trial for murder, but that I also believed him to be innocent. Of course, it wasn't my job to decide on the question of his culpability in the disappearance of his companions, but such a conclusion would be obvious if I stated that he was in full possession of his faculties, *and* he was telling the truth about what happened to the Konstantinov Expedition during their time in the forest.

I regret to say that at that time I was more concerned with the damage this could potentially do to my reputation than anything else. For one thing, my report would go to Dr Pletner, the Director of Peveralsk, as well as to the militia, and I couldn't imagine that he would read it with much sympathy...

Such were the thoughts chasing each other through my mind following my tenth session with Strugatsky, when Mrs Holender knocked on my door and announced that Senior Investigator Komar was here to see me. I asked her to show him in.

Komar strode through the door and closed it behind him, right in Mrs Holender's face. He looked terrible, as if he'd been up all night and had neither shaved nor changed his clothes.

'Investigator...' I began, but he waved me to silence and shook his head vigorously. Then he took a small electrical device from his coat pocket and proceeded to wave it over every object in the room.

After a couple of minutes, evidently satisfied, he returned the device to his pocket and sat down heavily in the chair in front of my desk.

'What's going on?' I asked.

'I've just swept the room for bugs. It's clean. We can talk here.'

'Bugs? What on earth are you talking about? What's wrong? I waited for you this morning, but...'

'I know, Doctor. Something came up.'

'Serious, obviously.'

'You might say that. Eduard Lishin is missing.'

'*Missing?* What ... how do you know?'

'His landlady reported it. She lives in the same building as Lishin. They play chess once a week, on Friday, and when she went up to his apartment on that day, there was no answer. She assumed he was otherwise engaged, and thought no more about it. But he didn't answer his door the following week either, and the week after that, his rent became due, and he didn't pay it. His landlady says he's never late with his rent, and so she became concerned that something might have happened to him. She let herself into his apartment with her key. There was no trace of him, so she reported it to the militia. She's quite adamant that his disappearance is totally out of character for him, and I believe her.'

'Do you have any idea what's happened to him?' I asked.

'I have a hunch, Doctor; and my hunch is that Lishin's former employers got wind of what he did.'

'You mean leaking the documents to Strugatsky and Konstantinov and ... and giving them access to the antiprism.'

'Which he apparently stole from them in the first place.'

'My God, you're right, of course! In order to have access to such an artefact, Lishin *must* have been a member of Project Svarog. If they are responsible for his disappearance, where do you think they've taken him?'

'I have no idea, and to be honest with you, I don't particularly want to know. But you can be sure they'll have sweated all the details out of him. That's why I've just swept your office. We can't take any chances.'

I felt a cold dread take hold of me, and yet I also felt a strange sense of inevitability, as if it could only ever have been a matter of time before the people in charge of Project Svarog uncovered Lishin's plan to release information on the Dyatlov Pass incident, and moved against him. Perhaps they had already suspected him, and had waited until his own actions condemned him.

And then I thought of Strugatsky, and myself, and Nataliya, and I broke into a cold sweat.

'Where does this leave us?' I asked. 'Should I expect a visit from Svarog? Here? At my home?'

'I doubt it. Viktor Strugatsky isn't some old man living alone; he's in the custody of the Peveralsk Psychiatric Hospital, at the request of the criminal militia. Of course, that doesn't put him beyond their reach, but it does make things more complicated for them. They won't want to move against the hospital, since that *would* raise too many questions. It's my guess that they'll now wait to see how this all plays out, *then* they'll decide what to do.'

'Somehow, Investigator, that doesn't reassure me,' I said.

'In that case, you won't like what I'm going to say next. Lishin must have been abducted very soon after he passed the dossier to Strugatsky. I'm willing to bet that his interrogation began almost immediately. Now, I suspect that he managed to hold out for a while – which is why Strugatsky and the others managed to embark on their little expedition to Kholat Syakhl without being apprehended also. But I'm also willing to bet that he couldn't have held out for long; he *must* have folded at some point...'

'At which he told them everything,' I completed. 'You're suggesting that Project Svarog knew that Strugatsky and the others were in the Northern Urals, and what they were doing there.'

'That's what I'm suggesting, Doctor,' Komar said. 'And how likely do you think it is that Project Svarog would have allowed them to go about their business in that forest?'

'Not very,' I conceded.

'I think there's something Strugatsky isn't telling us.'

'Or something he hasn't told us *yet*,' I said.

At that moment, Komar's cell phone rang. He answered it, and as he listened, a frown crept across his brow. 'Yes, sir,' he said. 'I'll be right there.' He broke the connection and, in response to my expression of curiosity, said: 'That was my boss.'

'Prosecutor Glazov?'

He nodded. 'He wants to see me right away.'

'What about?'

'He didn't say. But I didn't like the tone of his voice. When is your next session with Strugatsky?'

'Two o'clock this afternoon.'

'All right. I'll try and get back here by then.'

'And if you're not?'

'Go ahead without me. You can fill me in afterwards.'

After Komar left, I remained seated at my desk, thinking about Eduard Lishin and his probable fate. Now that I considered it, it stood to reason that he had been intimately involved with Project Svarog. How else could he possibly have gained access to the antiprism? When had he stolen it and placed it in that bank vault? I wondered. And what of Beloretsk-15, where it had originally been taken? The settlement's name meant that it was in Bashkortostan in the Southern Urals, but I didn't know where it was precisely. Evidently, it was one of the many classified cities that existed, and still exist, across the country. There was a lot of information on such places in the public domain, so I turned to my computer and ran an internet search for it.

Even after all I had learned so far in my investigation of Viktor Strugatsky and the Dyatlov Pass incident, I was not prepared for what I found.

The city of Mezhgorye, which was formerly the twin secret cities of Beloretsk-15 and Beloretsk-16, is located in the Beloretsk region of Bashkortostan in the Southern Urals, and is one of the oldest mining and metallurgical centres in the region.

On 16 April 1996, the *New York Times* reported that something strange was happening beneath Yamantau Mountain to the southwest of Mezhgorye:

> In a secret project reminiscent of the chilliest days of the Cold War, Russia is building a mammoth underground military complex in the Ural Mountains, Western officials and Russian witnesses say.
>
> Hidden inside Yamantau Mountain in the Beloretsk area of the Southern Urals, the project involved the creation of a huge complex, served by a railroad, a highway, and thousands of workers.

Yamantau Mountain is 500km south-south-west of Yekaterinburg and 1,500km east-south-east of Moscow. Its name means 'Evil Mountain' in the Bashkir language. According to the articles I found, the complex beneath Yamantau is truly vast, covering an area of some 400 square miles; it is, quite literally, an underground city, capable of supporting a population in excess of 60,000 with adequate food and water for a period of several months. Satellite photographs of the mountain show that construction work on the complex's above-ground support areas is still continuing.

Needless to say, the Americans are rather perplexed at this, and have requested an explanation for the presence of the Mount Yamantau complex; Russia has responded by offering several different explanations, including that it is a mining site, a repository for artistic treasures, a food storage area and a bunker to ensure continuity of government in the event of nuclear war or some other catastrophe.

In the archives of the *Washington Post*, I found an article by Bruce G Blair, originally published on 25 May 2003, which stated that:

the Yamantau and Kosvinsky mountains in the central and southern Urals ... were huge construction projects begun in the late 1970s, when US nuclear firepower took special aim at the Communist Party's leadership complex. Fearing a decapitating strike, the Soviets sent tens of thousands of workers to these remote sites, where US spy satellites spotted them still toiling away in the late 1990s. Yamantau is expected to be operating soon. According to diagrams and notes given to [Blair] in the late 1990s by SAC [Strategic Air Command] senior officers, the Yamantau command center is inside a rock quartz mountain, about 3,000 feet straight down from the summit. It is a wartime relocation facility for the top Russian political leadership. It is more a shelter than a command post, because the facility's communications links are relatively fragile. As it turned out, the quartz interferes with radio signals broadcast from inside the mountain. Therefore the main communications links are either cable or radio transmitters that broadcast from outside the center.

A little further investigation led me to an article by journalist Ron Rosenbaum. According to this article, entitled 'The Return of the Doomsday Machine?', Bruce G Blair is a former ICBM launch control officer and an expert on Russian weaponry, who is now head of the World Security Institute, a liberal think-tank based in Washington DC. In 1993, Blair revealed that the Soviet leadership had authorised the construction of an automated communication network in the early 1980s, which would be able to withstand a direct nuclear attack. This network was controlled by a sophisticated computer system, codenamed *Perimetr*, which, Rosenbaum notes, bears a striking resemblance to the 'doomsday machine' in Stanley Kubrick's satirical masterpiece *Dr Strangelove*.

The terrifying premise of *Dr Strangelove* is that the Soviet Union has secretly placed 50 cobalt-jacketed hydrogen bombs at various locations throughout the world, which will be automatically detonated should the system's sensors detect a pre-emptive nuclear attack on the nation. Once the system is in operation, no one can stop it, and when a nuclear-armed B-52 bomber makes an unauthorised attack on a Soviet missile launch facility, the doomsday machine detonates the bombs. The resulting cobalt fallout ends all human life on the planet.

According to Rosenbaum, Blair and others, including nuclear-age historian P D Smith of University College London, the Russian *Perimetr* system is a real-life counterpart of the doomsday machine in Kubrick's film, a so-called 'dead-hand' system which, if it senses a nuclear explosion in Russian territory and then receives no communication from Moscow, will assume that the leadership is either dead or incapacitated, and will then grant a single human being the authority and ability to launch the entire Russian nuclear arsenal. That person will most likely be stationed in the command complex within Mount Kosvinsky.

In response to questions from the journal *Aviation Week & Space Technology*, a Pentagon spokesman stated that Washington still doesn't know exactly what is going on beneath Mount Yamantau, adding that: 'the Russians have offered nonspecific reassurances that it poses no threat to the US'. Nevertheless, the facility has been built to withstand half a dozen direct nuclear hits.

I found further evidence of how seriously the US government takes the existence of the Yamantau complex in an online copy of the Congressional Record for 19 June 1997. Under the heading *PROVIDING FOR CONSIDERATION OF H.R. 1119, NATIONAL DEFENSE AUTHORIZATION ACT FOR FISCAL YEAR 1998 (House of Representatives - June 19, 1997)*, the record reads in part:

SEC.___. SENSE OF CONGRESS ON NEED FOR RUSSIAN OPENNESS ON THE YAMANTAU MOUNTAIN PROJECT.

(a) Findings.--Congress finds as follows:

(1) The United States and Russia have been working in the post-Cold War era to establish a new strategic relationship based on cooperation and openness between the two nations.

(2) This effort to establish a new strategic relationship has resulted in the conclusion or agreement in principle on a number of far-reaching agreements, including START I, II, and III, a revision in the Conventional Forces in Europe Treaty, and a series of other agreements (such as the Comprehensive Test Ban Treaty and the Chemical Weapons Convention), designed to further reduce bilateral threats and limit the proliferation of weapons of mass destruction.

(3) These far-reaching agreements were based on the understanding between the United States and Russia that there would be a good faith effort on both sides to comply with the letter and spirit of the agreements, that both sides would end their Cold War competition, and that neither side would seek to gain unilateral strategic advantage over the other.

(4) Reports indicate that Russia has been pursuing construction of a massive underground facility of unknown purpose at Yamantau Mountain and the city of Mezhgorye (formerly the settlements of Beloretsk-15 and Beloretsk-16) that is designed to survive a nuclear war and appears to exceed reasonable defense requirements.

(5) The Yamantau Mountain project does not appear to be consistent with the lowering of strategic threats, openness, and cooperation that is the basis of the post-Cold War strategic partnership between the United States and Russia.

(6) Russia appears to have engaged in a campaign to deliberately conceal and mislead the United States about the purpose of the Yamantau Mountain project...

It was then that I came upon a website which expressed a possibility that had gradually been growing in my mind as I scanned page after page dealing with Yamantau Mountain. The website asked a straightforward question: what if the secret underground city was *not* intended as a refuge for the Russian government in the event of nuclear war?

What if it was intended as a refuge against something else?

The website suggested three alternatives: one, impending environmental collapse; two, an approaching asteroid or comet that would cause catastrophic damage to the planet; and three, another, unspecified threat from deep space...

I sat back in my chair and ran a shaking hand through my hair. *An unspecified threat from deep space*, I thought. *My God...*

Those who knew about Yamantau Mountain suspected that it was part of Russia's plan to survive a possible nuclear war, accidental or otherwise. It seemed that even at the highest levels of the United States government, the assumption was that the vast underground complex was intended to ensure the continuity of the Russian government in the event of such a catastrophe.

Taken in isolation, that seemed a reasonable enough assumption; but placed within the context of the Dyatlov Pass incident, Project Svarog, the Konstantinov Expedition and the theories of Dr Valerey Uvarov ... the evidence seemed to point in another direction entirely.

The evidence seemed to indicate that the Russian government was afraid, *terribly* afraid – but not of America or any other nation on Earth. They had spent the last three decades preparing for something.

Something the rest of the world didn't know about.

———

When Komar returned a couple of hours later, I told him what I had learned about Beloretsk and Yamantau Mountain. I could see that he was distracted; in fact, I had the impression that my words were barely registering with him. I asked him if anything was wrong.

'I've been ordered by Prosecutor Glazov to drop the case,' he replied tonelessly.

'*What?* Drop the case? Why?'

'It wasn't Glazov's decision. The order came from higher up the chain of command, Doctor – *much* higher. It would be an understatement to say he was angry, but it looks like his hands are tied. He told me the Konstantinov case has been transferred to another department of government...'

'The FSB?'

'Officially, maybe ... but I think we can both guess who's really taking over.'

'Project Svarog.'

'Precisely.'

'And the men you've got searching the forest?'

'They're to be pulled out and reassigned immediately.'

'What about Strugatsky?'

Komar sighed and looked at me with a pained expression. 'He's to be released from Peveralsk. All potential charges are to be dropped. Your Dr Pletner is going to be contacted shortly.'

'Good God. Strugatsky was right.'

'Right? About what?'

'In one of our previous sessions, he said that if your men found what they were looking for, he'd be out of here within the hour, and would then probably suffer a "tragic accident", as he put it. Well, your men *haven't* found what they're looking for, and it looks like they're not going to. But Strugatsky *is* going to be out of here very soon.'

Komar nodded. 'We're clearly thinking along the same lines, Doctor. Strugatsky knows more than he should, and has apparently seen more than he should have, as well. Lishin must have folded under interrogation and spilled everything to Project Svarog. And they're not going to let Strugatsky walk around as if nothing happened.'

'Can you place him under militia protection?'

'Unlikely.'

'But surely you can go to Prosecutor Glazov and tell him that Strugatsky is in danger.'

'He'll want to know why.'

'Then for God's sake tell him!' I cried.

'And do you think he'll believe me?' Komar said angrily. 'I'll probably end up in Strugatsky's room, getting my head shrunk by you people!'

'I'll back you up.'

Komar laughed harshly. 'You? You'll be out of a job if you do that. Or maybe worse.'

'We can't do this, Investigator,' I said forcefully. 'We can't just cut Strugatsky loose and leave him to the wolves.'

'Do you think I like this any more than you do? We have no choice!'

'Then let's get him out now. Right now! Don't wait for the release order to come through. We'll take him to a safe place...'

'Even if there were such a thing as a "safe place", Doctor, they almost certainly have Peveralsk under surveillance. How far do you think we'd get?'

He was right, of course: we'd be apprehended the moment we left the hospital's grounds. I looked at him helplessly. 'Then what can we do?'

Komar regarded me in silence for some moments. Then he said: 'I want to get the rest of Strugatsky's story. I want to know everything else that happened to them in that forest. I want all the facts relating to the disappearance of Konstantinov and the others, *all the facts.*'

'Do we have time for that?'

'Transferring an investigation between government departments and ordering the release of a psychiatric patient can't be done instantly. They'll want to do this by the book, and that means red tape. I think we have time to get the rest of Strugatsky's story. And then...'

'Then?'

Komar sighed. 'I'll make a decision on what should be done.'

———

Strugatsky took one look at our faces as we entered his room and said: 'Well, well ... I guess a lot has happened since we last spoke. Good to see you again, Investigator.'

As Komar and I sat down, I said: 'Viktor, we need to begin this session without delay, and you must tell us everything else that happened while you were at Kholat Syakhl.'

'Why?'

'Never mind *why*,' said Komar. 'Just tell us.'

'Something *has* happened, hasn't it?' Strugatsky said.

I leaned towards him. 'Viktor, it looks like you're going to be released soon.'

He regarded me in silence, and then whispered: 'Oh, shit.'

'The Konstantinov case is being taken out of Investigator Komar's hands, and my own evaluation of your mental state is to cease.'

'Eduard Lishin has gone missing,' said Komar. 'My belief is that he was apprehended by Svarog soon after he passed the documents to you, and that he eventually succumbed to whatever interrogation techniques were brought to bear upon him. He must have told them everything.'

Strugatsky sighed. 'Then it *was* them in the forest. They're the ones who found us. I can't blame Lishin for telling them. God knows what they did to him.'

Komar and I glanced at each other.

'What are you talking about, Viktor?' said Komar.

Strugatsky sat back in his armchair and heaved a great sigh. 'You want to know everything else that happened in the forest. All right. This is what happened.'

SIXTEEN

Alisa believed that whatever had killed the bear was not hostile, since the human race is still here; but Viktor wasn't so sure, and said as much.

'What are you basing that on?' she asked.

'The bear may not have been killed in exactly the same way as the Dyatlov group, but they're all still dead – and who knows how many other animals are out here, mangled by some unknown force? The forest could be littered with them.'

'I doubt that.'

'Why? How do you know?'

'You may both be right,' said Veronika. 'Whatever it is, it could be dangerous without *intending* to be: it might simply be so *different* that no life as we know it can survive being close to it.'

Alisa glanced over her shoulder. 'Veronika has a point.'

'So where does that leave us?' asked Viktor.

'In Prokopy's capable hands,' replied Konstantinov, with a meaningful glance at Alisa.

'You can rely on mysticism if you like, Vadim,' she replied. 'I'll rely on science. Anything generating that much power will announce its presence in no uncertain terms, through an intense electromagnetic field which we'll be able to detect with the equipment I've brought along – and also by making a hell of a lot of noise.'

'Noise?' Viktor said. 'Like the sound we heard in the village?'

'Exactly. And we'll also hear its effect on the environment: the shattering of wood as it passes amongst the trees, for instance. It may even leave a trail that we can follow...'

'Assuming we want to follow it.'

'Interesting,' said Konstantinov. 'But I don't recall seeing any shattered trees back there, where we found the bear carcass.'

'True,' conceded Alisa. 'It really does look like the animal was dropped there from a great height. But the phenomenon had to have been on the ground at some point, to touch the bear.'

'What's that?' said Veronika suddenly.

Konstantinov immediately brought the car to a halt. 'What?'

She pointed through the left hand window. 'There's something down there, in that hollow amongst the trees.' Viktor was sitting next to her, between her and Prokopy, and he felt her body stiffen as she repeated: 'There's something down there.'

He leaned across her and peered out of the window, through the frozen ranks of trees, into the distance. About a hundred metres away and maybe five metres below them, he could see a circular shape, pale, almost silvery-grey in colour and perfectly flat. It was lying in a clearing at the bottom of the depression, which was like a shallow, inverted cone, quite regular and symmetrical in shape.

Konstantinov looked at it, consulted his map, then the GPS display on the car's dashboard, and shook his head. 'If I didn't know better, I'd say that we've found the mercury lake. Although it's not where it's supposed to be.'

'Maybe there's more than one,' Viktor suggested.

'There must be...' he agreed.

Before anyone could say anything else, Alisa opened her door and got out of the car.

'What the hell are you doing?' shouted Viktor.

'What we came here to do,' she called back as she opened the tailgate and took out a large black canvas bag.

Konstantinov glanced at the shaman. 'Prokopy?'

'Let her go,' he replied.

'It's safe?'

'Let her go.'

That didn't sound like much of a confirmation, so Viktor reached across and opened Veronika's door. She jumped out and he followed.

Alisa shut the tailgate and slung the bag over her shoulder. 'Got your camera?' she said to Veronika, who nodded. 'Then let's go.'

Vadim and Prokopy got out of the car, and together they moved off through the trees and over the edge of the shallow depression in the ground, stopping every twenty metres or so while Nika took a picture of the lake (or whatever it was) at the centre of the clearing.

When they got to within ten metres of its edge, Alisa opened her bag and took out a small box, the top of which was studded with several knobs and a meter, and which was attached by a thin cord to something that looked like a shower head.

'What's that?' Viktor asked.

'It's a Geiger-Mueller probe. It detects alpha and beta emitters.'

'You think there might be radiation?'

She didn't answer, but when she continued towards the centre of the clearing, she did so more slowly.

The 'lake' was perhaps fifteen metres in diameter, and was perfectly circular. Its surface was so flat and calm that Viktor wondered whether it was actually frozen, and they were after all looking at nothing more sinister than a body of ordinary water – albeit one whose topography was unsettlingly regular.

'It looks almost like an impact crater,' Konstantinov observed in a hushed voice.

'But what did the impacting?' asked Veronika, pointing to the lake. 'That?'

No one said anything. They continued their approach, the crunch of their footfalls in the snow the only sound to break the primordial silence of the surrounding forest. Alisa swept the detector slowly back and forth in front of her, watching the needle of the meter as she did so. It remained resolutely and mercifully still. Evidently satisfied, she stopped and put the Geiger-Mueller probe back in her bag, and took out another instrument.

'Multi-channel analyzer,' she said before Viktor could ask her what it was.

'Oh. And what does that do?'

'It automatically identifies and displays various types of radioactive materials – if any are present, that is. Very useful when dealing with unknown sources of radiation.'

'So you still think there might be radiation here?'

'I don't know, but I'm thinking of the condition Dyatlov and the others were found in. I just want to be sure.'

Her mention of Dyatlov reminded Viktor of the photographs in Lishin's dossier – in particular, the one showing Rustem Slobodin running away from what Project Svarog had termed the mercury lake. He recalled the look of abject horror and panic on the man's face, that grimace of uncontrollable terror, and he shuddered.

Alisa glanced at him and smirked. 'Cold, isn't it?'

'I'm not thinking of the cold. I'm thinking of Slobodin's reaction when he got too close to something like this.'

Viktor looked at Prokopy, wondering whether he thought this was a good idea or not. His expression gave no clue: his face was completely impassive, his eyes locked on the surface of the lake. Viktor told himself that his silence was all that was required – that and the fact that he was still there and not running away. *It's okay*, Viktor thought. *If he's still here, we're okay ... but if he turns around, I'm damn well turning around too.*

Almost without realising it, he had begun to defer to the shaman's authority, watching *him* for signs of danger rather than Alisa's gadgets. The feeling had come upon him that science would not help them as much as this old man's knowledge of a world that was his more than theirs – even if his people had shunned it for centuries.

They drew up to the edge of the lake, and as Viktor looked down at it, the thought that it might simply have been ice was wiped instantly from his mind. This was not made of water, frozen or otherwise.

This was something else.

Whoever had called it the mercury lake had named it well: its surface had a bright, metallic, almost mirror-like sheen; and yet, strangely and unaccountably, there was little sense of solidity. Somehow, Viktor had the impression that if he even breathed on it, it would ripple like water. The snow-capped tops of the surrounding trees and the mottled grey clouds in the sky were reflected without distortion on its perfectly still surface. And as they slowly and cautiously drew up to its edge and looked down, they saw their own reflections looking back at them.

'It *does* look like it's made of mercury,' said Konstantinov.

'Is it liquid or solid?' asked Veronika as she clutched Viktor's arm tightly. Her camera was hanging by its strap on her shoulder; she seemed to have forgotten all about it.

'It looks ... like it's *both*,' he replied.

'There's a way we can find out,' said Alisa. She bent down and picked up a handful of snow from the ground.

'What are you doing?' Viktor asked, although he already knew the answer, and didn't particularly like it.

'She's going to throw some snow into the lake,' said Prokopy, his voice quite calm and uninflected. 'And it will be a mistake.'

Konstantinov glanced sharply at him. 'Why?'

'Because the lake is asleep ... and if you throw anything into it, you will wake it up.'

Alisa looked at him as she hefted the small lump of snow in her hands. Her lips were curled in a slight grin, whether of amusement or contempt it wasn't clear – perhaps it was both. 'More fairy stories, Prokopy? What happens if I do wake it up? Will Baba Yaga come out of it, in her hut with chicken's feet?'

The shaman returned her grin. 'Perhaps not. May I ask a favour?'

'What's that?'

'Allow the rest of us to return to the car and get a little way into the forest before you throw that handful of snow. I promise we'll wait for you.' Prokopy's eyes never left Alisa's as he said this, nor did he blink. He simply stood there, smiling at her. 'Will you do us that favour, Alisa?'

She looked at the lump of snow, which she had stopped hefting and now held still, as though it were a hand grenade and she had just pulled out the pin. 'You're messing with my head, old man,' she said.

'Why would I do that?' Prokopy asked, still holding her in his unblinking gaze. 'Tell me ... what would be the point?'

As he looked at Alisa's face, Viktor could tell exactly what was going through her mind. She desperately wanted to throw that handful of snow; to test the physical consistency of the lake, to defy the shaman's authority, an authority which she refused to recognise, to prove that she was not afraid of this place or the things it contained, that she could force it to give up its secrets. She wanted to do all of these things, and knew that they could all be accomplished with a simple flick of her wrist.

She looked at the shaman again.

'All I'm asking,' he said, 'is that you give us a couple of minutes to get clear.'

'I thought you said you were here to protect us,' she said.

'I offer you my protection. It's up to you whether you accept it.'

Alisa looked at Viktor, and he could see the uncertainty in her eyes ... and anger that she *was* uncertain.

He turned to Prokopy. 'What happens if we disturb the lake?'

'You will wake it up.'

'Yeah, you said that. But *what happens* if we wake it up?'

'Difficult to say.'

'Will Alisa die if she throws that snow?'

'Difficult to say.'

'Old man,' said Alisa, and there was an ugly snarl in her voice, 'you're talking shit!'

Prokopy looked at the surface of the lake, and frowned, as if something had just occurred to him. 'Alisa, I'm going to show you something that will prove I'm not just a foolish old man who believes stupid things. Will the rest of you please take a few steps away from the edge of the lake?'

Viktor looked at Konstantinov, and saw fear in his eyes: he knew he didn't want Alisa to throw the snow, and was hoping that Prokopy would be able to dissuade her. Of course, one of them could have made a grab for it, but there was no guarantee that she wouldn't have flung it before they reached her, just to make her point.

'Nika, Viktor,' Konstantinov said as he walked a few paces away from the lake's edge. They followed, and together the three of them looked back at Alisa and Prokopy.

The shaman said to her: 'Look into the lake, Alisa.'

She did so.

'What do you see?' he asked in that calm, uninflected voice.

Viktor was totally unprepared for what happened next.

Alisa cried out, dropped the lump of snow, turned and ran from the edge of the lake. So desperate was she to get away that she shrugged off the bulky canvas bag she had been carrying over her shoulder and let it fall to the ground. She didn't even glance at it as she ran up the gradual slope of the clearing towards the car.

'What the hell...?' Viktor began, as Prokopy joined them.

'We should leave now,' he said. 'It seems that our presence alone was enough to awaken it.'

Konstantinov picked up Alisa's bag and said: 'All right, let's go.'

'Quickly,' said Prokopy. 'Please, quickly.'

'What did she see?' Viktor asked as they hurried up the slope. Alisa was already in the car; he could see her sitting there, bolt upright, staring straight ahead. 'What did you show her?'

'Something I noticed before I asked you to step away. I did so to make it absolutely clear to her, so that there wouldn't be the slightest doubt in her mind.'

They had reached the car. They clambered in and Konstantinov started the engine.

Nika leaned forward and touched Alisa's shoulder. Alisa recoiled as if she had been hit with a cattle prod.

'Christ, take it easy!' said Nika. 'What did you see?'

Alisa turned around in her seat to face them. In a tremulous voice, she replied: 'I saw our reflections. All of us, looking up at me, even after the rest of you had left the lake's edge ... you were still standing there ... reflected ... *you were still standing there!*'

At that moment, something in Alisa's bag started bleeping loudly. She grabbed the bag, thrust her hand into it and withdrew another detector. There was a red light flashing on it, and the digital display appeared to be going crazy.

'What is it?' asked Vadim as he threw the car into gear.

'EM detector,' said Alisa. 'There's a very powerful electromagnetic field ... looks like it's originating in the lake. Christ, Vadim, get us out of here!'

Veronika suddenly grabbed Viktor's arm. 'Oh God, look ... *look!*' She pointed through the window at the lake.

He turned and saw the metallic substance rising into a tall, slender pinnacle, as though it were a sheet of rubber which was being stretched by some sharp object rising from below.

What Alisa said next made him realise that that analogy was completely, horribly wrong. 'There must be something above it ... something drawing it upwards ... something generating incredible gravitational force!'

At that moment, they were nearly deafened by a horrific torrent of sound that flew out from the lake and jostled the big SUV as if it were a toy – a grinding, metallic sound like that of two battleships colliding with each other right above their heads.

Vadim floored the accelerator and Viktor felt the wheels spin on the snow beneath them. The car barely moved.

'Not that way!' he shouted above the cacophony. 'You'll dig us in!'

'I know,' he said. 'I wasn't thinking.' He shifted to a lower gear ratio and gently nudged the pedal. The car jerked forward a little way, but then slid back to its previous position. 'I ... think I've already dug us in.'

'Try again,' Viktor said, looking over his shoulder at the lake. The silver pinnacle was still there; it must have been about fifty metres tall, looking like some distant skyscraper in an alien city. He still couldn't see what was causing it, but he was more than ready to go with Alisa's guess.

Vadim tried again, and again they lurched forward a few centimetres before slumping back into the four depressions their initial wheelspin had created. 'It's no use!' he cried. 'We should leave the car and get away on foot.'

Alisa shook her head furiously. 'We won't stand a chance if we do that!'

'We'll stand more chance than if we...' Vadim's voice faltered into appalled silence as he glanced through the side window at the lake.

The quicksilver pinnacle was leaning towards them, as if it were the sense organ of some submerged leviathan searching for prey.

'Why's it doing that?' Veronika cried. '*What's it doing?*'

'It's the gravity source,' Alisa shouted back. 'It's coming this way, bringing the lake-substance with it.'

Vadim gunned the engine again, but even with the low gear ratio it was no use. They weren't going anywhere. He looked back at Viktor with panic in his eyes. 'We can't stay here. We *have* to leave the car behind and take our chances on foot.'

Viktor turned away from him to look at the approaching spire of glinting silver. As he did so, he caught a glimpse of something behind the rear seats, nestling amongst the supplies they had brought.

It was one of the spare blankets.

'Shit,' he said, more to himself than to the others. 'I think I know a way out of this.' Reaching over the seats, he grabbed the blanket and opened his door.

'What are you doing?' shrieked Alisa when she saw him jump out of the car.

There was no time to answer her. He ran around to the front of the car, staggering beneath the onslaught of sound. He had never heard anything as loud in his life, not even the roar of jet fighter engines when his parents took him to an air show when he was a kid. He wanted to clap his hands to his ears, although he knew that it wouldn't do any good. This sound filled the world; it *was* the world. It blasted its way right into Viktor's head, and he could feel his lower jaw vibrating in its socket. He had a sudden vision of his brain turning to superheated steam and blowing his skull apart.

His vision began to blur, and he thought he might faint; but somehow he managed to get to the front of the car. He caught a glimpse of three terror-stricken faces staring back at him through the windscreen. Yes, three … for Prokopy did *not* look terrified. His face was … serene … resigned. He seemed quite prepared for whatever was going to happen next.

Viktor thought of the bear carcass, with its bizarrely stretched and compressed hindquarters; he thought of the same thing happening to Nika, to Alisa, to Vadim and Prokopy … to him … and he decided that he was most certainly *not* prepared.

He shook the blanket so that it was completely unfolded, and as he glanced up at the approaching pinnacle, he noticed also that the tops of the surrounding trees were bending towards it, the snow flying from them in white streaks towards the invisible source of the gravitational field.

Oh, Christ.

He dropped to his knees and tucked one edge of the blanket under the car's front wheels, then half staggered, half crawled back to the open rear door. Nika and Prokopy reached out and hauled him in, and he yanked the door shut behind him and shouted to Vadim: 'Try it now!'

He gunned the engine again, gently, ready to lift his foot off the pedal at the first sensation of spin from the wheels. But the tyres bit into the blanket, found sufficient purchase, and hauled them away.

'Into the forest!' Prokopy shouted.

Vadim floored the accelerator, and the car shot away from the clearing and into the trees. Although they quickly lost sight of the mercury lake, the sound did not abate: it remained as loud as ever, and was punctuated by splintering cracks which at first Viktor couldn't identify ... until he looked through the rear window and saw the trees behind them being ripped from the ground and pummelled to matchwood by the incomprehensible thing moving through the air above them.

Alisa glanced over her shoulder and cried: 'Faster, Vadim. If it gets above us...'

'I know!' he shouted back as he wrestled with the steering wheel, trying to keep to the less densely-packed areas of the forest.

Viktor shut his eyes tight and thought: *Dear Christ, let us get out of this! Whatever it is, please don't let it get us!*

He heard Veronika moaning, and opened his eyes and was about to grab her and hold her in his arms, when he saw that she was looking out of her window and shaking her head. 'No!' she said, over and over again. 'No! No! No!'

He saw what she was looking at ... and felt something like nausea hit him. At first, he didn't know quite what he was seeing, and then his mind shook itself free of its shock and began to process the image properly.

It was a dog, running through the trees, keeping pace with the car, perhaps ten metres away. Viktor thought it looked like a greyhound: it was long and sleek, and dark grey in colour ... but it wasn't a greyhound, not really. Its limbs were much too long – almost skeletal in their slenderness; and its snout was too elongated. It ran with vast strides that were so great he had the impression that it was moving in slow motion, while its tiny, jet-black eyes were firmly fixed on the trees ahead of it.

It was a dog ... and yet it wasn't.

Further off in the forest, he saw something else running through the trees. It looked like a large cat - a lynx, judging by the long tufts of black fur rising from the tips of its ears. Unlike the dog, there was nothing wrong with the animal's proportions: it looked exactly like a big wildcat should look ... until it turned its head towards them.

Its eyes were much too large ... and even at this distance, Viktor could tell that they were those of a human being.

Veronika screamed when she saw the lynx's eyes, and Viktor grabbed her and turned her head away and held her close. She began to sob into his chest. 'What are they?' she cried. 'What are those things?'

'I don't know,' he said. 'I don't know.'

Alisa was looking at them, too, and Vadim snatched the occasional glimpse as he continued to steer amongst the trees. Viktor was about to ask Prokopy if he knew what they were; but the shaman had suddenly sat forward, his hands gripping the headrests of the driver's and passenger's seats, and was looking through the windscreen, his expression set in an intense frown, as if he were searching for something. At that moment, Viktor had the distinct impression that it would not be a good idea to distract him.

Alisa looked out of her own window. 'There's something on this side, too!' she said.

Viktor looked where she was pointing, and saw perhaps half a dozen wild hares bounding through the forest alongside the car. Like the dog, their leaps were far too big for animals of their size.

What the fuck is happening? he thought.

And then Prokopy shouted: 'Ahead! Ahead!'

It was the first time Viktor had heard genuine panic in the shaman's voice, and as he looked through the windscreen, he saw why.

Directly ahead of them, something was protruding from the frozen ground. It was large, at least ten metres in diameter, semicircular, and concave, its interior hidden in thick shadow.

It was a Cauldron.

'Get away from it!' Prokopy shouted.

Vadim twisted the wheel to the right, and they were all thrown towards the left-hand side of the cabin as the car veered away from the object.

And then there was only the sound of the car's engine.

The sound that had been rending the air all around them had ceased as suddenly and completely as if a switch had been thrown. Vadim brought the car to a skidding halt, and sat there, gripping the wheel and panting. They all sat perfectly still, not daring to move, listening to the car's idling engine. Viktor heard ringing in his ears, but he knew that that was just a side effect of exposure to the shattering cacophony generated by whatever had been pursuing them.

'Is everyone all right?' asked Vadim presently.

'Where are the animals?' asked Veronika, ignoring him. 'Where are they? Are they still out there?'

'I can't see them,' said Alisa, craning her neck to look through all of the windows.

'You should never have been able to see them,' said Prokopy.

Viktor looked at him. 'What do you mean by that?'

'Just what I say. They are not for people like you to see.'

'People like us? You mean, people who aren't shamans?'

'That is exactly what I mean. And yet, you saw them.'

Viktor could hear the confusion in his voice. It seemed that, for the first time since they had come to the forest, he was genuinely surprised and unnerved. That was not a good sign.

'Did you see them earlier?' asked Vadim. 'I mean ... before this happened? When we first entered the forest?'

The shaman shook his head. 'It doesn't work like that. We don't see these things as a matter of course. We only see them when our spirits travel, when we enter the other world. You should not have been able to see those animals ... and neither should I, without the necessary preparations. I don't understand this ... it's very strange.'

'Yeah, it's strange all right,' said Alisa, still looking through the rear window. 'But not as strange as the fact that the thing we nearly drove into is gone. The Cauldron has disappeared.'

———

They got out of the car and looked around at the forest. There was no sign of the strange animals that had run alongside them during their flight from the mercury lake; and there was no sign of the Cauldron. Everything appeared to have returned to normal – or what passed for normal in this place.

'How could something that big have disappeared into the ground so quickly?' asked Veronika. 'I mean ... that's what they're supposed to do, isn't it? At least, according to the legends.'

'Yes,' replied Konstantinov. 'That's what they're supposed to do.'

He walked back along the tracks the car had left in the snow, to the place where they had veered sharply to the right as he span the wheel to avoid hitting the Cauldron. The others followed him, and together they looked down at the ground where the object had stood. The snow wasn't even disturbed.

'Whatever that was,' said Alisa, 'it didn't sink into the ground.'

'What happened, then?' asked Viktor.

She shrugged. 'I can speculate, if you like.'

'Be my guest.'

'Well, if I hadn't been here myself and seen it with my own eyes ... and if I hadn't seen the other things that have happened ... I would have said that it had to be an optical illusion of some kind. Of course, I don't believe that now. There's only one explanation I'm willing to consider: that thing, whatever it was, is capable of travelling instantaneously between here and ... somewhere else.'

'You're talking about teleportation,' said Veronika.

'Yeah, that's what I'm talking about – incredible, *unbelievable*, as it sounds. But there's something else, something that tells me teleportation isn't *quite* the answer.'

'What's that?'

Alisa pointed to the undisturbed snow where, just a few minutes before, the Cauldron had stood half buried in the ground. 'If it really did teleport away from here, it should have left a crescent-shaped hole ... but as you can see, there's nothing, no sign whatsoever that it was ever here. That's puzzling. Unless...'

They all looked at her, waiting for her to continue; but she simply gazed down at the ground, lost in thought.

'Unless what?' Viktor prompted impatiently.

'Unless it has to do with time. Yes ... *time*.'

He shook his head. 'I don't get it. What are you talking about?'

'I lost it back there at the lake,' she said. 'When Prokopy showed me ... I mean, it was such a shock, seeing us all reflected there, even though you three were no longer standing at the edge. Maybe Rustem Slobodin saw something like that just before that picture was taken – at any rate, he looked as scared as I felt just then. But less than a minute before, we *were* all standing there looking down at the surface of the lake. It's as if time were moving more slowly in the lake than in the surrounding environment.'

'A dislocation in time,' Konstantinov said thoughtfully.

'Exactly,' said Alisa. 'When Prokopy asked me to look at the lake's surface, I was seeing something in the immediate past.' Her voice rose a little in excitement as she continued: 'And that's what could have happened just now, with the Cauldron. It isn't here now, but it *was* here in the past...'

'But not the immediate past,' Viktor said. 'We're not talking minutes here, are we?'

'No, that's right. Certainly not minutes. Years, perhaps, or even centuries.'

'Christ,' he said. 'Can this be possible? Dislocations in time?'

'It's the only thing I can think of that even comes close to making any kind of sense. And ... it might also explain what happened to the sky last night.'

He looked at Vadim and Nika blankly for a few moments; and then Vadim realised what she was getting at. 'You mean ... there were no recognisable constellations because we were looking at the sky not as it is now, but as it was in the remote past.'

Alisa nodded. 'Of course, you *always* see the sky as it was in the past, due to the speed of light being finite. When you look at a star that's a hundred light years away, you're not seeing as it is now, but as it was a hundred years ago, since it takes that long for the light to reach you. But the total lack of any familiar star patterns last night ... that means that we were seeing the sky as it was in the *very* remote past – *millions* of years.'

'And the animals?' said Nika. 'What about them?'

'I'm not sure,' Alisa replied. 'Maybe the same applies to them.'

'How could any of this happen?' Viktor said. 'How could these time dislocations occur? What's the mechanism?'

'I don't know. Usually, when we think of time travel, we think of a person moving through the time dimension into the past or future; we don't tend to think of other time periods doing the travelling!'

'Well, whatever's happening, we aren't prepared for it,' Viktor said.

Alisa glanced at him sharply. 'What are you getting at?'

'What I'm *getting* at is that we're in a pretty bloody dangerous situation, and I don't know if we should stay here any longer.'

'You think we should *leave*?' said Alisa incredulously.

'Yeah, I think we should leave. I don't know what I was expecting to find here, but I sure as hell wasn't expecting *this*. This is too weird.' He looked at Vadim. 'There are things happening here that we can't handle.'

'Viktor's right,' said Veronika. 'We very nearly died back there ... we nearly ended up like that bear we saw. That thing, whatever it was ... it was ripping up trees like they were weeds, blasting them to pieces. It nearly did the same to us. We can't stay here.'

Alisa gave her a disgusted look. 'So you just want to turn around and head home. You want to turn your back on what's happening here – the incredible *mystery* of it – and go running back to Yekaterinburg like some kid who doesn't want to play anymore.'

'This isn't a fucking *game*, Alisa!' Nika shouted. 'It isn't about not wanting to play anymore. It's about wanting to stay alive!' She turned to Konstantinov. 'Viktor is *right*: we can't stay here.'

They all looked at Vadim, waiting for him to speak. For several long moments, he said nothing, and Viktor could tell that he was torn between the two options open to them: stay and continue their exploration of the forest and the perilous wonders it contained ... or go back to the city, and safety. If it had been Viktor's decision alone, there would have been no contest. He hadn't signed up for *this*, and he was more than happy to call it quits and go home. Maksimov wouldn't be happy with the tale he'd have to tell – shit, he'd probably fire him on the spot – but that was fine. He didn't care; he just wanted to get away from there before they wound up like that poor bastard of a bear, flung into a tree with half its body stretched into its component molecules.

Vadim, of course, was the leader of the 'Konstantinov Expedition' (and how stupidly hubristic *that* sounded now), and the decision on whether to stay or leave was his. Viktor tried to think of what he'd do if the professor decided to stay. Should he and Nika stage a mutiny, jump into the car and tell the rest of them that they could either go with them or go to hell? And what if they did that, and Vadim and Alisa elected to stay behind? Could they really just drive away and leave them out here, even if it *was* their decision? Would their consciences really let them do that?

All these thoughts were chasing each other through Viktor's head as they waited for Konstantinov to speak. Presently, he gave a huge sigh, and said: 'This is very difficult for me. You can't imagine how I've hoped for something like this to happen, to be here and to see what they saw, after fifty years of unanswered questions ... finally, *finally* to come close to discovering what happened to them.' He looked at each of them in turn, and then his gaze fell to the ground, and he shook his head. 'But I can't ask anyone to stay who doesn't want to. I couldn't live with myself if anything happened ... if they were to...'

'Vadim...' Alisa began.

He held up a hand. 'No. the decision has been made: we return to Yekaterinburg immediately.'

'But you'll come back,' said Alisa.

'Oh yes, I will come back ... soon.'

Alisa looked at Viktor and Nika. 'I'll come with you,' she said.

Veronika met her contemptuous gaze squarely, and replied: 'Good luck. You're going to need it.' Then she turned to Prokopy, who had been standing still, listening to all this in silence. 'Are you ready to go home now?'

He said nothing; instead, he turned and walked back to the car.

'I'll take that as a yes,' Veronika muttered.

The rest of them trudged back after him, not speaking, not even looking at each other. Konstantinov climbed into the driver's seat and turned on the engine as Alisa joined him up front and slammed her door quite a bit harder than she need have. Nika and Viktor looked at each other, and she nodded and gave him a brief smile, for which he was grateful. The fact that she had insisted on coming with them to Kholat Syakhl was irrelevant; if Viktor hadn't called her in the first place, she wouldn't have been there, and he felt enormous relief that they were getting out while they still had the chance. If anything had happened to Nika, he wouldn't have been able to live with himself. As far as he was concerned, the Dyatlov Pass incident could remain a mystery for evermore – he no longer cared. *Let it stay buried in the past, where it belongs*, he thought. *I don't want to know about it, and I don't want to know why all this weird shit's happening now. I just want to forget about it. Is that cowardly? Fine. So I'm a coward. Fuck it.*

Then he thought about Vadim, and suddenly felt terribly sorry for him; not because he had decided that they should leave the forest, but because he knew that soon the professor would return to confront whatever existed here. Viktor didn't know what would happen to him, then; he had no idea where his destiny lay. Would he succeed in solving the mystery? Or would he be destroyed by it? What had begun as relief gradually transformed itself into despondency as they drove through the forest, back to their camp near the treeline on the edge of Dyatlov Pass.

The first inkling that something was wrong came when Alisa muttered: 'We should be there by now.'

Vadim brought the car to a halt and consulted the GPS screen on the dashboard. He had made a note of the camp's coordinates and entered them in the system before they had set out that morning.

'What's up?' Viktor said.

'Something strange,' Vadim replied. 'According to the GPS, we're at the camp's coordinates. But ... I don't see it.'

Veronika leaned forward. 'Is it working properly?'

'Seems to be. We should be able to see our camp – it should be right in front of us, but...'

'It isn't,' said Alisa.

'This is bullshit,' Viktor sighed, opening his door and climbing out of the car. He looked around at the massed ranks of trees extending in all directions. Something suddenly occurred to him, but he ignored it, realising it was true but not wanting to confront it just then. But he had no choice. He climbed back into the car and said to the others: 'There's no sign of the camp, but there's something else, as well.'

Vadim turned in his seat to face him. 'What?'

'Are you *sure* the GPS is working properly?'

'Yes, I'm absolutely sure.'

'Then we're in trouble.'

'Why?'

'Because we set up camp close to the treeline at the edge of the forest. But there *is no treeline*. We're nowhere near the edge of the forest.'

'But that makes no sense,' whispered Alisa.

'It makes perfect sense,' said Prokopy, who hadn't uttered a word since they fled from the mercury lake.

Alisa looked at him. 'What do you mean?'

'Did you really think you could leave the forest, just like that? Did you really think that, having faced what is here, you could simply turn your backs on it and leave? It has noticed you, and it will not accept your sudden farewell, your confident resolve to depart.'

'Are you saying that the forest *isn't going to allow us to leave?*' said Alisa.

'That's precisely what I'm saying,' the shaman replied. 'Your presence here is a question that has been asked of the forest, and the forest is going to answer you; and the fact that you are no longer willing to receive the answer is irrelevant. The answer will be given.'

'Are we going to die?' asked Nika in a small, quiet voice. 'Will this ... answer ... cost us our lives?'

'That is not for me to say. And in fact, I don't know. How *can* I know? My people have shunned this place for hundreds of years. Otorten and Kholat Syakhl keep their secrets, and we are content with that.'

'But your spirit came here during your initiation as a shaman,' said Vadim. 'If you know *anything* about this place, you must tell us...'

'I will keep my own council on what to tell you. But I promise you that I will do my best to keep you alive, when the forest gives you its answer. But for now, we must wait here.'

'Wait?' said Alisa. 'What for?'

'For whatever happens next. Viktor is right: we are nowhere near the edge of the forest.'

'How far away is it?'

'Too far to walk, in this or an infinite number of lifetimes.'

Viktor was about to ask him what the hell he meant by that; but just as he opened his mouth to speak, he stopped himself. Suddenly, he knew exactly what the shaman meant, as surely as he had ever known anything in his life. As he looked out of the car's windows at the surrounding forest, he knew exactly what Prokopy meant, and he strongly suspected that he was right.

Viktor strongly suspected that the forest went on forever.

SEVENTEEN

And so they waited. And waited. And the hours crawled past while the unseen sun slowly drifted down to the horizon, and the forest breathed out into dusk and then darkness. No one seemed inclined to talk, although occasionally one of them would leave the car and pace back and forth outside for a few minutes.

On one of these occasions, Veronika opened her door and took Viktor's hand, clearly wanting him to join her. She walked to the rear of the car and leaned against the tailgate. He stood beside her, hands thrust into the pockets of his padded coat.

'Vitya,' she said. 'What's happening to us? I mean, what *is* this place?'

'I don't know.'

'This isn't the way the world is. Things like this just *don't happen*. They can't!'

He looked at her, and saw the tears welling up in her eyes. 'I'm sorry, Nika,' he said. 'I'm sorry I got you involved in this...'

'I wanted to come.'

'It's still my fault. I shouldn't have called you that night ... shouldn't have asked you to meet me.'

She gave a small laugh as she wiped the tears from her face. 'You didn't know what was going to happen. How could you have known that this ... this *insanity* would happen? It's not your fault.'

'We're going to get out of this, Nika. I promise you we're going to get out of this.'

'I love you for saying that, Vitya. But you don't know what's going to happen anymore than I do.'

'Prokopy will help us.'

ALAN K. BAKER

'You really think he can?'

'I believe he can. It's funny, I'd never taken much of an interest in that kind of stuff before ... traditional beliefs, shamanistic cultures, all that. I never saw the point – it had nothing to do with me, after all. I just thought it was mumbo-jumbo, primitive bullshit. I used to laugh at all the New Agers who are into it. But I can see that that was a mistake.'

'Why did we break up, Vitya?' she asked, and he was so surprised by the question that for a few moments he couldn't think of anything to say.

'You made me so fucking sad, you know ... I hated you. It was so weird, going from love to hate like that, so suddenly – like I'd turned into a different person, without wanting to, without even realising it ... and I hated you even more for that.'

Viktor suddenly wanted to cry, not so much at what Nika had said, but at the torrent of thoughts that seemed to have been released by her words: thoughts of her weeping and hating him; thoughts of Dyatlov and the others lying frozen solid in the depths of a white hell; of Ludmila Dubinina lying at the bottom of a ravine with the inside of her mouth gone; of Nikolai Thibeaux-Brignollel's shattered skull; of the unknown abomination that had been visited upon the bear they had found; of the impossible animals bounding beside them with unnaturally long leaps as they fled from the mercury lake...

There's only so much strangeness a human being can take before they crack. As he stood beside a person whom he had loved, whom he *still* loved, in the depths of a forest that went on forever, Viktor knew that he had reached his limit.

'Christ,' he said, taking hold of her and hugging her tightly as his own tears came. 'Oh Christ, Nika...'

She wrapped her arms around his waist. 'I love you Vitya.'

'I love you too,' he whispered. 'And we *will* get out of here. I *promise* you we'll get out of here.'

———

It was Alisa who first noticed that the camp had returned – or that they had returned to the camp. There was no sense of movement, of anything

230

changing in any way; she simply glanced through her window, gave a small gasp, and said: 'It's there.'

The tent was about five metres to their right, and a little further on, the treeline, beyond which the slope of Dyatlov Pass rose in the darkness towards the rounded summit of Kholat Syakhl.

Alisa reached for the handle of her door, but Konstantinov stopped her. 'Just a moment,' he said, and then he lowered his window and directed the small spotlight that was mounted on the driver's door towards the tent. It appeared to be intact and undamaged in the spectral beam from the spotlight; and then Viktor realised that there was no reason why it *should* have been damaged. Their camp had been there all the time: it was *they* who had been somewhere else, even though the GPS had placed them right there.

'Do you think it's safe?' said Nika.

'There's only one way to be sure,' Viktor replied, opening his door and climbing out.

Nika followed him, and together they walked towards the tent. The remains of last night's fire were still there in front of it, a black stain on the snow. Viktor looked around in the freezing darkness. His breath, misting the air in front of his face, was the only sound to break the absolute silence. Even without everything that had happened to them so far, he knew he could never have got used to that silence: for someone who had spent his whole life in an urban environment, where there was always something or someone making a sound of some kind, there was something unnatural and profoundly disturbing in such total silence – something eerie and unearthly, as if the world had died and become a ghost of itself.

He and Nika looked around and then looked at each other. Everything seemed to be in order, so they beckoned to the others, who piled quickly out of the car, like passengers who had just come to the end of an intolerably long journey, and joined them. Konstantinov immediately busied himself with lighting the gas stove, while Alisa brought out a couple of camping lanterns from the tent and lit them.

Before long, the camp had become a cosy little home-away-from-home again – or at least, that was what Viktor tried to tell himself. In fact, he did start to feel a little better after some dinner and a couple of mugs of hot, strong coffee; but he still couldn't free himself of the feeling that they were all standing on the edge of a bottomless precipice, and the ground beneath their feet was crumbling...

He gathered that everyone else felt the same way, judging by the lack of conversation as they ate, and the way Vadim, Nika and Alisa threw frequent glances into the surrounding darkness. Prokopy, on the other hand, seemed to have regained his former equanimity: he accepted his food with a nod of thanks and gazed up at the sky as he ate. The clouds had returned, obscuring whatever lay beyond; Viktor wondered whether that made any difference to Prokopy, whether the shaman could still see what was above them, and what he thought of it.

They had decided, for obvious reasons, to wait until morning before breaking camp and returning to Yekaterinburg. Now that the decision had been made, Vadim's spirits seemed to have risen a little, and Viktor suspected that, deep down, he was more than glad to be leaving this bizarre place behind. There was little doubt that he would be true to his word and return as soon as he could, but for now he really did seem to have had enough.

After they had cleaned away the dinner things and retreated inside the tent for the evening, Vadim confirmed Viktor's suspicion. 'You know,' he said, 'the more I think about it, the more I'm convinced that to return to the city *is* the best thing to do.'

Viktor glanced at Alisa, expecting some kind of dismissive remark, but she remained silent and merely nodded. It looked like she, too, had had more than enough of this place.

'There's a great deal to think about,' Vadim continued. 'A great deal of information to study, theories to be formulated, comparisons to be made with the data we already have on the Dyatlov Pass incident. Of course, this trip was only ever a preliminary one, a brief reconnaissance – and in that regard, in terms of what we've experienced, it's been an astonishing success.'

'That much is true,' said Alisa with a humourless chuckle.

Viktor turned to Prokopy. 'What do you think? You said earlier that the forest isn't going to allow us to leave. Do you still think so?'

The shaman considered for a moment, then he replied: 'It has delayed our departure. It didn't want us to leave today. As for tomorrow ... I don't know. We shall see.'

Veronika sighed and said: 'Well, has anyone got any theories on what the hell is happening in this place?' She looked at Alisa. 'You're a physicist, you must have some idea, even if it's only an educated guess.'

'Right now, the only thing I can think of is that these phenomena might be evidence for M theory.'

'M theory?' said Viktor. 'What's that?'

'It's short for Membrane theory, which, er, is going to take some explaining.'

'We're not going anywhere,' Nika said with a shrug.

Alisa took out a cigarette and lit it. No one objected. 'All right. It has to do with the origin of this universe. Right now, cosmologists are virtually unanimous in their acceptance of what's called the Standard Model of the origin, which states that approximately fourteen billion years ago, the universe emerged from a colossal explosion...'

'You're talking about the Big Bang theory,' said Konstantinov, 'first put forward by Edwin Hubble.'

'That's right, except that Hubble wasn't quite the first to suggest it. That honour goes to a Belgian astrophysicist called George Édouard Lemaître, who ironically enough was also a priest. In the 1920s, Lemaître suggested that the universe emerged out of a "primeval atom" or "cosmic egg" between twenty and sixty billion years ago. He believed that the point of origin was a sphere about thirty times the diameter of the Sun. In this, and in his estimate of the universe's age, he was mistaken; but his basic idea was sound, and was quickly built upon by other scientists, including Hubble, who had noted from his own observations of distant stars and galaxies that the light from the furthest ones had a longer wavelength than that from nearer ones. The light was *redshifted*, stretched towards the red end of the spectrum. Hubble calculated that the redshift of a galaxy was proportional to its distance from Earth: in other words, the further away a galaxy is, the faster it's receding from us.

'This is known as Hubble's Law, and its inevitable conclusion is that, since the universe is expanding, it must have had a single point of origin in the distant past – fourteen billion years ago, to be more or less precise – when all of the matter and energy we now observe was compressed into a region far smaller than Lemaître's cosmic egg. In fact, it was infinitely small and infinitely dense, and no one knows how it came to be, or where it came from, or how it managed to expand outwards, given the infinite gravity associated with such an object.'

'All this is fascinating,' Viktor said. 'But what does it have to do with this Membrane theory you mentioned?'

'Patience, Viktor. I'm coming to it. The idea of this primeval singularity being able to expand into the universe we see around us today is a considerable problem for cosmologists. It shouldn't have been able to do that; its gravity would have been too great...'

'It would have been like a black hole,' said Nika.

'Exactly. Now, all kinds of problems arise when you talk about "infinite" this and "infinite" that. In fact, our current understanding of physics doesn't allow us to say anything meaningful about what happens in a region of infinite minuteness and density ... so cosmologists prefer to think of the universe as emerging from a region the size of the Planck length.'

Viktor frowned. 'Excuse me. The Planck length?'

'It's the smallest distance that can be meaningfully described with our current understanding of physics. And it's *very* small: 10^{-35} metres. In addition, the idea of "inflation" was introduced to account for the universe's initial expansion: it was a force which gave the universe a violent outward push, in effect accelerating its expansion before gravity could overcome it and cause it to fall instantly back into the singularity.

'This is where Membrane theory comes in. It has given rise to a new model of the universe's origin, which does away with the need for "inflation". This new model is called the Ekpyrotic model, named after the process of *ekpyrosis*, meaning "conflagration", in Stoic philosophy, whereby the universe is periodically consumed by fire and regenerated. And it states that our universe is a four-dimensional membrane embedded within a five-dimensional realm known as bulk-space.'

'I ... think you've lost me,' Viktor said.

'Okay. Think of this universe as a sheet of paper floating inside a room...'

'Done that,' he nodded.

'The piece of paper has two dimensions: length and width. And the room in which it floats has an extra dimension: height. Now, if you add a dimension to the sheet of paper, and a dimension to the room, you have our universe floating in bulk-space. Our universe is a "membrane" floating in this boundless higher-dimensional realm; and what we call the Big Bang was caused by the collision of two membranes moving through bulk-space. When the two membranes collided, the kinetic energy of the impact was converted into the fundamental particles of which our universe is composed, and which are confined to movement within the three space dimensions of the membrane.'

'Okay,' he said. 'That makes sense ... kind of. But what does it have to do with the things we've seen here?'

Alisa dropped her cigarette butt into her coffee mug, thought about lighting another, then changed her mind. 'It might explain how things can appear and disappear, how they can change. The more I think about it, the more I'm coming to suspect that dislocations in time are *not* the answer. What if M theory is true? What if the universe really is embedded within a four-dimensional membrane, which in turn is moving through five-dimensional bulk-space? And what if there are countless other membranes out there, and they don't always *collide* with each other, but interact in some other way ... some gentler way. What if they can intersect *without* the catastrophic energy release which gave rise to our universe?'

'That's a hell of a lot of "what ifs".'

Alisa sighed. 'I know. But I can't help wondering about the sky last night – the way it looked, the absence of recognisable constellations. I suggested that it might have been because we were looking at the sky of another period in history ... but maybe we were looking at the sky of another *dimension*, through the intersection between our cosmic membrane and another.'

'And the Cauldron?' said Veronika. 'The way it disappeared? You're saying that that wasn't the result of some kind of shift through time, but...'

'But was the result of another intersection of membranes. Yes, that's what I'm saying. The Cauldrons, and the Installations too, whatever they are ... are from another dimension.'

They were all quiet for some moments, trying to take all this in. It was crazy, of course, utterly bizarre. Shifting dimensions of spacetime intersecting with one another through 'bulk-space'? Christ. And yet, didn't it make sense? Viktor recalled hearing someone say once that extraordinary claims demand extraordinary evidence. Well ... didn't outrageous phenomena demand outrageous explanations?

Veronika voiced his doubts succinctly and eloquently. 'If this is true, then why is it only happening here? Why not all over the world, all the time?'

But Alisa had a quick answer. 'Maybe it is. Think about all the UFO sightings that have occurred over the years – literally thousands of them – most of them circular, like the objects the other skiers saw on the night Dyatlov and the others died. In fact, the shape isn't even important: whether we're talking about spheres, or discs, or cigar shapes – whatever, it doesn't matter. What matters is that people have been seeing strange objects in the skies for hundreds if not thousands of years. Don't let the sceptics tell you any different: most of them haven't even looked at the evidence. The fact is, *something* is there. But these things aren't spacecraft from another planet in this galaxy; they're something else, something much stranger.

'And there have been thousands of reports of strange objects on the ground. Witnesses and researchers have always assumed them to be spacecraft that had recently landed ... but maybe they weren't. And then there are the orbs...'

'Orbs?' said Viktor, glancing at Konstantinov, who was leaning forward intently, a smile spreading slowly across his face.

'For years, strange spherical objects – most of them only a few centimetres in diameter – have been showing up in people's photographs. Sometimes they're in reputedly haunted houses, but often they're in perfectly mundane situations and locations. But these things keep showing up on developed film. They're usually dismissed as lens flares or accidental double exposures, but now I'm wondering if that's the right explanation. Ball lightning as well ... it's an accepted phenomenon, but it's incredibly difficult to duplicate under laboratory conditions...'

Alisa was talking faster and faster, carried away by her own realisation and the network of speculations into which it had led.

Viktor held up his hands. 'Wait, wait a minute! Let's just say for the sake of the argument that you're on the right track with this, and that these membranes do intersect, allowing ... *things* ... to come through from some other dimension. The traffic seems to be all one way. Why is all that stuff coming through to us, and none of our stuff going the other way?'

Alisa looked at him with an expression of utter incredulity. 'Viktor, I can't believe you're asking me that.'

Evidently, he had just made a fool of himself, at least in Alisa's eyes. He decided he could live with it. 'So, enlighten me.'

'You're wondering why nothing from this membrane ever falls through an intersection, into another? Do you have any idea how many people go missing around the world every year? Hundreds of thousands. Okay, granted, most of them show up sooner or later, either alive or dead, but there's still a sizeable number who are never found, their disappearance a total mystery – even the *circumstances* of their disappearance a mystery.'

'That doesn't mean they've fallen through a doorway into another dimension,' he said, finding himself strangely reluctant to give credence to Alisa's theory. After all that they had seen out here, he should have been grateful for any suggestion of a possible mechanism by which it could have occurred. But so strange was her 'explanation' – stranger, it seemed, than the phenomena that had given rise to it – that he felt himself recoiling from it, refusing to believe that the world could really be like that.

Alisa sighed. 'All right. I'll give you an example: a case which is very famous in the literature on the paranormal. In the winter of 1873, a young couple were arrested for disorderly conduct at a railway station in Bristol, England. They had staggered into the station, dressed only in their night clothes, and had demanded that the police be called. While they were in police custody, the couple described how they had booked into a hotel near to the train station. They were passing through Bristol on their way from the town of Clifton to Weston-super-Mare, and wanted to get an early start so that they could complete their journey in good time.

'According to the couple, they went to bed at midnight, and had been asleep for only an hour or so when they were woken up by strange noises, which were immediately followed by the floor of their hotel room opening up into a whirlpool-like hole, filled with impenetrable darkness. The husband was pulled half into the hole, and had to be dragged out of it by his wife.

'As the vortex sucked in various objects from the room, the couple realised that they could not reach the door without the risk of falling into the depths, and so they decided to jump from the window to the street four metres below. They ran in panic to the railway station, where they were later arrested for disorderly conduct.'

'Interesting,' Viktor said, and was about to wonder aloud whether it was actually true. But then he realised the utter stupidity of such a question: in view of everything they had seen and experienced since arriving in the forest, did it really serve any purpose to question the veracity of a story which was no stranger than their own experiences?

Instead, he said: 'So, you think what happened to those people might be an early report of ... what? The intersection of two cosmic membranes?'

'Exactly,' said Alisa. 'I think that there was a pressure differential between our world and whatever was on the "other side". The environment in the other dimension had a lower air pressure, or it might even have been a vacuum, which is why the vortex sucked in several objects in the hotel room – and nearly sucked in one of the witnesses. But that's just one story out of many, and I haven't even touched upon the disappearance of aircraft and ships all over the world, in places like the Bermuda Triangle, that have been occurring for decades – if not centuries.'

'Well,' said Veronika, 'if what you're saying is even close to the truth, that's all the more reason to get the hell out of here. Fair enough, it can happen anywhere in the world, but the fact is, it seems to be happening *here* quite a lot.'

'Pressure differential,' said Konstantinov, more to himself than anyone else.

'What?' said Nika.

'Alisa, you said there might have been a pressure differential between the hotel room in which the couple were staying, and the world on the other side of the membrane intersection.'

'That's right. It's a logical enough explanation for the sucking effect.'

'And what if such an intersection were to open onto an environment with a *greater* atmospheric pressure?'

Alisa shrugged. 'It would have the opposite effect: instead of air rushing into the opening, it would rush *out* of it.'

'And if the pressure on ... the *other side*, as you put it, were very much greater than in this world, it would result in a very powerful blast.'

'That's right. I mean, think what would happen if the dimensional rift opened onto the interior of a gas giant planet, for instance, where the pressure is thousands of times that of the atmosphere on Earth.'

'Anyone in the vicinity would be pummelled by it – killed instantly, yes?' said Konstantinov.

Alisa looked at him in silence for a moment. Then they all realised what he was getting at.

'My God,' said Viktor. 'The injuries suffered by Dubinina, Thibeaux-Brignollel, Zolotarev, Kolevatov ... the injuries that were compared to those of a high-speed car crash...'

'A "compelling unknown force",' said Konstantinov. 'I wonder if we have just stumbled upon the true meaning of that enigmatic phrase.'

'It might well explain what happened to them,' said Alisa. 'And not just the concussive injuries, but the colour of their skin and hair. They might have been exposed to an alien atmosphere with a radically different chemical composition to ours.'

'What about Project Svarog?' Viktor said. 'Surely they must have figured all this out as well: I mean, they had a fully-equipped scientific research station set up here, didn't they?'

Konstantinov nodded. 'Which raises the question: why did they abandon it? Did they really get all the answers they needed? That strikes me as unlikely. If Alisa is even half right, there's potential here for a hundred years of research and investigation. There's no reason I can think of why they would have ceased their activities in this region.'

'What about the danger?' Nika suggested. 'I mean, there's no defence against what happens here, is there? Maybe they wanted to stay, but they simply lost too many personnel, too much equipment. Don't forget the debris you found last time you were here, what Yudin called the "metal graveyard". Or maybe they *did* get all the answers, or at least discovered something that rendered all further research pointless.'

Konstantinov gave a soft laugh. 'Here we are again, confronting the central problem of the Dyatlov Pass incident: every theory put forward raises more questions than it answers.' He stifled a yawn. 'Well, one thing's for certain: I'm tired, and I'm sure the rest of you are too. I think we should turn in for the night.'

Everyone agreed. It had been a long and eventful day, and they were all ready for some sleep. They quickly got into their sleeping bags, and Vadim wished them a good night and switched off the lantern.

And that was when they heard the sounds.

EIGHTEEN

They began very softly: at first they were no more than distant, faint disturbances of the silence, like the pale hint of a breeze heard on the edge of sleep. Viktor sat up and listened, holding his breath.

Gradually, in creeping increments, the sounds grew louder.

Someone hissed: 'What *is* that?'

Someone else said: 'Shh!'

In the pitch blackness, they listened.

The sounds were not like those they had heard in Yurta Anyamova, or in the forest when the thing had appeared above the mercury lake. These were of a completely different order, of a completely different origin. They were softer – gentler, more *organic* in nature. There was the sound of something vast inhaling and exhaling, which seemed to envelop another sound which was like bubbles forming and bursting in some thick, viscous liquid. There was a sound like that made by crickets or cicadas, although they knew that there were no such things in this frozen forest: a rapid, chitinous clicking that seemed to echo through the trees across infinite distances. And there was a sound like that of voices speaking an unknown language, which rose and fell in volume, as if they were issuing from a badly-tuned radio.

Viktor sat there, unable to move, paralysed with terror. He could hear Nika's ragged breathing right next to him, her little, sharp intakes of breath. He knew she was trying not to make any sound. He heard her swallowing, and then her shallow breaths again.

And then he shut his eyes tight as he heard the sound of swallowing coming from *outside* the tent: a loud, wet peristaltic spasm. Nika moaned in horror, and Viktor pulled her close and held her tightly, feeling her tremble uncontrollably.

And then, suddenly, mercifully, there was silence again.

Little by little, he felt Nika's body relaxing in his arms, heard her breathing grow more regular as the panic slowly subsided.

He heard someone whisper: 'Is it gone?'

No one answered; they simply lay there in the silence, the blessed silence, drinking it in like it was water and they were dying of thirst.

Viktor was about to say something. He was about to say that yes, he thought it was gone, whatever 'it' had been; but the words died in his mouth as another sound drifted into the tent.

It was the sound of footsteps in snow.

They listened to the soft crunching sounds as they approached the tent, and Viktor was so afraid that he wanted to die. He wanted his consciousness to flee, to plunge into insensate oblivion forever. For the first time in his life, he begged God to destroy him, begged for quick and painless annihilation.

But of course, it didn't come.

Of course, he remained alive, listening to the footsteps that slowly circled the tent. The most terrifying thing about them was their very normality, after the incomprehensible, ghostly sounds they had just heard. Viktor had no idea what could have made those other sounds ... but the footsteps were clearly those of a person.

But what person? Who could have been out there with them on that night?

Clearly, the solution was to open the tent flap and look. But he didn't want to do that. God, he didn't want to! He was so afraid of what he might see.

And so he lay there in the darkness, holding Nika close, listening to her tiny sobs and her whispered words: 'Who is it? Who is it?'

It would have been the easiest thing just to sit up and unzip the flap. It would have been so easy to clamber out into the night, to stand up and confront the person outside, to face them, to seize them and demand to know what the hell they were doing there.

Yes, it would have been very easy ... but for one question which echoed in Viktor's mind over and over again.

What if it isn't a person?

He heard Konstantinov whispering: 'We should go out ... we should go outside and see who it is...'

'Are you *crazy*?' Alisa hissed.

'It might be someone lost ... someone in trouble who needs our help.'

'Then why aren't they calling out?'

'It sounds like a person ... the footsteps.'

What if it isn't a person?

You're lying here shivering like a fucking child. Do something!

What – if – it –isn't – a – person?

The footsteps continued to circle the tent, slowly, almost ... *tentatively.* Three more times, the soft crunching circled them. And then the footsteps paused, and moved off into the forest, gradually fading, becoming less and less distinct.

'It's going,' said Konstantinov, his use of the word 'it' betraying his own unspoken fears and speculations.

He sat up suddenly and crawled towards the flap.

'What are you doing?' Alisa demanded.

Viktor felt a jolt of terror pulse through him as he heard the sound of the zip being undone. But the sound was brief, and he guessed, correctly, that Vadim only wanted to open it enough to peek through.

'Can you see anything?' he asked, not knowing if he really wanted to receive an answer.

Vadim said nothing for a moment. Viktor went to crouch beside him. In the darkness he could just make out the profile of the other man's head, pressed against the flap, peering through the chink he had opened.

'Can you see anything?' he repeated.

'I can see...' he began, and then he drew in a sharp breath and pushed himself away. 'We were right,' he whispered.

'What do you mean?'

'We were right not to go outside.'

'What did you see, Vadim? Tell me!'

'I only caught a glimpse, just before it disappeared amongst the trees ... but whatever it was, it wasn't a person.'

———

They passed the rest of that night in a strange and horrible combination of frightened vigilance and exhausted lapses into light and troubled sleep. They took turns keeping watch, of course, although no one knew what they could do if the sounds or the visitor returned; and for the next few hours Viktor tried to banish from his mind all thoughts of the Dyatlov group's ripped tent, which had so ominously suggested a panic-fuelled flight from their campsite on that night fifty years ago.

Never in his life have the hours crawled by so slowly; never have he wished more fervently for the arrival of daylight, while dreading what the daylight might bring.

No one said anything during those long hours of darkness, partly because they didn't want to draw any more attention to themselves beyond the presence of their camp, but mostly because nothing they could have said would have done anything to ease their minds.

And so they lay there, waiting for the dawn.

———

When the first rays of daylight appeared through the tiny chink in the tent's flaps, Viktor sat up and thanked God that they were still alive and sane. The others also roused themselves immediately, and began to make preparations for their departure from that forest and its mysteries.

As he zipped up his backpack, Viktor noticed Prokopy sitting by the entrance with his back to them. He was staring straight ahead at the flap – although the reason was unclear, since he clearly couldn't see anything. Viktor had the impression that he was waiting for something, or perhaps waiting for them to become aware of something he already knew. He was cradling his shaman's drum in his lap, as if it were some talisman of protection...

Konstantinov moved towards the entrance. 'Excuse me, Prokopy,' he said; but the shaman did not move.

With a frowning glance at the rest of them, Vadim edged past him awkwardly, and unzipped the flap. He was about to crawl out, when he stopped, and remained in the open entrance on his hands and knees, clearly transfixed by something outside the tent.

Viktor looked at Veronika and Alisa, who returned his gaze with expressionless faces; that is, their *faces* were expressionless, but their *eyes* ... well, their eyes held all the fear and uncertainty he felt at that moment.

'What is it, Vadim?' he asked.

Without answering, Konstantinov crawled the rest of the way out of the tent. Taking a deep breath, Viktor followed, and stood up beside him, gazing with an open mouth at what stood there, about ten metres away.

Last night, there had been nothing there but the trees, sparsely scattered through the clearing where they had made their camp.

Now, there was an Installation.

NINETEEN

It was not quite like the one in the photograph in Lishin's dossier: this one was almost entirely buried, so that only the upper dome and the smaller secondary dome perched on top were visible above the frozen, snow-covered ground. Viktor and Konstantinov stood together, staring at it, and presently they became aware of Prokopy standing beside them, and together they continued to look at this impossible thing, rising out of the ground before them in the dawn silence.

'It came during the night,' Viktor whispered. It was an obvious thing to say, of course; but he said it merely to establish the fact of it in his disbelieving mind.

Veronika and Alisa came out of the tent. They both gasped.

'Oh God,' Nika said breathlessly. 'Oh, Jesus Christ. What ... what do we do now?'

'We explore it,' Alisa answered without hesitation.

'What do you mean "explore it"?'

Alisa pointed up at the small secondary dome, and the dark opening it contained. 'We explore the interior.'

'You're insane,' said Nika. 'I'm not going inside that thing – no fucking *way* am I going inside that thing!'

Alisa threw her a withering glance. 'Do you really think we have a choice?'

They all looked at her.

'What the hell are you talking about?' Viktor demanded.

She nodded towards Prokopy. 'He knows.'

'I believe that Alisa may be right,' said the shaman. 'Yesterday, when you made the decision to leave, the forest hid your camp and became infinite in extent, to prevent your departure. Now it has brought an iron house to your threshold. Your presence inside is required.'

'You're not serious,' said Nika. 'You can't be...'

'I assure you I'm quite serious,' the shaman replied, without taking his eyes from the Installation. 'I do not believe we will be allowed to leave until we have entered the iron house. By coming here, you have asked a question. I believe that this is the response.'

'I think it came here for a reason,' said Konstantinov.

'The antiprism,' Viktor said. 'It knows we've brought it back.'

Prokopy glanced at him. 'What have you brought?' he asked.

'An object,' Vadim replied. 'Taken years ago from a thing like this, an Installation. We don't know what its purpose is, but it doesn't belong with humans ... it belongs here.'

'Then I was wrong,' said the shaman. 'You have not asked a question: you have provided an answer.'

'Why can't we just leave it here?' said Nika. 'We don't have to take it *inside*. We can just leave it and get out of here.'

'I don't think that will be sufficient,' Prokopy replied. 'What was taken must be returned to the place from which it was taken.'

Viktor felt the bitter cold of the forest dawn seeping through his clothes and clutching him like a fist. He felt trapped by bizarre circumstance, like a laboratory rat forced to enter a maze, with no comprehension of its true nature, or what might lie at its centre. And yet ... he also felt the excitement of unknown vistas of exploration and discovery that had been opened before him by the prospect of entering this incredible artefact, this product of a vastly superior civilisation. At least, he assumed it to be so, for the thought had occurred to him that whatever inconceivable alchemy had resulted in these breaches between worlds and dimensions, it might not be a natural phenomenon, but rather the result of some grand scientific enterprise.

Part of him, of course, wanted to do just as Nika had suggested: leave the antiprism beside the Installation and flee the forest, return to Yekaterinburg and obliterate the memory of ever having been here; but he also wanted to enter the Installation without delay, to probe its mysteries alongside Vadim Konstantinov, whose entire life had been haunted by the ghosts of nine people who had encountered similar things. The fact that they had died as a result filled me him fear ... but it was the fear of the child climbing a tall tree, knowing full well that he may fall and injure himself or worse, but who climbs higher and higher nevertheless, who cannot and will not return to the safety of the ground.

He heard Nika's voice, as if it were drifting through the forest from far away. 'Vitya ... please.'

He looked at her, and shook his head. 'I'm sorry, Nika. I really think we have no choice.'

When she heard that, her face lost its expression, and her gaze dropped to the frozen ground. She looked like someone who had just been condemned, and had instantly accepted the sudden trajectory of her fate.

The thought appalled Viktor, and he took her face in his hands. 'You don't have to come. You can wait here in the camp.'

She took his hands in hers and shook her head. 'No ... I'm not going to do that. I'm coming with you, Vitya. It's what I wanted.' She gave him a tremulous smile. 'It's what I wanted.'

And then he knew that it had not been out of curiosity that she had insisted on joining the expedition. No ... it had not been out of curiosity...

He held her close, and as he did so, he saw Prokopy looking at him. The shaman nodded, and returned his attention to the Installation.

————

They filled their backpacks with energy bars and flasks of water, since they had no idea how long they would be spending inside the Installation. Alisa quickly gathered her equipment together in her pack and slung it over her shoulder, while Vadim retrieved the antiprism, still in its quartz container, from the car's glove compartment and placed it in his own backpack.

As they stood at the base of the dome, Viktor thought of the photograph in Lishin's dossier, and imagined the parts of the structure that were buried beneath them. A cylinder, approximately twenty metres tall, surrounded by column-like features, each bevelled like the blade of a sword. The main hemispherical dome was about fifteen metres in diameter; however, it was partially buried, allowing them to step onto it and climb without too much difficulty. In fact, their boots found good purchase on the gunmetal-coloured surface, and they were able to ascend with relative ease to the smaller secondary dome which sat atop it, and which was about three metres in diameter.

The opening was an ellipse of complete darkness, two metres tall and a metre wide. Konstantinov stood in front of it and, very slowly, leaned inside.

'What do you see?' asked Alisa.

'A staircase,' he replied, withdrawing his head. 'It looks like a spiral staircase, descending into darkness.' He took a quartz-halogen flashlight from his pocked and switched it on; then he looked at each of them in turn. 'Well...'

Alisa smiled at him and indicated the opening. 'I think the honour should go to you, Professor.'

He returned her smile, took a deep breath and stepped through the opening.

One by one, they followed him: first Alisa, then Viktor, then Veronika and finally Prokopy. Viktor took out his own flashlight for extra illumination. Alisa was about to switch on hers, but he stopped her, suggesting that she should conserve its battery power for now. She nodded and replaced it in her pocket.

'You're right, Vadim,' she said. 'It *is* a staircase, which suggests that whoever built this thing is humanoid, and roughly the same size as us.'

As he descended, Viktor noted that the stairs had a slight give to them, as if they were coated with a substance similar to rubber. They and the shaft containing them were the same dull gunmetal colour as the exterior of the dome, possibly indicating that they were made of the same material – whatever that was.

Alisa ran a hand over the curving wall. 'On our way back, I'd like to try and get a sample of this,' she said. 'God knows what it is ... it's smooth, but there's a kind of granularity to it, almost like Teflon.'

Something caught Viktor's eye, and he peered closely at the wall. 'Turn off your flashlight for a moment,' he said.

Konstantinov glanced back at him. 'Why?'

'Something about this material ... please, just for a moment.'

They switched off their lights, plunging them all into complete darkness.

Veronika's voice sounded in Viktor's ear. 'Vitya, what are you doing? Turn the lights back on, please.'

'Look,' he said. 'Look at the wall.'

The granular flecks which Alisa had noted were glowing faintly, like softly glittering inclusions in a dark matrix.

'Built-in light source?' wondered Alisa.

'But I didn't see them from the doorway when I looked inside,' said Konstantinov.

'Maybe the daylight drowned them out,' Alisa suggested.

'Or maybe they're responding to our presence,' said Veronika. 'Maybe this thing really *does* know we're here.'

Gradually the illumination increased, until they could make out the stairwell fairly easily. All the same, it was a totally unfamiliar environment, and Viktor suggested that Vadim switch his light back on, just to make sure they could clearly see where they were going.

After a couple more minutes of their descent, Prokopy's voice drifted down. 'We are now underground.'

Viktor suspected that no one really wanted to hear that.

'Can you see anything down there?' Alisa asked.

'Not yet,' said Vadim. Then: 'Wait! I think I *can* see something...'

He said nothing more for several moments, until Alisa hissed: 'Christ, Vadim! *What* can you see?'

'The bottom of the stairwell. Wait there. Viktor, come with me. I'm going to check it out.'

'I appreciate your chivalry,' said Alisa, 'but I'm coming too.'

Konstantinov sighed. 'Sorry, Alisa. Very well.'

Of course, Alisa's use of the word 'chivalry' made it impossible for Viktor to remain where he was, so he continued down after them.

They emerged through a narrow archway into a large, circular chamber, the enclosed stairwell forming a central column which rose to the domed ceiling. Alisa took out her flashlight and switched it on, and all three of them played their beams across the curving wall, which contained what looked like several arched doorways leading off into other chambers.

'This room appears to be the same diameter as the upper dome,' Konstantinov observed.

'Which means that the Installation is more than just a cylinder,' Alisa added. 'There's evidently a lot more of it underground. I wonder how far it extends...'

At that moment, Veronika and Prokopy emerged into the chamber, prompting Konstantinov to sigh and mutter irritably: 'I thought I asked you two to remain in the stairwell.'

'Right,' said Nika. 'So what are going to do, send us both home?'

'There could have been something dangerous in here,' he persisted.

'If there's something dangerous in here, we're all screwed,' she shot back. 'Doesn't matter whether we're here or back there.'

He hesitated before conceding: 'I suppose you're right. I suppose we *should* all stick together.'

'Damn right.' Nika looked around the room, at the ceiling and the curved wall containing the doorways. 'What the hell is this place?'

'A vestibule of some kind, I would guess,' Vadim replied. 'I think we should explore further.'

'Through one of the doors?' Viktor said. 'Fine, but which one?'

'They all look exactly the same,' said Alisa. 'Pick one, Vadim.'

He nodded towards the doorway directly ahead. 'All right ... that one.'

Alisa took out her EM field detector and followed Konstantinov towards the doorway.

They stepped through the doorway and onto a ramp-like structure which descended at a shallow gradient. Konstantinov played his flashlight beam across the walls and ceiling, and in the fitful, dancing light they saw carvings the likes of which Viktor had never seen or even imagined. Their style was totally unique, and deeply unsettling. There were ribs and miniature buttresses extending at all angles from the curved walls; there were curiously asymmetrical panels containing carved objects that might have been elaborate hieroglyphics, or scenes from some mythological landscape; there were representations of things which looked like stars and galaxies – all rendered in sinuous curves and wildly flowing lines.

Silence can be an astonishing thing: the complete absence of sound can take on very different characteristics depending on the situation and one's state of mind. The silence that greeted them on that gently descending ramp was unlike any that they had yet encountered in the forest. It was of an entirely different order and intensity: it was beyond the silence of night in remote places, more profound than the silence of the grave: it was the silence of the utterly unknown, where all thought is halted and the animal instincts take over, the reptilian brain hiding at the centre of every human being suddenly awoken and uneasily aware.

They continued their descent for some time, Konstantinov playing his flashlight across the sloping floor, while Viktor cast his beam upon the walls and ceiling. He pointed to the walls, at a curious feature which ran laterally along the passageway, bisecting the carved panels. It was in the form of a wave, with oval, egg-shaped panels containing the representations of stars and galaxies nestling in its troughs.

'What do you make of this?' he asked Konstantinov.

'I'm not sure,' he replied. 'It could almost be an image of … an ocean?'

'The ocean of space, perhaps,' ventured Alisa. 'Or perhaps the foundation of the cosmos, since the stars seem to cling to it, as if depending on it for their existence.'

'Like fruit from the branches of a tree,' added Prokopy.

Presently, they reached the foot of the sloping passageway, and found themselves in a wide, low arched corridor. The bizarre carvings and bas-reliefs were no longer present. The walls of the corridor were heavily ribbed, with deep recesses which their flashlight beams failed to penetrate.

Viktor felt his fear suddenly increase, for who knew what lurked within those recesses?

They proceeded slowly along the corridor, their steps falling gingerly, as if they were deep-sea divers walking across a treacherous ocean floor. Viktor couldn't help casting frequent glances into the inky depths of those recesses in the walls … but nothing emerged to challenge them.

As they approached the end of the corridor, they could see that it opened into another chamber.

Konstantinov walked through the doorway – and stopped suddenly.

'What is it?' Viktor asked.

'I'm not sure,' he said. 'I've just had the strangest sensation.'

Viktor played the beam of his flashlight across the professor's face. 'What kind of sensation?' As far as Viktor knew, Vadim was in the best of health; but he was not a young man, and after all that they had been through, he was suddenly worried that the strain might have become too much for him. He had a terrible vision of the older man succumbing to a heart attack or stroke down there. 'Are you in pain?'

He shook his head in puzzlement. 'No, no. I just felt as if something passed through me ... or as if I passed through something.'

'I don't understand.'

'It was as if...' He struggled to find a comparison. 'As if I'd just walked through a cobweb.' He glanced up at the lintel of the doorway.

Viktor stepped through and joined him. 'I didn't feel anything.'

Vadim smiled. 'You think it was my imagination? Well ... perhaps you're right.'

Viktor shrugged apologetically. 'These are far from normal circumstances.'

Vadim hesitated another beat, then he nodded. 'Yes, of course, that's true ... quite true.'

Viktor's first impression upon looking around the room was one of confusion, and for some moments he thought that they had emerged into a natural cave. The walls of the chamber were angled strangely, as if huge stone blocks had been thrown together haphazardly, and the misshapen gaps thus created filled in with smaller stones. If it had been designed, then the mind which had conceived it must have been utterly unlike anything imagined by rational humanity. In fact, although he was not a religious man, Viktor felt that there was something almost blasphemous in those chaotic lines, something that had its true and rightful home in unplumbed depths of space and time, in places where no human would, or should, ever venture. Moreover, it was completely out of keeping with what they had seen of the Installation so far; and yet there could be no doubt that it was indeed a part of it.

Viktor was about to comment on the place, when Vadim suddenly cried out and shrugged off his backpack, letting it fall to the floor.

'What is it?' Alisa asked, turning to him.

'The antiprism,' he gasped. 'I felt it *move!*'

TWENTY

They all looked at the backpack lying on the floor of the chamber. There was indeed movement inside; it was quite obvious. The canvas rippled and undulated in sudden spasms, as if the bag contained a small animal that was trying to free itself.

'Open it,' said Alisa. 'Open it quickly!'

Vadim hesitated, his face creased in an expression of confusion and consternation.

'It's what we came for,' Viktor said. 'Do it.'

Vadim crouched beside the bag, unfastened the zip and stepped back quickly.

A thin, red filament shot out from the interior of the bag, like a laser beam, and terminated at the exact centre of the chamber, about three metres above the floor.

And then the antiprism emerged, and they all watched – disbelieving, fascinated, horrified – as the object moved upon the red filament like the shuttle of a loom along a line of thread, climbing slowly but steadily towards the centre of the chamber. Accompanying this inexorable movement was a faint hum, partly electrical, partly organic, like a woman's voice distorted by some acoustic device.

When the antiprism reached the centre of the chamber, the red filament withdrew into it, and the hum ceased. They looked up at it, as it hung there motionless for a few moments. And then it seemed that a fire was kindled within it, and the intersecting planes and impossible colours seemed to extend into the air around it, while simultaneously being contained within its constantly moving edges.

Within its depths, Viktor could see landscapes, entire worlds composed of dancing geometrical shapes which constantly broke apart and recoalesced into other shapes. He felt himself being drawn towards it, only dimly aware of his companions, who were also walking slowly towards the centre of the chamber where this incomprehensible *thing* floated.

Viktor came to a halt in front of it, and looked into its limitless depths. And as he looked, it seemed to him that he was drifting above the plane of the universe, so that everything was laid out before him: galaxies in small groups and larger clusters and titanic superclusters. And he saw the pearl-hued, mottled patterns of galaxies in other universes, suspended upon their own planes like raindrops upon infinite sheets of glass.

The cosmic membranes, he thought. *Are they the cosmic membranes?*

He saw the great sweep of Creation in its entirety, stretching into the infinity of higher-dimensional space: membrane upon membrane floating within the void, each a universe teeming with island complexes of galaxies and the tiny pinpoints of nomad stars drifting between them; each membrane of spacetime cast at a slightly different angle, drifting and drifting in endless movement.

Perpendicular upon the limitless horizon of their universe, two other galaxy-dappled membranes drifted towards each other, swaying towers of light without end. And as Viktor watched, the curvature of each membrane, rippled by quantum vacuum fluctuations within its own spacetime, increased by a barely perceptible degree, producing two shallow bulges. The bulges moved towards each other and collided, producing a gargantuan spray of light, their kinetic energy instantly converted to untold trillions of particles expanding outwards along the dimensional lines within each membrane.

The birth of a new universe...

Gradually, the infinite membranes began to fade, the light from their galaxies becoming less substantial, like milk diluted in water. And then they faded completely from view, and Viktor found himself looking into an unending void of intense sapphire blue. And yet, he had the impression that the void was not empty, that it seethed with the invisible foam of quantum events, just as the vacuum of our own spacetime seethes with its own infinite, submicroscopic potentialities.

But this seemed different, quite apart from the fact that he was able to sense the underlying structure of the void. He sensed order here: cool, pristine and beautiful, the antithesis of the quantum foam that bubbles and thrashes across our own cosmic membrane.

He sensed the acausal echoes of all possible universes, moving across a spectrum of potentiality, from certainty to likelihood to unlikelihood to impossibility. He sensed universes that were, and universes that could never be, falling half-formed back into the oblivion from which they could not escape, like doomed matter plunging into the gravity well of a black hole.

And then the infinite blue void also began to fade, its beautiful light dimming and finally going out altogether.

In its place was horror.

He had the impression that he was floating at the centre of a vast sphere made of darkness, writhing, fetid, hateful. Upon the boundary of the sphere, a million shapes twisted, thrashed, slithered and ruptured. They were all around him, in every direction. There was no escape from them.

He wanted to scream. Perhaps he did: it was difficult to tell, such was the cacophony of vileness and terror that pummelled his mind, plunging him into a despair greater than any he had ever known.

The sphere closed in upon him, the walls contracting, bringing the shapes closer. The darkness quivered obscenely, as if its contents sensed his helplessness.

The sphere continued to contract – or was his mind, his awareness, expanding? He no longer knew. He only knew that the distance between him and the terror was rapidly diminishing, bringing it upon him from every direction.

He became aware of people screaming, and he realised that it was Veronika, Alisa, Vadim, Prokopy, and himself.

And then it seemed that the boundary of the sphere was upon him, and *through* him. But there was no pain, and the mental destruction he had expected did not come. And yet, some kind of change had taken place – he felt it: an alteration in his awareness, profound, monumental.

The perceived hostility of the things that had twisted and writhed upon the sphere's boundary had vanished; their filth and hatred, their obscene ravenous hunger, the mad thrashings of their aggression, were no more. Even their appearance had altered beyond recognition. Viktor still sensed the presence of the sphere; but now it seemed to have expanded into a colossal space, which could have held billions of universes within itself.

The shapes were still on the surface of the sphere, an unknown, an unthinkable distance away; and yet he was aware of them, as if the distance meant nothing. And he seemed to perceive the forms with a new awareness, transfigured by the realm in which he now found himself. And the forms were perfect, and beautiful in their perfection.

And Viktor wept.

He wept for every living thing in his universe, for the chaos that was mistaken for order, the harmony that was sought but never found because it was an illusion, an impossibility. For the first time, he became acutely, unbearably aware of the sadness of the matter of which he was composed, the chaos of its indeterminism, the desperate writhing of the superstrings and the sorrowful music of reality they produced.

And then the vision was gone, and he was once again standing in that strangely-angled room, looking at the shifting, impossibly-coloured planes and filaments within the object floating at its centre. He grew nauseous, and was dimly aware of Veronika, Alisa and Vadim falling to the floor. Prokopy tried to walk towards him, but he too succumbed, and sank to his knees.

As Viktor fell to his own knees and then onto his back, he saw something entering the room, something that looked vaguely like a man but which was not a man. It was tall and spindly, and approached with slow, languid movements of its impossibly long limbs. When he saw its face, Viktor wanted to scream, and would certainly have done so had not his sudden fatigue and nausea robbed him of the ability.

Its face was elongated to the point of utter hideousness, like an animal's: a horse, perhaps, or a dog with a particularly long snout. Its skin colour was a deep orange-brown, and it appeared to be almost completely naked, save for a few scraps of cloth which clung to its shoulders. Its hair was sparse, but what there was of it was a silvery white. Its eyes ... its eyes were human, but they did not belong in that face, any more than those human eyes belonged in the face of the lynx that had bounded through the forest alongside them as they made their escape from the mercury lake.

The figure paused and regarded each of them in turn, but Viktor couldn't move, couldn't even begin to crawl away from it. He tore his eyes away and looked at Nika, who was gazing up at it in an obscene ecstasy of terror.

And then it came towards him, and he was afforded a closer look at the rags that hung from its shoulders. They were the stained remnants of a lab coat, and they included a name-patch, on which he could see a printed name.

The name was SOLOVIEV.

In the moments before unconsciousness overcame him, Viktor found the strength to scream.

TWENTY-ONE

When he opened his eyes, he immediately realised that he was no longer in the chamber containing the strangely-angled, impossibly-coloured anti-prism. Although the nausea had abated, he still felt terribly weak, so much so that movement was all but impossible. The softness beneath him seemed to indicate that he was lying on a bed. He could see nothing but a white ceiling with a bare light bulb hanging directly above him, flickering inter-mittently. He opened his mouth to speak, but no sound would come. His throat was parched, and he spent several moments trying to gather enough saliva to swallow.

When he finally managed to do so, he murmured: 'Where am I?'

A voice replied, off to his left somewhere. It sounded barely human, as if its vocal organs had been damaged ... or altered somehow. It was deep and rasping, with a clicking element which suggested that something had broken in the throat of the speaker.

The voice said: 'You are in the infirmary of Zone 3 Station.'

Viktor winced at the sound of the voice, and his terror returned, threatening to overwhelm him and cast him once more into a pit of screams.

He closed his eyes tightly and, with a supreme effort, managed to contain his panic. 'How did I get here?' he whispered.

'Zone 3 Station is now part of this Installation.'

'How...?

'The Installation wished to examine it more closely. It has been part of the Installation for many years.'

'Who ... are you?'

'I am Dr Anton Soloviev, nominal commander of the Station.'

'Project Svarog.'

'Yes.'

Viktor sensed a stirring just beyond his field of vision, and braced himself for what he was about to see. The elongated equine head moved into view, and again he felt the screams rising in his throat, like a carbonated liquid that had been shaken in its bottle.

'Please don't be afraid.'

'You're Soloviev.'

'Yes.'

'*What in God's name happened to you?*'

The narrow mouth twitched, and Viktor had the impression that it was trying to smile. 'Too long in the Installation ... too long apart from my fellow beings ... too long in other places. These things have had their effect upon me.'

'Where are the others?'

'The others?'

'The people I came with.'

'They are here.'

Viktor finally found the strength to sit up and look around the room, which he found far preferable to looking at the apparition standing before him in its dreadful, etiolated semi-nakedness. The infirmary was in a state of near-total disrepair: the floor was littered with detritus and shards of smashed glass from the numerous cabinets lining the walls. Here and there were trolleys containing medical instruments of various kinds. The place obviously hadn't been used in years – decades, in fact.

There were four other beds next to Viktor's. He saw Veronika, Alisa and Vadim lying upon them. Their eyes were still closed. In the fourth bed, Prokopy had sat up, and was looking at the thing that had once been Anton Soloviev with his head cocked to one side, almost comically. He appeared to be completely calm, and Viktor guessed that he had seen so many strange things in the course of his shaman's life that he could meet his current situation with something approaching equanimity. Viktor envied him.

'You and the shaman are the first to awaken,' said Soloviev in his grinding, clicking voice, 'so that you may help the others to remain calm when consciousness returns. I understand that it will be intolerable for them ... for a while at least.'

Viktor stood up unsteadily, and moved across the debris-littered floor to stand beside Veronika's bed, while Prokopy moved between Alisa and Vadim, although his attention was focussed on Alisa.

Viktor took Nika's hand and held it gently, as her eyes flickered open and then snapped wide in renewed fright. 'Nika,' he said quietly. 'It's all right. I'm here. It's Vitya ... I'm here.'

She looked at him, and her mouth opened. She was about to scream, and he shook his head, desperately hoping that she wouldn't. If she did, he knew that he would join her, for the panic was still bubbling inside him, and it would take very little for it to come surging back in an unstoppable tide.

'Nika, don't. I'm right here, we all are...'

'What the fuck's happening, Vitya?' she groaned. She looked at Soloviev, who was still standing on the other side of the room. 'Oh, Christ! *Oh, Christ!*' Her body stiffened, and Viktor realised that she was paralysed with terror, otherwise she would surely have fled from the room.

'Don't be afraid, Veronika,' said Soloviev.

She shut her eyes tight, and hissed: 'Oh, God, it talks. The fucking thing talks!'

'He's human, Nika,' Viktor said. 'It's Anton Soloviev. You remember seeing his name in the documents, don't you?'

She looked at him again, and perhaps she saw the terror lingering in his eyes and felt some kinship with it, some source of strength, for she nodded and gripped his hand tightly in both of hers.

Alisa and Vadim were also waking up. Viktor glanced at them, and saw that they seemed to be coping better than Nika. Prokopy was speaking quietly to them, and they were sitting up and nodding slowly, without taking their eyes from Soloviev.

'Where are we?' asked Alisa.

Viktor told her, and repeated what Soloviev had said about Zone 3 Station now being a part of the Installation.

'Well ... at least that's saved us a trip.'

At first, Viktor couldn't believe that she had made that flippant remark; but it did more to ease the fear that was still coursing through him than he would have thought possible. He smiled at her and said: 'Yeah. Very convenient.'

'I'm thirsty,' said Nika suddenly, and Viktor was reminded of how dry his own throat was.

'Your water is there,' said Soloviev, indicating with a long, chitinous arm their backpacks, which were piled upon a nearby table.

Viktor went to them and retrieved the flasks, which he handed to the others.

'All right,' he said, when he had slaked his own thirst, and was about to continue, when Soloviev said: 'I know you have many questions. We will be more comfortable in the conference room. Please follow me.'

He moved with his strange, insect-like elegance to the door, and waited for them.

———

Nika continued to hold Viktor's hand tightly as they followed Dr Soloviev through the corridors of Zone 3 Station. He could see exactly what Soloviev meant when he had said that it was now a part of the Installation. The walls and ceiling of the corridors were ruptured in places, and through the openings they could see *other* walls of a dull, gunmetal colour. The Station appeared to have been literally plucked from its original location and placed within the confines of the Installation, evidently undergoing a significant amount of damage in the process.

Viktor recalled from the Lishin dossier that the Station had been constructed from prefabricated modules, which had been transported to the Northern Urals Sector in the aftermath of the Dyatlov Pass incident. This was plainly evident at certain points, such as corridor intersections, where bolts had been ripped from connecting ring assemblies to reveal broken power and ventilation conduits and twisted metal reinforcement braces. They had to watch where they trod, and step carefully over gaps in the floor where one module had become partially detached from another.

Presently, they reached a door, which Soloviev opened, ducking through as he entered the room. The conference room was as much of a mess as the infirmary, with papers and personal effects scattered across the floor. At the centre was a circular table with eight chairs around it. There was a bank of nine TV screens, all cracked and no longer functioning, on one wall, while on the opposite wall was stencilled the Project Svarog symbol:

'Please be seated,' said Soloviev.

As they took the chairs, Viktor glanced at Nika to see how she was coping. Her face was expressionless, and her body stiff, her movements jerky, as if she were just barely holding some explosive energy at bay. He could tell that she was on the very edge of uncontrollable panic, and he sympathised: the thing that had once been Dr Anton Soloviev was appalling to look upon – he could barely manage to do so himself. That a human being could have been so altered, so warped, so hideously transformed by any process that might have left him alive and sane was impossible to understand, or even to believe.

For his part, Viktor had lost the feeling of abject terror, and now felt quite calm. He assumed it was shock, and that his mind had shifted itself into that mode of detached observation which often occurs when some particularly violent, traumatic or unexpected event has taken place. He had interviewed enough witnesses to accidents or violent attacks to understand that this was what was now happening to him. The situation in which they found themselves was so strange, so utterly beyond the bounds of reason or belief, that his mind had indeed decided to become merely an observer of events, rather than a direct participant in them.

He looked at his other companions, and tried to gauge their own states of mind. Vadim, he believed, was like him, since outwardly he seemed quite calm, while his eyes remained fixed unblinkingly on the creature standing before them. Alisa was the same, although such was her vocation that he assumed that fascination and curiosity must have overridden her initial terror. A glance at Prokopy reinforced his conviction that long years as a shaman had inured him to the bizarre and outré. *All in a day's work for him*, Viktor thought.

Notwithstanding his newfound detachment, Viktor's mind was still crammed with questions that demanded to be answered, and so he leaned forward and asked: 'What happened to us in that room? What did the antiprism do ... and what did it do to us?'

Dr Soloviev remained where he was (it was quite clear that his three-metre frame would not fit comfortably into a chair) as he replied: 'The antiprism ... yes, that's what we used to call them. That was their designation, our way of giving a name to something that cannot be named. You brought it back ... returned it to the place where it belongs. You have done a good thing.'

'What *are* they?'

'Each antiprism belongs in its Installation ... although the word "Installation" is equally inadequate to describe what this place actually is. As to what happened to you in the presence of the antiprism ... all I can say is that you saw it, saw into its mind, experienced a single flicker of its mentation.'

'I saw the whole of Creation – countless universes embedded in their cosmic membranes. Alisa, you were right, you were *right!* I saw a universe being born ... and then I was in another place that filled me with terror, and then the terror was replaced with sorrow – *dreadful* sorrow, at ... at my own nature, and the nature of all matter in this universe ... and...'

Viktor stammered to silence, and shook his head, unable to continue.

Alisa said: 'I saw that, too.'

The others nodded their agreement.

'You caught a glimpse of the ones who have come to this world, to this universe,' said Soloviev. 'But do not try to understand what you have seen. Do not try to understand their nature, or the nature of their artefacts: this place, the other Installations, the Cauldrons, the mercury lakes, the roaming singularities. Your minds do not possess the architecture to encompass what they truly are.'

'What do you mean by that?' Viktor demanded. 'We're intelligent beings, members of a sophisticated technological civilisation ... we *can* understand, if you explain it to us.'

'No, we can't,' said Alisa. 'I always suspected that this would be the result of genuine alien contact, the utter tragedy of it. Total incomprehensibility: our absolute inability to understand what we were encountering. Like giving a computer to a Neanderthal: he couldn't *begin* to understand its function or purpose. He would just sit there, looking at it, and probably be terrified by it and smash it to pieces. That's the position we are in.' She gave a dry, humourless chuckle. 'We humans, who have only been *writing* for a few thousand years. How could we possibly hope to understand beings who are not only an unfathomable distance ahead of us technologically, but whose very *minds* and thought processes are inherently incomprehensible?'

'But I want to try,' Viktor said, a note of desperation in his voice. 'I want at least to *try*. I didn't come all this way to hear that. I didn't come here to be told that I'm too stupid to understand the answers!' He turned to Dr Soloviev. 'What are the Installations? The Cauldrons? The mercury lakes? The ... *roaming singularities*? What *are* they?'

Soloviev lowered his equine head in thought, and then raised it again and looked at Viktor with his human eyes. 'Perhaps you could think of them as components in a machine ... or a vehicle. Yes, a vehicle for travelling between universes, although "travelling" is not the right word. And nor are "vehicle" or "machine", for that matter. Do not ask about them further, for you will not receive any answers that will satisfy you.'

'There's something I want to know,' said Alisa. 'You said that the antiprisms belong in the Installations, but they're not humanoid. So why are there staircases leading down from the Installations' entrances?'

Soloviev attempted to smile at her. 'They are not staircases.'

'What are they, then?'

'Simply part of the mechanism. I am not certain of their exact function. But they are not staircases, just as the mercury lakes are not lakes, and the roaming singularities are not singularities. You yourself presented a useful analogy earlier, when you referred to the Neanderthal and the computer. Imagine giving a computer's hard drive to a man of the sixteenth century. He would, perhaps, look at the disc and assume it was a small mirror; he would never suspect its true purpose, and were you to tell him, he would think you insane, or perhaps an agent of the Devil! It is like that with everything you have seen. You cannot know its true purpose and function ... you simply cannot.'

'All right,' Viktor said. 'What are they, these "antiprisms"? Are they explorers? Scientists?'

'No. Exploration and science are human terms, belonging to this universe. They are not explorers and not scientists. They are not even *alive* in any sense you would understand. You are shackled by your own mind, your own nature; you think in hopelessly anthropocentric terms, just as I once did. You attempt to apply human concerns, human states of mind to that which is as far beyond human as the human is beyond the amoeba – infinitely further, in fact.

'Have you not wondered whether the ultimate purpose of this or any other universe has nothing whatever to do with life? Have you never considered the possibility that all life is nothing more than a negligible by-product of some *other* process that is forever beyond the comprehension of material intelligence?'

The entity that had once been Soloviev asked these questions without rancour: his voice was quiet, oddly compassionate, strangely *beseeching*, as though he fervently wished them to understand what he was saying.

Viktor was about to protest further, but the words stalled in his throat. He suddenly felt terribly afraid, although the fear he now felt was of a completely different order to that which he had felt before. Previously, it had been the visceral fear of the animal when it perceives danger; this was a purely *intellectual* fear, a dreadful sense of helplessness in the face of an impenetrable, transcendental mystery. He shook his head and lapsed into silence.

Vadim spoke up, for the first time since they had awakened. 'What happened to the soldiers and scientists who manned this research station? Where are they? And what happened to *you* Dr Soloviev? Can you tell us that, or will we not understand those answers, either?'

Soloviev was silent for many moments, and then he gave a great, rattling sigh, and spoke.

'Project Svarog was not initially a scientific enterprise: it was originally established in the 1930s as an anthropological research program to study the belief systems of traditional communities across the Soviet Union. An enormous amount of information was gathered on many myths and legends, including those of the Yakut people in eastern Siberia.

'They sent expeditions there, and gathered the tales the Yakutians told of the "iron houses" and "Cauldrons", of the fiery spheres that rose from the Earth to join in celestial battle with their enemies. One of those expeditions discovered that they were more than just tales. They discovered an iron house, an Installation, in the depths of a frozen swamp; and then they understood that *something* had come to our world from somewhere else, somewhere very far away. Of course, back then, they still thought in terms of distance, which is not the right way to think. But they began to learn.

'In the late 1940s, the remit of Project Svarog was radically modified, with the result that the organisation no longer dealt with anthropology and the study of ancient human societies; instead, it became a study group whose intention was to investigate and, if possible, make contact with non-human intelligences.

'They had no idea what the Installation actually was, only that it had not been built by human beings; and their efforts at analysis were curtailed by the object's disappearance soon after its initial discovery. From then on, the project was anxious to discover more of these objects. That was the real reason for the launch of Sputnik in October, 1957: it was not to demonstrate Soviet engineering prowess to the Americans, as most people believe; Sputnik was a remote sensor platform – primitive, yes, and merely the first of many; but its purpose was to search for more evidence of these unknown guests in our world.

'It was Sputnik 3, launched in May 1958, which first detected signs of activity in the northern Urals. Army units attached to Project Svarog were sent on several expeditions to the region, but their observations were inconclusive. And then, nine months later in February 1959, the Dyatlov Pass incident occurred in the vicinity of a small Army unit which had been posted there to make observations. When the Installation and its associated objects arrived, the soldiers were prepared, for they had been well-briefed on what to expect. What they were *not* expecting, however, was the arrival of nine civilians. They tried to warn them to get away from the area, but all were killed.

'Project Svarog immediately took control of the investigation, and arranged for the bodies of the soldiers to be removed and taken to the classified city of Beloretsk-15 for further analysis.

'That was when the first investigative teams entered the forest bordering Kholat Syakhl, and began to gather evidence of non-human technological activity here: animals killed in strange ways, sections of forest that appeared to have been exposed to localised sources of intense gravity, the kinds of things you yourselves have seen. And so the area was sealed off from the public, and this research station was established.

'We all knew the risks involved in this endeavour: the scientists despatched here to study the phenomena, the soldiers whom the authorities, with their typical arrogance, assumed would be able to protect us from any threats we might encounter. Yes ... we all knew the risks, for hadn't the Dyatlov group succumbed to some lethal force?

'Of course they had, but we believed that the forces which had killed them were not antagonistic in nature: they were not weapons, nor was that which had generated them remotely malicious. You, Alisa, guessed correctly when you suggested that their concussive injuries were caused by a pressure differential between this environment and another, at once infinitely far away and infinitely close. They were casualties of something that meant them no harm, for "harm" is also a concept of this universe, which has no meaning to those who came. Depending on one's point of view, it might be said that the deaths of Igor Dyatlov and his friends were either utterly pointless, or utterly magnificent. I believe that one day, I may be able to ask them what they believe, since they still exist...

'Ah, you look at me quizzically, but it is true, for one of the things we learned here is that consciousness is a non-local phenomenon, and does not rely on the brain, which is its mediator rather than its origin, for its continuation.

'But you asked me what happened to us, to the scientists and the soldiers who lived and worked here. For three years, we studied the Installation, the Cauldrons, the mercury lakes, the zones of high gravity, the spheres; we ventured out each day from Zone 3 Station, anxious to experience new wonders, while being mindful of the peril we faced.

We gathered our questions and our theories, and presented them to each other in rooms like this, and transmitted them back to Moscow.

'But as so often happens with human beings, increased confidence brought with it increased arrogance: we began to believe that these objects were ours to study. They had arrived in the USSR, therefore they *belonged to* the USSR. That was our great mistake. That was the mistake Dr Kozerski made, when he authorised the removal of the antiprism. Kozerski believed the antiprism to be no more than a component of the Installation, whereas I believed it to be the Installation's mind and soul ... or perhaps its companion. My objections were noted, and then dismissed. I suppose I was lucky to be allowed to remain attached to the project, and to remain here ... although I can see by your faces that you would hesitate to describe my present condition and situation as *lucky*.

'When the antiprism was taken, the Installation left this universe, but before it departed, it reached out and took Zone 3 Station within itself. I'm still unsure why ... as compensation for its own loss? I doubt it. As revenge? Definitely not. Curiosity? No. The fact is, nothing the Installations do can be explained or comprehended by human minds – perhaps not by any minds native to this spacetime continuum. There were ten people in the station at the time: five scientists, five soldiers, and we were brought with it.

'It took us into other dimensions, the other membranes across which the Installations travel. My companions all fared equally badly, in spite of the rigours of our training. One soldier looked in the wrong direction at the wrong time, went insane and died of heart failure soon after. Three of them simply vanished, while the fifth took his own life with his sidearm. My scientist colleagues attempted to record our journey with the equipment that still remained operational. They were brave to do so, knowing that they might well suffer similar fates to our military comrades.

'And they did ... they did.

'I myself looked in a certain direction whilst outside the station, and became like this. I don't know what I am now, or how I was transformed, or how I have managed to survive the Installation's journey across the membranes. But I am here ... I am still here.

'But you ... you are not Project Svarog. How did you find the antiprism? Where was it?'

'We were contacted indirectly by a man named Eduard Lishin,' Konstantinov replied. 'He told us where to find the antiprism, which he had stolen – perhaps *liberated* would be a better word – from Beloretsk-15. We assumed he wanted us to return it to the place where it belonged.'

Soloviev nodded his great horse's head. 'You assumed correctly. Eduard always believed that the antiprisms are more than mere technological devices. He believed that they were direct manifestations of the Installations' controlling intelligence. But why did he not come with you?'

'I think he was afraid. I'm sure he believed himself to be under surveillance by Project Svarog. We have never met him, and right now I don't know where he is.'

'That is a shame,' said Soloviev. 'I would have liked very much to see him again.'

Viktor voiced a question that had been nagging at his awareness for some time. 'Where was this Installation while the antiprism was absent?'

'It wandered amongst the universes, directionless,' Soloviev replied.

'And now?'

'I'm not sure. But it will not stay here.'

'It will leave this planet?'

'This planet, and this universe.'

'When?'

Soloviev lifted his great misshapen head, as if he were listening to something which none of them could hear.

'Now.'

TWENTY-TWO

Viktor still couldn't hear anything, but clearly Soloviev could – or perhaps he sensed something else, something which told him that the Installation was preparing to leave.

'I don't want to go with it,' said Veronika, standing up suddenly, a look of terror on her face.

'How long do we have?' Viktor asked Soloviev.

'If you wish to leave,' he replied, 'you should do so now.'

Alisa and Vadim also stood up, but Prokopy Anyamov didn't.

'Come on, Prokopy!' Vadim said. 'We have to get out, now!'

The shaman smiled and shook his head. 'I think I would like to stay.'

Viktor looked at him, appalled. 'Jesus ... are you ... are you *sure?*'

'I'm quite sure. Goodbye.'

Vadim put a hand on his shoulder. 'Good luck, my friend.'

Viktor wanted to say something to him, to try and persuade him not to stay, or just to thank him. He couldn't just turn around and flee without saying *something* to him. But right then he couldn't think of anything except getting out of there: the possibility of ending up like Soloviev, or worse, obliterated every other consideration.

'How do we get out of here?' he asked Soloviev.

'I will show you,' he said, moving towards the door. 'Follow me.'

Viktor grabbed Veronika's hand and made for the door, with Alisa and Vadim close behind. As they hurried along the corridors leading out of Zone 3 Station, Alisa said: 'Why does Prokopy want to stay in this place? Why does he want to ... to go to those other places?'

'Isn't it obvious?' replied Vadim breathlessly. 'The Installation is about to head for worlds of which he has only caught a glimpse during his life as a shaman. Other dimensions of spacetime, other universes. I can't imagine what he will see and experience ... in a way, I envy him.'

'But not enough to join him,' said Nika.

'No ... not enough to join him.'

As they entered the chamber containing the antiprism, Viktor was struck by a sudden wave of nausea, and stumbled. The impossible object was still there, suspended in silence at the centre of the chaotically-shaped room; but now it seemed to have grown, its constantly shifting planes and filaments reaching to the walls.

'We can't get through!' he gasped. 'It's blocking our exit!'

'No,' said Soloviev. 'You can move through it – it will not harm you. Keep going.'

Holding Nika close to him, Viktor staggered through the 'body' of the antiprism, feeling something like a light breeze on his face, as if someone were breathing on him. Within his mind, he caught vague glimpses of geometrical shapes: cubes, pyramids, spheres, polygonal structures, all intersecting each other within a dark void which seemed to be bordered by objects that looked like vast, lighted buildings...

He shook his head, trying to stay focussed enough to reach the corridor leading out of the chamber. He didn't want to look back, didn't want to see Soloviev again or say anything to him; he just wanted to get *out*.

And then they were out of the chamber and running along the corridor towards the ramp that led to the surface. The nausea and strange visions had abated. At the foot of the ramp, Viktor glanced back to make sure that Alisa and Vadim were still with them. They were, and they all looked back one last time, to see Anton Soloviev – or whatever he had become – standing there in the chamber. He raised a skeletal arm in a gesture of farewell, and then turned away, towards whatever new wonders awaited him.

Viktor thought of Prokopy Anyamov, and hoped for his happiness in worlds he had previously only glimpsed.

TWENTY-THREE

As they clambered up the structure they had mistaken for a spiral staircase, a grinding hum assaulted their ears, and grew louder and as they emerged from the top of the Installation and slid down the surface of the dome to the ground.

'Keep going!' Viktor shouted. 'We have to get as far away as we can!'

He barely noticed their camp as they ran past it into the forest, while the metallic hum grew yet louder and the air seemed to crackle with something much more subtle and powerful than mere electricity. He thought again of Igor Dyatlov and the others, fleeing their tent in blind panic, running down the slope of Kholat Syakhl in the darkness of their final night.

For how long they ran amongst the trees, Viktor had no idea; but eventually they exhausted themselves and stopped, falling to the ground and panting, sucking the cold air into their lungs and blowing it out like steam.

'Do you ... think ... we're far enough away?' Viktor said between breaths.

Vadim was about to reply, but didn't get the chance, for at that moment his chest exploded in a thick gout of blood. A fraction of a second later, a loud *crack* punched through the grinding moan from the Installation. Vadim looked down at the hole in his chest, raised his eyes questioningly to Viktor, and then pitched forward into the snow.

Alisa screamed his name, fell to her knees beside him and turned him over. Beneath him, the snow was stained bright red with arterial blood. 'What happened?' she shouted. 'What the fuck *happened?*'

'Oh Christ,' Viktor said. 'I think ... he's been shot.'

At that moment, the tree trunk next to him erupted in a shower of wood and bark. He dropped to the ground, dragging Veronika down beside him. 'Keep your heads down!' he shouted as he peered through the trees, trying to see where the shots had come from.

'Who's firing at us?' cried Veronika.

'I don't know. But whoever it is, they're using high-velocity rounds.'

And then he caught a glimpse of movement away in the distance: a white-clad figure flitting from one tree to another, perhaps a hundred and fifty metres away. A few moments later, the figure moved into view again, and he saw that it was dressed completely in white, and was wearing dark goggles and a face mask of some kind. The figure raised its rifle again, and Viktor pressed himself flat against the ground. There was another loud crack as the figure fired, and they were showered with more splinters of wood and bark.

'He's got us pinned down,' said Alisa.

'There must be more than one,' Viktor said.

Alisa repeated Nika's question: 'Who are they?'

'I think they're Project Svarog,' he said. 'They must have found out that we're here, and that the Installation had returned. They don't want any witnesses to it...'

'But how did they find out? People have been coming here for decades! Why now? Why us?'

'Lishin,' he said. 'He must have told them. We assumed he was afraid of contacting us directly, that he suspected he was under surveillance. If that's the case, then he was right. They must have taken him.'

'What are we going to do, Viktor?' she said. 'They've already killed Vadim...'

'I don't know,' he said. He looked at Veronika, who was gazing back at him with wide, terror-filled eyes.

Alisa raised herself to a crouch. 'We've got to run for it,' she said.

'Alisa, no!'

But she was already running. She hadn't got more than a few metres when another shot rang out, the bullet punching through her left thigh. She cried out, falling to her knees. Another moment, another *crack*, and her head flew apart in a shower of blood and bone.

'*Oh, Jesus Christ!*' Viktor screamed, his stomach churning, threatening to void itself.

He looked back in the direction from which the shots had come, and saw three more figures moving through the trees towards them, each aiming his rifle at them. He moved to Nika and covered her with his body in a pitiful attempt to protect her.

'I'm sorry, Nika,' he whispered.

And then the snow around them glowed as if ignited with golden fire. They looked up, and saw three spheres hanging in the air above the Installation. Their light flooded the forest – the very atmosphere – and yet they could look at them without shielding their eyes. It was as if they were generating something similar to light, but which was actually something far stranger, far more rarefied. The three spheres revolved around the point on the ground occupied by the Installation, and where they passed over the trees at the edge of the forest, there was a great cracking and splintering, and Viktor and Nika watched as storms of fragmented wood flew upwards towards a point directly beneath each sphere, where they vanished with bright flashes.

The men who were approaching looked up, clearly shocked, and immediately began to run for cover. It was useless, however: they were too close to the phenomenon to escape it. One by one, they were snatched off their feet by a force which may have been gravity, or may have been something else entirely. It didn't matter, for the effect was the same: as Nika and Viktor watched in horrified fascination, three of their attackers were stretched, compressed and swallowed by the invisible singularities beneath the spheres. The others managed to run only a few paces before a titanic shock wave blasted outwards as the Installation departed from this universe. They were lifted from their feet and thrown like rag dolls against the nearby trees.

'Come on!' Viktor cried as he stood up and dragged Nika to her feet. And then he felt her lurch against him an instant before one last *crack* echoed through the now-silent forest. 'Nika?' he said, looking down at her. She returned his gaze with that same quizzical expression as Vadim, as a trickle of blood escaped from her lips.

'*Nika!*'

He looked over his shoulder in time to see one of the men collapsing to the ground, having managed to squeeze off one final shot before he succumbed to his injuries.

Nika sank to her knees, and Viktor laid her gently on the ground. He drew his hand away from the centre of her back, and gazed in horror at the bright red blood smeared across his palm.

Oh Christ! Oh no ... no!

'Nika, it's all right. I'll get you back to the car ... we'll get out of here ... get you to a hospital...'

He looked into her empty eyes, and realised that he was talking to himself.

Nika was gone.

TWENTY-FOUR

Viktor sat there for a long time, cradling Nika in his arms. Evetually, he stopped crying, and still he sat, feeling the tears freezing onto his face. Somewhere in the depths of his mind, a small voice whispered to him that if he stayed there much longer, he would freeze to death. He ignored it. He didn't care if that was what happened to him. He would sit there, perfectly still, until the stillness became that of ice, with Nika in his arms and the bodies of Alisa and Vadim nearby, to keep them company...

But gradually that small voice grew louder and more insistent, refusing to be denied. He laid Nika down and tried to stand, but his limbs were half-frozen, and he only succeeded in pitching forward into the snow. One part of his mind wanted to give up and just lie there, until the cold of hypothermia became the pleasant warmth preceding the loss of consciousness; but the voice had begun to shout, demanding that he try again.

And so Viktor tried, and eventually managed to raise himself to his knees ... and then his feet. He was hardly thinking straight at that point; if he had been, he would have made his way back to the camp, would have lit the stove to warm himself, and then he would have retrieved his companions' bodies and placed them in the car and driven back to civilisation...

But Viktor didn't do any of those things. Instead, he staggered deeper into the forest, not knowing where he was going, and not caring. He quickly became irretrievably lost, lurching from tree to tree, his body tortured by cold, his mind reeling beneath the relentless onslaught of memories and images of the last few weeks. Dimly, he wondered whether this was what people meant when they described their lives flashing before their eyes in the moments preceding death.

Finally, he came to a halt, and leaned against a tree trunk, his breath coming in shallow, shuddering gasps. And that was when he saw the dog ... the same dog they had seen as they fled in the car from the mercury lake. It stood a little way off, watching him with its tiny black eyes, its unnaturally elongated body and skeletal legs perfectly still.

'What are you?' he whispered.

It took a few steps towards him, and then turned and walked slowly away, pausing once or twice to look over its emaciated shoulder at him. And the voice that had spurred Viktor away from death spoke again, and told him that he should follow this dog that was not a dog. And so he followed, as it made its way through the forest, periodically stopping and looking back at him, as if to make certain that he was still there.

Viktor had few memories of what happened after that: just disjointed images of whiteness, and the trunks of trees passing by. The last thing he remembered with any clarity was emerging from the treeline of a wide clearing, and seeing a collection of houses clustered together there...

BASKOV (11)

'Those houses were the village of Yurta Anyamova,' I said.

Strugatsky nodded.

'And the partial greyness of your hair is due to your brief exposure to the spheres when the Installation departed.'

'Yes, I suppose so.'

'It's obvious that your friends were killed by Project Svarog,' said Komar. 'Congratulations, Mr Strugatsky. You're off the hook.'

Strugatsky took in the Investigator's sour expression, and said: 'Thanks. Although I'm not sure how long I'll be a free man.'

'Not long,' said Komar.

'What about your men?' he asked. 'The ones in Novaya Bolnitsa. If Svarog knows that they've seen the spheres, and are suffering the effects of exposure to them ... you've got to get them out, Komar. You've got to get them to a safe place.'

'And how am I supposed to do that, Viktor?' Komar asked, and I was surprised at the gentle tone of his voice. 'How am I supposed to discharge three sick men and get them out of a hospital which is almost certainly under surveillance?'

Strugatsky shook his head. 'I'm sorry.'

'So am I,' said Komar. Then he asked: 'Do you know anything about Yamantau Mountain?'

I was surprised at the question, and Strugatsky gave him a blank look. 'Tell him, Doctor,' said Komar.

I did as Komar asked, and told Strugatsky everything I had learned about the Yamantau Mountain complex. 'They've been building it for the last thirty years, but no one knows why. It's vast, big enough to contain at least sixty thousand people. It's a *city*, inside a rock quartz mountain, but no outsider knows its true purpose.'

'It sounds like a refuge,' said Strugatsky. 'But ... sixty thousand people?'

'There are four possible reasons for a redoubt of that size,' I said. 'Nuclear war, a total environmental collapse, an asteroid or comet impact ... or an unspecified threat from elsewhere.'

'Elsewhere...' Strugatsky echoed.

'It's quite obvious that we haven't seen *all* the information Project Svarog possesses,' said Komar.

'They're afraid of something,' I added. 'Something no one else knows about ... perhaps something which is rendered partially inert by the presence of trigonal crystals like quartz.'

'And Yamantau Mountain is composed of rock quartz,' said Strugatsky. 'So the complex *is* a refuge, but not from anything as mundane as meteorites or nuclear war.' He paused for a few moments, then shook his head. 'If you're talking about an imminent invasion, I can't believe that. I can't believe they're hostile.'

'From what you've told us, Viktor,' I said, 'hostility doesn't come into it. They're neither benign nor hostile, since those concepts belong to this universe. I believe that the people running Project Svarog know that more of them are coming, for reasons we can't even comprehend.'

'But their very presence is going to have a catastrophic effect on the Earth,' said Komar. 'The government knows, but they're not sharing that knowledge with anyone else on the planet...'

'For God's sake, why not?' asked Strugatsky.

'Perhaps they believe that these ... intelligences, whatever you want to call them ... will eventually leave; and when they do, the Russian government will be in a position of unassailable strength in whatever's left of the world. With a gene pool of sixty thousand people, they could even repopulate the planet...'

'If this is true,' said Strugatsky, 'then we have to warn people ... we have to warn the rest of the world of what might be coming.'

At that moment, Komar's cell phone rang. He answered it, and listened. 'I understand, sir. Thank you for telling me.' When he hung up, he looked at Strugatsky and me. 'That was Prosecutor Glazov. He's just informed me that my three men have been transferred from the Novaya Bolnitsa hospital...'

'Transferred?' I said. 'Where?'

Komar shook his head. 'He doesn't know. He wasn't told.'

'The bastards are tying off the loose ends,' said Strugatsky. 'And I'll be next.'

'We can't allow that to happen,' I said to Komar. 'We have to get Viktor out of here without Svarog knowing.'

The Investigator sat in silence for some moments. Then he looked at me, and said: 'Your copy of the Lishin dossier – where is it?'

I went to my secure filing cabinet, took out the papers and handed them to him.

'Do you have anything relating to this case in your home?'

'Just some files on my computer, which I downloaded from the internet.'

'All right. When you get home, run the Recovery Manager and return your computer to its factory settings ... I take it you know what that means?'

'Of course: it will permanently delete everything on the hard drive except the programs that were loaded at the factory.'

Komar nodded. 'You're sure that there's nothing else in your house?'

I nodded. 'Quite sure. But what are you going to do?'

'I'm going to get Strugatsky out of here. You don't need to know how, although I dare say you'll find out soon enough.'

'Where are you going to take him?'

Komar smiled at me. 'Do you really expect me to tell you that, Doctor?'

'No,' I said, embarrassed at the stupidity of the question. 'I suppose not.'

Komar rose to his feet, went to the door, opened it an inch and peeked through the crack. 'Good. Your secretary is still at lunch. Unfortunately, there's something I have to do before we leave. You'll understand why ... when you wake up. Goodbye, Doctor Baskov.'

I caught a glimpse of Komar's fist flying towards my face, and then there was darkness.

AFTERWORD

That was the last I saw of Senior Investigator Stanislav Komar and Viktor Strugatsky.

I woke up with blood in my mouth and a splitting headache, which was made worse by Mrs Holender's screams when she found me sprawled on the floor of my office.

As my head began to clear, I realised that whatever Komar had planned, he needed as much time as possible in which to do it; and so I feigned confusion as first Director Pletner and then the militia were called.

Several members of the hospital staff testified to seeing Komar leading Strugatsky through the corridors, showing his badge and barking that he was on militia business and ordering them to go about theirs. No one argues with the criminal militia, and so they went unchallenged. Later, I learned that a laundry truck had gone missing. Komar clearly knew better than to use his own car.

Pletner didn't want to take any chances, and admitted me to the hospital for observation. I recovered fairly quickly, although I complained, falsely, of short-term memory loss, and offered only a confused expression when the name Viktor Strugatsky was mentioned to me. I soon discovered that Komar had aided me in this subterfuge by taking my recorder and all of the tapes of the sessions I had conducted.

As soon as I went home, I did as Komar had instructed and ran the Recovery Manager on my computer. I am no longer in possession of any information relating to my involvement with Viktor Strugatsky and his investigation of the Dyatlov Pass incident – apart, of course, from the text you have just read, which I am going to place in a safety deposit box.

I suspect that I am under surveillance by Project Svarog, although the fact that I am still free – and alive – means that they do not believe I am a threat to them. I also suspect that they are waiting for Komar and Strugatsky (wherever they are) to make their next move.

What that move will be, I have no idea; nor do I know when they will resurface. That they *will* one day reappear, I have no doubt, however. And when that day comes, I will make this document public.

Until then, I must wait.

And so must the world.

———

Made in the USA
Lexington, KY
01 March 2014